THE
MANDIE
COLLECTION

VOLUME ONE

Books by Lois Gladys Leppard

FROM BETHANY HOUSE PUBLISHERS

MANDIE: HER COLLEGE DAYS

New Horizons

THE MANDIE COLLECTION

VOLUME ONE

LOIS GLADYS LEPPARD

BETHANYHOUSE
a division of Baker Publishing Group
Minneapolis, Minnesota

Published by Bethany House Publishers
11400 Hampshire Avenue South
Bloomington, Minnesota 55438

Bethany House Publishers is a division of
Baker Publishing Group, Grand Rapids, MI.

Printed in the United States of America by
Bethany Press International, Bloomington, MN.

Previously published in five separate volumes:
Mandie and the Secret Tunnel © 1983
Mandie and the Cherokee Legend © 1983
Mandie and the Ghost Bandits © 1984
Mandie and the Forbidden Attic © 1985
Mandie and the Trunk's Secret © 1985

MANDIE® and SNOWBALL® are registered trademarks of Lois Gladys Leppard

Library of Congress Cataloging-in-Publication Data
Leppard, Lois Gladys.
    The Mandie collection / Lois Gladys Leppard.
        v. [1–]   cm.
    Summary: A collection of tales featuring Mandie, an orphan, and her friends as
they solve mysteries together in turn-of-the-century North Carolina.
    Contents: v. 1. Mandie and the secret tunnel ; Mandie and the Cherokee legend
; Mandie and the ghost bandits ; Mandie and the forbidden attic ; Mandie and the
trunk's secret —
        ISBN-13: 978-0-7642-0446-3 (pbk.)
        ISBN-10: 0-7642-0446-7 (pbk.)
    1. Children's stories, American. [1. Family life—North Carolina—Fiction.
2. Orphans—Fiction. 3. Christian life—Fiction. 4. North Carolina—History—
20th century—Fiction. 5. Mystery and detective stories.] I. Title.
PZ7.L556May   2007
[Fic]—dc22   2007023752

Cover design by Dan Pitts
Cover illustration by Chris Wold Dyrud

18   19   20   21   22   23   18   17   16   15   14   13

ABOUT THE AUTHOR

LOIS GLADYS LEPPARD worked in Federal Intelligence for thirteen years in various countries around the world before she settled in South Carolina.

The stories of her own mother's childhood as an orphan in western North Carolina are the basis for many of the incidents incorporated in this series.

Visit her website: *www.Mandie.com*.

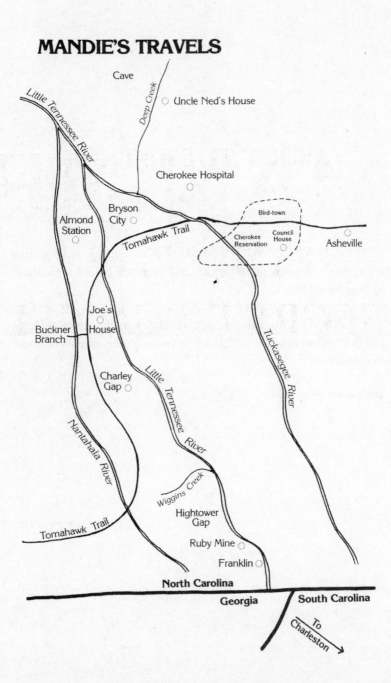

MANDIE'S TRAVELS

MANDIE

AND THE
SECRET TUNNEL

For My Mother,
Bessie A. Wilson Leppard,
and
In Memory of Her Sister,
Lillie Margaret Ann Wilson Frady, Orphans of North Carolina
Who Outgrew the Sufferings of Childhood

CONTENTS

"The Lord is my shepherd,
I shall not want—"
(Psalm 23:1)

CHAPTER ONE

MANDIE

"Don't get so close, Amanda. You might fall in." Her mother grasped the back of her long, dark skirt.

Mandie tried to pull free. Her tear-filled blue eyes sought a glimpse of her father through the homemade wooden coffin resting by the open grave.

"I want to go with you, Daddy!" she was mumbling to herself. "Take me with you, Daddy!" she tugged at her long, blonde braid in her grief.

Even in her sadness she was afraid of being scolded by her stern mother. She dared not cry out in anguish. Her voice trembled as she whispered, "How can I live without you, Daddy? You were the only one who ever loved me. I can't bear it alone!"

Preacher DeHart's deep voice echoed throughout the hills. "We all know Jim Shaw was a good man. He drew his last breath talking to God. We trust his soul is at peace."

His voice grew louder and more emphatic. "But, friends and loved ones, I am here to remind you of one thing! When the time comes for you to face your Maker, you will be damned to hellfire and brimstone if you have lived a sinful life!"

Mandie trembled as she heard the words.

"You will incur the wrath of God and your soul will burn in hell forevermore," he continued. "Above all, let us remember the Ten Commandments and keep them holy, live by them and walk the straight and narrow path in preparation for the hereafter. Otherwise, I admonish you, your soul will burn in hell! Your soul will be used to feed the fires of the devil! When you have sinned and come short of the glory of God, He will forsake you. He will punish you!"

The child was overcome by fear and grief as the final words were said for her father and the coffin was lowered into the ground. The clods of mountain woods dirt hit the casket with a thud. She gasped for breath and, falling on her knees beside the grave, she appealed to God, "What have I done to cause you to take my daddy away, dear God? You know I can't live without my daddy, God. I love him so much, dear God!"

The crowd standing nearby silently wiped away tears. The earth was smoothed into a mound and a rough marker was pounded into the soil with an axe. It read, "James Alexander Shaw; Born April 3, 1863; Died April 13, 1900." Such a small remembrance for such a big-hearted man. Jim Shaw had no enemies. Everyone had been his friend.

It was April, but it was still cold in the Nantahala Mountains of North Carolina. Mandie, trembling with cold and emotion, couldn't stop shaking enough to rise from her knees, so her mother grabbed her arm and pulled her up and away from her father's grave. Her legs would hardly carry her.

Through her blinding tears she caught a glimpse of Uncle Ned standing at the edge of the woods. Uncle Ned, the old Cherokee Indian, came often to the Shaws' neighborhood selling hand-woven baskets. He and Mandie's father had been good friends. He had loved her father, too. She suddenly jerked free from her mother, running to the tall Indian for comfort. Uncle Ned stooped to catch her in his arms, his necklace of shells softly brushing against her face.

"Uncle Ned, God doesn't love me anymore! He took my daddy away from me!" she cried.

"My papoose! Father—good man. Not gone far—only to happy hunting ground." His pronunciation was good, but his grammar was poor. He stroked her blonde hair as she buried her wet face against his deerskin jacket.

"Amanda, come now. We're goin' home. Right now!" The plump woman shouted to the girl. "Come, git in the wagon!"

"Uncle Ned, please come to see me. I love you." Mandie quickly kissed his redskinned cheek and turned to obey her mother.

The old Indian held her hand. "I make promise—your father. I look out for you. I keep promise." He smiled and released her hand.

Her heartbeat quickened as she heard his words. There would be someone to watch over her. But Uncle Ned could never overrule her mother; she had always bossed her father around. But then, Uncle Ned had his whole tribe behind him! He would indeed keep his word to her father.

Etta Shaw snatched the girl's hand and slapped her face. "Hesh up! Git in the wagon! This minute!" She gave the girl a shove and called instructions to her sister.

Mandie's sister, Irene, all but lifted her up as she forced the girl to climb into the waiting wagon, the same one that had brought her father's casket to the cemetery. All the other mourners had already turned down the long hill ahead of them.

"Now set down and shet up!" Irene was two years older, and eleven-year-old Mandie was afraid of her rough ways. She knew she couldn't resist. She gave one last pitiful look at Uncle Ned, who stood witnessing the scene with his keen black eyes, and fixed her gaze ahead.

She would go home now, but she would come back as soon as she got the chance. Her eyes stayed on the mound of earth until they were down the side of the mountain and the row of trees blocked her view.

Sitting in the back of the wagon with her sister, Mandie suddenly realized that her mother had not shed a tear. Neither had her sister. She turned to look at her mother. Etta Shaw was busily talking and laughing with Zach as they bumped on down the rough road. She didn't love my daddy, she was thinking. She acts like she's glad he's gone. How could she laugh as though she had already forgotten he ever existed?

Her thoughts turned back to the happy times with her father. He was always laughing, always ready to take her side in any disagreement with her mother and Irene. She could see his smiling face, his red curly hair, his blue eyes twinkling with some little secret between them. He had always been there to comfort his dear Mandie through the trials and tribulations of her eleven years, and then suddenly he was gone. God had taken him away.

Mandie was beginning to realize the way things really were. She could never remember being loved by her mother. Young as she was, she knew Irene was her mother's favorite. As far back as she could recall, Irene had always been given the new dresses which were later shortened to fit her, even though the dresses were made with rows of tucks around the skirts that could have been let out as Irene grew. She had never had a brand new dress in her life. The old, dark blue frock she was wearing had been made for Irene and, although it was almost threadbare, it had been hemmed yesterday for her to wear to her father's funeral. Mandie tugged at the faded fabric wishing she could be rid of the dress.

"Why don't they hurry up and get home?" she cried to herself. Her mother and Zach were leisurely riding along, talking too low for Mandie to understand what they were saying, with an occasional loud laugh from her mother. Irene kept herself busy snatching at the bushes as the wagon brushed past them on the narrow dirt road.

At last they got down to Charley Gap and their log cabin came into sight. It was huddled in the trees at the bottom of the slope. The hill to the north behind it gave protection against the cold mountain winds in the winter. The clearing around the house was already full of wagons and buggies and horses. People were standing around talking under the chestnut trees. Zach drove their wagon straight to the barn.

Mandie knew she would never be able to escape her mother that day. She would have to help wait on all these people who had come to eat and drink as soon as her father had been laid out in the front room on Friday. Today being Sunday, the whole congregation had come after the church services, which had included the last rites for her father. She knew none of them had been home yet to eat and that meant work for her. She had never been near a death before and she couldn't understand why they all acted like it was a party. Why don't they all go home and leave me alone? she wondered. I want to be by myself and think.

The chickens clucked and scattered as her mother jumped down from the wagon. "Let's git to the kitchen and see about the vittles."

She waited to see that Mandie was coming along behind her. Mandie scooped up her fluffy white kitten, who had come to greet her, and ran toward the house.

"See you in a little while, Zach. Gotta git this crowd fed. Better come on up and git something to eat yourself," Etta called back.

"Be along in a minute, Etta." Zach spit tobacco juice as he replied and began unharnessing Molly.

Irene jumped down from the wagon as a tall, gangly boy came up. She put on her best smile and smoothed her skirts as she tossed her dark hair.

"Hello, Nimrod," she giggled. "Wanta take a walk up to the springhouse 'fore Ma puts me to work?"

"Shore, Irene," the boy answered eagerly. "Druther slip off any day than work. Let's go git a long, cool drink of that sprang water."

The two hurried off behind the cabin before Etta missed Irene.

As Mandie walked through the crowd in the front room, she saw old Mrs. Shope take a dip of snuff, stick her sweetgum toothbrush in her toothless mouth, and then remark, "Poor child. He was all she had. Things is goin' to be rough now for all of 'em."

Mrs. DeWeese shook her gray head. "No, not so long as that thar Zach Hughes is around." She smiled a knowing grin.

Mandie fled through the door into the kitchen, not wanting to hear anymore, and, above all, not wanting to speak to any of these people. They were mostly her mother's kinfolk and friends. This was her mother's part of the country. Her father had always told her his people lived a long way off, but he had never said where.

The big, round oak table was loaded with food the people had brought, but it held no enticement to her nervous stomach. The warmth from the wood cookstove felt good to her. The heat thawed her somewhat and she wanted to talk.

"Mama," she began, unsure of herself, "where did my daddy come from?"

Etta Shaw stopped to look at her and she set down the plates from the cupboard. "What do you mean, where did he come from?"

"Well, you always said he was raised in a city somewhere—"

"That's right," Etta interrupted. "He was book read. That's all'n you need to know. Now git all the knives and forks out, and the glasses. We'll be needin' all of 'em. And run git that first piece of ham hanging on the right side in the smokehouse."

Mandie gave a sigh and obeyed. She longed for the day to end.

CHAPTER TWO

MANDIE LEAVES HOME

The full moon was coming up between the hills of Charley Gap as Mandie sat on the doorstep, wrapped in the quilt from her bed.

All the people had finally left and she, her mother, and Irene had gone to bed. She had listened, as she lay there on her cornshuck mattress, to be sure they were asleep, and then cuddling Snowball, her kitten, she had climbed down the ladder from the attic room where she slept with her sister. She couldn't go to sleep.

She was thinking of her past and wondering about her future without her father. She was remembering Preacher DeHart's words about God, "He will punish you!" What had she done wrong? Why was she being punished?

A soft whistle that sounded like a bird came from the nearby trees. She rose quickly as she saw Uncle Ned coming toward her, his soft moccasins soundless.

She ran to meet him, dragging the quilt and dropping Snowball. "Oh, Uncle Ned! I'm so glad you came!"

"I come find story why Jim Shaw go to happy hunting ground."

The old man put his arm around the child as they sat down on a nearby log.

"He had a bad cold, Uncle Ned, a real bad cold, and it just got worse."

"Cold?" The old Indian did not understand.

"Yes. Mama said it was new—ah—new moanie. He—he told me—he told me he was going to Heaven—that he would wait for me there." She broke into sobs.

"Don't make tears, Papoose. He wait. He always keeps promise." Uncle Ned wiped her eyes with the comer of the quilt. "When he go?"

"Today is Sunday. It was day before yesterday, Friday. Oh, why did he leave me? Why couldn't I go with him?"

"You little papoose now. Must be big squaw first. Big God, He say when you come. We do what He say. Remember? Jim Shaw, he tell us about Big God. Cherokee believe him. Jim Shaw one of our people."

She turned quickly to look at him. "My father, one of your people? But my father was a white man—red hair, blue eyes—and you are an Indian!"

"Yes. And his father look same. Your daddy never want tell you his Mama Indian squaw. Him one of our people. Him—"

Mandie interrupted excitedly, "My grandmother was an Indian? Are you really my Uncle Ned?"

"Jim Shaw—one brother. He never come see. Jim Shaw take me for brother."

"Is my grandmother still living?"

"No, she go to happy hunting ground when Jim Shaw little brave."

"What about my grandfather? Is he living?"

"I do not know. Jim Shaw never tell me when he come to see Cherokee."

"My daddy used to come to see you? Where do you live, Uncle Ned?"

"Over the hills. That way." He pointed toward one of the hills above the cabin. "Follow Nantahala River."

"Could I come to see you sometime?"

"No, bear get Papoose. Wolf, panther wait for Papoose to come."

"But they don't get you."

"I shoot with arrow." He patted the sling over his shoulder holding his huge witch hazel bow and his arrows with turkey feathers. "I kill."

"I've never been anywhere except to school and to church. The schoolhouse is just down the road apiece, and we go in the wagon to church at Maple Springs. And all the Sunday school teacher ever says is 'Honor thy mother and thy father,' and all that stuff. I never can remember the rest of it. Uncle Ned, do you think God really means for us to honor our mother?"

"Big Book say that?"

"Yes, that's what it says, the Bible."

"Then you do what it say. Jim Shaw say, we don't do what Big Book say, we don't get see Big God."

"But my mother—" she hesitated.

"I know. I see. I hear. She bad squaw."

The girl smiled at his description. "Even if she is bad, do I still have to honor her?"

"Book say that?"

"The Bible doesn't say whether your mother has to be good or bad. It just says honor thy mother."

"Then close ears, eyes. Honor mother." Uncle Ned stood up. "Papoose go sleep now. I come again soon. Go now."

Mandie scrambled to her feet and picked up Snowball, who was rubbing around her feet. She would go back to bed, but now she would have other things to think about. She was part Cherokee Indian! Why had her father never told her? If she could get enough courage, she would ask her mother about it.

Back in her bed, with Snowball curled up by her side, she finally fell asleep. Her mother woke her, yelling from downstairs. It was morning, but Mandie felt as though she had just closed her eyes.

"Git up, Amanda. Work to be done. Amanda, you hear me?"

"Yes, Mama." She sat up. Irene was still asleep. She reached over and shook her sister. "Irene, Mama is up."

"Leave me alone. I'm not ready to git up yet." Irene pulled the cover over her head.

Mandie quickly dressed in the early morning chill, remembering cold mornings when she was small and her father had held her in his lap by the fireplace downstairs while he put on her shoes and stockings.

Then she remembered her conversation with Uncle Ned. Maybe she could catch her mother in the right mood if she hurried and she could ask some questions about what Uncle Ned had told her. But when she reached the last rung of the ladder, her mother was waiting for her with the milk bucket.

"Go milk Susie while I start breakfast. Git a move on," Etta Shaw scolded.

Without a word, Mandie took the bucket, set Snowball down as she went outside and raced with the kitten to the barn. She didn't mind Susie at all. Susie was her friend. She always stood still and made mooing sounds while Mandie milked her, but when her mother tried it, Susie kicked up a fuss and would turn the bucket over if she got a chance. She would also use her tail to slap Etta Shaw in the face. Only Jim and Mandie were able to handle her and now that her father was gone, she could see the job falling entirely upon her.

"Good morning, Susie." She rubbed the cow's head. "You gonna give me a good bucketful of milk this morning? If you don't, Mama will scold me and I want to get her in a good mood so I can find out some things." She drew up the little three-legged stool. Susie looked back at her and began her mooing, and the bucket was soon full to the brim.

"Thank you, Susie. Now I'll let the bars down so you can get outside and get your breakfast. Please don't go too far away, because I know I'll have to come and get you tonight." The cow moved out into the pasture. She set the milk bucket down and followed. It was such a beautiful spring morning. Her eyes roamed over the fields, seeing her father as she remembered him and she fell to her knees on the soft, green grass.

"Dear God, please take good care of my daddy," she implored. "And, dear God, I still love you even if you don't love me anymore."

She hurried back to the house, certain that her mother would be pleased to see so much milk, but she only took the bucket and set it on the sideboard.

"Git a move on, Amanda. School today, as usual." Going to the ladder, she called, "Irene, git up. Breakfast is ready. School today."

Mandie sat down to her grits and biscuits with honey without another word. She kept staring at her father's empty place at the table. She could see it was no time to talk to her mother.

Irene joined her and then they prepared their lunch in baskets their father had bought from Uncle Ned. They put in sausage and biscuits, and buttermilk in tightly closed jars which would be warm by the time recess came at school. They took their sunbonnets down from the pegs by the door, tied them on, and together they began their mile-long walk down the road to the one-room schoolhouse. Even Irene was glad to get away from her mother to enjoy the company of her classmates.

There were only sixteen pupils in the school and one teacher, Mr. Tallant. They were divided into four groups of four, one group in each corner of the big schoolroom. Mr. Tallant would go from group to group giving assignments, listening to reading and recitation of arithmetic. He was not a strict schoolmaster and as long as a student made good grades he pretended not to notice the passing of notes during the time they were reading to themselves.

Mandie frequently received notes written in poetry from Joe Woodard, whose father was the only doctor in the vicinity. Joe had been her best friend from the day she had begun school, young, shy, and bewildered. Joe was two years older, an experienced hand in the schoolroom, and he immediately took Mandie under his protection. Irene was jealous and made life miserable for the boy.

Joe passed a folded note to Mandie with the explanation that he had had to return home with his mother after her father's funeral

21

because his father, the doctor, had to make some urgent sick calls. Even though he lived a good two miles from the Shaws, he showed up there quite often. Etta Shaw tried her best to get him interested in Irene, but Joe had eyes only for Mandie. His note told her that he had permission to walk home with her, and his father would pick him up on his way home.

The two strolled along the road, ignoring Irene who tagged by the side. Joe carried Mandie's books and she tried to listen to his attempt to cheer her up, but her thoughts kept reverting to the fact that her father would not be home when she got there. Her father usually finished the many chores around the farm by the time school was over each day and almost always lately he would be splitting logs at the chopping block for the fence he planned to put around the property. She knew this would take quite a while because the farm had one hundred and twenty acres. The pile had steadily grown and he had begun hauling the rails around the boundary line a few days before he became ill.

"I'm sure glad to feel the weather getting warmer," Joe remarked, throwing back his thin shoulders and taking a deep breath. "When hot weather comes I always feel better, for some reason."

"I never thought about it," Mandie remarked. "Yeh, I suppose I like hot weather better, too, even though there are spiders and bugs and snakes crawling around."

"I ain't afraid of them things. I'm bigger than they are," Irene put in.

"You might be bigger, but you'd still better not fool around with snakes," Joe told her.

"That's why Daddy planted the gourds, to keep the snakes away from the house," Mandie added.

"Yeh, I know," Joe said. "Here comes Snowball. It's a miracle to me how that kitten knows when you're coming home."

"He's smart. He always knows." Mandie stopped to pick up the kitten. "He knows when it's time to go to bed, too. He waits for me at the ladder every night."

As they walked into the yard, Etta Shaw saw them coming and was waiting to give out the chores.

"Change your dress, Mandie. The yard needs sweeping after all that mob of wagons and people here yesterday," and turning to Irene, she said, "You can churn the milk, Irene."

Mandie hurried upstairs and changed into her old faded dress and came back down to find Joe waiting with the broom in his hand.

"I'll help," he told her. "You pick up the trash, papers, and things around and I'll do the sweeping. We'll get it done in no time."

"Thanks, Joe," Mandie said.

The rough handmade broom always made blisters on her hands and then when she had to wash dishes her hands would feel like they were on fire.

She ran about collecting papers, moving rocks out of the way that had been used to prop wagon wheels. Joe swept furiously and they were soon finished.

Etta Shaw came to the front door with the water bucket. She took the gourd dipper out of the pail and handed it to Mandie. "Fetch me some water. And then take this bucket of slop down to the hog walla." She indicated another bucket sitting in the doorway.

So, between Mandie and Joe they brought the water from the spring and then went to feed the pigs. By that time, Dr. Woodard was pulling up in his buggy.

"And how are you today, Mandie?" the doctor greeted the girl.

"Fine, Dr. Woodard." She smiled shyly at the old man.

"Come in, Dr. Woodard," Etta yelled from the doorway. "You younguns come in, too. We'll have a piece of that pound cake Mrs. Shope brought yesterday."

"I only want a glass of sweetmilk," Mandie told her. She didn't want anything that would remind her of yesterday.

"Well, Etta, what are you going to do now?" Dr. Woodard asked, as they all sat at the round table in the kitchen.

"Marry the first man that'll have me, Doc. That's the only thing I can do. I'm poor as Job's turkey, you know." She smiled as she tossed her head.

Mandie's heart thumped loudly. *Marry—another man—soon as my father is gone,* she was thinking.

"Well, I suppose so. You could never make it on your own here with two girls and no man around. I certainly wish I could have saved Jim, Etta. He was a fine man. He'll be hard to replace."

Mandie jumped up and ran out the back door. Joe came closely on her heels. She had tears in her eyes and didn't want Joe to see. He followed her as she raced up the mountain road to the cemetery where her father was buried and fell on her knees beside his grave, weeping uncontrollably.

"Mandie!" was all Joe said as he caught up with her, but she understood.

Finally she rose and wiped her tears on her apron. Joe held her small white hand.

"Just wait, Mandie. One day you and I will grow up and I will see that you are taken care of."

"That's a long time, Joe. Things may get worse."

"But I'll be around to help in the meantime," he assured her.

Joe came to the Shaw house more frequently after that and went with Mandie to put wild flowers on her father's grave. It was always a silent affair, neither speaking until they were back down the rough road.

Only one month after Jim Shaw had been laid to rest, Etta Shaw and Zach Hughes went into town together and came back to say they were married, and he moved into their house.

Mandie had seen him around a lot. He belonged to the same church and he was always offering to bring supplies from the store for them, or take them somewhere. He had never paid much attention to Mandie, but evidently he had been doing a lot of thinking and she was shocked when she was told what was planned for her.

They were sitting around the supper table on Friday night, two weeks after the wedding, when it happened.

"Well, Amanda," began Etta, clearing her throat. "We're afixin' to send you to live with the Brysons over yonder at Almond Station. They have a new baby and need some help."

"Mama!" was all she could say.

"Now, no argument! It ain't but two hoots and a holler away. We can't make a livin' here as 'tis and you'll just be one less mouth to feed. They'll give you a better home than we got here and plenty to eat," Etta told her.

"But, Mama—"

"Now, Amanda," Zach Hughes cut in. "We have already made the arrangements. They'll be here atter you tomarra morning so git your thangs together tonight."

Mandie, knowing she was beaten, fled from the table and went outside to sit in the dark under the chestnut trees. Snowball followed her and spread himself out across her feet.

She wished with all her might that Uncle Ned would come to see her. He had promised to watch over her and he had shown up at least once a week since her father had died. But he had already been there on Wednesday night and she didn't have much hope.

"Please, God, help me!" she pleaded, her face turned toward the moonlit sky. "Even if you don't love me anymore, won't you please help me?"

"Papoose need help. Me help." She couldn't believe her eyes when Uncle Ned stepped out from behind the tree in front of her and came forward. "Me help Papoose."

"Uncle Ned, how did you know? I didn't expect you again this week."

The old man sat down on the uncovered roots of the tree. "I know things. I hear things. I walk, no sound. I watch Papoose. Sit. Pow-wow. Tell trouble."

She sat down next to the old man and put her head against his deerskin jacket. She repeated what her mother and Zach had just told her.

"I know. I listen to talk. So, I come back." He put an arm around the child.

"But what can I do, Uncle Ned?"

"Papoose must go. Uncle Ned watch over her at new house. I promise Jim Shaw. I keep promise."

"I wish you were really my uncle." She smiled wistfully at the old Indian. "Then I could go live with you. You said I'm part Cherokee. Couldn't I just go home with you, Uncle Ned, please?"

"No, Papoose must get book learning. Jim Shaw say, you must go to school. When Papoose big squaw, then Papoose live with Cherokees."

"Amanda! Amanda!" Etta was calling from the back door. "Where're you at? Git back in this house and rid up these dishes!"

The old man quickly rose. "I go now. I watch Papoose new house. Better squaw not see me. I come again—full moon." He kissed the top of her head and silently disappeared into the darkness.

"Amanda!" Etta still yelled for her.

She walked slowly back to the house, the house where she had so many memories of her father, the house her father had built, now taken over by another man. She would leave because she would be forced to go, but she would come back someday. She would return to her father's house.

Before the first streak of light was in the sky the next morning, Mandie quietly rose, dressed, and hurried up the mountainside to her father's grave. Snowball bounced along before her.

She hurried, stumbling over the rough rocks, because she knew her mother would be looking for her. The weather was warmer now, but it was still chilly early in the morning. She held up her long skirt to keep it from getting wet in the early morning dew, and then seeing Indian Paintbrush blooming along the way, she quickly let go of her skirt and picked a handful of the bright flowers and ran on. Out of breath, she dropped on her knees by her father's grave and made a hole with a stick to plant the tiny bunch of flowers.

She sat back and folded her hands under her chin as she looked toward the sky. "Dear God, what time I am afraid I will put my trust in thee. I don't know what I did to cause you to take my daddy. I don't understand it, but I still love you."

Rising, she fought back the tears and ran back down the dirt road. She saw Mr. and Mrs. Bryson arriving in their buggy as she hastily ran in the back door and was confronted by her mother.

"Where've you been? Why, your skirt's all wet." Etta bent to touch the fabric. "I hear the Brysons now, so you'd better git your grits there in a hurry if you want any breakfast."

Etta went on into the front room where Mandie could hear her greeting the visitors. She slid into a chair and spooned out grits into her plate. She ate quickly, without saying a word to Snowball, as she fed him beneath the table. It was all she could do to keep from choking on the food. She was so fearful of what lay ahead for her. She had never spent a night away from home in her life and now she was being sent away to live with strangers.

Etta stuck her head through the doorway, "Git a move on, Amanda. They're in a hurry."

She jumped up, snatched Snowball up in her arms, and turned to face her mother defiantly. "I'm taking Snowball with me!"

"Well, take him. Be one less cat around here. Now come in here and meet the people you're goin' to live with."

Etta pushed her forward into the front room. A very fat young woman, evidently dressed in her Sunday-go-to-meeting clothes, sat near the door and a short, thin man stood nearby talking to Zach.

"My, my, she's an awful little thing," the woman exclaimed. "Is she big enough to be any good around the house?" The man silently turned to listen and look.

"Course she is. She's eleven year old atter all. Be twelve next week," Etta told the woman. "Just the age for you to train her the way you want."

Etta gave the girl another shove. "Now git your things, Amanda."

Mandie climbed the ladder and blindly crammed her few belongings into the flour sack her mother had given her. She picked up Snowball and went back downstairs. The Brysons were in a big hurry to get going.

Etta attempted to put an arm around the child. "Now you be a good girl. And remember we still love you."

Amanda tore loose, fighting the tears and the hatred she felt at that moment and ran into the yard, the Brysons following. She did not look back as they rode off until she knew her mother would be gone from the yard. Then she wiped her eyes and took one long, last look at her father's house.

CHAPTER THREE

THE SECRET JOURNEY

Sarah Bryson was the same age as Mandie, and at first Mandie thought she had found a friend. But soon she learned that Sarah was doing things she shouldn't and blaming them on Mandie, telling lies and getting her into trouble. And the Brysons always believed their daughter. Mandie was punished with a hickory switch on her legs, which she had never experienced in her life. Her father had never allowed it. Mandie was desperately afraid of the Brysons and no matter what she did, she could not please them with anything.

The new baby was an adorable little boy named Andrew and Mandie loved him immediately. But he was not her only duty. She had to help hoe corn and bring in the cows. And with a sinking heart, she learned she would not be allowed to attend school. Furthermore, she had to stay home and watch Andrew while the Brysons went to church on Sunday!

Preacher DeHart came to preach on the first and third Sundays every month at the Brysons' church. The other Sundays he was at Maple Springs, the church Mandie belonged to back home. When he learned that the girl was living with the Brysons and was not allowed to come to church he came to see her.

"Remember the Sabbath Day to keep it holy, Amanda, even though you have to tend to the baby and can't go to church," he told her, as they sat in the Brysons' kitchen on Sunday afternoon after dinner. "You mustn't do anything to sin on the Lord's Day."

Mandie, always frightened by the big man's loud words, meekly said nothing, but, "Yes, sir, yes, sir."

She had known the preacher all her young life and she believed the bad things he said would happen to her if she did not live the right kind of life.

Her birthday came and went and no one even mentioned it. She wished the days by until the full moon when Uncle Ned had promised to visit her.

She sat in the swing under a tree in the backyard that night waiting for him, and when he made his stealthy appearance, she ran to him crying, pouring out her troubles.

"Don't cry, Papoose," he comforted her. "Cherokee think. I keep watch over Papoose. Cherokee think what to do."

The old Indian returned each week, but had not been able to come up with any solution to her problems. However, after Mandie had been living there for a few weeks, she happened to overhear a conversation which gave her some hope.

She was singing to the baby as she tried to rock him to sleep in his cradle in the room she shared with him. Mr. and Mrs. Bryson were in the next room and did not know the door was open.

"What are we going to do with that girl? She just can't do nothing right. We're gonna hafta git shed of her," Mrs. Bryson was speaking shrilly.

"Looks like Jim Shaw's brother over in Franklin would take care of her," Mr. Bryson replied.

"You know there's been hard feelings between Jim and John Shaw ever since Jim married—"

"That don't make no difference," Mr. Bryson interrupted. "This girl is the old man's niece and he ought to be responsible for her. He's got the money to support her."

"Well, I'm sure he knew Jim died and he never went near them." Mrs. Bryson changed the subject. "I think we orta git Dr. Woodard to look Andrew over. He's been lookin' mighty peaked lately."

"Seems all right to me, but I'll send word tomorrow if you want," her husband promised.

Mandie had stopped rocking the cradle when she heard the name and location of her father's brother. She would find him herself. And of all things—they were going to have Dr. Woodard come to see Andrew! That meant she could get a message to Joe. Maybe things weren't so hopeless after all. She didn't want to lose touch with Joe. He was her only connection with her father's house. Joe would be seeing her sister at school and would know what was going on.

Andrew had finally dropped off to sleep. She picked up an old catalogue lying nearby and tore off a corner of a page that didn't have much printing. She quickly found a pencil in her bag of personal belongings and wrote a message. "Going to Franklin to live with Daddy's brother, John. Terrible place here."

Dr. Woodard came two days later and Mandie was overjoyed to see the old man as he pulled up in his buggy.

"And how are you, Amanda? Joe hasn't been over to your ma's lately, but he says your sister is mean as ever." He laughed as he tweaked her long, blonde braid. "You all right?"

"I'm fine, Dr. Woodard," she said, watching for the Brysons as she followed the doctor into the house. "Please give this to Joe for me," she whispered, pulling the folded piece of paper out of her apron pocket and giving it to him. "Please don't tell anyone."

Dr. Woodard winked at her and put the paper in his vest pocket. "Be glad to, Amanda. Now I have to see the baby."

It was full moon that night and the old Indian showed up after suppertime. Mandie had rocked Andrew to sleep and was sitting in the yard when he appeared out of the trees. She got up and ran to him.

They sat down on the tree stump near the big black washpot hanging on its fork, with the two washtubs on a nearby bench shielding them from view.

"I have news, Uncle Ned," Mandie told him. "I overheard Mr. and Mrs Bryson talking about me. They said my Uncle John lives in Franklin. I have no idea which way that is. I need Cherokee help to get there, because I am going to live with him."

A big smile broke across the old man's face. "I glad. I am. Papoose go to uncle. No more trouble. Cherokee help. Find way. Bring food." He was almost as excited as the girl.

"When, Uncle Ned? I need to go as soon as possible. These people here don't like me and I'm afraid they might send me somewhere else."

"Next moon, I come back. I go now. Find way. Make plans with Cherokee. Must hurry." He rose.

"Thank you, Uncle Ned. Thank all of your people, or I should say, my people. They are my people, too, if they were my daddy's people."

"Yes, you Cherokee papoose. You go live with real uncle. Go to book school," he told her.

She wiped a tear of joy from her eyes, as he silently stole away into the darkness. "Thank you, dear God, thank you," she whispered as she looked up at the sky full of twinkling stars.

Doctor Woodard returned two days later to check on Andrew and he brought an answer to Mandie's message to Joe.

"I'm getting to be a regular mailman," he laughed, as he tucked a small piece of paper into Mandie's apron pocket when she followed him out to his buggy. She gave his big hand a quick squeeze and ran away to the outhouse where she could read the note in privacy.

"My father takes me to Franklin with him sometimes. Happy that you are going there. I will see you on my next visit there with my father—soon, I hope. Joe."

Mandie smiled to herself as she thought about the boy and his concern for her. It would be nice to see him again.

At the change of the moon, true to his word, Uncle Ned silently waited for Mandie in the darkness of the trees in the backyard. When Andrew was asleep, she quietly slipped out the back door and found him there.

"Franklin long moon away. We come, squaw and braves, to take Papoose. When moon rises three times we come here."

"Three days?" she asked.

He nodded.

"I will wait for you right here. Oh, I'm so—"

At that instant the back door opened and Sarah was calling to her as she came out into the yard. "Amanda, are you out there?" Sarah came into view and stopped. "Why, Amanda, who are you talking to out there?" She screamed as she came closer. "An Indian!" She turned to flee back to the house. Uncle Ned ran quickly away.

Mandie followed Sarah, running and calling, "It's all right, Sarah."

Mrs. Bryson appeared in the doorway. "What is going on?"

Sarah ran to her, clutching her long skirts. "An Indian! Amanda was talking to an Indian!"

"What!" Mrs. Bryson was shocked.

"It's all right. That was Uncle Ned. He was my daddy's friend," Mandie tried to explain.

"Your daddy's friend? An Indian?" Mrs. Bryson was white with fright as she turned back into the house.

"My daddy had lots of friends, all kinds," Mandie added.

"I never heard of Indian friends. What was he doing here?" The woman was furious now.

"He just keeps in touch with me. He promised my daddy he would," Mandie tried to reassure her.

"Keeps in touch with you?" Mrs. Bryson was still unsettled. "Now you listen here, young lady. Don't you dare let that Indian come back here again. Why, I'll have my husband shoot him! He'll steal us blind!"

"Oh, no, Mrs. Bryson!" Mandie broke into tears.

"Well, I'd better not catch him here again." She was very determined.

"You won't, Mrs. Bryson. I promise," she told her, silently thanking God that Uncle Ned was not to return again until he came after her. Then she would slip out and the Brysons would not see him.

The next three days dragged and it seemed as though the Brysons were meaner than usual to Mandie. They couldn't stop warning her about the old Indian. She tried her best to be patient and made her plans for the night when she would leave.

Andrew was more fretful than usual and she had a hard time getting him to go to sleep the night Uncle Ned was to return. She was almost sick with worry, fearing Uncle Ned would come with his friends and one of the Brysons would see them before she would be able to warn them.

At last the baby grew quiet and Mandie hastily gathered up her few belongings and crammed them into the same flour sack she had brought from home. Bending to kiss the chubby cheek of the sleeping infant and to scoop up Snowball in her arms, she picked up her bag and slipped outside into the warm summer darkness.

As soon as she had reached the shadows of the trees she saw Mr. Bryson come out the back door and settle down on the steps with his pipe. Her heart fluttered as she thought of the consequences should he catch the Indians there. She knew there was a pond nearby that was out of sight of the house and the Indians would probably pass it on their way. She hastened to the pond to intercept them.

The water seemed black and dangerous in the darkness, but Mandie sat down on a fallen log nearby to wait. After walking around in circles before deciding to curl up and sleep, Snowball softly purred in her lap.

Uncle Ned saw her first. He came quietly to stand at her side.

"Papoose, why you wait here?" he asked.

"Oh, Uncle Ned! I was afraid the Brysons would see you. They threatened to shoot you if you came back!" She stood up, catching Snowball as he fell. "Did the others come? Are we ready to go to Franklin?"

"Yes, Papoose. Come," he said and led the way back past the pond. There an old Indian squaw and two young braves waited for them.

Mandie ran to the old woman and hugged her tightly. It was so good to hug someone who cared for her. At that moment, a distant yell filled the air.

"Amanda! Amanda! Where are you, Amanda?"

The girl turned to Uncle Ned. "Quick! Let's go! That's Mrs. Bryson looking for me!"

The group ran through the cornfield, up the slope on the other side of the pond, and were soon hidden from the moonlight in the dark woods Uncle Ned led the way and the two braves brought up the rear.

The old woman took Mandie's bag, threw it across her shoulder with her own bag, and grasped the girl's hand tightly as she hurried along.

Snowball stiffened in Mandie's arms, frightened because of the speed at which they were traveling He didn't scratch the girl, but merely sank his claws into the shoulder of her dress and didn't move.

They did not slacken their pace until they reached the Nantahala River. There Uncle Ned stopped them.

"We cross here." He pointed to a narrow place in the river where the rocks rose in the moonlight on the water. There was a footlog extending from side to side. "Then pass through Charley Gap. Papoose must not be seen there."

"Charley Gap? We're going right by my father's house?" Mandie questioned, her heart pounding.

"Yes. Big trouble if Papoose seen," Uncle Ned cautioned her. "We rest now." He sat down on a boulder nearby.

The two braves drifted, one on each side, and likewise sat down some distance away. Mandie dropped gratefully to the ground. Her feet hurt and her legs were tired. It seemed hours and hours since they had left the Brysons' land, and she was also sleepy and hungry.

There was the clanging of church bells in the distance and Mandie knew, with a sinking heart, that the Brysons must have sounded an alarm when they discovered her missing.

"The bells, Uncle Ned. They are probably getting a search party together."

"Don't worry, Papoose. They not find us," he told the girl. "Now we eat."

The Indian squaw brought forth meat and dark bread from her bag and held it out to the girl. Mandie thankfully took it and turned to the old man.

"She doesn't speak English, does she?" she asked.

"No. She know Indian talk. She good squaw. Name Morning Star."

Mandie turned back to the squaw. "Thank you, Morning Star."

The old woman smiled and bit into her own ration of food.

"Uncle Ned, does each Indian carry his own food? You have yours, and the other two men—do they have theirs?"

"Yes. We bring meat. Long way to Franklin."

When they had finished eating, Uncle Ned urged them on. "We go in dark. Sleep when sun shines. No one see."

The ringing of the church bells grew dimmer and then could no longer be heard as they made their way across the Nantahala River, went down Buckner Branch, and crossed the Tomahawk Trail. They had to stop often for Mandie to catch her breath. It was all up and down hill and through thick underbrush, and the rough rocks hurt her feet.

A long time later they approached Mandie's father's land. Uncle Ned halted the group.

"Careful. Follow me." He indicated that they were to swing out in a circle away from the house.

Mandie kept her eyes wide open, staring toward the darkened house and outbuildings. Evidently everyone was asleep at this hour. She almost wished she could run right past her mother and let her know that she had defied her and had run away from the Brysons. But she obeyed the old Indian, knowing she would be stopped if some of her people did see her.

She came to a sudden halt at the nearest point to the house, gazed at the log cabin with tears in her eyes, and then furiously ran ahead of the squaw in the direction Uncle Ned was taking.

She thought of her father's grave up the mountainside and wished she could visit it, but she knew it was out of their way. She would have to wait until someday in the future.

She would come back someday. She knew she would.

Her tired feet carried her off her father's land and on toward Franklin.

CHAPTER FOUR

THE MANSION

The first streaks of dawn were lighting up the sky when Uncle Ned finally stopped the group to sleep. They had just crossed Wiggins Creek when they finally sat down to rest.

Mandie flopped down on the grass. "Guess I'm plumb tuckered out." She laughed wearily.

Morning Star quickly gathered branches and made a bed for her to lie on, hidden under the trees. The girl used her shawl for a blanket, knowing when the sun came up it would be warm again.

She was so excited she couldn't sleep, but the fatigue overcame the excitement and she dropped off to dream.

The sound of shooting woke her. She sat up quickly and almost smashed Snowball, asleep by her side. For a minute she couldn't remember where she was. Then the old squaw put an arm around her and she relaxed. She could see Uncle Ned standing near the creek. He came to her. She could tell by his shadow that the sun was fast moving into the west. She must have slept all day.

"Braves go see where gun shoot," he told her. "They come, we go."

At that moment there was the sound of voices in the trees nearby.

"Well, I reckon we done searched fur enough. That girl couldn't 'a got no futher than this," a man's voice came to them.

Uncle Ned quickly whisked Mandie behind a laurel tree and he and the squaw slipped behind the rhododendron bushes nearby.

"Yeh, let's go see what's goin' on up yonder. Must be Jed's search party," another male voice replied.

Two men came into view. They were carrying rifles and stomping the underbrush beneath their feet. One was a tall man with a white beard and the other was a short, fat man who was spitting tobacco juice as he went. Mandie peeped around the tree, but she did not recognize either one. She realized they must be looking for her. They paused while the tall man lit his pipe.

"Don't much blame that youngun fer not wantin' to stay at that Bryson house. Hear tell that female is a tiger," the tall one was saying.

"Yep, I hear tell they can't nobody please her. But I shore would like to find that youngun 'fore the wildcats git her. I wouldn't want to take her back to the Brysons, but I wouldn't want her to git lost on this mountain either," the short one said. "I knew her pa. Good man, he was." They walked on, out of hearing, and were soon lost from sight in the tall underbrush.

The squaw went to Mandie and put her arm around her. Uncle Ned followed.

"Be not afraid, Papoose. We go to Franklin. White men not stop Indians," he reassured the girl.

"I know. I know how smart the Indians are. I know you will get me to my uncle's house in Franklin," she replied, grasping the old man's hand. "I'm not afraid. After all, I'm part Cherokee, too."

The two braves came silently up to the old man.

"White men carry guns; coming this way," the taller one said.

"Two passed here," Uncle Ned told them. "Looking for Papoose. We go." He pointed in the direction of Hightower Gap away from the way the two men had gone.

The group slipped quietly through the woods, resting only when Mandie was tired, and they finally reached the Little Tennessee River. They took long detours for safety's sake but followed the banks of the river most of the way. They came on through Burningtown and up the main road that ran through Franklin.

The sight before her was unbelievable to Mandie. All the houses were so close together and there were so many of them. Then there were all the stores. They passed the livery stable. It was barely dawn, but there was the sound of voices and horses. She was speechless as she stared around her.

"John Shaw that way." Uncle Ned pointed down the long main road. "Take Papoose to house. White man must not see Indian."

He halted in front of an immense white house with a huge yard covered with green grass, flowers, and shrubs, and a small summerhouse at one side. A white picket fence enclosed the yard and a hitching post with a stepping-stone was at the gate. Across the road was an old church with a cemetery.

Mandie stood in frozen awe at the monstrous size of the house and the surrounding yard and gardens. So this was Uncle John's mansion. It must have twenty rooms, at least. She at once became nervous and excited at the prospect of meeting her father's brother. What if he didn't like her? What if she had to go back to the Brysons? But then, she would not think of such things, because she would not go back to the Brysons under any circumstances. She would go live with Uncle Ned's tribe if her uncle rejected her.

"Go, Papoose," Uncle Ned urged her. "I come later. Love."

"And love to you, Uncle Ned and Morning Star." She turned to hug the old Indian and the squaw, and then quickly opened the gate and ran up the steps to the front porch. She lifted a shaking hand to knock on the front door.

She could not hear a sound inside. No one seemed to be at home. Her heart sank. She turned to look at the Indians who were half hidden by the shrubbery. Then she heard footsteps coming closer to the door. She looked up to see a big, tall man, barefooted and in workclothes, standing before her.

"Are you John Shaw?" she asked nervously.

"No, ma'am. He's not home." The man scratched his gray head as he stared at her.

"When will he be back? You see, I'm his niece, Amanda Shaw," she explained.

"Well, come in, miss." The man held the door open and Mandie turned to catch a glimpse of Uncle Ned's smiling face.

She entered a wide hallway and followed the man to a room on the right, which she decided must be the company parlor judging from the rich furnishings. She sat down on the edge of a soft armchair and deposited her bag on the floor by her side. Snowball escaped from her arms and went running off into the other part of the house.

"When will Uncle John be back?" she asked.

"Oh, he's gone to Europe. He's been gone since March. I'm the caretaker, Jason Bond." He was still standing as he explained.

"Oh, goodness, to Europe!" She was dismayed to have come all this way and then not find her uncle at home. "What will I do?"

"Where're you from, miss?"

"I lived with my daddy, Jim Shaw, and my mother over at Charley Gap in Swain County until my daddy died in April and my mother got married again. Then they sent me away to live with some awful people at Almond Station and I ran away." She told the man the truth, knowing her uncle would have to know. "I—I don't have anywhere to live."

"Oh, well, plenty of room here. He oughta be back any day now. Come on, I'll find you a room." He picked up her bag and led the way up a long flight of stairs to the second floor, and then down a long hall and opened the door to a room furnished with blue and gold. Mandie stared in delight. Never had she seen such an elegant room.

"How about this one?" Jason Bond was asking as she stood there.

"Oh, it's beautiful! It's wonderful!" She stood in the middle of the room, gazing about.

"I'll get Liza to bring you some fresh water for your pitcher over there, and some breakfast if you ain't et yet."

"Oh, I am hungry," she said. "In fact, I'm starving!" She laughed.

"Well, we'll fix that." Jason Bond went out the door and she removed her wrinkled bonnet, tossed it on the bed and sat down in a big, soft chair. She had a strange feeling that she must be in the wrong house. How could her uncle have so much when her father had had so little?

An enormous old black woman knocked and then came on in with a tray of food, followed by a young black girl with a bucket of water.

"I'm Lou, Aunt Lou, they call me, my child. I keeps this house together." She set the tray on a table nearby and stood before Mandie. "Now, what might be your name?"

"Amanda Shaw, Aunt Lou. My daddy was Jim Shaw, John's brother." She lifted the cloth covering the food and exclaimed, "Oh, thank you, Aunt Lou. I'll eat every bite; I'm so hungry."

"Well, you'd better had if you gonna stay around here. Now this here's Liza. She'll be lookin' after you whiles you here." She beckoned to the young girl who still stood behind her. Liza came forward and poured the water into the pitcher on the washstand.

"Guess you'd better wash that dirty face 'fore you eat." Aunt Lou smiled at her. "Liza, you comb that pretty hair for my child. But let her eat first."

Aunt Lou left the room and Mandie went to wash her face in the bowl of water.

"I be back later, Miss Amanda," Liza told her. "You want anything, all you has to do is pull that cord over there."

"Pull that cord?" Mandie asked, looking to where Liza was pointing toward the drapery beside the bed.

Liza laughed and danced around the room. "That makes a bell ring down at the other end where I hear it and I knows you calling me." She danced on out the door, laughing.

Snowball came running into the room and jumped up into Amanda's lap as she sat down to eat.

"You just wait, Snowball. You have to eat on the floor. Here," she said, putting him down and giving him some milk in a saucer that had been on her tray. She added a bit of bacon. "Now you eat it all up because we're going to take a nap."

True to her word, she, with Snowball's help, ate every bite of the food and then, pulling down the silky bedspread, she flopped onto the big soft bed and fell fast asleep with the kitten curled up beside her.

At noontime Liza came to call the girl to dinner and had to wake her.

"Time to eat, Miss Amanda," Liza said, shaking the girl.

Mandie sat up rubbing her eyes. "Eat? I just ate. Oh, goodness, what time is it?" Snowball rose and stretched.

"It's time to eat again. Wash your face and I'll comb that hair," Liza told her.

The black girl quickly unbraided Mandie's hair, combed out the many tangles and then braided it again.

"I think I'll wash your hair later," Liza suggested.

"Oh, yes, it is dirty," Mandie agreed, remembering the bed of twigs she had slept on and the many miles she had walked through briars, dusty roads and river water.

"Later," Liza said. "Now you just follow me. I'll show you where the food be."

They went back down the long, carpeted hall, down the elaborate staircase and through another long hall into the most beautiful room Mandie had ever seen. A huge crystal chandelier hung over an enormous dining table covered with a crocheted tablecloth and set with one place at the end for her. Silver candelabra stood at intervals along the table. A whole wall was covered by a tapestry of peacocks and flowers. The opposite side of the room had long French doors opening onto a terrace. Mandie stopped to gaze about the room.

"Here, missy, down to this end," Liza beckoned to her as she pulled out a chair with a velvet seat. "You set right here and I bring on the food."

Mandie, still speechless, walked to the chair and sat down. Then she turned quickly as the girl turned to leave the room. "What do you have to eat?"

"Anything you want, missy. Ham, chicken, sweet potatoes, green beans, turnip salat, cornpone, biscuits, honey, preserves, anything you want. Now what must I bring you?" Liza waited.

"You mean you have all those things already cooked? All for one meal?"

"Well, missy, all us servants have to eat too, and there's two more 'sides me and Lou. There's Jenny, the cook, and there's Abraham, the yard man, what lives in the house in the backyard. Lou, she's the boss," Liza went on. "So we just cook everything at one time. That's the way Mr. Shaw tells us to do. Want me to bring you some of everything?" Liza grinned.

"Oh, no, I couldn't possibly eat so much. Just a small piece of ham, a spoonful of green beans, a huge sweet potato, a big piece of cornbread, and milk," Mandie told her. "My uncle must be an awfully rich man if he has all that for one meal."

"Oh, he is, missy. Richest man this side of Richmond, they say. So much money he'll never spend it all. And no one to leave it to—except—"

Aunt Lou came through the door at that moment.

"Liza, git a move on here. Take that cat there and feed it and git this child something to eat. And no more of that gossip, you hear?"

Without a word, Liza took Snowball and quickly left. the room.

"And how is my child feeling after her nap?" Aunt Lou put her arm around Mandie's shoulders.

"Fine, Aunt Lou. Liza says my uncle is unusually rich; is that so?"

"I don't knows about it being unusual, but he shore is rich. Liza ain't got no business meddling in his affairs like that, though."

"She wasn't meddling, Aunt Lou. I asked her. You see, my daddy was never rich."

"Many's a good man that don't git rich."

"You see, you can tell by my clothes that I am not rich. I don't have any pretty, fancy dresses and bonnets." Mandie smoothed her dark gray frock.

"Well, that's one thing we's can fix, my child. We's got a sewing room here that's just plumb spang full of pritty cloth. We'll just make you up some new clothes," Aunt Lou was telling her as Liza came back into the room carrying a silver tray loaded with dishes and the smell of hot food. "Now you just eat up, my child, and Liza can bring you 'round to the sewing room when you git done. I'll see what we can whip up."

"Thank you, Aunt Lou. I'll hurry," Mandie assured her, as she picked up her fork. The black woman left the room. "Don't go away, Liza. I'll be finished in a minute."

"I has to go eat, too, but I'll be right back. Just pull that little cord over there by the window if you want me. It'll ring in the kitchen," Liza told her.

"You haven't eaten yet? I thought I was the only one left to eat dinner," Mandie told her. "Go get your food and come sit right here." She pushed out a chair next to her with her foot.

Liza laughed. "You don't understand, missy. I'se a servant. Us servants has our own table in the kitchen."

"But I'm the only one at this big table. Can't you come and eat with me?"

"Nope, can't," Liza replied. "Nobody exceptin' Mr. Bond and Mr. Shaw eats at that table, and you, of course, 'cause you'se kin."

"Where is Mr. Bond?"

"He et early 'cause he had to go off and tend to some bidness," the dark girl told her. "Now you eat up. I'll go eat and then I'll be back."

Liza laughed and danced out through the door. Mandie, famished as she was, hurriedly ate the rich food in anticipation of getting a new dress made for her—a brand new dress made just for her—one that nobody had ever worn.

When Liza took her to the sewing room, Mandie was again amazed with the wonders of her uncle's house. It looked like a store. Fine materials, laces, ribbons, buttons of every color, were everywhere about the room. Aunt Lou, who was also the seamstress for the household, was waiting for her.

"You just pick out what you want and we make it," the old woman told her.

Mandie immediately spied a roll of pale blue silk in the pile. She stroked the soft material with her fingertips.

"This one, please," the girl murmured shyly. "I've never had a light-colored dress in my life."

"And a bonnet to match." Aunt Lou smiled at her. "We'll just put lots of trimming on it—lace, ribbons, and sech. We'll make a real baby doll out of you, that's what we'll do."

Mandie spent the afternoon in the room while Aunt Lou pinned, measured, and cut material. She just couldn't believe it would all turn into a dress just for her. When Aunt Lou was ready to sew, Liza came to tell Mandie she had a visitor in the parlor.

"Miss Polly, that lives in that big house next-door, she's come to see you, missy," Liza said. "She waiting in the parlor for you."

"In the parlor? I don't even know where the parlor is," Mandie laughed bewilderedly. "I've never seen such a big house in my life."

"Right this way." Liza led her. "Down this hall and on down these steps and it's the big double door on the left, next to the front door. 'Member the room where you first came in?"

"I remember the room, but I didn't remember the way. Thank you, Liza." Mandie went on through the double door and there stood a girl about her own size in front of the sofa.

She had long, dark hair and eyes as dark as chinquapins. She smiled and came forward.

"My name's Polly Cornwallis. I live next door, and Mr. Shaw's cook told our cook that Mr. Shaw's niece had come to visit, and so I came over." She rolled off this long speech without taking a breath.

"I'm glad you live next door," Mandie told her. "Sit down."

They sat on the sofa.

"My name is Amanda Shaw. My uncle is gone off to Europe and I'm here alone, so I'm glad you came."

They were friends at once and before they realized it, Liza was telling them supper was ready. Polly had to go home, but promised to come back the next day and bring her schoolbooks. But the next day brought more than Polly and her schoolbooks for Mandie.

CHAPTER FIVE

THE SECRET TUNNEL

Early the next morning, Jason Bond answered a knock at the front door. He found a messenger there from John Shaw's lawyer's office in Asheville.

"Mr. Wilson sent you this letter, Mr. Bond," the young boy told him.

Mr. Bond took the letter, withdrew a paper from the envelope, and stood there reading.

"What's this? What's this?" Jason Bond was plainly shocked. "Come on in, my boy. I'll get the cook to give you something to eat. I'll have to send an answer back."

He took the boy to the kitchen and left him there with Jenny. Then he hurried to his room and wrote a note. Hearing Mandie singing in her room, he knew she was up, and knocked on her door.

"I see you're up bright and early. Come on downstairs. I have something to tell you." He led the way down to the dining room and yelled through the door to Jenny.

"Send Liza in here with something to eat," he said and went back to sit down by the girl at the table.

"What's wrong, Mr. Jason?" Mandie asked him. She could sense he was disturbed about something.

"Well, it's like this," he began, as Liza brought in the coffee and poured it. He waited until she left the room. "I have a letter here from your uncle's lawyer."

"You do?" Mandie leaned forward.

"Yes, but I'm afraid it's bad news. He says—he says your uncle has—died in Europe and—"

"Died! Oh, no!" she gasped and brought her hand to her mouth. "Please, God, not my Uncle John, too!"

"I'm sorry," Mr. Bond said. "I couldn't think of any way to tell you. The letter says he was buried over there and—"

"When, Mr. Jason?"

"A few weeks ago. It took a long time for word to reach his lawyer and then his lawyer had to let us know," the old man told her.

"Oh, Uncle John, now what will I do?" she sobbed.

Mr. Bond held her hand and tried to comfort her. "Don't worry about what you're going to do. You're going to stay right here. I'm sending a note back to the lawyer, telling him you are here and you are going to stay here until the will is found."

"The will?" she asked.

"Yeh, until the will is found. Lawyer Wilson drew up a will for your uncle last year, but he says in this letter he believes your uncle made another one since then. At any rate, he thinks the will must be in his papers here in the house somewhere, so we'll have to look for it."

"What good is the will if Uncle John is dead?" she asked.

"Don't you know what a will is? It's a paper, a legal paper, stating who is to receive what of the inheritance when a person dies. Your uncle had lots of money and property and someone will get all that, depending on who is mentioned in his will," Mr. Jason told her. "There's a possibility you will be mentioned in his will as a legal heir."

"An heir?"

"Yes, that's the person who gets whatever is left to him by the person who dies."

"But he never even saw me that I know of. He might not have even known that I was born."

"Maybe, maybe not. Anyway, he knew he had a brother, who was your father; and since your father is dead, if he willed anything to him, then you would get it instead."

Mandie finally understood most of what Mr. Bond was telling her, and she became anxious to find the will. She also wanted to talk to someone her own age.

"May I invite Polly to spend the night with me, Mr. Bond?"

"Of course, but her mother will have to agree, you know."

So when Polly came over and heard the news, she returned home to tell her mother and came back to tell Mandie that her mother would come to call later in the afternoon.

Mrs. Cornwallis, a young widow, was very expensively dressed; her clothes were beautiful. Mandie was a little unsure of herself in the presence of such a lady.

"My dear, such a shock for you. And just the day after you got here, too. You must come over to our house and stay until things are settled," Mrs. Cornwallis told her.

"Thank you, Mrs. Cornwallis, but I can't leave. I have to help Mr. Jason look for Uncle John's will," Mandie said. "And I would like Polly to spend the night with me, if you would let her."

"Yes, yes, of course, dear," Polly's mother agreed. "But, doesn't anyone know where John Shaw kept his will?"

"No, not even his lawyer. He says it must be somewhere here in the house, so we have to find it."

"Mandie, can I help you look?" Polly put in.

"That's why I wanted you to spend the night," Mandie replied.

Mrs. Cornwallis rose to go. "Polly can spend the night, dear; but please get some sleep, girls." She laughed as she left.

"Will you have to go home now because your uncle died? I sure hope not," Polly said.

"Oh, no, Mr. Jason said I was to stay here until the will is found; and we're going to find it ourselves. Come on! We'll start right now."

The two girls left Polly's nightclothes in Mandie's room and then in whispers decided to take candles and go up to the third floor. Mandie had not yet been to the third floor of the house, and was anxious to do a little exploring.

They found the door to the stairs, turned the knob and it opened. Silently they gazed up the dark steps, then slowly began their ascent on the creaking stairway. They reached a landing halfway up and stopped to open the window and push open the shutters to let in the light and fresh air before climbing the last flight.

"At last!" sighed Polly, as they reached yet another door at the top of the stairs.

Upon opening it, they found themselves in a long hallway. Holding their half-spent candles at arm's length, they cautiously followed the corridor to the only door they could see in the hall, at the left. Mandie, arriving first, pushed it open.

Before them was a huge, impressive bedroom furnished with two ornately carved four-poster beds. Each was covered with a white crocheted spread and draped with matching canopy curtains. There were two full-length mirrors with heavy wood frames to match the beds. Four tall windows were covered with sheer Priscillas.

Before the girls could take in more in the meager light, the canopy curtain moved slightly on one of the beds and they heard a strange noise. At the same time, a draft from somewhere snuffed out their candles. With this, the frightened girls ran down the hall in search of the stairway. Just as they reached it, the door slammed violently and when they grabbed for the doorknob they discovered there was none.

Mandie gasped and clung to Polly as the two raced down to the other end of the hall. In the darkness they both stumbled into the wall, pushing a hidden panel open which led to yet another descending stairway. Just when they were beginning to wonder if the stairs would end, they came to a short hallway. They could see no door, but more stairs led downward and they took the plunge hand in hand.

To continue the maze, they found another door, opened it and stumbled into a dark room, managing to cross it without bumping into any furniture. A second door in the room led to another stairway, at which point Mandie cried, "Where in the world are we?"

"Don't ask me," was Polly's bewildered reply.

At the end of another hall they came upon a locked door, but this time Polly discovered a large key dangling on a nail beside the door. With a trembling hand she inserted the key in the lock.

Exhausted with suspense and fear she handed the key to Mandie and asked her to open the door. To the complete surprise of both the girls there were bushes and vines growing directly in front of them in the open doorway. They pushed through the shrubbery and exclaimed together, "We're in the woods!"

They could barely see the back of the house through all the trees.

"It was a secret tunnel, just like in the storybooks!" cried Polly.

"It's amazing! I can hardly believe this is happening," added Mandie.

"Say, I'm getting awfully hungry," murmured Polly. "It must be close to dinnertime."

"Yeh, me too. Come on, let's run," Mandie called as she bounded toward the other side of the house.

Polly caught up with her. "Let's keep this *our* secret. Then we can explore it all over again."

"All right. We won't tell anyone where we've been," Mandie agreed. "But I sure would like to know what was behind that curtain on that bed. Ooh, it makes me shiver just to think of it!"

"I know," agreed Polly. "Let's get Mr. Bond to go up there with us and see what it is."

"That's a good idea. Come on. Let's hurry and eat dinner." Mandie once again broke into a run.

As they came in the back door Aunt Lou greeted them. "Land sakes! Where you all done been? Vittles bein' put on the table. Git a move on and git washed. Quick!" She shooed them on through the kitchen with a big grin, as they obeyed.

They washed, hurried to the dining room and slipped into their chairs just as Mr. Bond came in right behind them.

"Well, well, where have you two been for so long?" he asked.

"We've been looking for the will," Polly said, quickly.

"On the third floor," added Mandie, watching for his reaction.

"On the third floor, eh? Well, did you find anything up there?" He began slicing the ham.

"Yes," Polly said.

"But we don't know what it is," Mandie reminded her.

"Well, what's that supposed to mean? How did you find something if you don't know what it is?"

"We found a big bedroom with ghost-white curtains and spreads over two big four-poster beds on the third floor, with white curtains all over all the windows. It makes chills run down my spine!" Mandie exaggerated.

"Mine, too! It made a noise, Mr. Bond, and made the curtains move and then it blew out our lights," Polly told him.

"Well now, if you'll eat up, we'll just go back up there and see what it is."

They were soon finished and Mr. Bond went to get some matches and an oil lamp.

Mandie absentmindedly slipped her hand into her pocket. "I still have the key to that tunnel," she whispered.

"Listen, let's tell Mr. Bond about it—just him—nobody else?" begged Polly.

"All right, but not till we see what the ghost is," cautioned Mandie as Mr. Bond returned.

They followed the kind man up the stairs silently, darting glances all around. When they reached the landing where they had opened the window, he closed it, commenting that the draft might cause their lamp to go out. Arriving at the top of the stairs he opened the door into the center hall of the third floor.

"Land sakes! Gotta replace that knob," he said, as he noticed the other side of it was missing.

The girls followed more closely behind him.

"It was in that room," Mandie said, pointing to the door on the left.

"All right, we'll just see what's in there," the caretaker told them. He walked over to the bed and the curtains moved. And there was that noise again!

As he touched the curtain a bat flew out from behind it. The girls screamed and ran into the hall. After a long chase, Mr. Bond finally ran the bat out through the window in the hall and closed it again, leaving the shutters open to allow some light from outside.

"Come on back in now and see for yourselves, girls. It's gone," he assured them.

The two slowly entered the room, looked cautiously around and were satisfied.

"Mr. Jason, we found a secret tunnel today right here in this house," Mandie blurted out.

"A secret tunnel?" the old man asked.

"Yes, come on! We'll show you!" Mandie fairly danced about.

"It goes into the woods," Polly said.

"I don't know anything about a secret tunnel in this house," Mr. Bond said.

The girls explained how they had found it. They led the way down the hall and searched for the loose panel. Instead, they found a door they hadn't seen before, which opened to a small room containing steps which led to the attic.

"Well, reckon that's it," Mr. Bond said. "We've looked everywhere and haven't found it yet. There's only one more door left and it's locked." He indicated a door near where they were standing.

"Oh, we missed that one," Mandie jumped.

"I've got the key. I know what's in there," Mr. Bond said.

"Here," Mandie pulled the key from her pocket. "I have the key to the door at the other end of the tunnel. We can come in from that end."

"Too late tonight for such things," Mr. Bond said. "We'll try it tomorrow in the daylight."

"Well, if you have the key to this room, can we see what's in there?" Polly asked.

Mr. Bond took out his keys and fumbling through them came up at last with the key that unlocked the door. The girls stepped ahead of him into the room and looked around in surprise.

There were shelves on three sides of the room filled with books. In front of a large stained-glass window was a huge desk with papers strewn about on it. All the shutters were open, letting in the moonlight from outside. On the opposite side of the room was a beautifully carved couch with big soft cushions. On the three sides with shelves there were wall sconces holding candles, as many as could possibly be placed between the rows of books.

Mandie noticed a smaller door in one corner which she tried to open and found locked. The caretaker had no key for it. She also noticed an ashtray with ashes in it on the desk and a pen in a bottle of ink.

"Wonder what your uncle used this room for—a private library?" Polly asked.

"He did his private book work up here," Mr. Bond told them. "None of the servants are allowed on the third floor."

"Do you know what's on the other side of that locked door, Mr. Jason?" Mandie wanted to know.

"Nope, can't say I remember ever seeing it before. Believe those curtains may have been pulled over it when I've been in here, and that's not been many times."

"Can we light the candles, Mr. Bond, so we can see how they look all burning at one time?" Polly begged.

Mr. Bond struck a match, lighted one candle, and the one on either side of it automatically burst into flame. He repeated this around the room.

"You see how close they are? That's what makes 'em all light up magic-like," the old man told them.

The room was brilliant, and Mandie's attention was drawn to a paper on top of the pile on the desk.

She picked it up and read aloud, " 'March 1st. Dear Brother Jim'—This is to my daddy!—'I am going on vacation to Europe for the summer and since one never knows what the future on a ship can hold, I would like to make peace with you while I can. I am an old man now, fifteen years older than you, you know, and I have no one to leave my belongings to, except you. I am taking the blame entirely for the disagreement between us all these years. I want you to know that Elizabeth is still in love with you, and she says she will never love anyone else. All that matters to me now is—' " Mandie looked up, puzzled. "That's all; it's unfinished. Who is Elizabeth?"

Mr. Bond took the paper and read it over again. "I'm afraid I have no idea who Elizabeth is."

"I wonder why it's not finished," Mandie mused.

"Might have been written over again on another piece of paper. See that ink blot?" He showed her a black smear of ink on the paper, which she had not noticed.

"You're right, Mr. Jason," Mandie's blue eyes filled with tears. "I hope my daddy received that letter before he—passed away."

"He probably did." Mr. Bond put the paper back on the desk and reached for a long rod.

"What's that?" Polly wanted to know.

"It's a snuffer, to put out all these confounded candles," he said, as he swung it around the room extinguishing each one as he went.

"Imagine doing this every day," Polly remarked.

"Yeh, and I'm glad I don't have to," he said.

Once in her room for the night, with only Polly for company, Mandie studied the paper again, which she had taken from the library. She was glad Polly's mother had agreed to let her stay with her until her uncle's missing will was found.

"I hope my daddy got this," she said again. "I have to find this Elizabeth who loved him."

"In the meantime, tomorrow we'll show Mr. Jason the tunnel," Polly reminded her. "What did you do with the key?"

"I put it on the bureau over there." Mandie pointed to it.

But, in the morning the key was gone. It was nowhere to be found.

CHAPTER SIX

THE GHOST

One morning, later that week, the two girls had wandered across the road through the cemetery, reading stone markers and commenting about the names, when they perceived someone knocking at John Shaw's front door.

They hurried across the road to find a tall young man with big hazel eyes, standing there with a black traveling bag in his hand.

He looked down at the girls, smiled, and asked, "Is this where Mr. John Shaw lived before he died abroad?"

"Yes, sir," Mandie told him. "I'm his niece, Amanda Shaw."

"You are?" he questioned her. "I'm his nephew. You live here?"

"Yes, come on in and sit down. I'll get Mr. Bond." She opened the door and met Mr. Bond in the hallway. "Mr. Bond, this is Uncle John's nephew."

The old man quickly looked the young man over and said slowly, "Mr. John Shaw didn't have any nephews."

"Well, I'm Bayne Locke, his sister's son. And since I *am* his nephew, I have come to claim my part of his property," the young man told him.

"I said, Mr. Shaw did not have any nephews; in fact, no living relatives, except his brother, Jim, and his family and they live in Swain County," Jason Bond was emphatic.

"I am John Shaw's *nephew,*" the stranger insisted, standing there in the hallway. "My mother died when I was born and I never have seen my uncle, but I'm sure I can claim at least part of what he owned. Where's his will?"

Mr. Bond looked puzzled, scratching his head thoughtfully. "To tell you the truth, we haven't found the will yet. But we have received word from his lawyer concerning the property—"

The young man interrupted, "I have as much right to stay here as anyone else until the will is found, if it *is* ever found." He plopped his bag on the floor.

"Oh, it'll be found all right," Mr. Bond told him.

"Well, until it is found, please show me my room. I've been traveling all the way from Richmond and I'm tired," Bayne Locke demanded.

"I suppose you can stay here tonight, but I'll have to have proof as to who you are," the old man said.

"I have it right here." Bayne pulled a paper from his inside pocket and handed it to Mr. Bond.

"All this says is that you are the son of Martha Shaw and Caro Locke. It does not prove you're John Shaw's nephew."

"Anybody that knows the Shaw family knows that he had a sister who died twenty-two years ago giving birth to a son in Richmond," Bayne told him.

Mr. Bond still stood there scratching his head. Mandie was left speechless with the matter. Then Polly suddenly looked from Bayne to Mandie and spoke up.

"Well, Mandie, you have a cousin!" she exclaimed.

"Well, sort of, I suppose I do," Mandie agreed. Then she turned to Mr. Bond. "I'll show my cousin to a room, Mr. Bond. Which room should I put him in?"

"Either one down the hall upstairs. I'll get Liza to go up and get things ready." Mr. Bond turned back down the hallway toward the kitchen.

The girls led the young man up the stairs, past Mr. Bond's room, to an unoccupied bedroom.

Mandie pushed open the door and peered into the room. It was well furnished with heavy furniture, red rugs and gold draperies.

"This will have to do," she said, standing aside for Bayne Locke to enter the room. "It's on the front of the house and won't get the afternoon sun."

"Fine, fine," Bayne muttered, throwing up the windows and opening the shutters.

Liza danced in with a broom and a dustmop.

"Shoo, shoo! You-alls just git out of the way now, so's I can git this place shuck up," the black girl ordered the girls.

Mandie turned back as she went out the door, followed by Polly.

"Dinner's at twelve o'clock on the button. Don't be late."

"Never been to dinner on time in my life, but I'll turn over a new leaf just for you," Bayne called back to her.

As the two girls sat in the swing on the front porch, Polly asked, "What are you going to do now? That man says he's your cousin, and he'll take what he came after, if you ask me."

"We'll see about that! Just leave him to me!" Mandie teased.

"But what can you do about it?" Polly wanted to know.

"Tonight's the night for Uncle Ned to come visit," Mandie said.

"Uncle Ned? Who's he?"

"He's the Indian who brought me here. Remember I told you?"

"Yeh, but so what? What can an Indian do about this Bayne Locke?"

"I'll ask Uncle Ned to get the Cherokees to check up on this so-called cousin. Uncle Ned has his own ways of finding out things."

The screen door opened and Aunt Lou stuck her head out. "Got that new dress done fuh you, my child."

Mandie quickly followed her back into the house with Polly close behind. The blue dress was finished and pressed and was hanging in the sewing room. Mandie could only stand and gasp. She had never owned such a garment in all her life.

"Well, don't just stand there, my child. We'se got to put it on to see if it fits." Aunt Lou smiled as she began to unbutton the dress Mandie was wearing.

The dress fit perfectly and Mandie turned and twirled in front of the long mirror with oh's and ah's and Polly admiring.

"It's beautiful, Aunt Lou." Mandie was tearful as she turned to hug the old woman tightly. "Thank you, Aunt Lou! Thank you!"

"It takes a pretty girl like you to make a dress pretty," Aunt Lou told her. "You look mighty fine, my child."

"Positively heavenly, Mandie," Polly agreed.

"Will you unbutton me now, Aunt Lou?" Mandie asked.

"Unbutton you? What for? There's more acomin' from where that one came from. Now you just keep it on and enjoy it, my child." The old woman patted her on the head.

"More, Aunt Lou?"

"Sho' 'nuff. Next one will be ready 'fore you git that one dirty," Aunt Lou assured her. "Gonna be the lady of the house, you is. And you gotta look like the lady of the house—no more countrified looks. You'se a city girl now. Gotta dress like city folks."

"But, Aunt Lou, I hate to make so much work for you. You have other things to do, I know."

"Ain't just me working on these dresses. Got help from old Miz Burnette over on the hill, too."

"Mrs. Burnette makes my clothes too, Mandie," Polly told her. "Mother says she does the best work in town."

"Somebody has to pay her," Mandie said.

"Oh, never you mind about pay. Mr. Bond done arranged all that. Now git on 'bout your business. I'se got other things to do," Aunt Lou gave the two girls an affectionate shove out the door.

Thank you, dear God, Mandie whispered to herself. Thank you for all these nice things.

That night, when Mandie met Uncle Ned in the summerhouse nearby, she wore her new blue dress. The old Indian was happy when she told him about all the nice things that had happened to her, but he was greatly disturbed when he heard that her Uncle

John had died and Bayne Locke had come to the house saying he was his nephew.

"Bayne Locke. You know where he come from?" he asked.

"He said he had come all the way from Richmond, Uncle Ned," Mandie told him. "I suppose he must have lived there before he came here."

"Cherokee go to Richmond. Find out. I know by next full moon," he promised.

"Thank you, Uncle Ned. I seem to ask you for so many things, but I don't have anyone else to ask," the girl said.

"No, no—is all right. You one of us. Cherokee keep watch over Papoose. I promise Jim Shaw. Anything you ask, I do," Ned reminded her. "You Cherokee, too."

"Isn't that wonderful, Uncle Ned? That I have such people, people who will always look out for me. Tell all the Cherokees I am grateful. I'm happy that I'm one of you and I long for the day when I can visit my people."

Not only was Mandie planning to check up on Bayne Locke, but Mr. Bond had immediately sent a messenger to Lawyer Wilson's office, requesting information concerning the young man.

Later that night when he thought everyone was sound asleep, Mr. Bond climbed the stairs to the third story in a determined effort to locate John Shaw's will and settle the matter once and for all as far as Bayne Locke was concerned.

John Shaw's library was directly over the room that Mandie and Polly occupied on the second floor and he tried to be very quiet, but despite his efforts, he stumbled into a chair in the darkness.

"Polly, did you hear that?" Mandie shook her sleeping friend.

"Yes," Polly said, sitting straight up in the bed.

"A ghost!" Mandie whispered.

"In Uncle John's library. Let's go see what it is," Polly said, jumping from the bed.

"This time of night?" Mandie was leery of such adventures.

"Ghosts only walk at night. Didn't you know that?" Polly informed her. "I read a book about ghosts once. They can't do you any harm. So why be afraid? We're more powerful than they are. Want to go see what one really looks like?"

"Oh, Polly, you aren't afraid of anything, are you?" Mandie reached for her slippers. "Let's go, if you insist."

Polly led the way up the dark stairs while Mandie carried the oil lamp from her room. They crept along the hall and found the door open to Uncle John's library. As they cautiously peeped in, Mandie began to laugh.

"Some ghost that is!"

Mr. Bond turned at the sound of her voice. "Why, what are you two doing up this time of night?"

"We heard a noise, so we came up to see who it was," Polly answered. "We had kinda hoped it was a ghost."

"Well, I'm not a ghost," Mr. Bond chuckled. "But I'd advise you two to be quiet and not disturb the rest of the house. I don't want that Mr. Locke poking his nose in here."

"No, that wouldn't do," Mandie agreed. "He might find the will before we do. Can we do anything to help?"

"Well, start at the corner there and look through every book on the shelves. If you find any piece of paper at all, or any handwriting in the books, let me see it," Jason Bond told them.

So the real work began on the search for the important paper.

CHAPTER SEVEN

SEARCH FOR THE WILL

The search for the will was more involved than anyone had dreamed. Jason Bond and the two girls covered every inch of the house—except the tunnel. The missing key had not been found either, after it had disappeared from Mandie's bureau.

Mandie spoke to Mr. Bond about it, "I've asked Aunt Lou, Liza, Jenny, and even Abraham, and nobody has seen a key of any kind."

"Could be that Mr. Bayne Locke has been in your room, Mandie, but don't ask him about it. We don't want him involved in what we're doing around here. The less he knows the better," Jason Bond told her. "You two girls just keep your eyes peeled. Maybe it'll turn up somewhere."

No one had been able to find the entrance to the tunnel from the inside of the house, and with the key lost, the door could not be opened from the outside.

Mr. Bond was leaving the dining room after breakfast one morning, when there was a knock on the front door. He went to see who it was, followed closely by the two girls.

A tall, middle-aged woman with gray, staring eyes, and a tall, brunette girl were standing there.

"I'm Mrs. Gaynelle Snow and this is my daughter, Ruby. I've come to claim my part of my uncle's estate," the woman announced to Mr. Bond.

"Well, dad-blast it! If everyone in the continent ain't gonna try to claim John Shaw's property!" he shouted angrily.

"What did you say?" The woman stared at him with her sharp eyes, then peered to get a glimpse of Mandie and Polly behind him in the hall. *"Well,* if you're not going to invite me in, I guess I'll just walk in!" She pushed the old man aside and stepped into the hallway. "Where are the servants? Tell one of them to show me to my room!"

"Room! You'd think we was running a hotel here!" Mr. Bond stood there ruffling his white hair, trying to resolve the situation.

Liza was crossing the hall just then and the woman, followed by her daughter, yelled at her, "Hey, you there, find me a room in this mansion."

Liza stopped and stared at the woman and the girl and then looked at Mr. Bond.

"Might as well take them up to a room," he sighed. "Claim they're kinfolk. I'll have to prove them a lie before I can throw them out."

The girl turned her nose up at Polly and Mandie as she followed Liza and her mother up the stairs.

"Stupid ain't the word!" Polly exclaimed.

"Right you are!" Mandie agreed.

After the unexpected arrival of Mrs. Gaynelle Snow and her daughter, Ruby, things took on an even livelier pace at the John Shaw house.

Mandie and Polly took the notion to move into a bedroom on the third floor. They had grown tired of the room on the second floor where Bayne Locke always seemed to be lurking in the hallway watching their every move. Jason Bond warned they would be too frightened up there and wouldn't stay one night, if that long. But they in turn said they would stay no matter what happened.

Polly's mother, young, widowed, and longing for companionship, saw her chance for a trip to Philadelphia without her daughter, as long as the mystery seemed to be prolonged. Polly eagerly moved more of her things over to join Mandie in their new room on the third floor. Liza thoroughly cleaned the large bedroom for them, but was anxious to get back downstairs. All the servants were leery of the third floor and the attic.

The two girls were putting their things away in the drawers and the wardrobe, when Polly handed Mandie a cut glass jar full of powder. "Here's your powder, Mandie." Just as she reached for it, it slipped and fell to the floor, sprinkling the carpet and dusting Snowball, who gingerly jumped across the room, shaking his feet and licking his fur.

Mandie and Polly were doubled up in giggles at Snowball's action, when Mandie suddenly bent closer to the floor. "Hey, look! The key! Here's the key to the tunnel!" She picked it up from the carpet.

"The key to the tunnel!" exclaimed Polly. "You mean it was in the powder jar?"

"It must have been, it's right here in this pile of powder," Mandie told her. "I wonder where Liza got this jar, anyway."

And at that precise moment, Liza came through the doorway, carrying an armful of Mandie's belongings.

"Say, Liza, where did you get this jar of powder?" Mandie questioned, holding up the jar.

"Land sakes! You done went and spilled powder all over this here rug just after I cleaned it! Now why you want to do that?" Liza scolded her as she dropped the things onto the bed and stood there staring at the powder on the carpet.

"Sorry, Liza, it was an accident," Mandie told her, "but look what was in this jar—the key we've been looking for! Where did you get the jar, Liza?"

"Now let me see," she pondered. "I think it was on the bureau in the room that Mr. Locke is staying in. Yes, that's where it was," Liza went on. "I didn't think he needed that good-smelling powder, so I took it for you."

"Liza!" Mandie laughed. Then she turned to Polly. "Then Bayne Locke must have taken it from my room—the key, that is."

"I didn't think we could trust that man," Polly added.

"Hey, come on. Let's find Mr. Jason and take him to the tunnel," Mandie excitedly brushed the white powder off her skirt. "Let's go!"

They found Mr. Bond on the front porch.

"The key! We found the key! Let's go to the tunnel!" Mandie called as she and Polly ran on down the steps. Mr. Bond scratched his head and followed.

Breathlessly, the two girls pushed aside the bushes in front of the door. Mr. Bond reached for the door to unlock it, but it was already unlocked and standing wide open.

"Well, how do you like that?" Mr. Bond said, as he stepped inside.

"Now, we go for miles and miles before we come to the door into the main part of the house," Mandie told him.

And they walked and walked—down halls, up stairs and down again, and no door appeared to lead into the house at all. Instead, they found a panel in the wall slightly ajar.

"Look, that wall is open a little," Mandie whispered.

As Mr. Bond reached to touch it, the panel closed back into place and they could not even tell it had been open at all.

"Well, looks like it's not meant for us to get through," Mr. Bond said.

"I wonder how that panel got loose," Polly speculated.

"You girls probably knocked something loose on your travels down through here," Mr. Bond laughed.

"Guess we'll just have to go back out the way we came in," Mandie muttered. "But we're not going to give up."

"Nope, we're not," Polly confirmed. "Must be somebody on the other side of that wall, the way it closed so fast, and I know it was open, 'cause I saw it."

"Probably one of those ghosts we've been trying to catch up with," Mandie teased.

"Maybe we can find the other side of this tunnel now that we know the panel opens," Mr. Bond told them.

They left the tunnel the way they had entered. Mr. Bond locked the door and put the key in his pocket.

The three of them went back into the house and were climbing the steps to the third floor when they met Bayne Locke coming down. He grinned at them and would have gone on down the steps, but Mr. Bond stopped him.

"Look here, fellow, where have you been up that way?"

"Why, I've been up to the third floor," Bayne sarcastically replied. "Where'd you think I'd been?"

"What reason did you have to go up to the third floor?" Mr. Bond wanted to know.

"Hey, mister, you just work here. I am the nephew of the man who owned this house." Bayne was not grinning any longer.

"And I also happen to be in charge of Mr. Shaw's affairs until the will is located," Mr. Bond replied.

At that moment, Mrs. Snow and Ruby appeared at the top of the stairs to the third floor.

Mandie turned to them, "And what were you doing on the third floor?"

Mrs. Snow hurried down the steps, with her daughter at her heels. "What business is it of yours? I have as much right as you do to this house and everything in it. So, don't bother asking me any questions, because you certainly won't get any answers." She kept right on going down to the second floor, her daughter following and turning to make faces at the girls.

"That woman is no relative of mine!" Bayne Locke loudly proclaimed.

The woman turned back. "And Mr. Locke is no relative of mine." She and her daughter disappeared down the hallway below.

"Well, why don't you throw her out? She's certainly not kin to John Shaw!" assured Mr. Locke.

"Same reason I'm not throwing you out right now. I have to prove you're no kin before I can oust you from this house. But that day will come. You can be sure of that." Mr. Bond passed the younger man and went on up the stairs, Mandie and Polly following.

"Guess we won that time," Mandie remarked.

"Yeh, but who's gonna win the final say-so?" Polly replied.

They climbed the stairs all the way to the attic. It was dark and spooky, even though there were gabled windows to let in the daylight. The floor was covered with boxes, old furniture, trunks, dishes, clothes, and even an old organ.

"Now, the best thing to do is to go around the wall like this and tap on it to see if it will move," Mr. Bond told them as he rapped the wooden wall with his hand. "You two go around that way and I'll go this way."

Mandie and Polly did as he told them, laughing as they went, banging on the wall. They were almost all the way around the attic when they realized Mr. Bond was no longer with them.

"Polly! Mr. Bond! He's gone!" Mandie cried. "Where did he go?"

"I don't know. He was here just a minute ago. Maybe he's behind some of that old furniture. You go that way and I'll go this way and maybe we can find him," Polly told her.

As they worked their way around the room, they kept calling, "Mr. Bond! Mr. Bond! Where are you?"

Finally they met again.

"He's not here!" Mandie gasped.

At that moment, something scampered across the floor and both the girls screamed.

"Let's get out of here." Polly shouted, running for the door to the steps. Mandie, her heart pounding, followed close on her heels, and then she stopped suddenly as she looked back and saw Snowball beating an old piece of wood around with his paws.

"Oh, Snowball! Polly, it was Snowball!" She picked up the kitten.

"Well, anyway, let's get out of here." Polly ran ahead to the door.

They came down the steps into the front hall so fast they almost collided with Liza who was passing through with her arms full of bed linens.

"Hey, where you two going?" Liza stepped out of their way just in time.

"Liza, have you seen Mr. Bond? He disappeared," Mandie told her.

"I ain't seed him since he went up the steps with you two," Liza answered. "Why? What's wrong? Something wrong?"

Mandie immediately tried to compose herself, knowing the black girl would become frightened if they told her what had happened.

"Oh, nothing, we just missed him, I guess," Mandie said.

"Yeh, we stayed too long in the attic," Polly helped out.

"You been in the attic? Lawsy mercy, what you two done been doin' in that spooky place?" Liza's eyes widened. "Ain't you'ns askeered to go up there?"

"We just went up there looking for something, Liza. Come on, Polly, let's go out in the yard."

Once the two girls were out of Liza's sight they ran for the entrance to the tunnel.

"He's gotta be in the tunnel. He must've found the panel that opened up," Polly declared.

"Right. Maybe we can find the way in from the tunnel now," Mandie said as she ran on ahead and pushed at the door. "Oh, no, Mr. Bond locked it when we left, remember? And we don't have the key!"

"Guess we give up and go home and wait for him to come back from wherever he's gone," Polly lamented.

To their amazement, Mr. Bond was sitting in the swing on the front porch when they came around the corner of the house.

"Mr. Jason! Where did you go?" Mandie ran to him.

"Where did I go?" the old man asked.

"Yes, when we were in the attic, you just disappeared," Polly added.

"Oh, the attic—why, I just came on back downstairs."

"But we didn't see you leave," Mandie insisted.

"No, because some of that old furniture is taller than you two, I suppose." He smiled at the girls. "Did you get scared because I left you alone up there?"

"Oh, no, Mr. Jason. We were just trying to find you. We thought maybe you had found the secret panel," Mandie told him.

"The secret panel? Oh, the panel to the tunnel. No, I don't suppose there's an opening into the attic after all," Mr. Bond said.

The two girls looked at him and then at each other and didn't say anything else, but they went on inside the house and up to their room on the third floor.

"I don't believe him!" Mandie was emphatic about it.

"Neither do I!" Polly flopped down beside Mandie on the big bed.

"But why would he lie to us, Polly?"

"Must have a good reason."

"Well, after all, this is my uncle's house and Mr. Jason shouldn't keep secrets from me," Mandie moped.

"Nope."

"Well, don't you have any ideas?"

"I just can't figure this one out, Mandie. Everybody seems to be trying to hide something from everybody else."

"I know. Guess it's the money my uncle has. Money makes people fight sometimes, my father always told me. He always said it was better to be poor. Then you would know who your friends really are."

"Oh, Mandie, I don't agree with that at all. I'd just die if we were poor." Then Polly realized what she was saying. "Sorry, I forgot. I mean, I know you told me how poor your family is. But, anyway, don't you think it's better now, with all those new dresses and so much to eat, and servants to do all the work?"

"Well, I suppose. But look at the difference in things since Bayne Locke and that Mrs. Snow and her terrible Ruby came here. They're all after my uncle's money!"

"So what are we going to do about Mr. Jason now?"

"I suppose we'll have to watch him now, along with the others."

CHAPTER EIGHT

JOE COMES TO VISIT

The people who sat around the dining table at mealtime after that acted like enemies. There was very little conversation between any of the occupants of John Shaw's house.

Mr. Bond tried his best to carry on a conversation at the table one day at dinnertime, but Bayne Locke and Mrs. Snow and her daughter completely ignored him. The girls did not talk either, but continued to listen and watch everyone else. Mr. Bond only got curt answers to any questions he asked in an attempt to draw the girls out.

"Well, if this ain't the quietest bunch I ever seed in all my born days," Liza remarked as she brought in the dessert. "What's the matter—cat got all your tongues?"

Mandie laughed. "No, Liza, we just can't do two things at one time. If we're going to eat, we have to eat, and if we're going to talk, we just can't eat."

"Oh, I sees," Liza smiled at her. "Everybody must be starved to death." She twirled on out of the dining room with her arms full of dishes. "Most nonsense I ever heard of!"

"Well, guess she's right," Mr. Bond remarked, looking straight at the two girls. "But if everyone's starved to death, why is everyone leaving so much food on their plates?"

"Don't include me in that. I eat whatever I'm served," Mrs. Snow haughtily informed him.

"So do I," her daughter piped in.

"I'm always hungry. I always eat anything I can get my hands on," Bayne Locke said. "Food's too good to waste."

"That leaves me to answer, I suppose," Mandie volunteered. "My stomach doesn't feel too well lately. Too much excitement around. Besides, I'm not used to so much food at one meal."

"Well, I think eating is a silly habit and a waste of time when you could be doing something more interesting. Therefore, I only eat enough to keep from starving," Polly told them.

"Maybe the food will taste a little better at suppertime," Mr. Bond said as he rose from the table. "Although I didn't see anything wrong with what we just had."

There was a loud knock on the front door. Everyone was silent and listened. There were indistinct voices in the hall and Liza came hurrying into the dining room.

"Missy, you'se got company—the doctor man and his son," Liza announced to Mandie.

"Joe!" Mandie rushed from the room.

She greeted Dr. Woodard and Joe in the front hallway.

She grasped the old man's hand. "Dr. Woodard, I'm so glad to see you, and you, too, Joe." She turned a little shyly toward the boy. "Seems like ages since I saw y'all. Come on into the dining room and meet everybody. You'll probably want something to eat, anyway."

"Wow! Your uncle sure does have a big house," Joe commented.

"Hope you've been all right, Mandie," the old doctor squeezed her hand.

"Everybody," Mandie addressed all who were still at the table, "these are my friends, Dr. Woodard, and his son, Joe."

Liza was already setting two more plates and she motioned for them to sit down.

"Jason Bond, Doctor," Mr. Bond said, shaking his hand heartily. "Sit down, eat. You, too, young fellow." As the two sat down, Mr. Bond resumed his seat. Mandie took her place again, and then introduced each one around the table. "This is my friend, Polly Cornwallis. This is Bayne Locke, Mrs. Snow, and her daughter, Ruby. Now do help yourselves, Dr. Woodard, there's plenty to eat."

"Yes, I can see there is," Dr. Woodard said, piling his plate high, and turning to Joe who kept his eyes glued on Polly. "Joe, dig in, boy."

"Oh, yes, sir," Joe answered and began filling his plate, still stealing glances at Polly who was openly staring at him also.

"Where are you from, Dr. Woodard?" Bayne asked him.

"We live near where Amanda comes from, in Swain County," he answered between mouthfuls of green beans and cornbread. "Had to come to Franklin on some business and just thought we'd drop in to see how she was getting on."

"You know that Uncle John died?" Mandie questioned.

"Died? Why, no, I hadn't heard. When? What happened?" Dr. Woodard asked.

"He died right after I came here," she told him. "He was in Europe."

"It was very sudden, Doctor, from what his lawyer told me, and he was buried overseas," Mr. Bond added.

"Well, I'm very sorry to hear that," the doctor replied. "Your ma and sister are fine, Amanda. I saw them at the store yesterday."

"Oh, Dr. Woodard, please don't tell them where I am!" Mandie begged, as she quickly studied the doctor's face. "You—you haven't already, have you?"

"Well, as a matter of fact, I have, Amanda. But, now don't you worry. It's all right with your ma, if you want to stay here—but then, what's going to happen now that your uncle is gone?"

"You *told* her?" Mandie felt betrayed.

"Yes, I had to. There was a posse out looking for you all over Nantahala Mountain after you ran away from the Brysons. Just happened you had written Joe where you were going," Dr. Woodard told her. "I didn't want to, Amanda, but I had to. Those men were wasting their time. But like I said, your ma doesn't care if you stay here. She told me so. Will you stay on here, now that your uncle is dead?"

"Yes, I will," Mandie replied. "Mr. Bayne Locke says he is my uncle's nephew and Mrs. Snow says she is his niece. But, we haven't found the will yet, so we don't know what he left to whom."

"Well, that's a nice kettle of fish. Can't find the will, eh?" The doctor continued eating as he turned to Mr. Bond. "Say he has a will to be found yet?"

"That's right. His lawyer believes it's somewhere in this house but we haven't turned it up yet," Jason Bond told him. "And until we do, nothing can be settled."

Dr. Woodard turned to Bayne Locke and Mrs. Snow.

"I don't recollect Jim and John Shaw having any other living close relatives," he told them.

"That's because my mother, who was John Shaw's sister, Martha, died when I was born," Bayne told him.

"When you were born? Now, let me see, you must be twenty-two or twenty-three?"

"Twenty-two."

"Well now, twenty-two years ago I was in school with Jim Shaw and he didn't have a sister. As a matter of fact, I had known the family probably four or five years before that." The doctor was emphatic about this.

"Sorry, but he did have a sister and I am her son," Bayne Locke smiled crookedly at the doctor.

The doctor grunted his disapproval and turned to Mrs. Snow. "And you claim to be a niece? He didn't have any niece except Amanda here."

"Well, I don't know who you think you are, but I guess I know who I am." Mrs. Snow jumped up from the table and threw down her napkin. "Come on, Ruby, we have things to do." And they left the room in a hurry.

"Guess she's mighty sensitive about it," Dr. Woodard mumbled.

"You're absolutely right, Doc," Jason Bond told him. "I know these people are not kin to John Shaw, none of them excepting Amanda here, but I got to get proof before I can put them out. And that proof should be on the way any day."

Mandie finally noticed that Joe and Polly were staring at each other. Thinking they were both just being shy, she tried to start a conversation. "Joe, you just ought to see all the nice clothes Aunt Lou has made for me since I came here."

"Clothes? Aunt Lou? Oh, yes," Joe turned and smiled at her. "I see you have on a new frock. It's awfully pretty."

"Joe, maybe Dr. Woodard would let you visit with us for a while. We have this huge house with all these rooms and all this food," Mandie began.

"Could I, Dad?" Joe turned to his father and watched Polly out of the corner of his eye. "Could I stay here till you come back next week? Please?"

"Well, I don't know about that. There isn't any—"

"Please, Dr. Woodard!" Mandie begged.

Jason Bond tried to help her. "He's welcome, Doc, if he wants to stay. Like Amanda said, plenty of room and plenty to eat."

"What about clothes? What did you bring with you?" his father asked.

"You said we were going to be in Franklin two or three days, so I brought a change of everything," Joe replied. "Please, Dad."

"All right. I'm not sure what your mother will say, but I reckon it'll be all right," his father finally agreed.

"Whee!" Polly spoke at last and jumped up. "Let's show Joe around—all over—you know."

Mandie understood the "all over" to include the tunnel and she quickly left the room with them.

Joe, who inadvertently found himself between the two girls, was speechless with all the finery and rooms in the house, and most of all, the story about the tunnel. Mr. Bond still had the key and Mandie had to return to secretly ask him for it. He smiled and handed it to her.

Curious about the tunnel, Joe was glad that his father had allowed him to stay to visit; but Mandie wanted to talk to him alone and it was near suppertime before she had a chance. Mr. Bond went with Polly to her house next door to get more clothes and

Mandie promptly asked Joe to sit in the swing on the front porch with her.

"I sure miss school, with you and everything, Joe," she told the boy.

"Me, too, Mandie. I never go over to your mother's house any-more, but I heard that Irene is getting seriously involved with Nim-rod," Joe told her.

"Nimrod! Oh, well, they are two of a kind!" she laughed. "Joe, have you—do you ever—that is, were you ever up at my father's grave since I left?"

Joe reached over and took her hand in his. "Yes, I've been up there several times when I was with Dad in the neighborhood. I've tried to keep it cleaned off. And once in a while, I find some flowers growing along the way and I put them on his grave."

"Thank you, Joe!" She reached over and kissed him on the cheek. "You're the only real friend I ever had."

Joe blushed and squeezed her hand. "You, too, Mandie. You know, we will grow up someday. And I still plan on looking out for you."

"Oh, Joe!" Mandie became shy.

Polly came around the corner of the house suddenly and broke the spell.

"Goodness gracious! Holding hands!" she teased, as she stood in front of them.

Mandie and Joe both blushed then and the boy nervously watched Polly as she went into the house. Mandie caught the look and sensed some feeling between Joe and her friend, and wise beyond her years, did not give away the fact that she was upset over it. After all, Joe was going to be around until the next week. And after all, she had known Joe all her life and she was sure she came first with him.

CHAPTER NINE

UNCLE NED'S MESSAGE

The messenger Mr. Bond had sent to Lawyer Wilson's office returned early one morning, tied his horse to the hitching post at the road and came to the door to give his report.

"Morning, Jason," he said as Mr. Bond opened the door. "I jest got back and came straight hyar."

"Come in, Daniel," Mr. Bond greeted the man. "Come on into the kitchen and I'll see if we can't rustle up a cup of coffee."

"That would be nice, Jason," Daniel said, following him into the kitchen where Jenny, the cook, was washing the breakfast dishes.

"How about some coffee and something to eat with it for my friend here, Jenny? We'll just sit right here," Mr. Bond told her as they sat down at the table where the hired help ate their meals.

"Sho, Mr. Jason, comin' right up," Jenny said, bustling about.

"Did you have a good trip, Daniel?" Jason asked, as the man eyed the food being placed before him.

"Well, Tiddlywinks threw a shoe smack-dab in front of old man George's mansion and that was lucky 'cause his smithy put on a new 'un right then and thar. Otherwise, I tended to my bisness and had to wait fer Lawyer Wilson to come back to town," Daniel told him. "Then when he did git back, didn't do no good. He ain't never heerd of this hyar man, Locke, or that thar woman, Snow. Said they probably thought they could worm their way into some easy money."

"Well, that's exactly what I figured. I didn't believe a word of their stories. Now, what did he say I should do about it?" Jason Bond asked.

"Hyar, he writ you a letter." Daniel pulled out a folded envelope from his shirt pocket.

Jason took it, withdrew a letter on the lawyer's stationery, and read parts of it out loud. " 'Just leave things alone for the time being and I will begin a thorough investigation in order to get the proof we will need to evict them from John Shaw's house.' "

"Sounds like you gonna hafta put up with 'em a whit longer, eh?" Daniel gulped down the last of the strong coffee.

"I 'spec so. We'll have to do things legal-like so there won't be no repercussions," Jason agreed. "Dad-gum, I was hoping I could put them out in the street when you got back. Well, reckon I'll have to wait."

"They been causin' you any trouble?" Daniel asked.

"Not really. It's just that I don't trust them and I can't keep them in my sight all the time."

"Does the girl keep a lookout on 'em, too?"

"Yeh, Mandie and Polly follow them around some—that is, when they're around. I sorta figure Mandie has decided not to trust *me* either. She won't talk about things anymore. And we've got Doc Woodard's boy staying here for a few days from over in Swain County. The girls are more interested in him right now than in our impostors."

"Well, I gotta be ramblin' on home 'fore Sadie hyars I'm done back and ain't come home yit." Daniel rose and turned to Jenny. "Thet was right good, Jenny—good food."

"Yessuh," Jenny replied, smiling.

"You comin' back to town on Saturday?" Jason asked as he led the way to the front door.

"Yeh, reckon I'll have to git some things from the store," Daniel answered, walking on out to his horse.

"Stop by and I'll have the money then to pay you for the trip," Jason told him.

Daniel waved and was off down the road on his horse.

Mandie and Polly came out the front door while Jason still stood there on the porch. Joe was close behind them.

"Well, 1see Mr. Daniel got back," Mandie remarked.

"Yep, and Lawyer Wilson don't know nothing atall about these people we got staying here," Mr. Bond told her.

"Does that mean you can make them leave?" Polly asked.

"Nope, he's got to do some investigatin' first."

"Well, I hope it won't take long," Mandie said.

Mandie remembered this was the night that Uncle Ned was supposed to return with his information on the Snows and Bayne Locke. She also knew tomorrow was the day that Polly's mother was supposed to return home, and she was glad because jealousy had sprung up between the two girls over Joe. Not a word had been said, but each one sensed it. Mandie had been subconsciously possessive of Joe from the first day he had smiled at her, and she always felt he had eyes for her only.

Joe was attracted to Polly, but he did his best to remain loyal to Mandie. Polly was attracted to Joe and did nothing to disguise the fact.

"We're going over to my house, Mr. Jason. Mother is coming home tomorrow and I have to tell the cook," Polly told him, as the three went on down the front steps.

"Well, be sure you get back in time for supper," the old man called after them.

Polly bounded along the lane to her house. "Can't wait to see what Mother brings me."

"Is this the first time your mother ever went off and left you?" Joe asked.

"She didn't exactly leave me. I didn't want to go, so I persuaded her to let me stay with Mandie. I've always gone on trips with my mother, but this time I just didn't want to go. Too many interesting things going on," Polly told him. She turned to Mandie. "We sure fell down on our job of finding the will, didn't we?"

"Yeh, but it's bound to be somewhere. It will eventually be found," Mandie said.

"If we could only find the way into the tunnel from inside the house!" Polly sighed.

"Let's try again tonight. Three heads are better than two," Joe suggested.

"All right, except it'll have to be real late, because Uncle Ned is coming as soon as it gets dark," Mandie warned.

"Uncle Ned is coming? How do you know?" Joe asked.

"Because I sent him to Richmond to find out about Bayne Locke and this is the night he said he'd be back. He never fails to keep his word," Mandie assured him.

"Can I see him, this time? Please?" begged Polly. "You always tell me about him but I've never seen him."

"Oh, he's just a real old Indian," Joe told her.

"He's also kin to me somehow. I told you I'm part Cherokee," Mandie put in.

"That's right. I forgot you're an Indian papoose," teased Joe.

"That's not funny, Joe," Mandie snapped.

"Sorry, Mandie, I didn't mean any harm. It's just that I can't get used to the fact that your father was half Cherokee," he said, taking her hand in his, causing her heart to flutter.

"Well, you didn't answer my question. Can I see this kinfolk of yours, Mandie?" Polly tried to break the mood.

"I guess so. But you'll have to wait until I talk to him and tell him you want to meet him. Otherwise he'll run away if someone besides me shows up."

"Well, here we are," Polly said, as the huge house she lived in came into view behind the trees. "Come on, we'll beat Cook out of something good to eat."

Mandie met Uncle Ned that night in the summerhouse after dark, while Joe and Polly waited in the swing on the front porch.

"Uncle Ned, I knew you would come. You always do," she greeted the old man as he appeared from behind the big walnut trees shadowing the porch. "Sit down, Uncle Ned."

The Indian sat across from her and smiled. "Papoose have visitor, doctor son?"

"How did you know?" Mandie asked, smiling.

"Cherokee knows all," the old Indian told her. "Cherokee find people named Locke in big city."

"In Richmond?"

"In Richmond. People know Bayne Locke. People *not* know if Bayne Locke kin to John Shaw."

"They don't?"

"Cherokee stay in Richmond. Find people who know. Then I tell Papoose," Uncle Ned told her.

"So he did come from Richmond and he has relatives there. Well, at least we know that much," Mandie said.

"Must go now. Morning Star send love to Papoose," he said.

"Give her my love, too, Uncle Ned. But, before you go, please, wait a minute." Mandie grasped his arm as he rose. "My friend, Polly Cornwallis, wants to meet you. She and Joe are on the front porch. Is it all right if I bring them out here to see you?"

"Yes, but hurry," he grunted.

Going around the corner of the house, she beckoned to the two and they came hurrying toward her.

"Polly, this is Uncle Ned," Mandie proudly introduced him. "And Uncle Ned, you know Joe already."

Joe nodded and held out his hand to Uncle Ned. The Indian solemnly shook hands with a grunt.

Polly smiled up at the tall Indian. "How do you do, Uncle Ned? I've heard so much about you that I wanted to meet you."

"Pleased to see Papoose number two," the old man said.

Everyone laughed at his name for Polly. The sound carried to the house. Jason Bond stuck his head out of the upstairs window directly above.

"What's going on down there?" he yelled.

"Nothing, we're just getting some fresh night air," Mandie quickly replied, looking up at him.

At the sound of the other man's voice, Uncle Ned darted out of sight, whispering as he went, "Must go. See Papoose next moon."

Mandie silently waved to him as he disappeared into the shadows.

The three walked back to the front porch and sat down in the swing.

"Say, that was close, Mandie," Joe sighed.

"Sure was, but somehow I don't believe Mr. Jason would mind if I had an Indian friend—unlike the Brysons, who were out to kill every Indian they could find."

There was a slight stirring in the doorway behind them.

"No, I don't mind, Mandie," Mr. Bond said. "I see him every time he comes. And I know who he is."

"Oh, Mr. Jason, you scared me," was all Mandie could say.

"I'm sorry, didn't mean to frighten you. Did he get any information for you?"

"Well, how did you know that?" Mandie was surprised.

"I heard you talking to him the night you asked him to find out about these people," the old man said.

Mandie dropped her voice to a whisper and told him what the Indian had told her.

"That's good. I'll let Lawyer Wilson know. Now are y'all going up-stairs? The parties in question are already turned in for the night."

"Let's do," Polly said.

"Sure, Mr. Jason. We haven't given up. We're going to look upstairs again for an entrance to the tunnel," Mandie chirped.

"Well, get to it then. I'm going back to my room. See you tomor-row." And he disappeared back into the dark hallway.

"Well, what are we waiting for?" Joe laughed.

The three softly crept up the steps to the third floor on their unending mission, being careful not to be heard by their mysteri-ous visitors.

CHAPTER TEN

THE SECRET DOOR

Joe led the way, carrying an oil lamp, Mandie close behind with matches in her pocket in case it went out. Polly brought up the rear as they noiselessly tiptoed on up the steps to the attic. Even the old door cooperated by not creaking this time when Joe pushed it open. They moved very slowly and carefully around, whispering softly to each other as they made an inspection of the attic. Joe, still in the lead, held the lamp at arm's length, the light picking up the debris, as the girls closely peered at everything in their path.

Joe carefully inspected the walls and the ins and outs of the eaves and the dormer windows.

"It seems to be awfully solid. I don't see how this wall could open up anywhere and there isn't room for any steps behind it," Joe whispered to the girls.

"But, it has to open somewhere," Mandie insisted.

"Well, look at it. You can see the wall all the way around the house up here, except where it goes into the eaves and the eaves are not high enough to have steps going down," he insisted.

"All right, maybe that's the way it looks, but there's sure an opening somewhere because we found it on the other side in the tunnel," Polly told him.

"Well, if you want to, we can keep moving and check the wall out all the way around," Joe said.

The three silently pushed on the wall as they went, reaching high and low, examining every foot of it. They were all tense with the spooky atmosphere when suddenly there was a loud noise on the third floor.

"Sounds like someone is below us!" Mandie whispered.

"Could be that Mr. Locke or Mrs. Snow," Polly added.

"Come on, let's slip up on them and see who it is," Joe suggested, as he moved toward the door to the steps. "Stay close behind me, because I'm going to blow out the light."

"All right," Mandie said softly, as she and Polly held hands and Joe put out the lamp.

They felt their way down the dark steps to the door leading into the hall of the third floor. Joe put out his hand to caution them to be quiet as he slowly pushed the door open. It was still dark on the third floor hallway and there was no sign of a light or anyone around.

Mandie pulled at Joe's shirt. "Psst! Go left toward Uncle John's library."

Joe followed her directions and the three slipped along the passageway to the door of the library Mr. Bond had shown them the other day. As they reached it they heard a slight movement in the room.

"There's someone in there!" Joe whispered, putting his hand on the doorknob, the girls close behind him.

"Push it open," Mandie urged him.

With that, the three burst into the room which was in total darkness. A man's figure outlined by the moonlight from the window moved quickly toward the small door that had been locked the day Mr. Bond was with them, and to which no one had the key. Just as the figure reached the door, the three dived at him, pulling him to the floor.

"All right, we've got you!" Joe cried, as he held onto the man's coattail. The girls were snatching for his sleeves and kicking him in the shins.

"Hey, wait a minute! Let's get some light in here!" the man said quickly.

"No!" Joe shouted. "Here, Mandie, take the lamp and light it. I'll hold onto him!"

The man quit struggling and Mandie quickly lit the lamp with a match from her pocket. Then, holding the lamp, she stared into the man's face, her hand shaking violently.

"Oh, no!" she cried, unable to move.

"Mandie!" the man said, smiling at her.

"You can't be my Uncle John!" Mandie shook her head.

The man reached for her and took her into his arms as he passed the lamp on to Joe.

"But, I am!" He kissed her hair. "My dear little niece!"

"Then, you really are my Uncle John?" Mandie's voice trembled with excitement.

"Yes, I guess I played a mean trick on you," he told her.

Joe and Polly stood there staring and listening.

"But, Mandie, how do you know this man is your Uncle John? You said you had never seen him," Joe insisted.

"Yes, it is Mr. Shaw, Joe. My next-door neighbor, remember?" Polly assured him.

"He's just like my daddy! Can't you see that, Joe? You knew my daddy. He looks just like him, except maybe a little older." She leaned back to gaze into the smiling face—so familiar, yet different.

"Good guess. I'm fifteen years older," Uncle John said.

"But why did you make us think you were dead, Mr. Shaw?" Joe asked.

"Well, I guess I just wanted to see what would happen to my property when I do die. When I heard of my brother Jim's death, it was too late to see him, of course, but, thank the Lord, I had written him a letter before he died," he said, sitting down at the desk. "You see, there's been hard feelings between the two of us since before you were born, Amanda. Then when I learned that he—was gone, I knew you were my only living relative, and since you are so young, I had to find out just whom I could trust to look out for you if anything happened to me."

"Then Bayne Locke and the Snows are no kin to you?" Mandie sat on the floor at his knee, while Joe and Polly hovered nearby fascinated with their discovery.

"Absolutely none! And I want them out of my house immediately! I had to take my lawyer into my confidence to send the message of my demise and of course he knows they are no kin, but he would have to prove it to stand up in court."

"But, Uncle John, where have you been all this time?" Mandie wanted to know. "That is, since I've been here."

"I've been living with my people—the Cherokees." He smiled at the girl. "Remember, we *are* part Cherokee."

"You've been living with the Cherokees? Then Uncle Ned must have known all along what was going on!" she reasoned.

"Yes, I came home with him when he saw you out in the yard earlier tonight. I could see things were getting out of hand, with no one able to find my will and all. However, I didn't know you children were occupying rooms on the third floor, and you almost caught me when you got the lamp from Amanda's room and went to the attic."

"Well, where is that will?" Polly put in.

"It's under the carpet over there by the door," he said, pointing toward the small door which was still closed.

"Under the carpet?" All three gasped and then laughed.

"What a good place to hide it!" Joe exclaimed.

"Where does the door lead to, Uncle John?" Mandie questioned. "Mr. Jason tried to open it, but it was locked and he didn't have the key."

"Oh, he has no idea where that door leads. He has never had a key. I have the only key." He pulled it from his pocket and got up to walk to the door. "Here, you want to see what's behind here?"

Mandie scrambled after him, Polly and Joe crowding closely behind her. John Shaw put the key in the lock, turned it with a click, and pushed open the door. Behind it was a paneled wall. Reaching to one side he pushed a latch and one panel swung aside. And there before them was the entrance to the tunnel.

He smiled as the three gasped in surprise.

"Uncle John!" Mandie covered her mouth with her hands.

"If we only could have found a way to unlock that door!" Polly moaned.

"And all this time you have been trying to open a wall in the attic!" Joe laughed.

"The tunnel stops here. It doesn't go up to the attic," Uncle John told them.

"But, what is the tunnel for?" Mandie asked.

"My grandfather, your great-grandfather, Amanda, who was also named Jim Shaw, built this house at the time the Cherokees were being run out of North Carolina. He didn't believe in the cruel way the Indians were being treated and he had this tunnel built for them. He hid dozens of Cherokees in there, fed and clothed them, and then helped them on their way when things calmed down along about 1842, and they could set up living quarters somewhere else," John Shaw told her. "That was the way my father met my mother. He was twenty-eight years old and had never been married when he met my mother. She was only eighteen, a beautiful young Indian girl."

"She was beautiful, Uncle John?" Mandie grasped his hand.

"Very beautiful, Amanda. I have her portrait. The frame needed redoing. It's in Asheville now, being refinished. You'll see it when it comes back."

"Oh, Uncle John, I'm so happy!" Tears filled Mandie's eyes as she looked up into her uncle's face. "I'm so happy you are—not—are still alive!"

At that moment, there was the sound of footsteps in the hall. Jason Bond appeared in the doorway and almost dropped the lamp he was carrying when he saw John Shaw standing there.

"Mr.—Mr.—S—Shaw!" he stammered.

"Yes, it's me, Jason. Sorry I couldn't let you in on the secret, but no one knew I was really and truly alive except Ed Wilson,"

John Shaw told him. "And I must say you've played your part well, Jason. You can be trusted." John Shaw explained everything to Jason Bond, who still stood there gaping and trembling.

"Oh, dear," Jason muttered as he learned the truth. "I—I'm sure glad you're back, Mr. Shaw. It sure straightens out a lot of problems. Like these people that moved in here—"

"Yes, I know. I knew about them as soon as they arrived. Uncle Ned kept me informed as to what was going on. Sorry you had to put up with them, but as soon as the sun rises they will be hitting the road."

And that was the way it happened. Upon being confronted by the real, living John Shaw, Bayne Locke, Mrs. Snow, and her daughter were all too glad to pack up their belongings and leave the next morning.

Mandie stood on the porch holding her uncle's hand as the three made their abrupt exit. She breathed a sigh of relief.

"Now maybe things will simmer down!" she exclaimed.

"Well, no, actually things are just beginning to happen! I'm expecting company from Asheville." He squeezed her hand.

Joe and Polly, standing nearby, looked at each other and Polly said, "Well, my mother is coming home today. So that eliminates one more guest from this house."

Joe scratched his head. "Don't know when Dad will come back for me, but it should be sometime this week."

John Shaw turned to them and said, "Well, let's not everybody leave at once! I thought we could have a little party when the company arrives from Asheville."

The three young people grinned at each other. *A party? What fun!* Mandie had not the faintest idea as to the importance of the party or the people who would be visiting. She merely knew it would be her very first *real* party.

CHAPTER ELEVEN

THE TRUTH REVEALED

The return of John Shaw was truly a happy event in the household. Every piece of furniture in the house was polished, silverware was cleaned, the best linens laid out for use, and two guest rooms readied for the two mysterious visitors who were coming from Asheville.

Mandie moved back to her room on the second floor. Joe also moved his things down to a room on the same floor. Everyone was excited, but no one could find out the names of the expected guests and John Shaw remained secretive about the whole thing.

Polly's mother returned and Polly moved back home, but came to visit Mandie every day. Joe received a note from his father saying there was a sudden outbreak of fever and he was needed so badly he couldn't come for him until things were under control.

Early one bright, sunshiny morning John Shaw drew Mandie off into the parlor.

"Today is the day the company's coming. Now, I want you to put on your loveliest dress and brush your hair until it shines—that is, if it will shine any more than it does already."

"Oh, Uncle John, I'm *so* excited! I don't even know these people, but I'll do my best to look and act like a lady," she promised him.

"That's all I ask, and I know you will." The old man smiled and her heart melted as the memory of her father's smile flooded back to her.

Mandie hurried off to her room and enlisted the aid of Liza to button her up in the newest dress that had been made for her. It was made of snow-white muslin covered with sprigs of bluebells that matched her blue eyes. Liza combed out her long blonde hair and let it hang loose in ringlets.

"Miss Amanda, you are really and truly beautiful today," Liza said, admiring the finished product.

Mandie laughed nervously. "Why do you say that, Liza, because you made me that way with all your fussing?"

"Nope, you just got that natural bloom today. Wouldn't doubt but that Joe boy tries to put some sugar on them lips if he catches you by yourself," Liza teased her.

Mandie blushed. "Oh, Liza, quit that silly talk. You know Joe has been my friend all my life. But, he's *not* my boyfriend."

"No, he ain't no boyfriend yet, but I can tell he'd *like* to be," Liza answered solemnly. "One of these days you'll know."

"Do you really think so, Liza?" Mandie turned to stare at the black girl.

"Sho as I'm astandin' here." Liza crossed her arms over her bosom. "You wait and see. And 'member I told you so."

Mandie's cheeks were still rosy. "Liza, do you think Uncle John will approve of the way I look?"

" 'Course he will. Now, you'd best be gittin' on down there to the parlor and act like a lady. Company comin' any minute now." Liza hurried her down the steps to the parlor where Uncle John was waiting.

"Where's Joe? Isn't he dressed yet?" Mandie looked around.

"First of all, my dear niece, you are absolutely lovely," her uncle told her. "As for Joe, I sent him on an errand. He won't be back for a while."

"Oh," was all she could say. She had been counting on Joe's support at her side to meet these important strangers who were coming to visit.

At that moment, there was the sound of creaking wagon wheels and horses stopping out front, and John Shaw turned quickly to her.

"Supposing you wait right here, my dear. I'll meet the company at the door and bring them in to meet you shortly."

"Yes, sir, Uncle John," she agreed and he quickly left the room.

Mandie could hear women's voices at the door, one sounded older and one quite young; there was also the soft speech of a black woman, and Aunt Lou was directing them inside with the baggage.

"John Shaw, you could give a person more time to get things together for such a trip," the younger voice was teasingly greeting Mandie's uncle.

"My, yes, you'd think someone was dying, instead of it being a party we are coming to," agreed the older woman.

"Well, I think you'll find the party well worth your sudden trip. Come on in here to the parlor. I want you to meet my other guest," John Shaw was saying.

"Really, John, we should freshen up a bit first," the younger woman was hesitating.

"Nonsense, you never looked lovelier. Come on," he insisted.

John Shaw appeared at the doorway to the parlor, accompanied by the most beautiful young woman Mandie had ever seen. She was dressed in rich silks, with diamonds sparkling on her fingers, and the scent of perfume came with her into the room. She had piles of shining golden hair, sparkling blue eyes, and a complexion that looked as though it had never been exposed to the sun's rays.

Mandie could hardly take her eyes off the younger woman, but snatched a look at the heavy-set, bustling matron, also dressed in the finest and most fashionable clothes Mandie had ever seen.

John Shaw hesitated. "Amanda, this is Elizabeth—you read about her in my letter to your father that night—"

The young girl was overwhelmed. So, this was the woman who had loved her father. She rushed forward to take her dainty hand. Elizabeth kept staring at Mandie and the older woman caught her breath and stood as if frozen to the spot.

Elizabeth was quite flustered as she turned to John Shaw. "John, who is this girl?"

John Shaw put one arm around Elizabeth and the other around Mandie.

"Elizabeth, this is your daughter, Amanda Elizabeth—"

The young woman trembled violently and John led her to a sofa to sit down, while Mandie, not quite comprehending the situation, trailed along, still holding onto her hand.

"Sorry it had to be such a shock, but I only found out the truth myself just a few months ago," John told her.

The older woman had finally found her voice. "John Shaw, just what kind of trick are you playing?"

"It's no trick, Mrs. Taft. You, of all people, know that. You knew that Elizabeth's baby didn't—"

John was interrupted by Mandie's urgent tugging at his coat. "Uncle John, what—who—"

Elizabeth and Mandie were staring at each other, speechless.

"John, it can't be. You know my baby died," Elizabeth kept repeating. Then she turned to Mandie, "Do you know your birth-date, child?"

"Oh, yes, I was born June 6, 1888," Mandie managed to say.

"Your baby did not die, Elizabeth. This is your baby—grown to a full twelve years old, never knowing who her real mother was," John was telling the young woman.

"John Shaw, you are only making trouble, you know that," Mrs. Taft was warning him as she sank into a deep chair.

"Uncle John, please—" Mandie begged.

"Yes, my child, this is your real mother, and this dear woman is your real grandmother," John finally turned to Mandie.

"It is quite a long story. Your mother, Elizabeth Taft, ran away and married your father thirteen years ago, but her parents opposed the marriage because your father was half Indian. Your father had lived here with me before that. Elizabeth's parents managed to have the marriage annulled and moved to Asheville to get away from your father's influence. Then, they discovered Elizabeth to be expecting a child. So, they sent her to an aunt's house in Madison County where you were born. They told your mother you died at birth, and persuaded your father to take you, telling him that Elizabeth had agreed she had made a mistake and didn't even want to see you. Then Jim pulled up stakes—"

"Oh, no, no! It must be a lie! To think my own mother and father could have done such a thing to me!" Elizabeth sobbed.

"Jim took you, Amanda, off to Swain County and had the misfortune of meeting Etta McHan, a widow with a daughter, who immediately latched onto him and got him to the altar. He never came to Franklin again, that I know of. You see, he and I were both in love with Elizabeth and he figured I had a hand in breaking up his marriage, but, so help me God, I never even knew you existed until a few months ago," John Shaw continued.

"That, that—woman—in my father's house—is not my real mother?" Mandie could hardly believe it.

"That's right. Not one whit kin to you, nor is her daughter. And I have Uncle Ned to thank for informing me of your father's death and of your existence. And, Amanda, he did get my letter about Elizabeth before he passed on and after I put two and two together, he wrote me about you."

"Then, you actually didn't know about me, Uncle John?"

"No, not until just before your father passed away. You see, Jim never came back to the house here. He just went off without ever seeing me and I had no idea he had taken a baby with him. I also fell for the lie about your death," her uncle said.

"Honor thy mother," Mandie was mumbling to herself.

Elizabeth, trying to recover from the shock, suddenly stretched out her arms to Mandie. "I've always had a strange feeling—Come to me, my—my daughter!" Mandie rushed into her arms and their tears mingled, as Mandie babbled incoherently, "Oh, Mother, Mother, my very own *real* mother! I'm so, so glad! I'm so happy! Thank you, dear God! Thank you, dear God!"

John Shaw turned to Mrs. Taft who was silently wiping tears from her chubby cheeks. "I'm sorry I had to do that but, but I had to. Let's leave them be, now. Come on, I'll show you to your room where you can be comfortable." He offered his arm and without a word the old lady rose and left the room with him.

"Let me look at my beautiful daughter!" Elizabeth held Mandie at arm's length. "And all those years I've missed being with you. Oh, my baby!" She held Mandie close. "I won't miss another minute away from you. You can be sure of that, my darling. And your father, Amanda—I loved him so much." Tears glistened in her eyes. "It's too late now for that, but it's not too late to claim my own daughter."

"My father never loved that—that woman. I'm sure of that," Mandie told her. "She never loved him either. Oh, *why* didn't my father tell me who my own mother was?"

"Don't blame him, my child. If anyone is to blame, it's myself. I shouldn't have given him up so easily," Elizabeth told her as she stroked the girl's soft, blonde curls. "And believe me, I will never give you up."

"Oh, Mother!" Mandie cried.

"And you know—we have the same name. Your father named you Amanda Elizabeth, which is my own name. That proves he loved me, doesn't it?"

"Yes, yes, Iknow he must have loved you, Mother, because he never loved anyone else."

Upon learning who the visitors were, Joe was overwhelmed and Polly could only stare at the beautiful young woman. And Mandie would not let her mother out of her sight, and was reluctant to go to bed that night, even though she would be close by.

Mandie knelt by her bed that night and thanked God. "Oh, God, you are so good to me! I know now that you do love me. All the trials and troubles I had to go through were necessary to bring back my own real mother. Please forgive me for ever doubting that you loved me. I should have remembered—*'The Lord is my Shepherd, I shall not want!'* "

And while Amanda tossed and turned in her bed, too excited to go to sleep, John Shaw and Elizabeth Taft were alone in the parlor. Mrs. Taft had retired early, complaining of being tired from her journey, but, actually, glad to get away from the two who had stirred up the secret past.

It had started to rain after supper, and John lit the fire in the parlor to keep out the sudden, damp chill that so often came in the mountains. He and Elizabeth were sitting on a low sofa in front of the fireplace, silently watching the flames jump and sing as they raced up the chimney. Neither had spoken a word after bidding Mandie and Mrs. Taft good night.

Finally, John leaned closer, covering her small white hand with his larger rough one. "Elizabeth—"

"Yes, John—" Elizabeth breathed softly, placing her other hand on top of his.

"It's—it's been a long time—" John faltered.

"Too long, John. And even now, Mother didn't want to come to your house. I threatened to make the trip by myself and then she gave in. I really believe she was afraid to face you after all these years," Elizabeth said.

"Well, I imagine she must have realized that somehow your trip here concerned Jim."

"Yes, an old friend of thirteen years ago doesn't just suddenly invite you to 'a most important occasion' at his house without good reason, and what good reason it was, John!" She smiled at him as tears of happiness filled her eyes.

"Elizabeth, I wish I had known the truth years ago. Even though I was in love with you, I would have done anything I could to get you and Jim back together."

"John, I can never thank you enough for giving me back my daughter," she said, squeezing his hand between hers.

John turned to her, "Then, Elizabeth, would you consider sharing her with me, now that—"

"Oh, John, no, don't say that. 1don't want to hurt you, but you know how much I loved Jim. I've never looked at another man."

"I know that, Elizabeth. But he was my brother and he is no longer with us. I would be willing to take a chance because I love you so much."

"But that wouldn't be fair to you—" she hesitated.

"That's for me to decide. It would be enough to know that you were finally mine."

"John, I just don't know. I really am truly fond of you, but in a different way from the way I loved Jim."

"I know that. But, I'm hoping that with time you will love me, too. It would be wonderful to share Amanda with you, too. She is the only living relative I have left, except some distant Cherokee cousins."

Elizabeth was silent for a few moments. "Let me think it over tonight. And I'll see you at breakfast—early," she said, rising as he still held both her hands.

"Fine, Elizabeth. I hope you sleep well and have pleasant dreams of me." He laughed. "I don't imagine you will sleep a wink after all the excitement, but, anyway, you are right. It is time to retire. I'll be up with the birds in the morning, and I hope I have something to sing about." He bent and kissed her lightly on the lips.

Elizabeth looked solemnly up into his face. "Until then, John."

CHAPTER TWELVE

THE WEDDING

After hours of tossing, unable to sleep, Mandie finally slept soundly for two hours then awoke with a start. She sat straight up in bed, trying to remember what was so special. The first streaks of light were in the sky and she could hear the twittering of the birds in the tree outside her window.

Then it suddenly came to her. Her mother—her real mother—her very own mother was here in this house!

She bounced out of bed and hastily snatching clothes from the drawers and the wardrobe she was quickly dressed. She quietly opened her door and crept down the long stairway.

The smell of fresh coffee was in the air and she knew Jenny must be up. Slipping into the kitchen, she found Aunt Lou busily giving the day's instructions to Jenny, who was rolling out the dough for the morning's biscuits.

"Aunt Lou, is my mother up yet?" Mandie quickly asked the old woman, who was startled by the sudden presence behind her.

"She ain't been in here if she is, my child," Aunt Lou smiled and put her arm around the girl. "Set yo'self down over there. I'll get fresh milk for you while you wait on dat important lady."

Mandie smiled and sat down at the table. Aunt Lou wiped one hand on her apron and poured a glass of milk from the pitcher on the sideboard.

"Here, you drink this. You ain't et a bite since them people come here. Your stomach's gonna be stuck to your backbone, first thing you know."

Mandie laughed and gulped the milk down. "Thank you, Aunt Lou. My stomach does feel kinda hungry."

Liza breezed into the kitchen. "Lady's in the dining room. Mr. John, too."

Mandie scrambled to her feet and ran for the door, "Oh, I have to go. Thank you, Aunt Lou. Thank you, Liza." Then turning back, she added, "And thank you, Jenny! *Thanks, everybody!*"

She hurried through the door, then slowed down to approach her mother and Uncle John who sat at the table. They both turned to smile at her.

"Good morning, Mother. Good morning, Uncle John," she greeted them, slipping into a chair at the side across from the two of them. The thought of her real mother being present still seemed a bit strange to her.

"Good morning, my darling. I hope you slept well." Elizabeth reached over to pat her hand.

"Good morning, my dear," Uncle John said, watching the two.

"Mother, I thought about it all night last night. Where are we going to live?" Mandie questioned.

"Why, we'll go back to Asheville, of course," Elizabeth told her.

"But, couldn't we stay here with Uncle John? You see, I've just found him, too, and I'd like to get to know him. He looks so much like my father." Mandie looked from one to the other.

"Well, Elizabeth?" John queried.

"Well, John—" the young woman began.

Mandie nervously interrupted. "I was thinking about this so much I couldn't sleep last night and I think I have a good solution to our problem."

"Why, what's that?" Uncle John asked.

"Well, it's like this," Mandie began, and then paused to look from one to the other. "Mother, if you and Uncle John would just get married, then we could all stay together here for always!"

Elizabeth laughed hysterically. "And here I was afraid to express my own mind for fear my daughter wouldn't like it."

John laughed, too. "Has Amanda answered my question, then, Elizabeth?"

Mandie was confused by the conversation, and was trying to figure out what they were talking about, when Elizabeth turned to her daughter. "You see, dear, your Uncle John asked me last night to marry him—"

"He did? Oh, Mother! Oh, Uncle John!" Mandie cried, and got up and ran around to embrace them both.

Elizabeth finished her sentence. "And I told him I had to think about it overnight. I was really afraid you wouldn't approve."

"Oh, Mother, he's my father's brother!" Mandie exclaimed.

"Amanda, my child!" Uncle John got up to put his arms around the girl. She looked up into his face and saw the strong resemblance of her father. She buried her face against his chest.

"You have my answer, John dear," Elizabeth told him.

Just then, Mrs. Taft came through the doorway. Mandie ran to her, grabbing her hand and leading her to the table.

"Guess what, Mrs.—Grandmother—you are my grandmother, you know," she told her as she pulled out a chair across the table from her mother.

"Yes," the old lady grudgingly admitted as she sat down.

"Guess what, Grandmother?" Mandie plopped down beside her. "My mother and my Uncle John are going to get married!"

Mrs. Taft darted a glance at the two. "This is quite sudden, isn't it, Elizabeth?"

"Not as sudden as you think, Mother. You see, John has been asking me to marry him for the last fifteen years, through the mail," Elizabeth told her mother, and winked at John.

"That's right, Mrs. Taft. I never gave up," John laughed.

Mandie cut in. "But it was my idea, really. I told them if they would just get married, then Mother and I could live here. We wouldn't have to go to Asheville."

"Oh—so you won't live in Asheville?" the old lady asked. "Well, Amanda, you haven't seen our home in Asheville yet. Your grandfather was one of the richest men in the country and when he died ten years ago, he left a fortune to your mother and me."

"Oh, that's very nice, Grandmother, but I'd really prefer living here where my father used to live," Mandie told her. She looked around the huge room. "Just think. He used to eat in this very room. Oh, I loved him so much."

Elizabeth turned to her mother. "You don't really need me, Mother. You have all the servants. I think Amanda has a good idea. We'll just live here and be on our own."

"Don't tell me you are allowing a child to make such important decisions for you!" the old lady rebuked her daughter.

"No, Amanda did not make any decisions for me. John asked me last night to marry him and I was ready to say yes this morning, provided we lived in this house. You are welcome to stay, Mother, of course, but this will be our home."

"Well, I was just—I didn't—" the old woman was quite ruffled at having her daughter speak to her in such a way.

"It is better this way, Mrs. Taft," John added. "I would never think of parting with this house. It's to be Amanda's at the time of my death, and I trust she keeps it in the family."

"Have it your way, then. I'll go back to Asheville where I have friends," Mrs. Taft replied curtly, then added, "After the wedding, that is, so I hope you won't delay too long with your plans."

Plans were indeed rapidly made. Dresses were ordered, the house refurbished, and guests invited. Elizabeth insisted on having Uncle Ned come to the wedding. After all, he was kinpeople to her new family.

Dr. Woodard finally came for Joe, but promised to return with Mrs. Woodard for the wedding. Mandie was surprised to learn that Dr. Woodard and her mother seemed to know each other from way back.

Polly and her mother paid them a formal call and Mandie was again surprised to find that Polly's mother also knew her mother from long ago. Actually, Mandie's mother had been born and raised and lived in Franklin until her father moved to Asheville when she was sixteen. And there he had built their mansion.

It seemed to Mandie that everyone in town was talking about the forthcoming wedding and had been invited to attend. Things moved along quickly and the day soon was upon them.

Uncle Ned arrived and was given a guest room, even though he felt very uncomfortable among the white people. Mandie and Polly were the bride's attendants. Joe and his father stood for Uncle John. The ceremony took place on a warm September afternoon in the chapel of the church across the road where John Shaw was a member and where Elizabeth Taft had belonged before moving out of town.

Everything seemed like a dream to Mandie—all white, full of clouds and scents of flowers, soft music, and whispering voices. Her feet never seemed to touch the floor as she floated down the aisle with her bouquet. She was so happy, she was afraid she would awaken and find it was not true. She faintly heard the wedding march. She barely understood the words of the pastor. And when her mother and her uncle floated back down the aisle together and out through the door of the church, she pinched herself to be sure it was real.

The drawing room of Uncle John's house had been transformed into a wonderland for the reception. There were flowers, greenery, and candles everywhere. Mandie darted in and out through the room to keep from missing anything. She had never known there could be such happiness. She caught a glimpse of her grandmother sitting alone in a corner and tried to talk to her, but the old lady had little to say to anyone except Jason Bond, whom she had charmed.

"Hey, slow down, Mandie," Joe said as he caught her arm at the corner of the long table holding the cake and punch bowl. "Where're you going in such an all-fired hurry?"

"Ain't goin' nowhere," she teased him.

"Ain't goin' nowhere? I think you'd better go somewhere—back to school if that's the way you're going to talk," Joe laughed.

"Oh, yes, I'm going back to school, all the way through, with years and years of education," Mandie continued to joke with him.

"But not *too* many years," Joe said, as he moved closer. "I don't want you to know more than I do."

"Know more than you do?" she asked, twirling her long silk skirts.

"That's right. I don't want my wife to be smarter than I am," he said, reaching to grasp her hand.

"Wife?" Mandie shot back.

"You heard right. I said my wife. I'm asking you now to become my wife—that is, when we get all educated and grown up, and all that, of course," he said, looking seriously into her blue eyes.

"Oh, Joe Woodard, you're not old enough to propose," she teased.

"I'm old enough to know what I want," he said. "Well, what is your answer? Will you be my wife—someday?"

Mandie became solemn. "I'll have to think about it, Joe. Too much has happened lately."

"I'll wait for your answer. Whenever you make up your mind let me know," he said, squeezing her hand hard.

"Holding hands in public! Shame! Shame!" Polly appeared at Mandie's side.

"Well, shame on you for being so nosy!" Mandie retorted.

"I have to look where I'm going, don't I? I couldn't just close my eyes as I passed," Polly scolded.

"Let's go talk to Uncle Ned. He looks kinda left out over there in the corner," Mandie remarked, and the three moved across the room to where the old Indian was sitting on a stool quietly taking in the whole scene.

Mandie was so happy she was giddy. As she approached the old man, she laughed, "Uncle Ned, will you come to my wedding? Joe has asked me to marry him!"

Polly stared at Joe in disbelief. Joe blushed and slipped away across the room.

"When Papoose gets to be squaw, then I come to wedding," Uncle Ned smiled.

"Joe!" Mandie called after him. "I didn't mean—don't be angry with me!" But he ignored her and kept going.

"Uncle Ned, I guess I said the wrong thing, but everything is so out-of-this-world right now, I can hardly cope." Mandie put her arm around the old Indian. "I'm so glad you came."

Mandie didn't get a chance to see Joe again, alone, and he and his father left early the next morning. Then she learned that her mother and her new stepfather were going to Swain County to visit her father's grave and his Cherokee kinpeople, and she was to go with them.

Uncle Ned went ahead to prepare the Cherokees for the visit. Mandie still could not comprehend; so much was happening. All her young life she had never known what it was to be really and truly happy. She thanked God every night for being so good to her.

To top off the excitement, they went by train. Mandie had never been inside a real train before. It was stuffy and dirty, but to her it was like a chariot from Heaven. At the station, Dr. Woodard, his wife, and Joe met them, and they went to spend the night at their house. Mandie knew she would get a chance to see Joe alone, sooner or later.

After supper, as the older people were sitting around discussing old times, Mandie asked Joe to show her his dog's new puppies. They went outside and into the barn where Samantha was giving her four offspring their supper. She flapped her tail when she saw Joe approaching, but kept right on with her duties. She was a golden brown mixed breed and her puppies were a variety of colors.

"Joe, they are beautiful! But, they're so little! Watch that black one! What a little pig. He keeps rooting the others away," the girl laughed.

"They might let him push and shove, but they get their share," Joe assured her. Then he turned abruptly to her, "Well, did you make up your mind?"

Mandie blushed. "Oh, Joe, I'm really and truly sorry for the way I acted at the wedding. I was just plain in the clouds during the whole time. I acted so foolishly."

Joe dropped his head and kicked at the straw on the floor. Then he looked straight into her eyes. "That's all right, Mandie. I understand. After all, it isn't every day one finds their real mother and then gets a stepfather, too."

"It's all so unreal," she said quietly.

"But, you still didn't tell me. Did you make up your mind about us?" He was determined.

"I've been thinking about it, Joe. I'll—I'll let you know tomorrow," she promised him.

"All right, tomorrow I'll expect your answer," He turned to the doorway. "Let's go back to the house. I'm hungry. How about you?" He took her hand and they laughed together.

The next day was like opening an old scrapbook and reliving the old memories. They all piled into the Woodards' wagon and began their journey up the mountainside. They approached the cemetery from the opposite side and did not pass Jim Shaw's house.

At the sight of the graveyard, Mandie jumped from the moving wagon and hurried to kneel at her father's grave. There were several withered bunches of wild flowers which Joe, true to his word, had put there. The Woodards stayed in the wagon while John helped Elizabeth down and together they joined Mandie in silence, standing hand in hand, and gazing at the mound of dirt which had settled considerably from the rain.

Mandie's memories of the day of the funeral came flooding back and tears flowed down her cheeks. If only her father could see them all now. She suddenly burst into uncontrollable sobs, and in a flash Joe jumped from the wagon and flew to her side.

Elizabeth blinked back the tears as John squeezed her hand and pulled out a clean white handkerchief, carefully wiping first her tears and then his own.

"We all loved him, John," she whispered as she moved closer.

"Yes, we all loved him, my darling," John replied, holding her tightly.

Joe was whispering. "Mandie, he can't hear you. He's in Heaven."

"I know that! I know that!" she sobbed.

It was a silent group who came down the mountain through Charley Gap in sight of Jim Shaw's house. As soon as she spotted the house, Mandie reached instinctively for Joe's hand.

"Joe, I'll marry you when we get grown, if you'll get back my father's house for me." A sob caught in her throat.

Joe put his arm around her. "I will, I promise I will, Mandie." He roughly planted a kiss on her cheek as the wagon jolted them along the bumpy trail and Amanda slid closer and smiled.

"Guess we'll be seeing your Cherokee kinpeople next," Joe said.

"Yes," Amanda whispered, afraid to breathe for fear she would awaken and find it all a dream. "Thank you, God. Thank you for everything. My cup runneth over." She lifted her face to the morning sun.

Somehow, the secret tunnel back home seemed far away and unimportant.

MANDIE

AND THE
CHEROKEE
LEGEND

For My Brother and My Sisters,

James Matthew Leppard,
Margaret Louise Leppard Langer,
Sibyl Belle Leppard Langford,

In Memory of Our Childhood Joys and Sorrows.

CONTENTS

MANDIE AND THE CHEROKEE LEGEND

"Blessed are they which are
persecuted for righteousness' sake;
for theirs is the kingdom of heaven."
(Matthew 5:10)

CHAPTER ONE

MANDIE AND THE PANTHER

Mandie sat with her feet dangling in the cool water of the Tuck-asegee River. Her white kitten, Snowball, played at the edge of the rocks. It was a hot day for the North Carolina mountains and Mandie was tired. Slipping away from the others, she had hastily pulled off her shoes and stockings, thrown her bonnet on a nearby bush, and run down the bank to the river.

She had left her fine clothes at home and traveled in calico. Mandie and her new family were on their way to visit her Cherokee kinpeople, none of whom she had ever seen. She was wondering if the Cherokees would like her. After all, she was only one-fourth Cherokee herself, and not only that, she didn't even look like an Indian with her long blonde hair and bright blue eyes.

It was so important to Mandie that the Cherokees like her, because they were her father's people, and her dear father was now in heaven.

A faint sound behind Mandie startled her, bringing her out of her reverie. She was so frightened, it took all her willpower to turn her head to see what it was. To her horror, directly behind her the beady eyes of a panther watched as it crouched menacingly in a chestnut tree, ready to spring. She froze, her heartbeat pulsating wildly in her throat as she gasped in fright. The others were all up at the wagon on the road. There was no one to help her. No one, that is, but God. *Please, dear God, make the panther go away,* she silently prayed, her eyes never leaving the animal. She knew she shouldn't have slipped away by herself. The beady eyes still watched her.

Then out of the corner of her eye, she caught a glimpse of a young Indian boy standing in the nearby bushes. He looked at her, then at the panther, then turned to walk away.

"Help me! Please!" she whispered hoarsely.

The boy glanced back but continued on his way. Never in her life had Mandie hated anyone as she did that boy right then.

Suddenly, from another direction, an arrow winged through the air striking the beast in the tree. Mandie held her breath—appearing through the trees was Uncle Ned! The thrill of relief flooded her body.

"Don't move, Papoose." the old Indian cautioned, as he quickly moved forward.

The panther, severely wounded, loosened its grip and fell from the tree. Mandie scrambled up the bank, her white kitten leaping after her.

"Uncle Ned! Where did you come from?" she asked as she paused to put on her shoes and stockings over her wet feet.

"Papoose take too long to get to Cherokee house. I come see why," he replied, turning the panther over. "Go back to wagon, now. I come soon. Wait there."

The girl snatched her bonnet from the bush where she had left it, calling back as she ran up the hill, "Hurry, Uncle Ned. We'll wait for you."

She hurried through the trees, and as she caught sight of the others at the wagon on the road, she called out, "Mother! Uncle John! Uncle Ned is here!"

Her mother and Uncle John, standing under the shade of the trees, turned to look at her. Her friend, Joe, came from around the wagon.

"Where, Mandie?" asked Uncle John.

"Down there—down at the river," she replied, pointing back at the way she had come. "Oh, it was awful! I was washing my feet and this panther was up in the tree getting ready to attack me when all of a sudden Uncle Ned came out of the woods and shot him with one of his arrows!"

The other three looked at one another, startled.

"Slow down, Amanda," her mother told her. "You're out of breath."

"Oh, and there was this Indian boy standing there in the woods, but he wouldn't help me at all; and he saw the panther, too," she continued. "He just turned around and walked away, leaving me there helpless and alone."

Uncle John lifted a rifle from the wagon and started down the hill. "Let me go see what Uncle Ned is doing. He might need some help."

"Guess I'll go, too," called Joe, hurrying after John.

"Amanda, dear, please don't *ever* go off alone like that again," her mother pleaded. "Something awful could have happened to you."

"I'm sorry, Mother," Mandie said soberly, putting her arm around her mother's waist. "But it was so hot I just had to wash my feet to cool off a little. It has been such a long journey all the way from Franklin. Wonder how much farther we have to go?"

"I know, I know," her mother replied, stroking the blonde curls. "We are all hot and tired. It shouldn't be much farther. Uncle Ned will know."

When the men came up the hill with Joe, Mandie ran to meet them. She hugged the old Indian. "You always come just in time, Uncle Ned."

"I promise Jim Shaw I see after Papoose when he go to happy hunting ground," the old Indian reminded her.

"I know, Uncle Ned, but now that I have found my real mother and she has married my Uncle John, you don't have to worry about me," the girl replied.

"May be fine, but I promise. I keep promise. Even when Papoose get to be squaw and marry Joe here, I keep promise," he told her, with a twinkle in his eyes.

Joe blushed and kicked at the stones under his feet. He intended to marry Mandie when they grew up, but he certainly didn't want people talking about it. He stole a quick glance at Mandie. She was looking at him.

"I'm glad, Uncle Ned. If you had not come along when you did, I don't know what might have happened to me. I probably wouldn't be here to tell about it," Mandie admitted. "Did you see that Indian boy in the woods there? He just looked at me, and then at the panther and walked away."

The old man turned quickly toward her, his eyes squinting. "I no see Indian boy. Where he go?"

"I don't know. He just disappeared into the woods," she replied.

The old man tightened his lips and murmured, "Mmm."

"All right, let's get going," Uncle John said, changing the mood. "We want to get to Uncle Ned's house before sundown."

The road they traveled on ran parallel to the Tuckasegee River for many miles. After a while Uncle John turned the wagon onto an old wooden bridge and crossed to the other side, traveling upward along the banks of Deep Creek.

"Oh, how I'd love to get into that water!" Mandie exclaimed, as she peered at its clear, shallow stillness.

Joe leaned out to look. "There're enough rocks to walk plumb through it."

"Won't be long now," Uncle John called back to them from his seat at the front.

And it wasn't long before cornfields started showing up along the way. Here and there tobacco was growing. At one place a hog ran grunting across the road in front of the wagon, causing the horses to buck and snort. There was an odor of food cooking, and as they came around a sharp bend in the road, a settlement of log cabins came into view. Mandie and Joe became excited.

"Looks like we're here!" exclaimed Joe.

"I can't wait to meet all my kinpeople!" Mandie cried.

"Just better not be any boys among them casting their eyes on you," Joe warned.

Mandie's mouth dropped. "I do believe you have a jealous streak in you, Joe Woodard."

"Remember, you promised. I get your father's house back from that woman he was married to, and you'll marry me!" Joe reminded her.

"Oh, Joe, it'll be years and years before you'll be old enough," Mandie replied.

"Not so long. I'm past thirteen already."

They were slowing down in front of the largest cabin in the group. There was a barn at the rear and horses could be seen behind a split-rail fence. The house looked very similar to the one in which Mandie had lived with her father. It was made of logs chinked together, with a huge rock chimney at one end. The door stood open, and they could smell the strong odor of food cooking.

"This is where Uncle Ned lives," Uncle John called back to the two young ones. He stopped the wagon by the barn and helped Elizabeth down as Uncle Ned took the reins to unhitch the horses. Mandie and Joe jumped down and looked around. There, standing across the road, was the Indian boy she had seen in the woods.

"Uncle Ned, look! There's the boy I saw in the woods!" she called, pointing to the boy.

Uncle Ned turned to look. "Oh, that Tsa'ni. He go to school. He not good Indian. I not know why he not kill panther."

An Indian squaw with a red kerchief tied around her head appeared at the door of the cabin. Mandie ran to hug her.

"Morning Star! I'm so glad to see you!" she squealed.

The old Indian woman grunted and held her tightly.

"She can't speak English, but she understands what we say pretty well," Uncle John told Mandie.

"I know. She came with Uncle Ned when he brought me to your house in Franklin," she replied. "But how did you know?"

Uncle John winked and smiled. "I stayed here at Deep Creek with the Cherokees while you were at my house hunting for my will, remember?"

"Oh, yes, of course," she laughed.

Uncle Ned and Morning Star motioned for them to come inside the log cabin. Mandie set Snowball down and looked around. It was very similar to her father's house in Charley Gap. There was a huge rock fireplace with the kettles hanging in it. A homemade table nearby was draped with a cloth, and when Morning Star removed the cloth, Mandie saw that the table was set and supper was ready and waiting.

At the far end of the room were several beds built into the wall and covered with cornshuck mattresses. Curtains hanging between them could be pulled around each one. Over in the other corner was a spinning wheel and a loom. And against the wall was a ladder going upstairs where Mandie knew there would be more beds.

"Food sure smells good!" Joe exclaimed.

Uncle Ned was speaking Cherokee to Morning Star, explaining who Mandie's mother was. All the Cherokees had known her father and now Morning Star embraced her mother. With tears in her eyes, Elizabeth smiled at the old woman.

In his Indian fashion, Uncle Ned tried to make the white people feel welcome. "Wash! Eat!" he told them, pointing to a washpan on a shelf. A clean towel was hanging on a nail beside it. A bucketful of fresh drinking water was also nearby with a gourd dipper hanging on a nail over it. Ned was a full-blooded Indian, but he knew how the white people lived.

"Save food for Snowball," Uncle Ned told Mandie, handing her a pan from the shelf. She understood they were to save the scraps from their plates for the kitten.

A beautiful young Indian girl about Mandie's age came through the open door. She was wearing a long, full skirt with a ruffled blouse; multicolored beads hung from her slender neck. Her long, black hair was held back by a red ribbon. Moving silently in her soft mocassins, she smiled as she came forward.

Uncle Ned put his arm around the girl. "This my son's papoose. She Sallie," he told the others.

"Hello, Sallie, I'm Amanda Shaw—Mandie for short," Mandie greeted her. "This is my mother, Elizabeth Shaw; my stepfather, who is also my uncle, John Shaw; and my friend, Joe Woodard, the doctor's son."

"Welcome," Sallie replied. "I know John Shaw. We are so excited to have you all visit us." Her speech indicated she was well educated.

Elizabeth took her small brown hand in hers. "Sallie, we are so happy to be here."

"Yes, we are, Sallie," John Shaw added.

Joe stole a glance, admiring her dark beauty, and then put in his greeting. "Sallie, we love your grandfather, Uncle Ned."

Morning Star spoke quietly to Uncle Ned and he announced loud and clear, "We eat now! Eat! Sit! Sit!"

The adults gathered at one side of the table and were soon deep in conversation. Mandie found a place on the other side between Joe and Sallie. Morning Star took the plates to the kettles over the fire, filled them, and brought them back to the table. Uncle Ned passed them around.

"Give thanks, John Shaw," Uncle Ned spoke again, as Morning Star sat down.

They all bowed their heads as Uncle John raised his voice in thanks. "We give thanks to thee, O Father, that we are all together, and for the wonderful food prepared for this meal. Bless this house and the people that dwell here. Amen."

"Guess we can eat now," Joe remarked.

"Yes," Sallie told him and then turning to Mandie, she said, "I was very sorry to hear about your father. I remember Jim Shaw. He used to visit us now and then."

Mandie was surprised. "You knew my father! Well, yes, I suppose you did. Uncle Ned said my father used to come to visit his people here."

"All the Cherokees loved Jim Shaw. He was a good man," the Indian girl said. "My father is dead also. I live here with my grandfather and my grandmother."

"And I have known your grandfather all my life. At least, ever since I can remember. He always came to sell the baskets the Cherokees made. And I never even knew I was part Cherokee until Uncle Ned told me, after my father went to heaven. My grandmother was Talitha Pindar, a full-blooded Cherokee," Mandie told her.

"I know. The Cherokees all know who you are," Sallie said. "Eat. It is owl stew. It is very good."

Joe, who was listening to their conversation, almost choked as he stuttered, "Owl—st-stew?"

"Yes, it is something special Morning Star makes."

Mandie swallowed hard and lowered her spoon into the delicious-smelling bowl of stew in front of her. She sipped it, blinked her eyes, and smiled. "It *is* very good." Then she dug in, thinking, *This is what the Cherokees eat and I am part Cherokee.*

Joe had to follow suit. There was no way he could let a girl outdo him. Then he also smiled and said, "Say, we'll have to get Morning Star's recipe for this to take back home." He reached for a piece of beanbread and washed it all down with a huge swallow of coffee.

"I suppose you know Tsa'ni?" Mandie asked Sallie.

"Of course. He lives right down the road. He is the grandson of your father's uncle, Wirt Pindar, who lives in Bird-town," the Indian girl told her.

"Now, let me think that one out. In other words, he is my great-uncle Wirt Pindar's grandson? That would make him my cousin!"

"Yes. He goes to school and is very intelligent, but has no common sense about him," Sallie said. "He—he thinks too much."

"I see. Well, I guess he was thinking too much, or something, today, when he left me with a panther staring at me." Mandie told her about the incident by the river.

"You might as well know. He does not like white people," Sallie said. "The English for his name is John, but he refuses to use it and goes by his Cherokee name. Most of us are called by our English names."

"He doesn't like white people? Why?" Mandie wanted to know.

"Because the white people destroyed our nation and took our people's land and homes and forced them to move away," Sallie said.

"I know that was wrong, terribly wrong, but that was a long time back in history. The white people living today had nothing to do with it," Mandie protested. "Besides, it was my grandfather who rescued my grandmother and her people."

Joe leaned forward. "Oh, Sallie, you've got to come to Franklin and see Mandie's Uncle John's house. It's complete with tunnels and hidden rooms, and all. Her grandfather had all this done to hide the Cherokees who didn't want to leave that area."

"I must see it, then," agreed Sallie. "It sounds very interesting. Is that where you live now, Mandie?"

"Yes, since my father died," she replied. "Uncle Ned helped me get to Uncle John's house. And then Uncle John found my real mother, and here we are!"

"Most of your kinpeople live in Bird-town," Sallie said.

"That's what Uncle Ned said. After we visit with you a day or two, we'll be going over there. Is it far to Bird-town?"

"No, but by wagon you have to follow the road instead of cutting through the woods and that makes it longer. Probably two, three hours."

The grown-ups were getting up from the table.

"You men go sit and visit and you young ones go along with Sallie outside. I will help Morning Star clear the table," Elizabeth volunteered.

"I have to feed Snowball first," Mandie told her, and holding out the pan Uncle Ned had given her, she waited for her mother to fill it with food left on the plates, which was very little, except for Joe's. He had not eaten all the owl stew, she noticed. She took the pan over to the hearth and the kitten purred contentedly as he hastily ate the food.

"He was hungry!" Sallie laughed.

"Come on. He'll follow us outside after he finishes," Mandie told her.

"Yeh, you sure can't lose that cat. He follows you like a shadow," Joe said as they went out into the yard.

Tsa'ni was sitting on a log under a hickory nut tree nearby. Sallie steered them in his direction. He stared at them silently as the group approached. Mandie could sense hate emanating from his dark eyes.

"Tsa'ni, this is your cousin, Mandie Shaw, and her friend, Joe Woodard," Sallie told him.

The boy looked from one to another and merely nodded his head without saying a word.

Mandie did not like the boy, but she knew she must at least speak to him because he was her cousin. She could still visualize the panther sitting in the tree and Tsa'ni walking away.

"Hello, Tsa'ni. Could we sit with you?" she ventured.

He immediately moved all the way down to the end of the long log.

"Sit. The log belongs to Sallie's grandfather. It is not mine," he told them.

They sat down, Mandie next to Tsa'ni.

"Mandie lived at Charley Gap with her father before he died," the Indian girl told him.

"Charley Gap? Tsali, our great warrior, whom you white people call Charley, lived in a cave near here before you white people killed him," Tsa'ni said.

"He did? I know the story of Charley, how he fought with the soldiers during the removal and killed one—" Mandie told him.

Tsa'ni interrupted, "—and how your soldiers forced Cherokee prisoners to shoot him down when he surrendered. You killed his brother and his two sons."

"I didn't kill anyone, Tsa'ni. Let's get this straight. What we are talking about was long ago in history—" Mandie's voice raised.

"I know, I know," he interrupted again.

"That was something I was not responsible for, nor my family," continued Mandie. "You can't live in the past, and you can't change history. As far as that goes, the Yankees killed my grandfather during the War of Northern Aggression, but I don't hold a grudge against the people living in the North now. They had nothing to do with it."

"Cherokee blood must be thicker than white blood then," Tsa'ni said.

"Well, just remember my grandmother was a full-blooded Cherokee," Mandie reminded him.

Joe, anxious to smooth the feelings between the two, spoke up, "Could we go see this cave, Tsa'ni?"

The Indian boy hesitated a moment, looking at Mandie. "Sure. It is not far. I will take you there tomorrow, all of you."

Mandie spoke up, "I'd really like to see it, Tsa'ni."

"I will go with you," Sallie added.

The sky was almost completely dark and the air was becoming much cooler. Snowball came bouncing across the yard and jumped into Mandie's lap.

"And so will Snowball," Mandie laughed, snuggling the kitten on her shoulder.

Tomorrow would be a day long to be remembered.

CHAPTER TWO

LOST IN THE CAVE

Mandie awoke the next morning to the sound of a rooster crowing, and she had to think for a minute before she knew where she was. Sallie was asleep on the cornshuck mattress next to her, and she knew Joe was sleeping on the other side of the rough hand-sawed wall dividing the room. She pulled the long cotton nightgown over her head and quickly reached for her dress hanging on a nail. Today was not a day to be wasted sleeping. She was in Uncle Ned's house, among the *Cherokees!*

The Indian girl looked up at her and smiled.

"You are in a hurry," she said.

"Yes, I don't have a minute to spare. I want to enjoy everything I can about our visit," Mandie replied.

From beyond the wall, Joe called to them, "Right. We gotta get going so we can go with Tsa'ni to the cave. Remember?"

"Of course," Mandie agreed.

"I smell coffee. Someone else is already up," the Indian girl commented as she, too, pulled on her skirt and blouse.

The three hurried down the ladder and found Uncle Ned, Uncle John, and Elizabeth sitting at the table. Morning Star was tending a pot over the fire.

"Good morning," Mandie called, as she came down the ladder.

"Come, eat," Uncle Ned said as they lined up at the washpan to wash their faces in the cool creek water from the bucket.

"You won't have to say 'eat' twice to me this morning. I'm starving!" Joe joked as he sat down across from Uncle Ned.

The girls joined them, and the Indian woman placed bowls of steaming hot oats and slices of homemade bread, with thick slices of ham between, in front of them. Elizabeth filled the coffee cups and passed them around.

"Good morning, Morning Star," Mandie smiled as she caught the old squaw's hand. The Indian woman smiled too and patted the girl's long blonde curls.

"Love," she whispered, and Mandie returned the word.

"Love. Oh, Morning Star, you are learning English!"

Sallie was listening. "She can understand some of what you say in English, but I have never heard her say an English word before. You are a good influence, Mandie."

After the chores were done and the noon meal eaten, the three wandered outside, waiting for Tsa'ni. Soon he arrived, carrying a lantern.

"Sallie, get the lantern from your grandfather's barn, too. It will be dark in the cave," Tsa'ni told her.

Sallie got the lantern and gave it to Joe to carry.

"Ready?" Tsa'ni asked.

"Yes, but I should tell my mother that we are going now," Mandie told him.

"Never mind. I will tell your mother, and your grandfather, Sallie." The Indian boy hurried up to the open door of the cabin with Mandie right behind him. Looking inside, he said, "I am taking the boy and the girl to see the mountain, the woods, and the creek. Sallie is going with us."

Elizabeth spoke up. "How kind of you, Tsa'ni. Amanda, you won't be long, will you?"

"No, Mother," she replied, turning to join the others waiting in the yard. "Tsa'ni, you didn't mention the cave."

"That is all right. The cave is included in the mountain and the woods. Come, let us go." He started off down the road toward the creek.

Mandie picked up Snowball and carried him on her shoulder. At first it was great fun, skipping along by the creek bank, throwing pebbles at the fish, plucking wild flowers, chasing butterflies, but after a while it became an uphill climb, and it was beginning to get hot. There was no definite trail, but Tsa'ni seemed to know the way all right. The other three grew more quiet and slowed their pace as they became more and more exhausted.

"Whew! Tsa'ni, how much farther?" Mandie complained, holding her skirt close to her legs through the thick undergrowth.

The Indian boy laughed. "Not far."

"Not far to you must mean miles to us," Joe sighed, as he pushed a brier away from his pant leg.

"Tsa'ni, where *are* you taking us?" Sallie demanded.

"To the cave, Sallie. I know the way," the boy replied.

Mandie turned to the Indian girl. "Don't *you* know where the cave is, Sallie?"

"No, I have only heard of it. I do not wander around the way the boys do." Sallie smiled. "And I have not lived long with my grandfather, so I do not know this land."

"Do not worry. I will not get you lost. I know exactly where we are going," Tsa'ni assured them.

A long time later a rushing, roaring waterfall came into view. Mandie stopped to admire it.

"Oh, how beautiful!" she exclaimed.

"That is where we are going," Tsa'ni told her.

He ran ahead of them and when they reached the falls, he stopped and gave them directions. "Now, you must walk across the rocks in the creek behind the waterfall. The entrance to the cave is behind the falls," and he started forward.

"We'll get all wet!" Mandie screamed above the noise of the water.

"No, you will not get wet if you stay against the cliff away from the water when you walk through. Just watch where you step. The rocks are slippery sometimes," Tsa'ni yelled back and continued on.

Mandie followed, with Sallie behind her, and Joe bringing up the rear. Snowball was frightened of the water and clung desperately to Mandie's shoulder.

Once under the falls, Mandie looked up and could see a ledge protecting the walkway as the water cascaded down into the creek. It felt terribly damp under there and the rocks were awfully slippery. There was no use trying to talk. No one could be heard above the sound of the water.

Joe lost his footing once, and if the girls hadn't grabbed for him, he would have fallen into the creek. The slip caused the girls to almost lose their balance, and Mandie felt her free hand scrape a rock as she grabbed for a hold. Regaining her footing, she stuck her hand out into the waterfall to wash away the grit and slime. The water was ice cold.

Tsa'ni had stopped ahead of them, and when they caught up they found him waiting in front of a huge, dark hole in the cliff which appeared to be the mouth of the cave. He had taken a match from his pocket and was lighting his lantern, motioning for Joe to light the one he carried, and then he entered the cave.

Once inside, the loud roar of the falls became a muffled sound and Mandie looked around, afraid to go any farther. Joe, right behind her and Sallie, swung the lantern around, lighting up the cave. They could see huge, moss-covered boulders around the entrance. The floor seemed to be solid rock.

"Come." Tsa'ni called, going deeper into the cave. "I want to show you something."

The three hurried on, passing into another part of the cave with enormous, long spears of rock hanging from the ceiling and sprouting up from the floor. They looked around in wonder.

"What are those things?" Mandie asked, breathlessly.

"That is what I wanted to show you. The ones hanging from overhead are stalactites and the ones sitting on the ground are called stalagmites," Tsa'ni explained.

"Well, what caused them?" Joe asked.

"They are formed by the water dripping from above," the Indian boy replied.

"It must have taken an awfully long time," Sallie remarked.

"Hundreds of years, maybe thousands," Tsa'ni nodded.

Mandie set Snowball down, and he began to check out the scent of the floor.

"You mean this cave has been here that long?" Mandie asked.

"And this is the cave where Tsali lived?" Sallie queried.

"Yes. People are born, live, and die, but mountains stay forever," the Indian boy replied. "This cave has several tunnels and other sections. Come, I will show you."

The group followed as he went down a long tunnel which led into another section of the cave, and then continued into another tunnel. It was all so dark and cold. The lanterns made a soft glow and cast eerie shadows. Snowball seemed nervous. He leaned against Mandie's skirt and meowed to be picked up. She consented and he snuggled against her shoulder.

"Oh, Snowball, I think you are lazy today," she laughed.

"Look, there is a stream over there. Look closely and you can see minnows in it," Tsa'ni told them, pointing to the other side of the large cavern they were in.

Everyone hurried over to the stream and huddled on the ground to watch for minnows in the flowing water.

Tsa'ni, with a sly grin on his face, silently crept away, heading for the entrance. He knew his way around inside, and the trail for home, but he knew the two white children didn't know the way, and neither did Sallie. *The white girl claims to be part Indian,* he thought. *Well, we'll just see how much Indian she is. A real Indian could find the way out. White people—always coming to mess in Cherokee business!*

Joe turned to speak to Tsa'ni. "I don't see any minnows." And then realizing the Indian boy was nowhere in sight, he called, *"Tsa'ni,* where are you?"

The girls were startled at the alarm in Joe's voice. They saw no sign of Tsa'ni. Mandie once again felt the hatred rising in her heart.

"He has left us," Sallie spoke angrily.

"Oh, no, Sallie! How will we ever find the way out—and home?" Mandie cried.

"We can only search around and hope to see familiar things," the Indian girl told them.

"Thank goodness, we have a lantern," Joe added.

Mandie sighed. "Well, let's be on our way." She started forward and then stopped. "Joe, you'd better go first with the lantern so we can watch our step."

"Please, be careful," Joe warned them. He stepped ahead and flashed the light into the next section of the cave. "Did we come in from here or over there? There's another opening over there." His voice echoed.

The girls turned to look. There *was* another opening. They were both puzzled.

"This one, I—I think," Mandie said, indicating the one nearest where they stood.

"No, I think it is that one over there," Sallie disagreed.

"Hey, now, we can't go two ways at once," Joe said.

"All right, which way do you say, Joe? We'll go the way two of us agree on," Mandie said.

"I just don't know!" Joe sounded confused. "I suppose we could *try* this way and then come back if we don't find the way out."

"And maybe get thoroughly lost doing it!" Mandie moaned.

"But there is nothing else we can do but try," Sallie reasoned.

"Agreed," Joe said. "So here we go." He led the way into the next cavern, and to their dismay it had several openings.

"Listen for the sound of the water," Sallie told them. "If we can get headed toward the water, we will find our way out."

The three stood still, holding their breath, listening for the faint roar of the waterfall. Simultaneously they pointed in three different directions. Then they all laughed.

"I've always heard two heads are better than one, but I'm not so sure three heads are any good at all," Mandie sighed.

"Let's do it this way," Joe suggested. "We'll take turns deciding which way to go."

"All right, you choose first," Sallie replied.

"This way," Joe said, pointing to his right, and the girls followed.

Now they were in a long tunnel with no end in sight within the dim light of the lantern.

"Mandie, you choose next," Sallie said, as they stumbled along the rough floor.

"Right now I would choose to go back the other way. It looked smoother and I don't remember a floor as rough as this one. No, wait! I see a dark place on the right up there." She hurried forward. "It's an opening."

"Well, let's go through it," Joe said, flashing the lantern light inside the next cavern. At that moment it seemed like hundreds of dark birds came flying at them. Flapping wings buzzed around their heads and a wild cackling sound filled the air. Joe and Mandie froze in terror.

"Bats." Sallie yelled. "Get down low and go back out!"

The three almost crawled out of the cavern into the tunnel they had just come down. Two of the bats circled here and there, and then disappeared.

"Sorry, I picked the wrong way," Mandie said breathlessly, as they ran through the tunnel.

"Here is another opening on the left," Sallie said.

"Joe, hold the light inside first so we can see."

Joe flashed the lantern around but no bats appeared. Directly across the passageway was yet another opening.

"There's another tunnel over there."

The girls followed him on through. It was a large cavern with a huge hole in the middle of the floor. They gathered around to look. Even though Joe held the lantern as far over the hole as he could bend, they could not see the bottom.

"Oh, how spooky!" Mandie shrieked.

"Do not get too near the edge!" Sallie warned them.

Joe turned to look at the girls. "I think we are completely lost."

"That Tsa'ni! Just wait until I tell my grandfather what he has done to us!" Sallie cried.

"There's only one thing left to do," Mandie told them. "We must pray. In fact, we should have prayed long before now."

"Pray?" asked Sallie.

"Yes. I know you must go to church, because Uncle Ned does. Whenever I am afraid or confused I ask God to help me," Mandie told her. "And He always does."

"Yes, I go to church and I believe in God," the Indian girl replied.

"Then, let's all repeat this verse together: 'What time I am afraid I will put my trust in Thee.' " And the three did as Mandie suggested.

"Oh, dear God, please help us! We need your help now!" Mandie pleaded, turning her eyes upward.

"Now let's not worry anymore. God will help us find the way out," Joe added.

"Yes, but I cannot hear Him telling us which way to go, can you?" Sallie was serious as she looked at the other two.

"No, but we have to trust Him to put it into our heads which way to go," Mandie explained.

"I think I'll check what's over on the other side," Joe said, walking slowly around the huge hole in the floor.

The wall on the other side had stones of all shapes and sizes piled up against it, and there was no opening.

Mandie, following Joe, accidentally stubbed her toe on a rock near the bottom of the pile, and all of a sudden the whole stack seemed about to tumble. She jumped out of the way and bent to look closer at the stones. As she was straightening up, her eyes caught a glitter in the pile.

"Joe, hold the lantern over here! I saw something shiny in the rocks!" she exclaimed.

"Oh, it's probably mica," Joe said.

As he swung the lantern the light revealed more glitter and the three began pulling at the rocks to see what was there, breaking fingernails and rolling rocks onto their shoes. All at once a large stone rolled down, uncovering a pile of gold nuggets.

"Gold!" whistled Joe, furiously digging away the loose stones.

"Gold!" murmured Mandie.

"Gold!" repeated Sallie.

Then the three of them broke into hysterical laughter.

"Here we are, lost to civilization, with a fortune in gold at our feet!" Mandie cried, picking up a nugget.

"Yes, we'd better be trying to find our way out," Sallie reminded them.

"Find our way out? Oh, Sallie, aren't you interested in seeing how much gold is here behind the rocks?" Joe asked, as he kept digging.

"Gold—that is what caused the Cherokees to lose their land, their homes—everything!" Sallie replied, sadly

Mandie turned to her, understanding. "I know, Sallie. If that gold had not been found in Georgia, the white people might not have ever made the Cherokees move out." She dropped the nugget into her pocket.

"Daylight! I see daylight!" shouted Joe as he continued to pull away at the rocks. "There's an outside opening behind all these rocks!" In his excitement he broke the lantern on a rock he was rolling away and they were suddenly in the dark.

But he was right. Together the three soon had a hole dug big enough for them to squeeze through to the outside. The terror of being lost in the dark, cold cave was over.

"It's a little uphill out there, I think. Let me go first and then I can help you two crawl out," Joe suggested.

All thought of the gold left their minds. Joe climbed through the hole they had dug and pulled the two girls after him. Snowball scrambled ahead of Mandie. Sallie went through last and barely cleared her foot when the whole side of the cave seemed to come tumbling down and the opening disappeared.

"Thank you, God! Thank you!" Mandie cried.

"Amen!" Joe added.

"Me, too!" Sallie said.

They stood up and looked around. They were in a thick forest of balsam firs and it seemed to be growing dark rapidly. Hours must have passed since they left Uncle Ned's house and now they were lost in the woods. There was no sign of the waterfall or the creek. It would be dark soon, and they had no lantern.

CHAPTER THREE

CAPTURED IN THE DARK

Tsa'ni waited for hours outside under the waterfall for the three to find their way out of the cave, but they never came out. He smiled to himself. *That white girl claimed to be part Cherokee. If she was part Cherokee she would find the way out.* He sat down to whittle on a piece of pine he took from his pocket. It got later and later and then began to grow dark, and still there was no sign of the three!

Suddenly he heard voices and saw lights flashing through the waterfall in front of him as they came nearer. He stood up and put his knife and the piece of wood back into his pocket. Evidently a search party was coming and he had better be prepared for them.

A group of men appeared through the trees, swinging lanterns in the dark. One stepped forward and Tsa'ni recognized him as Uncle Ned.

"Cave under water," he said, motioning to the waterfall. "Papooses might go there."

Uncle John walked to the edge of the creek, swinging a lantern. "Where is the cave, Uncle Ned? I can't see a thing beyond the water."

"Follow me," the old Indian told the others. He took them across the rocks and under the waterfall.

Then they were face to face with Tsa'ni.

"Tsa'ni! Where Papooses?" Uncle Ned demanded.

"We went into the cave and they ran off and left me. I went back inside to look for them, but could not find them," the Indian boy lied to the old man.

"Lost in cave!" Uncle Ned muttered.

"Do you know your way around in there?" asked Uncle John as the old Indian approached the entrance and flashed his lantern light inside.

"Little," Uncle Ned replied. "Big place, many rooms. Drumgool, pull trees. We make trail." He spoke in Cherokee to another Indian in the group.

Drumgool, understanding his friend's language, turned back and ordered the other men to gather small branches from the trees. Soon they returned with their arms full, while Uncle Ned and Uncle John waited at the entrance to the cave.

"We make trail," the old Indian repeated, entering the tunnel into the cave. The other Indians, understanding perfectly what he meant, began breaking twigs from the branches they carried and dropping them on the floor as they followed him.

Tsa'ni followed along in the rear. Now that the three were really lost, he was afraid of what they might tell. He had better prepare a good argument for when they were found. *Palefaces, why didn't they stay out of Cherokee territory? Always causing trouble!* He thought to himself.

Led by Uncle Ned, with Uncle John close behind, the search party thoroughly combed the cave.

"No one come to cave anymore. Rocks slide," Uncle Ned said, pointing to a rockpile that had evidently fallen from above in one of the sections.

"But Tsa'ni, knowing this, took them inside?" Uncle John questioned.

"Tsa'ni bad brave." Uncle Ned was angry.

"I don't think the boy likes us, even though we are kinpeople," replied Uncle John as they entered another tunnel.

"Tsa'ni no like white people," Uncle Ned explained. "He have no heart." He swung his lantern up and another rockpile came into sight. "Rocks dangerous."

"Where, oh, where can those kids be?" John sighed. "Tsa'ni said they ran off and left him while they were in the cave. Maybe they are already outside somewhere, or have already gone back to the house."

"Papooses come home; Morning Star send word. No, Papooses not home," the old man said as he flashed his light into the room with the huge hole in the floor. The opening the young ones had dug in the wall to escape through was now completely obliterated, and a pile of rocks hid the gold nuggets. "Papooses not here."

They went into the other sections and surprised the bats as the three lost ones had done.

Tsa'ni, still tagging along at the rear, was growing more and more positive that the three had just completely disappeared. He knew only the one way in and out of the cave, and they had certainly not come out. On the other hand, they weren't to be found in the cave. They had just vanished.

It was a big cave and the men were tired, but Uncle Ned insisted on going through the entire place one more time. This time the men laid bare twigs for their trail. They walked slowly and poked into every crevice, looked into every nook and cranny, and finally ended up back at their starting place.

Uncle Ned shook his head in dismay. "Not here. Now we look in trees, bushes," he told the men, explaining how they would work.

"Please, God, let us find them before some harm comes to them," Uncle John implored, as they gathered to leave the cave.

Mandie, Sallie, and Joe stumbled along in the darkness after they left the cave. It was some time before their eyes became accustomed to the dark night so that they could detect outlines of bushes and trees.

"Where do you think we are, Sallie? Do you have any idea?" Joe asked.

"I do not know this land, but I think we should keep going downhill because we went uphill all the way to the cave," she replied, pushing the limbs of a bush out of her face.

Mandie, carrying Snowball on her shoulder, was having the roughest time of all because the kitten insisted on clinging to her dress; and every time she took an uneven step because of unlevel ground or rocks and underbrush in the way, Snowball tightened his claws. And with the nightfall, it had become cold on the North Carolina mountain.

"I hope we're not too far away from food. I'm hungry!" Joe exclaimed.

"Me, too," Mandie added. "And I'm cold."

"Here is food," Sallie said, stopping by a huge bush and pulling berries from its limbs. "Serviceberries. They are good to eat."

"Oh, yes," agreed Mandie as she and Joe joined the Indian girl for a berry supper. They sat down on a boulder nearby. She offered one to Snowball. He turned his nose away from it. "Snowball, if you don't want these berries, you're going to have to wait, and no telling how long."

"Cats don't eat berries, Mandie," Joe laughed at her.

"Well, Snowball eats tomatoes, so why can't he eat berries?" Mandie told him. "Goodness gracious, I'm tired." She took a deep breath and stretched.

"Me, too, but we must keep moving on. There may be dangerous animals here," Sallie told them as she stood up.

"Of course! And we don't have a thing to defend ourselves," Joe said, as he and Mandie got to their feet and Snowball clung to the shoulder of Mandie's dress.

"Joe, what did we do in that cave?" Mandie admonished him. "We said we would trust in God. Have you forgotten so soon?"

"Well, no, but it would help if we had a rifle," he answered.

"Since we do not have one, I suggest we make haste," Sallie said, going ahead downhill through the bushes. The other two quickly followed.

It was a cloudy night with no moon to light the way. The three hurried along, slipping, sliding, sometimes falling over huge boulders along the path they took, sometimes getting caught in the briers of a bush, sometimes being struck in the face by an unseen branch. On Sallie's advice they tried to keep on a downhill route, but it was so dark and the trees and brush were so thick, they could not be sure which way they were going.

A small animal brushed by Sallie's legs in the darkness, and in her fright she lost her balance and went sliding downhill straight into a stream. Mandie and Joe ran after her.

"Here I am. Here!" the Indian girl called to them as she rose from the edge of the water. Luckily the wet sand had stopped her and only her feet had gone into the water.

"I can't see you," Joe called.

"Keep talking," Mandie told her. "We'll follow your voice." She put Snowball down so she could hurry.

"I landed in a stream down here," Sallie called to them.

"I can hear you," Joe yelled back to her. He went running down the hill and suddenly ran into what sounded like a bunch of huge tin cans.

Mandie, frightened by the noise, called out. "Joe, are you all right? What was that noise?"

"Looks like a whole lot of big cans," he said, as Mandie and Sallie both got to his side.

The Indian girl walked slowly around, feeling the cans and trying to see in the darkness. "I think it is a still."

"A still?" asked Mandie.

"A real moonshine still?" asked Joe.

"That means someone has been here and may be somewhere close around," Mandie figured.

"Sure does, and it means they must be bootleggers," Joe laughed.

Sallie did not understand his language. "Bootleggers?"

"Yeh, that's people who make liquor illegally," the boy said.

"Bad Cherokees make liquor, but not here," Sallie replied.

They were talking loudly enough that their voices carried in the dark, still night.

Mandie cautioned them. "The bootleggers might be around. We'd better be quiet. You've already made enough noise banging against those tin cans."

Out of the darkness a pair of hands grabbed Joe from behind and at the same time another pair latched onto Sallie, pushing her against Mandie and causing the girls to fall. The two dark forms were barely visible.

"Hey, what are you doing to me?" Joe demanded, as he felt his hands being tied behind him. He put up a struggle but the hands were too strong.

"They ain't nothin' but younguns, Snuff," a woman's coarse voice said as she held onto the two girls.

There was a strong, sickening smell about the two strangers. Evidently they had been drinking what they made in the still.

"Ne'er mind what they be, they done found somethin' that ain't none of their bidness and they's aliable to be atellin' the wrong people 'bout it," Snuff replied as he finished tying Joe's hands, and with the end of the long rope started to tie Sallie's as well, leaving a short piece of rope between the two.

"Please, Mr. Snuff, we won't tell anyone we saw you, or whatever it is you don't want us to tell," begged Mandie, the woman still holding her tightly.

"No, we'll just do as you say, Mr. Snuff," put in Joe.

"Shet up!" Snuff replied.

'Ysee, Snuff, they don't even know what we're atalkin' about," the woman told him.

"Shet your smacker, too, Rennie Lou," the man said. He jerked Mandie's hand from the woman, causing the girl to slip as he jerked her around. She almost fell head first into a bush. As she stumbled, her hair ribbon fell out and caught on a twig unnoticed.

Snuff pulled Mandie's hand behind her, and leaving a short space in the rope for Sallie's hands, he tied Mandie's, letting the long end of the rope dangle. Now all three were tied to the same rope.

"We are lost," Sallie tried to explain. "We do not even know where we are. If you would just show us the way back to Deep Creek, we would be most grateful."

Snuff turned quickly to look at Sallie in the darkness. "An Injun, by George! We've captured an Injun here!"

"Now, how do you know?" It's so dark I can't even tell what color hair they've got," Rennie Lou said.

"Don't you catch that Injun accent? No matter how much eddication they git, you kin always hear that kind of lisp they have," Snuff said, trying to look closely at Sallie in the dark.

"Yes, you are right. I am Cherokee," Sallie proudly told him, as she tried to straighten up in pride.

"Well, well, well, whadda ya know!" Rennie Lou slapped her skirt and laughed hoarsely. "And is the udder two Injuns, too?"

Snuff was trying to see what the other two looked like but it was too dark.

"Nope, don't think so. That 'un has got yellar hair," he said. "Well, now that you'ins can't git away too well, mind tellin' me whar you thought you was goin' this time o' night?"

"Sallie told you the truth, Mr. Snuff. We are lost," Joe replied.

"That's right. We are," Mandie added.

"Lost? Everybody that believes that stand on your head," the man growled. He pulled the rope, almost causing the three to lose their balance. "Now, where was you'ins goin'?"

"We were in the cave and got lost," Sallie told him. "There are probably search parties out right now looking for us."

"In the cave? What cave?" the man asked.

"The cave where the Indian Charley hid," Mandie told him.

"The cave whar the whut?" he howled and stomped his foot. "Now that's a good 'un. Ain't no cave nowhere 'round hyar, much less an Injun called Charley."

"Well, we were in a cave," Joe said, "whether you believe it or not. We were in a cave."

"I know every leaf and stone in these hyar woods. Ain't no cave hyar," the old man argued.

"But Joe's right. We were in a cave. The Indian boy with us ran off and left us and we got lost," Mandie insisted.

"Snuff," the woman said as the old man jerked Mandie around on the rope. "Make 'em show us if thar's a cave. A cave might come in handy sometime."

"All right. We'll keep 'em in the barn till daylight and then they will show us the cave," Snuff agreed, pushing the three together in front of him. "This way. Rennie Lou, lead the way and watch out for any sudden-like tricks."

O God, please help us! Mandie prayed silently as they were herded forward. She had never been so scared in all her life. The old man and woman didn't seem to have any common sense about anything, and there was no telling what they might do to them. Besides, everyone would be out looking for them, and her mother would be awfully worried.

They stumbled about in the darkness trying to follow the woman as they were ordered to do. Snowball, unseen by the man and woman, scampered along near Mandie. All three were already tired, hungry, and worn out. Now they were about to collapse from their weariness in avoiding the branches that scratched their faces and the thorns and briers that tore their clothes. Mandie slipped on a rock and pulled the other two down with her as she fell.

"Now, look ahyar. None of that stuff!" the old man yelled, jerking cruelly at the rope. "You're agoin' to the barn whether you like it or not. Git up! Now! Rennie Lou, give 'em a hand!"

The old woman tried to help in the dark but she wasn't much help. They finally managed to get to their feet.

"I'm sorry, Sallie, Joe. I accidentally fell. I didn't do it on purpose," Mandie apologized.

"It's all right, Mandie," Joe calmed her.

"It could have happened to either one of us," Sallie said, as they moved on.

Soon they could make out the blurred outline of a building in the clearing ahead. As they came closer they could see it was a rough log cabin, and to their dismay they were pushed on past it. Snowball followed.

"Go on! This ain't the barn," Snuff told them.

"Ain't far," Rennie Lou looked back and informed them.

After passing a clump of bushes behind the house, another structure showed up in the darkness. Rennie Lou walked on toward it and stopped at the door. She swung it open on creaky hinges.

"All right, inside!" Snuff prodded them on through the doorway into the darkness.

"Want me to light the lantern, Snuff?" the woman asked.

"Course not, woman. You want them to see us?" the old man growled. He pushed the three forward. "There's a pile of hay over thar. You kin sleep thar till it gits daylight!"

"Could we have a drink of water?" Joe asked. "We haven't had any food or water since noon yesterday."

"Water? Well, reckon you kin. Rennie Lou, git the water bucket over thar," Snuff said.

The woman picked up something in the darkness and came toward them, Joe felt a metal bucket in her hands as she pushed it in his face. "Hyar you air. Sorry we ain't got no dipper," she said. "But I tell you whut. There's apples in that haystack if you kin manage to eat one without usin' yer hands!" She laughed hysterically, holding the bucket to Joe's mouth.

"Rennie Lou, leave 'em be," Snuff warned her. Turning back to the three captives, he said, "Now we'll be back as soon as the sun cracks that darkness. Meantime you'd better rest good 'cause you're gonna find that cave for us, or else."

The man and the woman left the barn then, slamming the door behind them. The three prisoners gave a sigh of relief. Snowball moved around Mandie's feet.

"Now, we've got to think fast," Joe whispered to the others. "How can we get loose? We've got to get loose before they come back, so we can get away."

"Yes, they are definitely drunk," Mandie agreed. "I'm afraid of people who drink liquor."

"You never know what they will do when they have been drinking spirits," Sallie said. "But what can we do?"

"Oh, I don't know offhand but I suggest we start thinking," Joe replied. "I have no idea how you go about sitting down when you are all tied together like we are, but why don't we just take a plop all together?"

"All right, on count of three we'll all sit at once," Mandie agreed.

"One, two, three!" Together they landed in a pile of hay in the dark. Snowball prowled around them and started playing with the end of the rope hanging from Mandie's hands.

"We'll never be able to get up again," Sallie told them.

"We've got an awful lot of thinking to do first," Joe said.

"Yes, we've got to get back to Uncle Ned's, so we can go back to the cave and get the gold," Mandie reminded them.

"I do not want any of that gold, but I will go with you," Sallie told her.

"Yeh, we've got to get back to that gold somehow. There must be a fortune there," Joe said.

"I wonder who put it there," Mandie mused as she twisted her hands in the rope. "Do you suppose these people here did?" Snowball's paw caught at the rope behind her.

"No, because they don't even know about the cave," Joe said.

"Maybe some bank robbers left it there," Mandie suggested.

"I doubt it because it is too hard to get to the cave from any road or trail," the Indian girl replied. "Besides, they would probably guard it. And Tsa'ni seems to know his way around in there."

"You don't mean *he* could have put it there?" asked Mandie.

"No, he would never have gold like that," Sallie answered. "I mean someone would have seen him around if they were guarding the gold."

"You're right. But how did it get there? And who put it there?" Joe asked.

"We could ask Uncle Ned about it," Mandie said.

"First, we have to get away from these people, so we'd better concentrate on that," Joe reminded the two girls.

It was going to take an awful lot of thinking to get them out of their predicament.

CHAPTER FOUR

DIMAR

Elizabeth Shaw could sit still no longer waiting for her daughter to come back or to be found. It was a long time after midnight and no word had come from anyone. She decided it was time she helped in the search.

"Morning Star," she began, trying to talk to the old squaw. "You and me—" she pointed to the squaw and to herself—"let's go to Bird-town and get Mandie's kinpeople to help find them."

Morning Star understood part of it. "Bird-town," she said.

Elizabeth smiled and made motions like she was riding a horse and then pointed to the old woman and to herself again. "Bird-town," she said again.

The Indian woman grinned as she understood what Elizabeth meant. She got up and motioned to Elizabeth to follow her. She went outside to the barn. There was a small cart inside and Morning Star hastily opened a door to a stall and led out a pony. Elizabeth helped her harness it to the cart and they started out for Bird-town.

Meanwhile the three prisoners in the barn were still talking and trying to figure out a way to escape from the old man and woman.

"If we could only see in this darkness, we might find something we could cut the rope with," Mandie said.

"How is either one of us going to cut the rope when all our hands are tied?" Joe wanted to know.

"If one of us had something we could hold in our hands, we could back up to each other and cut each other's ropes apart," Sallie said.

"That's right," Mandie replied and then jumped as Snowball clawed her hand as he played with the rope. "Oh, Snowball, you stuck me with your claws!" Then she caught her breath. "Snowball! Snowball! He can do it!"

"Do what, Mandie?" Joe asked.

"Untie the rope. If I shake it for him to play with, he can claw at it.until it comes undone!"

"Oh, Mandie, how could a cat untie a rope?" Joe asked.

"Well, it does feel looser and besides, I am the last one on the rope." She shook her hands behind her, and Snowball jumped and began playing and clawing at the rope.

"Mandie, it'll never work," Joe told her.

"Snowball is smarter than you give him credit for. Don't forget, I am the one who educated him," laughed Mandie, still shaking her hands as the kitten played. "It's looser! It's looser!"

"Please keep trying," Sallie told her as she shifted from her cramped position to lean back against a post. Then she jumped forward again. A nail had scratched her back. "Mandie, there's a nail behind me. If Snowball has the rope loose enough, you might be able to hang it on the nail and pull it apart."

"Where, Sallie, where?" Mandie was excited.

"Do not lose your sense of direction. It is directly behind me on the post. I am going to move so you can slide over here in my place," the Indian girl said, moving slowly closer to Joe, who began edging farther away to give the girls room to move. Mandie kept sliding until she felt the post behind her. She leaned back trying to locate the nail.

"I've found it!" she cried. "Now if I can just catch the rope on it!" She maneuvered her hands until her fingers found the nail, and then she slid her wrists around until the nail caught the rope.

"Did you find it?" Joe wanted to know. "Or I should say, did the nail find the rope?"

"Yes, now I have the rope caught on it. If I can only catch the right loop so it will start untying."

"Be careful. You might hurt yourself," Sallie warned her.

Snowball had followed Mandie and was again pulling at the rope with his claws. One foot caught and he pulled with all his might trying to get his paw free. Mandie felt the rope give way. She rubbed her wrists together and slipped one hand out of the noose.

"It worked! I have my left hand free!" she cried. "There! I have it all off! Now, let me get you two untied."

She slipped behind Sallie and freed her hands and then removed the rope from Joe's hands. The three sat there rubbing their bruised wrists in the dark.

"That man must not have tied the knots very tight," Joe said.

"Probably because he was too drunk to realize what he was doing," the Indian girl said.

"Well, let's get going!" Mandie stood up, picking up Snowball.

"I will leave a signal for our people if they come here looking for us," Sallie said, as she removed the beads from around her neck and hung them on the nail. "My grandfather will see these and will know we were here."

"I hope we find them before they get this far," Joe said.

"We'd certainly better be careful going by the log cabin," Mandie reminded them as they stepped out of the barn. The first signs of dawn were in the sky.

"We will circle the clearing and stay away from the house," the Indian girl told them. She led the way, keeping the house at a distance as they tried to find their way back into the woods and downhill.

While the three were trying to find their way, Uncle Ned's search party had fanned out across the mountain. He and Uncle John stayed together while the other men scattered out. Sometime later the old Indian found the bright blue ribbon from Mandie's hair hanging on the bush by the creek where she had lost it in the scuffle with the old man and woman.

"Papoose ribbon!" he cried excitedly as he pulled the ribbon from the bush. "They been here!" He looked around on the ground. "Feet make marks!" He pointed to the footprints in the soft sand by the water.

Uncle John anxiously bent to look.

"Looks like quite a few different feet," he remarked.

"Yes," the old Indian said, as he straightened up to follow the direction of the footprints. "Go this way." He walked on up the hill, bending low to see the prints as he continued. The old cabin came into view.

"At least we know they got out of the cave," Uncle John said.

"I hear people coming," Uncle Ned said, listening as he turned his ear toward the sound. "Walk like white people."

Snuff and Rennie Lou appeared in the distance, their heavy shoes noisily clopping on the rocks here and there. Uncle Ned stepped behind a tree and motioned for Uncle John to do the same.

As the couple drew nearer, the old Indian stepped out directly in front of them. They stopped in their tracks.

"Where Papoose—wear this ribbon?" Uncle Ned held up Mandie's ribbon for them to see.

"What papoose?" Snuff asked. "We ain't seen no papoose, Injun."

"Papoose feet make prints to your house," Uncle Ned said, pointing to the tracks in the dirt. "Where Papoose?"

Rennie Lou held tightly onto Snuff's arm. She was frightened of the old Indian. Snuff tried to bluff his way out.

"I told you we ain't seen no papoose. Now git out of our way!" Snuff gave Uncle Ned a shove.

At that instant Uncle John, his rifle in his hand, stepped out from behind another tree and Uncle Ned gave a loud whistle to round up his braves. The man and woman stood still without saying a word. Indians came from every direction out of the woods as they heard their leader's call for help. Snuff and Rennie Lou, quaking in their boots, were soon surrounded.

"Hold man, woman," Uncle Ned ordered. "Me and John—we go look." The circle of Indians closed in around the frightened pair.

Following the footprints, Uncle Ned and John went on past the cabin and into the barn. The old Indian looked around and grunted as he picked up Sallie's beads from the nail on the post.

"Papooses been here," he said to Uncle John, holding up the beads.

"But evidently they are gone now," Uncle John replied.

"Left different way. Prints going opposite way," Uncle Ned said, motioning to the footprints left by the three as they had detoured around the house.

Suddenly the dark, cloudy sky broke loose and the rain came pouring down. The old Indian looked up in dismay.

"Rain wash feet marks away!" he exclaimed. "Must hurry!"

"And the children are out in this," Uncle John fretted. "Unless they found the way back, which I doubt very much."

The old man whistled for his braves once more and they came on the run, pushing the man and woman along with them in the downpour.

"Must hurry. Rain clean trail," Uncle Ned told them. "We follow feet marks now!" He pointed to the footprints remaining in the sand.

"What we do with palefaces?" Drumgool asked, pushing the two forward.

"Let go. Must hurry," the old Indian instructed him.

"I think we should send the authorities back up here, Uncle Ned," John said. "These people are kidnappers."

Uncle Ned nodded in agreement.

Snuff and Rennie Lou heard all that was said and looked at each other anxiously. They were sober this morning and the realization of their crime began to dawn on them.

"Look, we ain't meant no harm. We didn't hurt the younguns," Snuff pleaded. "In fact, we'll hep you hunt 'em if you want."

"No! We don't need your help," Uncle John told them, firmly. "You have broken the law. It will all be taken care of as I said. I am reporting this to the authorities. You're not going to get away with it."

"Please, mister," the woman begged. "We won't never do it again. I 'spect we jest had too much partyin' 'fore they showed up. We didn't hardly know whut we was doin'. Can't you unnerstan' that?"

John shook his head and ran to follow Uncle Ned, with the braves bringing up the rear. The rain was quickly obliterating the tracks of the three, and they were hurrying as fast as they could go. Their clothing was heavy with the dampness, and the wet rocks had become slippery, but they knew they were on the trail of the missing children.

Far ahead of them, Mandie, Joe, and Sallie pushed their way through the dripping bushes and mostly slid downhill when they came to huge boulders now and then. Snowball registered his complaint by clinging tightly to Mandie's dress.

"Sallie, do you think we are heading in the right direction?" Mandie asked.

"I am not certain but I do know we are headed toward the foot of the mountain, and once we get down there we'll be able to find the way home," the girl replied.

"Whew! I'm still hungry!" Joe complained as he led the way. "We sure were dumb not to load up with apples from that barn."

"It's too late now," Mandie replied. "When we get back to Uncle Ned's I'm going to eat everything in the house." She laughed, tossing her long, wet hair back out of her face.

"Even owl stew?" Joe teased her.

"I said everything," she replied.

"Everyone must be worried about us by now," Sallie said. "I am certain my grandfather has a party searching—if we only knew which direction they were coming from."

"Looks like a level place for a while here," Joe remarked as they came down into a meadow.

At that moment an arrow suddenly shot through the trees near Mandie, who was carrying the kitten. Snowball, frightened by the sudden movement, jumped down and darted ahead. He ran up the first tree he came to and peered down from a limb.

Mandie, not noticing the kitten, stared and pointed to the arrow imbedded in another tree. "Joe! Sallie! Look!"

"Land o'Goshen, don't stand there! Come on!" Joe grabbed her hand and turned to grip Sallie's hand. They ran along until they came to a thick clump of bushes, where they hid. From there they saw a young Indian appear in the clearing and go to the arrow in the tree.

Sallie immediately felt relief. She was certain the boy would help them. She broke out of the bushes, calling back, "That is an Indian boy. He will help us. Come on!" She ran toward the boy. "We are lost! Please help us!"

Mandie and Joe, not trusting the boy, stayed behind the bushes. The boy turned to look at Sallie. "Where did you come from?"

"I am Sallie Sweetwater. My friends and I are lost. Will you help us?" she asked as she stood before the boy who seemed to be not much older than she was.

The boy looked around. "Your friends? Where are they?"

"They are behind the bushes because you almost hit us with your arrow and they are frightened," she told him.

"I am very sorry. I will not harm any of you. Tell them to come out," he said.

Sallie called to her friends. "Come on, Mandie, Joe. He will help us find the way!"

Mandie and Joe reluctantly appeared from their shelter and came forward. The boy's eyes lit up when he saw the blonde-haired girl.

She is the most beautiful girl I have ever seen, he was thinking as she came nearer. *And blue eyes! How beautiful!*

Mandie returned his stare, thinking what a handsome boy he was!

"Where are you going?" the boy asked.

"We are trying to find the way to Deep Creek where I live with my grandfather," Sallie told him.

"Deep Creek." he repeated. "You are going in the wrong direction!"

"Oh, no!" Joe moaned. "I'm starving to death!"

"Yes," the boy said. "My name is Dimar Walkingstick. I live with my mother not far from here. I will take you to her for food and dry clothes. Come!" He turned, expecting them to follow him.

"I am certain my grandfather has a search party looking for us by now," the Indian girl said. "We shall leave a trail for him."

"Of course. I will go ahead and break the twigs as we go. He will see them and find the way to my house," Dimar said, as he began marking their way.

"Food!" Joe murmured. "At last, some food!"

"That's what he said," Mandie replied, following along with Joe as Sallie stayed with Dimar, marking their trail. "And a fire to dry our clothes. This rain will never stop!"

Snowball was completely forgotten in the excitement. He clung desperately to the limb of the tree, too frightened to descend.

CHAPTER FIVE

UNCLE NED TO THE RESCUE

Elizabeth and Morning Star arrived at Bird-town, hurriedly told Mandie's great-uncle, Wirt Pindar, what they had come for and in no time flat they were riding toward the mountain with Wirt leading a group of men. Elizabeth insisted on going along and was given a pony to ride, but Uncle Wirt reminded her that she would have to climb the mountain on foot when they reached it.

By the time the foot of the mountain was in sight, the rain began.

"Well, looks like we're going to have a wet hike," she remarked as she dismounted. Gathering her long skirt about her, she tucked the hem into the waistband so as not to be slowed down by the weight of the wet material about her feet.

"Yes, will be hard find trail in rain," Uncle Wirt told her. He motioned for his men to come together and then gave them directions to spread out up the mountain as they climbed.

Morning Star took Elizabeth's hand and motioned toward the men. Together they followed Uncle Wirt up the incline in the downpour.

"Morning Star, pray," Elizabeth told her, clasping her hands together and looking toward the sky. She knew the Cherokees always looked up to God in the sky rather than bowing their heads when they prayed. "Pray!"

Morning Star understood and stopped to raise her face and hold her hand on her heart as she prayed in Cherokee.

"Please, God, guide and direct us to our lost children!" Elizabeth implored. "We put our faith in you!"

They quickly caught up with Wirt as he climbed through thick, wet underbrush. Morning Star was experienced in this kind of thing, while Elizabeth was hardly a match for the dense undergrowth in the pouring rain. But in her determination to find the children, she quickly adapted to the way the Indians were stepping and making their way.

"We climb opposite side. Ned climb from Deep Creek. We climb from Bird-town," Wirt explained as they kept going.

"Yes, I realize that," Elizabeth replied, pulling a brier from her skirt. "That is good; we will be covering two sides of the mountain between us,"

It was a long, tedious journey up the mountainside in the heavy rain. The Indians were watchful for any sign of a trail and now and then paused to send a loud whistle through the woods in hopes of being heard by the children.

Covered with bruises and scratches, Elizabeth forced herself to keep up with Morning Star who, in spite of her age, was as agile as the men in the party. She paused only a second to catch her breath after a steep climb over boulders that were constantly in their way. She kept a prayer in her heart that no harm come to the missing ones. She had lost her twelve-year-old daughter when she was a baby and had only recently been reunited with her. Those memories kept her diligent on the path now.

Wirt, worried about the white woman trying to keep up with the Indians, called for a rest stop at the bottom of a huge boulder.

"We sit," he commanded, pointing to a clearing under a ledge projecting from the boulder above. "Rest."

"Please don't stop on my account," Elizabeth called breathlessly. "I can keep up with you."

"Sit, rest," he told her. "Morning Star need rest, too." He pointed to the old Indian woman who sat down on the rocky floor under the ledge.

Elizabeth followed her, glad for the rest. The men also came under the shelter to get out of the rain.

"While we rest, we send message," Wirt told them. Stepping back out into the rain, he gave his loud whistle that rang through the trees. Turning, he instructed the men, "You next, then you, until all give message."

The men, one at a time, stepped out and repeated the loud call through the woods. As the last one turned to sit down, there came an answering call in the distance, barely discernible through the sound of the rain.

"Ned near us. His call." Wirt cried excitely as he ran up the face of the boulder, whistling again. His men followed.

Morning Star and Elizabeth smiled joyfully. Maybe Uncle Ned had some good news. They lifted their skirts and ran after the men as fast as they could manage.

Uncle Ned, hearing the call and answering, turned to Uncle John as they stopped beneath a tree.

"Wirt must be near. That his call," the old Indian said.

"Someone must have let him know," Uncle John replied. Then he spoke up excitedly. "Elizabeth! Of course—she wouldn't sit there all this time and do nothing. She has rounded up our kinpeople at Bird-town."

Uncle Ned grunted and the two men, with the others following, started out in the direction from which the call had come.

It didn't take the two parties long to meet. Elizabeth ran forward as John came to meet her.

"Any word?" they both asked at once.

They both shook their heads in the negative as their arms flew around each other.

Wirt was speaking in Cherokee to Uncle Ned. Elizabeth, raising her head from John's shoulder, heard a soft meow. She looked up to see Snowball still clinging to a limb in the tree.

"Snowball!" she cried, pointing.

Everyone turned to look. John quickly scaled the tree, picked up the frightened kitten and brought it down to Elizabeth.

She stroked the wet kitten who clung to the shoulder of her dress. Her voice trembled as she spoke, "Oh, John, where can Mandie be without Snowball?"

Uncle Ned walked over to the tree. There his quick eyes caught sight of the broken branches on the bushes.

"Trail!" he said, quickly pointing to twigs jutting out at angles on the bushes ahead. "Quick! Follow trail!" He hurried ahead, watching for the marked bushes.

The two parties of searchers fell in behind him and made their way through the brush.

Meanwhile, the three children arrived at Dimar's mother's house and were welcomed in to dry by the fire and to partake of a meal. As soon as they had gotten inside the log cabin, the rain stopped.

"This is my mother, Jerusha," Dimar told them, and turning to his mother, he said, "These are friends I found lost in the woods—Mandie, Sallie, and Joe."

"Ah, my papooses," she said, hurrying to them. "Come." She took the girls by the hand and led them behind a curtain at the far end of the room. "You wrap in blanket," she said, handing them each a blanket from the beds.

Sallie explained in Cherokee that they must find the way back to her grandfather's house as soon as their clothes had dried and they had eaten.

The girls went back to the fire, and Jerusha spread their dresses to dry. Dimar helped Joe find a blanket and hung up his wet clothes.

"Now, we eat," the woman said smiling.

She brought them tin plates filled with ham, corn, and beanbread, and cups of steaming hot coffee were set on the hearth. The three ate as though they had not eaten in a week.

"Oh, how good." Joe said, with his mouth full as he continued to cram in the food.

"This is the best meal I think I've ever had," Mandie added.

"Good food," Sallie agreed.

Dimar and his mother sat nearby, having their meal and watching the three. Jerusha kept turning the clothes so the heat would dry them.

"Eat. Much food," she told them. She rose and refilled Joe's plate but the two girls refused.

"I just can't eat anymore," Mandie told her. "I'm full up to here." She touched her throat and laughed.

"Me, too. The food was very good. We thank you." Sallie smiled as she pulled the blanket closely around her.

Even though it was summertime and terribly hot during the day, the rain cooled the air considerably. All the homes had a fire in the fireplace for cooking, and today it felt especially good.

Everyone jumped at the sound of voices outside. Mandie was the first to look out.

"It's Uncle Ned!" she cried and, securing her blanket, ran to open the door. Joe and Sallie joined her.

Uncle Ned cried with joy as he took the three into his arms. John and Elizabeth crowded in behind him.

"Uncle Ned! Mother! Uncle John!" Mandie cried excitedly.

Elizabeth handed the wet kitten to Mandie.

"Snowball! How could I not have missed you?" she said, cuddling the kitten to her blanket. She ran to the fireside and fed him the scraps on her plate, which he swallowed at once and began searching for more. Jerusha was quick to comply.

It was a joyous occasion and everyone was talking at once. Jerusha made them all feel welcome and brought out more food. The cabin was filled with so many people, there was only room to stand. Tsa'ni sulked over in a corner, afraid to mingle with the crowd. His eyes kept darting from Mandie to Sallie to Joe. Mandie ignored him. She could feel the hatred in the air between them, though she knew she shouldn't hate him. She shouldn't hate anyone. But it was so hard to be nice to an enemy. She was afraid all her

Cherokee kinpeople would be like Tsa'ni and would not like her because she was mostly white.

Uncle John grabbed her hand and led her to Wirt Pindar.

"Mandie, this is your Great-Uncle Wirt. He is your grandmother's youngest brother,"

The old man bent to embrace her.

"My real uncle!" she exclaimed, backing off a little to look at him. He was also looking her over. "My very own uncle!"

"Jim Shaw's papoose." the old man said softly. "Look like Jim Shaw, but have Indian thumb." He was holding her hand and examining it.

"Indian thumb?" the girl questioned him.

"Short, blunt thumb," he explained, holding his own next to hers. They were similar in shape.

"I have a Cherokee thumb!" she cried. "I'm so glad!" She turned to John. "Uncle John, let me see your thumb."

He held out his thumb and laughed. "We both have one like Uncle Wirt's."

"Little one come to Wirt's house," the old man said.

"Oh, yes, Uncle Wirt. We *are* coming to visit you," Mandie replied.

"Today," he said. "Not far to Bird-town."

Uncle Ned was standing nearby listening. "Close to Bird-town. Far to Deep Creek. We go to Bird-town."

"Now," began Elizabeth as the three gathered around her, "I want to know exactly what happened. *Where* have you been?"

Tsa'ni, wide-eyed and listening from across the room, moved in closer to hear what they would say. Mandie saw him and took pity on him. She thought, *I won't tell a lie. I just won't tell everything.*

She looked back at her mother. "We got lost in the cave and couldn't find Tsa'ni," Mandie told her.

"And we couldn't find the way we came in so we dug our way out," Joe added.

"Yes, and then those strange people in the woods tied us up and left us in the barn," Sallie explained.

"But how did you get separated from Tsa'ni?" Uncle John asked.

"Well, we stopped to look into a pool of water and I guess it was then we got separated," Mandie replied.

Tsa'ni was holding his breath as he eavesdropped. He did not understand why the girl did not tell the whole story.

"Do not see how got lost from Tsa'ni," Uncle Ned said.

Sallie answered her grandfather. "I suppose he thought we were right behind him, but we stopped to look into the water and then we lost him."

"And how did you dig your way out of the cave?" Elizabeth wanted to know.

"Well, there was a pile of rocks and—" began Joe.

"—and a pile of gold," Mandie interrupted. "And I mean a pile of gold! And then we could see the daylight through the rocks, so we dug with our hands until we had all the rocks out of the way."

"Gold?" Uncle John asked as he looked at Uncle Ned. "You saw gold in that cave?"

Tsa'ni moved a little bit closer. They had found gold in the cave? They must be lying.

"Yes," Mandie affirmed. "It was all under the rocks we dug through to get out."

"But then the rocks all fell in and the hole closed up as soon as we got through it," Joe added.

"Do you know of any gold in that cave, Uncle Ned?" John asked.

"No. No gold. Maybe mica in rocks," Uncle Ned said.

"But it was *gold,* Uncle Ned. We saw it!" Mandie insisted, forgetting about the nugget in her pocket.

"No one goes in cave. Dangerous. Rocks fall in," the old Indian said.

"Maybe it was mica you saw, but, anyway, we're so thankful you are all safe," Elizabeth told them. "Now, don't you think we'd better get going so we can get to Uncle Wirt's house before dark?"

The three scrambled for their clothes. As Mandie put on her dress behind the curtain, the gold nugget fell out of her pocket and lay unnoticed on the floor by the bed.

Tsa'ni, breathing a sigh of relief that he was not implicated by the three, swaggered up to Mandie and said in a low voice, "You have no Indian blood in you. You could not even find your way back. You are just white, that is all."

Dimar, standing nearby, overheard and spoke up, "Tsa'ni, you are a disgrace to the Cherokees, talking like that to your own blood."

Joe advanced toward Tsa'ni. "You look here, Tsa'ni, Mandie is a well-seasoned traveler. She made a journey all the way from Almond Station to her Uncle John's house in Franklin, through the woods, across the rivers, and over the mountain. And that is rough terrain. Why, she even—"

Mandie caught him by the arm and interrupted. "Never mind, Joe. We have to go now. Come on." She turned to Sallie who was also listening. "Just ignore him."

Sallie nodded in agreement.

Wirt came over to Tsa'ni, who was his grandson. "You go to Deep Creek; bring John Shaw's things to my house. They stay with me. Make haste."

Tsa'ni looked at the old man. "I am on my way," he said. He turned and gave the three a know-it-all look and walked out the door.

Tsa'ni had no plans to do what his grandfather had asked. He had plans of his own.

CHAPTER SIX

CHEROKEE KINPEOPLE

Uncle Ned and his group went to Bird-town with the others. They were all tired and it was the closest place to go.

Mandie, who had ridden behind her mother on the pony from the foot of the mountain, looked around, her eyes taking in everything. This was part of the Cherokee Indian Reservation here at Bird-town. This was the original land where her Indian ancestors had lived. It was like a small town with a wide dirt road running through it. Rows of log cabins were spaced apart by crops.

There seemed to be an unusual number of women and children waiting along the road. Most of the men had gone with the search party, and they were now returning to their families.

Elizabeth followed Wirt Pindar to his house. It was the largest in the group and was in the center of the community. Aunt Saphronia, Wirt's wife, embraced them and made them welcome. She was a tiny Indian woman with a million wrinkles in her face. She had food cooked and waiting. Her neighbors, some of whom were relatives, opened their doors to the extra men from Deep Creek.

Saphronia then spotted Mandie.

"Jim Shaw's papoose!" she cried as she hugged the girl. "Love!"

"Mandie, this is your Uncle Wirt's wife, Aunt Saphronia," Elizabeth told her as John Shaw came up behind her.

"I love you, too, Aunt Saphronia," Mandie said, blinking back tears as her father's name brought back memories.

"Aunt Saphronia." John Shaw smiled as he put his arms around the little woman.

Saphronia looked up into his face. "Take care Jim Shaw's papoose."

"Yes, I will, Aunt Saphronia, together with her mother Elizabeth here," he replied.

"You forget," Elizabeth reminded him. "I have already been here. When we came to get Uncle Wirt, I met Aunt Saphronia then." She smiled at the old squaw.

"Right. I'd forgotten in all the excitement," he replied, grinning as he put one of his arms around Elizabeth and tried to include Mandie.

The girl laughed. "I don't think your arms are long enough to hug three of us at one time."

"Eat. Food ready," Saphronia told them, leading them to the table.

As they sat at the long table Mandie turned to her Uncle Wirt. "Tell me about my grandmother, Uncle Wirt, when she was a young girl. What did she look like'?"

Uncle Wirt cleared his throat as he strove for the right words. "Talitha beautiful—more than others. She sing, she dance, she smile. Braves follow her. She like everyone. Everyone love her. She born here."

"She was born here?" Mandie was surprised. She had never thought about that. "Before our people were made to move out and give up their land?"

"Yes. She oldest papoose. Me youngest. All gone to happy hunting ground, but me," he said sadly.

"I love you, Uncle Wirt. I thank God that I am able to come to see my Cherokee kinpeople. He has been good to me," she said.

The old man's face brightened. He smiled. "Love, Papoose. Jim Shaw's papoose."

The others had been listening and now Uncle John spoke up.

"Talitha was my mother, you know, Mandie. But I didn't know her well because I had to go away to school as a small boy, and she was very ill. It was a long time before I had a chance to come back, but I have been back many times since then. Your father also came to visit, at least once a year, but he never knew our mother. She died not long after he was born.

"When she died our father lost all interest in life. He just pined away. He died when your father was only five years old," he said.

"Five years old," Mandie said thoughtfully. "Then you took care of my father while he was growing up."

"Yes, Jim and I lived in the house in Franklin until he got married," Uncle John said. "Uncle Ned and Morning Star lived with us for several years. He taught us both how to fish, swim, and how to use a bow and arrow."

"They lived with you and my father" Mandie was surprised. She turned to the old Indian. "Uncle Ned, you never told me that."

Uncle Ned smiled. "Take many moons tell Papoose many things."

Dimar Walkingstick came in through the doorway and went straight to Mandie. Everyone was surprised to see him because they had left him at home with his mother when they came to Bird-town.

He held something out to Mandie. "Here. I think this is yours. It was on the floor where your dress was hung to dry."

Mandie took the gold nugget and gasped, "Oh, Dimar, thank you! I had forgotten about it entirely."

"Sit. Eat," Uncle Wirt told the boy, sliding closer to Uncle Ned to make room for him. Dimar squeezed into a place between the two old Indian men, directly facing Mandie. His eyes fastened on her and remained fixed as she showed the others what he had brought.

"You *did* take a nugget with you!" Sallie exclaimed.

"Holding out on us, huh?" Joe teased.

"You see, Uncle John," she said, handing him the nugget. "There *is* gold in the cave. It *is* gold, isn't it?"

"It certainly is," Uncle John said, passing the nugget on to the two Indian men. "Look at that!"

Uncle Ned grunted. "Cherokee not know gold in cave."

Uncle Wirt agreed. "No, Cherokee not know."

The two old men looked at each other and seemed to be concerned.

"How much do you think was there?" Uncle John asked.

"Probably a bushel basket full, wouldn't you say, Joe, Sallie?" Mandie answered.

Sallie nodded. Joe said, "Oh, probably more than that. I'd say several tote sacks full."

"Let's see, you said you found it under some rocks when you were digging a hole to get out of the cave?" Uncle John questioned.

"Yes, sir," Mandie said. "We found this pile of rocks and could see the daylight through a tiny hole in the middle of them so we started digging to see if there was an opening. There was only a small layer of rocks over the pile of gold."

"Between the three of you, could you find the pile again?" Uncle John wanted to know.

"I don't know. You see, as soon as we got through the hole all the rocks came tumbling down from above and covered up the opening we'd dug," Mandie said.

"Unless the rockslide changed things drastically inside the cave, I think I would recognize the place," Joe added.

Uncle John turned to Sallie. "What about you, Sallie? Would you remember where it was?"

"Gold has always been bad luck for the Cherokees. I would rather not look for it," the Indian girl replied.

Everyone turned to look at Sallie.

"I know what you are referring to—the removal of Indians because of the discovery of gold in Georgia. But it wouldn't be like that now," John reminded her.

Uncle Ned spoke up. "Cave dangerous. Cherokee not need gold."

"But, Uncle Ned, there must be a fortune there," John said.

"Cave not too dangerous. Tsa'ni go there many times," Uncle Wirt put in.

"That's right. Tsa'ni goes there. Has he ever found any gold'?" John asked.

"No," Wirt said. "We go to cave when sun up."

"Uncle Ned, will you come with us?" John asked.

"Papoose go, Ned go. I promise Jim Shaw." He nodded his head. "But—gold bad for Cherokee."

"May I go, too?" Dinar spoke up.

Everyone had forgotten about him.

"Of course, if you want to," John told him.

Dimar rose. "I must return home now. I will meet you at the cave tomorrow morning."

So plans were made for another search—this time for a pile of gold. And this time they wouldn't get lost.

Meanwhile, Tsa'ni had gone straight to the cave from Dimar's house. He did not bother to go on to Deep Creek and deliver the Shaws' belongings to Bird-town as his grandfather had asked. He felt sure the others would return to look for the gold and he wanted to beat them to it.

He didn't have much oil left in his lantern, but he would hurry before the light went out. He knew his way around inside the cave pretty well. He hurried from one room to another, swinging the light close to the wall as he went. According to what he had heard them say, they had found the gold next to a wall.

Once, as he paused to look carefully at a pile of rocks, he thought he heard voices. He stood still and listened but could hear nothing.

"Hmm, probably the echoes of old Tsali," he said to himself, and went on about his search.

He knew which room the bats lived in so he carefully avoided them. He was certain gold couldn't be in there anyway. They would never have stayed long enough to dig out a hole in the wall with the bats flying about their heads.

As he carefully searched tunnel after tunnel, the light in the lantern began to grow dim as the oil was being used up. He shook it and gave a sigh. He would have to leave, go home and refill the lantern before he could continue his search.

As he wound his way back toward the entrance, the light finally sputtered and died, leaving him in total darkness. He felt his way forward slowly. As he crossed the cavern with the huge hole in the middle of the floor, he stumbled on a broken rock. Losing his balance, he grabbed desperately for the rocks, but slid back and fell directly into the pit. Just as he thought he'd never hit bottom, he landed with a splash, his head cracked against a stone, and he knew no more.

CHAPTER SEVEN

THE PIT

"Are y'all ready to go prospectin'?" Joe called through the wall in the upstairs room the next morning as the rooster crowed in Uncle Wirt's yard below.

"Yep!" Mandie yelled back as she jumped out of bed and stretched. Snowball followed her.

"I will go with you," Sallie said as she rose to reach for her dress hanging on a nail.

"Beat you downstairs!" Joe called, and the girls could hear him scrambling down the ladder.

The adults were already sitting around the table. It seemed no matter how early the young ones got up, the older ones were always there first.

"I was just going to wake you," her mother said. "On this trip to the cave we are going prepared. You must eat a good breakfast, and we will carry more food. I understand we have an uphill climb on a footpath after we leave the wagon on the road, so we can't carry anything heavy."

"Besides, we have to carry lots of lanterns," Mandie told her. "It's awfully dark in that cave."

"Yes, and I have lots of rope handy, too," Uncle John added.

"Shouldn't we take something to bring the gold back in?" asked Joe as he sat down to eat beside the girls.

"Oh, yes, the men will take something to put it in—if we find it," John smiled.

"Gold—bad luck," Uncle Ned mumbled as he rose from the table.

"Hurry. We go soon," Uncle Wirt told the young people as he also stood up. "Eat."

Mandie laughed. "That's one English word my Cherokee kinpeople all know—eat." She dug into her bowl of cornmeal mush.

"Eat—that's a good word to know," Joe said.

"Do you like what our people eat? Do you eat the same thing when you are at home?" Sallie asked the two as she began eating her mush.

Mandie and Joe looked at each other.

"Well, yes, almost the same thing." Mandie paused. "Everything I have eaten since I came to Cherokee country has been delicious."

"At home we have fatback and red-eye gravy sometimes, and grits," Joe added.

Elizabeth was packing meat and bread in several separate packages. "Let's make haste now," she called. "We don't want to be too late coming back." Turning to John, she asked, "Tsa'ni never came with our things from Uncle Ned's house, did he?"

"No," he replied. "We can stop and get them on the way back."

As they went through the community at Deep Creek, they asked several people, but no one had seen Tsa'ni. They left Morning Star at her cabin and said they would stop for their things on the way back. Tsa'ni's mother was not in her cabin as they stopped by.

Uncle Ned mumbled, "Bad Cherokee."

Uncle Wirt, his grandfather, agreed, "Tsa'ni not good."

However, there was one Indian boy they could depend upon. Dimar was sitting on a rock near the waterfall waiting for them when they got there. His eyes fastened on Mandie again. He rose and came forward.

"Good morning," he greeted them.

"Good morning, Dimar," Uncle John replied. "You haven't seen Tsa'ni around, have you? He never did come to Bird-town."

"No, I have not seen him," the boy said. "I have not seen anyone around here."

"Tsa'ni—bad Cherokee," Uncle Ned muttered. "Go." He motioned for the others to follow him under the waterfall and into the cave.

"Since we aren't sure what direction to take, we'll all scatter out in different directions, but you three be sure to stay together," Uncle John told them. "Now let's all go looking for a pile of rocks!"

Elizabeth took one look at the cave and shuddered as she turned to the three children. "To think you were lost in here! I would have been frightened to death!"

"It sure wasn't any fun," Joe answered, shifting the coil of rope he was carrying over his shoulder.

"No, it wasn't." Mandie agreed.

Sallie took a lighted lantern from one of the men. "Come, we will look together." She motioned for Mandie and Joe to follow her.

"I'm glad you decided to come with us," Mandie told the Indian girl.

"Since my grandfather was coming, I decided I should try to help, too," she answered.

"Please be careful," Elizabeth warned them.

Uncle John called after them. "Yes, you be *very* careful. We don't want to have to go looking for you again."

"We will," Mandie promised as she picked up Snowball. "I think we can find it."

"Don't worry, Mrs. Shaw. We can't get lost with everyone in here," Joe said.

With Sallie leading the way with the lantern, the three went off down a tunnel. This time they were laughing, feeling very secure with the grown-ups nearby. They stopped to look at every little pile of rocks they could find along the way.

"That can't be it," Joe said as Mandie and Sallie walked over to a rock-covered wall. "The place we went through had a smooth wall all around except for the pile of stones covering the gold."

"No, Joe, it had lots of rocks stacked all along the wall," Mandie disagreed.

"Now wait a minute, Mandie. It did not!" Joe countered. Turning to the Indian girl, he asked, "Didn't it, Sallie?"

"I do not know, Joe. Do you not remember the lantern went out and we were digging in the dark?"

Mandie and Joe looked at each other.

"That's right, Sallie," he said.

"Yes, you dropped the lantern, Joe! It must be wherever you dropped it," Mandie reminded him. "We'll find the broken glass—"

"Aw, now, come on, Mandie. All those rocks fell on top of it. It's probably well buried by now," Joe interrupted.

"We have not passed the room with the bats in it yet," Sallie said. "The bats flew at us before we found the gold."

"Oh, goodness, I had forgotten about the bats," Mandie groaned. "Do you suppose we could pass quietly so they won't get stirred up again?"

" 'Course not, Mandie. There's no way you can sneak up on bats. They are very sensitive," Joe admonished her. "We'll just have to watch out and get away fast when they come out."

They rounded a corner and a whirring, cackling noise greeted them.

"Here they come!" Sallie yelled as they bent low and ran down the passageway.

The terrifying black creatures circled and circled before they finally roosted again in their hiding place.

"Whew, that was close," Mandie said, breathlessly, pulling Snowball's claws loose from her shoulder, "Snowball, calm down. Let go!"

"We are getting close to the place," Sallie said. "Remember, it was not long after we saw the bats that we found the opening."

"There was a large hole in the floor of that room where the gold was," Mandie reminded them. "We walked around it before coming to the pile of rocks."

"Right," Joe agreed.

Meanwhile, Uncle Ned was leading Elizabeth and John around another way. Uncle Wirt had taken Dimar with him in still another direction.

Uncle Ned pointed to cracks in the walls and ceiling and kept muttering, "Dangerous! Cave not good!"

"But Uncle Ned, these cracks look like they have been here a long, long time," John replied, examining them closely.

"Long time. Ready to fall now," the old Indian said.

"John, if this thing started caving in we'd never get out," Elizabeth fretted.

"This is a huge cave, Elizabeth, and the walls look like pretty solid rock. Even the floor is mostly rock," John said. "Anyway, we'll hurry." He put his arm around her tightly.

"John, I wonder where the children have gone," she said.

"Papooses not lost," Uncle Ned reassured her as he continued on through the tunnel they were in.

"I would like to know what happened to Tsa'ni," John remarked.

"Tsa'ni—bad Indian," Uncle Ned repeated.

They wandered on through the tunnel, searching for the pile of rocks that might be covering a pile of gold.

In another tunnel Joe was leading the way with the lantern when he yelled, "Here's the room with the hole in the floor!"

The girls joined him to look at the place. There it was—the hole in the floor of the cavern where they had found the gold.

"Now, our opening must have been over there," Joe said, pointing across to the other side.

At that moment the three heard a low moan and then a weak cry, "Help!"

They stood absolutely still with fright.

"W-w-w-wh-what was th-that?" Joe whispered.

"It may be the spirit of Tsali," Sallie replied.

"But Charlie didn't die in this cave," Joe said.

Again there was a call for help, this time a little louder.

"Sounds like it came up from that hole in the floor," Mandie said, not moving an inch.

"Who is it?" Sallie called in a loud voice.

"It is me, Tsa'ni. Please help me!" he answered, more clearly now.

Mandie was suddenly seeing another day, another call for help. She was remembering the panther and her terrible predicament. Tsa'ni had turned and left her alone. But she couldn't do that to him. No matter how mean he had been, she would have to help him now.

"Where are you, Tsa'ni'?" Mandie called to him.

"I fell in the opening in the floor. I am down here at the bottom of it," the boy said.

"Tsa'ni!" Joe ventured to the edge of the hole, and swinging the lantern he could faintly see something at the bottom of the pit. "Why should we help you after what you did to us?"

Mandie hesitated, fighting with her own feelings.

"No, Joe, we must help him," she said, coming to his side.

"He must have come back here looking for our gold." Joe frowned. "He's not honest. I won't help him."

"Oh, but Joe, the Bible says we should return good for evil," Mandie reminded him. "You know that."

"Well, anyway, there's nothing we can do to help him. The hole is too deep," the boy argued.

"Are you hurt, Tsa'ni?" Sallie called down to the boy.

"Yes, I cannot move," he answered in a weak voice.

"Joe, let's tie our rope around that stalagmite over there and I'll scoot down to see what's wrong with him," Mandie suggested.

"Are you crazy? There's no telling what's down in that hole," Joe argued.

"I will help," Sallie told Mandie.

"You can't climb down a rope," Joe reprimanded.

"I can so. It's not much different than climbing a tree, and I've climbed quite a few trees in my life," Mandie said, as she put Snowball down and began to pull the end of the rope from Joe's shoulder, "Come on. Unroll the rope."

Joe set the lantern down and did as Mandie asked. They fastened the rope as tightly as they could knot it and pulled it over to the hole as Mandie prepared to descend.

"Go very slowly," Sallie warned.

Pulling up the slack in the rope, Mandie finally wriggled around on the edge of the hole so that she was swinging down. Joe held the lantern as far out as he could over the hole.

Snowball, watching Mandie slide down the rope, reached over with his paw and started to claw at it.

"Snowball, stop that!" Mandie commanded, looking up at him.

Sallie picked up the kitten. "I will hold him. He might fall."

Mandie slid on down until her feet touched the bottom. She looked around in the dim light until she saw Tsa'ni lying on his back watching her. She let go of the rope and bent over him.

"What's wrong, Tsa'ni?" she asked. "Where are you hurt?"

"I do not know. I cannot move," he said.

The girl saw a stream of water near where he lay. She took off her apron and dipped it.

"Here, let me wash your face," she said. "But I'll warn you. It's pretty cold."

She wiped his face gently and he didn't move.

"Tsa'ni, we have to figure out a way to get you out of here," she said.

"Please, go for help," he begged. "Get some strong men to help me."

"Uncle Ned and Uncle John and your grandfather are all in the cave somewhere," she told him. "You just lie still and we'll go find them. It shouldn't take very long." She dipped her apron into the water again, squeezed it out, and placed it across his forehead.

"There, I'll leave that right there. Maybe it'll help. Now I'll go back up the rope and get help."

"Please hurry," the Indian boy moaned.

"We will," Mandie called back as she caught the rope. By pulling it tight and bracing her feet against the wall of the pit, she was able to work her way back up to the top. Sallie and Joe pulled her onto the floor at the top.

"Well, what's wrong with him?" Joe asked.

"He can't move, Joe. We must find the men as fast as we can."

Mandie picked up Snowball as they hurried through the tunnels and caverns calling the men's names. It was a few minutes before they finally got an answer.

"Here, Papoose. Stay there. We come," Uncle Ned called from somewhere out of sight.

"That's Amanda," Elizabeth said.

"Maybe they've found the gold," John said as they followed Uncle Ned in the direction of the voices.

Turning a sharp corner they were met by a flood of light from Mandie's lantern.

"Uncle Ned, Uncle Ned, we found Tsa'ni! He's hurt—bad. He's in a deep hole. It will take some strong men to get him out."

"Show us, Mandie," Uncle John said, and turning to Uncle Ned, he added, "So he came back here looking for the gold."

Uncle Ned nodded his head and grunted. Then he gave his whistle for help. Uncle Wirt and Dimar were not far off and came on the run. Soon they were all in the cavern with the hole in the floor.

"There!" Mandie said, pointing. "He's down there. I went down to see what was wrong with him. He can't move."

She showed them the rope still fastened in place.

"Papoose good Indian," Uncle Ned said, putting his arm around her.

Mandie, pleased beyond expression by the compliment, looked up in his face with a big smile. "Thank you, Uncle Ned."

"This is the room where we found the gold," Joe told them. "I think it was over there where all those rocks are spilled all over the floor."

"Over there?" Uncle John was trying to distinguish the rocks he was talking about in the dim light from the lanterns.

"But first we have to get Tsa'ni out!" Mandie reminded them.

The two Indian men were already making a rope ladder to get down inside the pit.

"If he can't move, Uncle Ned, it's going to take some doing to get him out," John said, helping with the rope.

"Make basket. Put basket down hole," the old Indian replied. He was busy weaving the rope they had been carrying into a crude basket. Wirt and Dimar were helping, evidently knowing exactly what he had in mind. Uncle John finally understood. He walked around the hole to the other side, carrying the end of the rope from which they were making the basket. The other end stayed on the other side. The rope was fastened on each side to the basket so it could be lowered into the pit and then pulled back up.

Dimar volunteered. "I am young and strong. I will go down and put Tsa'ni in the basket."

"Go," Uncle Ned told him, and he slid down the rope Mandie had used.

"I am at the bottom," Dimar called. "Send down the basket."

The crude basket was lowered and Dimar pulled it flat on the rock floor of the pit. He and Tsa'ni were about the same size, and it was no easy job to lift the other boy and lay him on the rope basket. Neither spoke a word.

"All right, pull! He is in the basket," Dimar called.

The men carefully pulled on the rope from either side of the hole, and soon the basket with Tsa'ni in it appeared.

"That way," Uncle Ned motioned to the men on both sides to walk to the far end of the pit, holding the rope taut as they went. Then they lowered the basket carefully to the floor. Uncle Wirt bent to examine the injured boy.

"I cannot move," Tsa'ni told his grandfather. His face was pale and he looked frightened in the lantern light.

"We take Tsa'ni to wagon," Wirt told the others.

Tsa'ni turned his head away.

Joe protested as they prepared to leave. "What about the gold?"

"We'll have to use the wagon to get Tsa'ni to a doctor. We'll just have to come back tomorrow," Uncle John told them.

Mandie sighed. "Oh, me. All this work all over again." She was feeling hatred again toward Tsa'ni for interfering with their plans. After all, he had fallen into the pit because he was trying to beat them to the gold.

"Yeh, all because of that stupid boy," Joe said.

Sallie looked at the two, "He will be sorry."

"I hope he is," Joe said. "First thing you know, someone else will get the gold, and we'll never know what happened to it. So many people know about it now."

Mandie and Sallie agreed. Too many people knew about the gold. They must hurry back the next day.

CHAPTER EIGHT

THE BROKEN WAGON WHEEL

Uncle Ned pulled the wagon to a halt in front of his cabin and motioned to the others. "Wirt and me take Tsa'ni to doctor. You stay here. Morning Star make food."

"Are you sure you won't need any help?" Uncle John asked as he helped Elizabeth down from the wagon.

"No. You watch papooses," Uncle Ned said, laughing.

"I don't think they'll go anywhere. It's past suppertime and I know they're hungry," Uncle John told him.

Mandie, Joe, Sallie, and Dimar jumped down and headed for the cabin. Dimar had told his mother he would be gone for a day or two, so he decided to stay at Uncle Ned's house for the night.

Morning Star had the food cooking and Elizabeth helped her finish. The four young people sat on the doorstep with Snowball.

"Where are they taking Tsa'ni to a doctor?" Mandie asked Sallie.

"To Dr. Carnes. He is a white doctor. He lives between here and Bryson City," the Indian girl replied.

"He probably won't find anything wrong with him. I think it's all put on so he won't get into trouble for trying to steal the gold," Joe remarked, as he drew lines in the sand with a stick.

"But, Joe, he didn't say a word all the way back. He had his eyes closed," Mandie said, secretly thinking the same thing as Joe. She was desperately trying to rid her mind of the mean thoughts.

"Well, I could do that, too. Saves answering a whole lot of questions," Joe chided.

"I do not think so, Joe," Sallie disagreed. "I really believe he was hurt. He looked pale and weak."

"Well, he sure slowed things down for us."

"You're right there, Joe," Mandie said.

"Your uncle said we would return tomorrow," Dimar reminded her. His eyes never left her face. His admiration was plain to see, but Mandie was not aware of it.

"But, Dimar, we have to go all the way back up there to the cave and then all through those spooky rooms until we find the right one again," Mandie said.

"That will not be hard this time. I think I can remember exactly which way we went." Sallie was confident.

"Yeh, like that." Joe drew a rough diagram of the cave in the sand. "Here's the entrance, and we went this way." He pointed. "Then this way and that way," He sketched a line through the outline.

"That is right." Sallie was watching.

"But there's still the problem of actually finding the gold. It's buried somewhere under all those rocks, and they all look the same," Mandie reminded them.

"That should not take long with so many people to help dig," Dimar said.

Elizabeth came to the doorway. "Eat!" She laughed.

"Eat! That word is good in any language!" Joe exclaimed as they stood up and hurried to the table for their evening meal.

"Amen!" agreed Mandie.

Dimar managed to sit between Mandie and Sallie with Joe on the other side of Mandie. Joe was beginning to notice Dimar's behavior around his friend. He didn't say anything, but kept a watch on the two of them during the meal. Mandie still did not seem to notice the extra attention.

Uncle Ned returned after a while, alone. Everyone looked up, anxious for news of Tsa'ni.

"Tsa'ni go home. Wirt go with him," the old Indian told them as he sat down to eat. "Doctor say—stay in bed."

"Well, did he think it was serious? I mean, can Tsa'ni move now?" Uncle John asked.

"No," the old man replied. "Hurt back, legs."

"Well, I hope he doesn't have a *bad* back injury. He may never walk again," Elizabeth said.

Everyone became serious. Mandie was fighting elation over the fact that Tsa'ni really was injured. In the back of her mind she knew she should feel sorry for him. But she couldn't help feeling he deserved it.

She spoke up to clear her thoughts. "Can we go to see him tomorrow?"

The old Indian nodded. "Yes—Tsa'ni bad Cherokee."

"You mean because he tried to get the gold?" asked Joe.

The old man nodded again. "Gold bad for Cherokee. Tsa'ni bad, too."

Mandie turned to her Uncle John. "Are you still going back to the cave tomorrow?"

He turned to Uncle Ned. "What do you think? Should we go back up there tomorrow?"

"Go tomorrow. Be done!" the Indian grunted.

Uncle John laughed. "You still aren't happy about looking for the gold. Uncle Ned, the Cherokees could use the gold for a lot of things they need—a hospital, a school closer by, even a new church. Depending on how much is there, the gold could buy lots of things which would take years and years to get otherwise."

"Gold make people crazy. Bad for Cherokee. Bad for Tsa'ni." He was very firm about it.

"I know, but we'll see what good we can do with it," John continued.

"You mean we can't *keep* the gold?" Joe asked, surprised at the conversation between the two men.

"Of course not, Joe," Uncle John told him. "This is Cherokee territory, so it rightfully belongs to them."

"But the cave is not on the Cherokee reservation," Joe argued.

"I know that, but it's almost one hundred percent Cherokee territory around here. Besides, that cave belongs to their history. Remember, Tsali hid in there," John added.

"Couldn't we just keep a little sample for a souvenir?" Mandie ventured.

"Depends on how big the sample is," Uncle John laughed. "Anyhow, we'll cross that bridge when we come to it."

Morning Star had been sitting at the table listening to the conversation. No one had any idea how much she had understood until she spoke up with great conviction, "Jim Shaw's papoose have gold!"

Everyone turned to look at her, startled.

She tried to explain. She pointed to herself and then to Mandie. "My gold Papoose's gold."

Mandie jumped up to hug her. "Oh, Morning Star, you are learning to speak English! I wouldn't take your gold. Like Uncle John says, it belongs to the Cherokees living around here."

Morning Star shook her head furiously and rattled off something in Cherokee. Uncle Ned listened and turned to explain.

"Morning Star say gold bad for Cherokee. Morning Star remember Cherokee move. I remember, too."

"Times have changed, Uncle Ned," John insisted. "I can guarantee you no harm will come to the Cherokees when the gold is found. It won't be like it was before."

The old man grunted and got up to go outside. John followed him.

"Early to bed, early to rise," Elizabeth told the children.

The four went to bed early, but there was a great deal of talking going on over the wall. Dimar and Joe were on the one side and the girls on the other. Joe, knowing the Indian boy was interested in Mandie, tried to monopolize the conversation.

"Mandie, this is even more exciting than looking for your uncle's will, don't you think?" Joe began.

"Well, I don't know about that," she said. "I suppose it is just *as* exciting. Of course, I've never seen so much gold before."

"Neither have I," Sallie put in.

"I sure hope we find it," Dimar said. "There must be a pile of it if it can buy a hospital and all that other stuff your Uncle John was talking about, Mandie,"

"A *huge* pile of it. I have no idea how much it's worth, though," said Mandie.

"Your uncle will know," Dimar assured her.

"I'm sure glad he's around to handle everything because Uncle Ned is certainly not interested," she said.

"He can remember the removal," Dimar reminded her.

Joe, becoming jealous of the boy, faked a yawn and said loudly, "Well, time to go to sleep. Have to get up early."

"Yes, we have to get up early," Sallie agreed.

"I almost forgot something. If we are leaving early in the morning for the cave, how are we going to see Tsa'ni?" Mandie asked.

"Well, I have no intention of going to see Tsa'ni. You will just have to wait until we come back if you insist on visiting him," Joe replied.

The question was settled at early dawn when the four, wide awake with excitement, went downstairs for breakfast. Uncle Ned and Uncle John were just coming in the door from outside. They looked disturbed.

Seeing the four youngsters at the table, Uncle John explained, "Well, it looks like we won't be going back to the cave today. The wagon has a broken wheel and we have to get the part from Bryson City, which is going to take some time."

The four spoke as one, "Oh, no!"

"It wasn't broken when you came home last night, was it, Uncle Ned?" Mandie asked.

The old man shook his head. "Broke today."

Uncle John explained. "No, it wasn't broken last night. It looks like someone has been prowling around and deliberately damaged the wheel."

The four looked at one another.

"Well, since Tsa'ni can't walk, it couldn't have been him this time," Mandie said.

"How about the old man and woman that captured us in the woods?" Joe asked

"Snuff and Rennie Lou?" Mandie asked.

"Yeh, maybe it was them."

"I hardly think they would come down here and do a thing like that," Uncle John said.

"You said you told them you were going to report them to the authorities," Sallie reminded him.

"Yes, as a matter of fact, I did tell them that."

"But why would they want to do something like that?" Uncle John added.

"Maybe they know about the gold," Dimar suggested.

"And maybe they know we are going after it," added Mandie.

"Well, anyway, however it happened, we will have to wait until the wagon is repaired," John Shaw said.

"Couldn't we borrow a wagon from one of the neighbors? After all, Uncle Ned knows all of them," Mandie said.

"No, we'd rather not do that. We'd have to keep it all day, and we'd have to explain where we were going. Uncle Ned and I are going to ride into Bryson City when we get the horses saddled up and see what we can get to fix the wheel."

"Are you going to talk to the authorities about the old man and woman?" Joe asked.

"I suppose we'll do that while we're there," John said.

"They must have a still up there. Remember, we told you they thought we were spying on their still," Mandie added.

"I remember."

"May we go visit Tsa'ni while Uncle John is gone, Mother?" Mandie asked Elizabeth.

"If you want to, but you mustn't stay too long. Tsa'ni is probably too sick to be bothered with company," her mother told her.

As the men rode away to Bryson City, the four waved good-bye from the front of the cabin.

"Anyone want to go see Tsa'ni now?" Mandie asked.

"I will go with you," Sallie replied.

"I don't know. I think he is dishonest with us," Joe mumbled.

"I will go," Dimar said, eager for the chance to be with Mandie.

Joe was quick to notice, and he thought he'd better go along just to keep an eye on the two. He shuffled his feet around in the sand and looked up. "All right. I'll go, too, but I won't have anything to say to him."

Tsa'ni lived about a mile down the road from Uncle Ned's house, but the road had such a sharp curve that it was easier to cut through the backyards of several neighbors. Mandie had already decided that all the Cherokees' cabins were alike and so she was not surprised to find Tsa'ni's home a duplicate of Uncle Ned's. The door of the log cabin was open and as they approached, a kind Indian woman came to welcome them.

"Come in. I am glad you could come to see Tsa'ni," she said, as they entered the house.

The boy was on a bed at the far end of the room, and Mandie could feel him staring at her.

"I am Amanda Shaw, and you must be Tsa'ni's mother," Mandie introduced herself.

"Yes, I am Meli," the woman said. "Your father was my husband's cousin."

Mandie nodded. "That's right. How is Tsa'ni today?"

"Not good. But, go—see," she said, directing the four over to the bed.

Tsa'ni stared but did not speak.

"We came to see how you are," Mandie spoke cheerfully.

There was no answer.

"What did Dr. Carnes tell you about your injuries?" she asked.

Tsa'ni seemed determined not to speak.

"You could at least answer," Dimar told him. "You are being rude."

Tsa'ni took a deep breath. "Why should I speak to the white girl? White people! They are always causing trouble for the Cherokee!"

"No one caused trouble for you, Tsa'ni," Dimar retorted. "What happened to you was your own fault. And you *were* rescued because Mandie cared about what happened to you."

"The white people come here poking into the Cherokees' affairs," Tsa'ni said. "I do not want to see any more white people!" He turned his face toward the wall.

"You are a very narrow-minded person, Tsa'ni," Mandie told him.

"Tsa'ni, if you had not been trying to find the gold first, you would not have been injured," the Indian girl said.

"Go away! I do not wish to communicate with white people! I do not wish to have any company!" He still kept his face turned away from them.

Joe was filled with anger. "You may not wish to communicate with white people, but you must admit you tried to get the gold which we found first."

"The gold belongs to the Cherokees, not the white people!" Tsa'ni turned to glare at Joe.

"We found it and we will do what we please with it!" Joe insisted.

"Do not be too sure about that! Now, get out!" Tsa'ni yelled, flushed with anger.

The four backed off to leave. They stopped to say good-bye to his mother who had been watching the whole scene.

As they walked back through the yards to Uncle Ned's house, Mandie asked, "I wonder what he meant when he said we shouldn't be too sure about doing what we please with the gold?"

"Just talking," said Joe. "He wants to frighten us away from it."

"He could have told someone else about the gold," Sallie suggested.

"Yes, and they could be looking for it right now," Dimar added.

"I hope not," Mandie said. "You all heard what Uncle John said could be done with the gold, and I sure hope the wrong people don't get it."

They all felt their plans were strangely threatened. Mandie hated Tsa'ni more that ever in spite of her intentions to forget the wrongs he had done them. He was such a revengeful person. How could anyone like him?

CHAPTER NINE

TSALI'S MESSAGE

Uncle Ned and Uncle John were back from Bryson City in time for the noontime meal. As they all sat around the table, they discussed their journey.

"Did you get the piece to fix the wagon?" Mandie asked before anyone had eaten a bite.

"Yes, as soon as we finish eating, we'll get it back in working order, and tomorrow we'll go back to the cave," Uncle John told her.

The four looked at one another and smiled.

"Eat," Uncle Ned commanded.

"Yes, sir, Uncle Ned," Mandie replied, picking up her fork, and starting on the beans. The other three followed suit.

Elizabeth turned to John. "Did you talk to anyone about those two people up in the mountain?"

"The old man and woman? Yes, we told everything we knew about them. There will be men scouting the mountain looking for a still in a few days," he said.

"We went to see Tsa'ni and he was rude to us," Mandie said. She related the conversation between them. Uncle Ned listened closely.

"Tsa'ni bad Cherokee," he mumbled. "Up to no good."

"Bad," echoed Morning Star.

"Well, there's nothing he can do if he can't get about," Uncle John told them.

"I don't trust him at all," Joe said. "I think if he *could* walk, he wouldn't let us know it."

"Joe!" Elizabeth admonished him.

"Sorry, Mrs. Shaw, but I don't trust him," Joe told her.

"I don't either, Mother," Mandie said. She had decided to give up believing the Indian boy.

"I cannot trust him either," Sallie added.

"Neither can I," Dimar joined in.

"Well, in that case, maybe there *is* some reason not to trust him," Elizabeth replied.

"Reason—Tsa'ni bad," the old Indian repeated.

"Oh, Uncle Ned, you've been saying Tsa'ni is bad ever since we got here. How about telling me why you say that?" John asked Ned.

"Leave Papoose with panther. Try to steal gold. No bring things to Bird-town," the old man explained. He took a deep breath. "Now he make bad talk to Papoose."

"The Bible says repay evil with good, remember, Uncle Ned?" John reminded him.

"Big Book not say Tsa'ni can be bad Indian," the old Indian muttered.

Everyone smiled.

Mandie couldn't understand why one should keep on doing good to a person who kept on doing bad things in return. She was quite exasperated and was losing her determination to be kind. Then she remembered her father had taught her to pray for her enemies, so she decided she would start praying for Tsa'ni. In the meantime, she hoped he would recover from his accident—but not in time to beat them to the gold!

Uncle Wirt went with them the next morning to the cave. He was still angry with his grandson and would not talk about him. He had gone on to his house in Bird-town the day before and had not seen Tsa'ni since.

After arriving inside the cave, Sallie led them straight to the cavern where they had seen the gold.

"Here is the place," she told them, pointing to the pile of rocks along the far wall.

Mandie agreed. "Yes, this is it."

"Well, let's start digging," Joe said, pushing up his sleeves.

With the three men to help them, it didn't take long to move the piles. Elizabeth watched from a safe distance as they threw the rocks behind them out of the way. Sallie found the first nugget.

"Gold," she said, handing the nugget to Uncle Ned who was working beside her.

He turned it over in his hand, didn't say a word and passed it on to John. The others crowded around.

"The real thing," John Shaw said. "Let's see how much we can find."

Mandie and Joe were moving the rocks at the bottom of the pile when she stooped and squealed. "Here it is! All of it!" They had uncovered the gold they had found before.

"At last!" Joe gasped.

The men bent to inspect the gold.

"You were right, Mandie. It is about a bushel," her uncle told her. "Now let's get it into these sacks and get out of here."

Everyone was stuffing the sacks with the gold when Sallie, cleaning off the floor under one end of the pile, called out, "Look! Writing!" She was pointing to the wall of the cave behind the rocks.

The group gathered to see what she had found. They all worked to clean the wall and the rest of the writing. Soon large Indian sign language appeared and also some words in English.

Sallie bent close to read it. "This gold left here for good of Cherokee after white man makes peace. This gold belongs to us who are hiding here to save our lives. Curse on the white man who takes it. Tsali." She gasped as she finished the words.

All were speechless as they stared at the crude letters on the stone wall.

Joe turned to Ned. "Could it really have been Tsali who wrote this message and left the gold?".

The old Indian nodded. "His name." He pointed to the symbol under the English "Tsali."

"He did not forget his people," Dimar said very solemnly. "He gave his life and left them a fortune."

"After all these years!" Mandie exclaimed. "And to think we were the ones who discovered it!"

"Someone else must have written the message for him," Uncle John said.

"Probably the white man, William H. Thomas, who came to ask him to surrender to save his people," Sallie added. "He was the trusted friend of the Cherokee people."

"Of course," Uncle John agreed.

"Would it be possible to take the message, too, with the gold?" Mandie asked.

"You don't mean that?" Joe laughed. "That's a stone wall."

"I just don't know. I suppose we could get somebody to look at it to see if the piece of stone could be chiseled out," Uncle John suggested.

Elizabeth asked, "Wouldn't it be better to leave it here for history's sake?"

"Well—" began John.

"On, no, Mother," Mandie protested. "You see, the wall caved in on us when we climbed through the hole we dug, and sooner or later rockslides will completely cover it again and maybe even break it up. Besides, we don't want to spread word about the gold yet, do we?"

"You're right," her uncle said. "We'll see about getting it chiseled out."

"We take message out," Uncle Ned told them.

Wirt nodded.

"Please, could I help?" Dimar asked.

Uncle Ned nodded. "Strong brave."

"Let's hurry," Uncle John said, bending to help fill the sacks. "We want to get back before sundown. Uncle Ned, you and Uncle Wirt can come back whenever you get ready and see what you can do about cutting out the message."

Carefully sorting through the rocks to be sure they got it all, they finally finished filling the sacks and carried them to the wagon. It was time-consuming and back-breaking work, but it seemed worth the effort. With all this gold the Cherokees could accomplish a lot.

As they prepared to return to Uncle Ned's cabin, Uncle John warned them, "It's better that we don't discuss this with anyone outside our little group here until we can come to some decision as to how to give this gold to the Cherokee people."

Uncle Ned looked fiercely at the others. "No talk!"

Uncle Wirt added, "No talk."

The others agreed. Some plan would have to be made for distributing the gold to the Indians, and until something was finalized, it would be safer not to let anyone else know about what they had found.

It was dark when they arrived at Uncle Ned's cabin. Morning Star had the table set with food to greet them. They hurriedly unloaded the gold in the barn and covered it with hay.

"Should be safe here until we can decide something further," Uncle John said as they shut the door. He took the nail hanging on a leather strap and dropped it into the hook, the only way there was to secure the door.

They were all happy as they walked toward the cabin, not realizing they were being watched in the darkness.

CHAPTER TEN

THIEVES IN THE NIGHT

The four young people were talkative and restless long after they had gone to bed. Snowball sensed their mood and bounced around between them. There was a small window next to Mandie's bed, and she and Sallie kept peering out at the barn.

"Just think what's in the barn!" Mandie exclaimed.

"Yes, and think of how much fun it will be giving it to the Cherokees," Joe called over the dividing wall.

"It is such a dark night. If the moon were only shining, we could see the barn more clearly," the Indian girl said.

"I do not think we need to stay up all night watching the barn," Dimar said from the small room he occupied with Joe.

Sallie tensed up suddenly. "Mandie! Look! Is that someone out there?"

Mandie pressed her face against the windowpane. "Where, Sallie?"

"At the corner. There!" Sallie poked at the window.

"I can't see anyone, Sallie," Mandie was getting excited.

"Oh, I suppose it was just my imagination," Sallie admitted. "We should go to sleep."

"I can't believe those girls," Joe sighed.

"Hey, wait, I see a light! Look!" Mandie shouted.

The two girls stared hard into the darkness. Then gradually the light grew stronger.

"It's a fire! The barn is on fire!" Mandie screamed. She ran to the ladder and screamed again. "Uncle Ned, Uncle John, the barn is on fire!"

Dimar and Joe hastily pulled on their trousers and ran to see. They took one look through the window and flew down the ladder. The girls, pulling their dresses on over their heads, followed, Snowball close behind.

Uncle Ned and Uncle John were already out the door by the time the boys' feet hit the floor. Elizabeth and Morning Star were getting dressed.

"Bell!" shouted Uncle Ned to Dimar as he ran. The boy understood and ran to the huge iron bell hanging in the tree and pulled the rope. The clapper sent out a loud gong and in seconds neighboring Indians began appearing from all directions carrying water buckets.

"Oh, please, dear God, don't let it burn up," Mandie prayed as she was held back by her mother.

There were so many men fighting the fire that it was soon extinguished with little damage done, thanks to the girls who had seen it start. Uncle Wirt had gone to his son's house for the night, and he was among the fire fighters who had answered the call of the bell.

The volunteers all went home and Uncle Ned, Uncle Wirt, and Uncle John stood surveying the damage.

"Thank goodness we caught it in time," John said. "That was deliberately set. I just hope whoever it was doesn't come back tonight."

"I will guard the barn," Dimar offered as he stepped forward. "I will stay out here."

Joe, not to be outdone, spoke up, "I'll help you. One of us can sleep inside while the other one watches and then we can switch."

So it was agreed. The boys stood watch for the rest of the night. The girls, more restless than ever, kept watching at the window.

"Who do you suppose set that fire?" Mandie asked as they lay by the window.

"I do not know," the Indian girl said. "But whoever it was I wish we could catch him."

"I have a feeling whoever did it knew about the gold," Mandie said.

"Yes, I think so, too," Sallie agreed.

"Tomorrow Uncle John will repair the barn and Uncle Ned and Uncle Wirt will go back and start work on chiseling out the message in the cave. And when they get done, we can do something with the gold. Uncle John said they wanted the message to show the people when they present the gold to them."

"That will be a great day for the Cherokee!" the Indian girl said.

Tired and worn out, the two girls were soon asleep in spite of their excitement. But while they slept peacefully, things were not so peaceful in Uncle Ned's yard.

Joe was trying to sleep inside on the haystack, while Dimar was on guard outside the barn. He couldn't get comfortable, his ears attuned for intruders. Finally he gave up trying to sleep and went outside to join Dimar.

"I might as well forget it," he told the Indian boy. "I can't go to sleep in there."

"I can't sleep either," Dimar said.

"How about if you stay in the front here and I'll stay at the back?" Joe asked.

"All right. Sounds good to me." Dimar was too tired to argue.

Joe walked around to the back and stretched out in the grass. He had been lying there for what seemed like hours to him, when he heard the soft snap of a twig. He didn't move, but his ears perked up to listen. The night was so dark it was impossible to see very far. Then he heard another pop in the underbrush behind the barn. Now he was certain someone was there. He waited, his heart pounding furiously. Whoever it was, he must be out of sight lying in the tall grass.

Quietly turning on his side with his eyes trained on the brush in front of him, Joe finally distinguished the figure of a man. He took one step forward, pausing to listen, took another, then paused again. Joe waited until he was almost within reach, then bolted upright.

He could hardly believe his eyes, "Tsa'ni! You liar! You're supposed to be in bed!"

Tsa'ni stared in surprise at the sudden outburst. As he turned to run, Dimar, having heard the commotion, joined the chase. He was as surprised as Joe to see Tsa'ni.

"Tsa'ni! You are a disgrace to our people!" Dimar shouted at the fleeing Indian, who, knowing the area so well, was soon far from the reach of his pursuers.

The two boys finally gave up the chase. "Looks like we lost him," Joe said, exhausted and gasping for air.

"Yes, but now we know who started the fire, don't you think, Joe?" Dimar replied, wiping the perspiration from his forehead.

"Shall we wake up his mother and Uncle Wirt and tell them?" Joe asked. "We must be somewhere near his house. I'm sure he's the culprit all right."

"No, I think it best we wait until daylight. We can keep watch until morning, and then we'll tell Uncle Ned," thy Indian boy said.

"Yeh, Uncle Ned will know what to do," Joe agreed, as they returned to the barn.

In spite of their good intentions, they both fell fast asleep and didn't awaken until daybreak, when they heard Morning Star open the door of the cabin.

They waited until everyone was gathered around the table, and then relayed the excitement of the night before.

"Uncle Ned, we think we know who set fire to your barn," Joe told the old man.

Every head turned in his direction. Just then, Uncle Wirt came in through the open door, unnoticed.

"Who?" Uncle Ned asked.

"Tsa'ni," Joe replied.

Uncle Wirt stopped in his tracks, his presence still undetected.

"Tsa'ni?" Uncle Ned repeated, shaking his head There were a few seconds of shocked silence; then the questions began.

"How do you know, Joe?" Uncle John asked.

"We caught him prowling around the barn last night, only he escaped," Joe said.

"Joe caught him by surprise. We know it was Tsa'ni We chased him a long time," Dimar added.

Uncle Wirt stepped forward to the table and everyone noticed him for the first time.

"Tsa'ni?" Uncle Wirt asked incredulously.

"Yes, Uncle Wirt," Joe replied.

"Tsa'ni—gone last night," Uncle Wirt nodded.

"I'm sorry, Uncle Wirt. I know he's your grandson," Uncle John sympathized.

"No. Tsa'ni bad Indian," Uncle Wirt affirmed. "He make lies."

"We chased him all through the woods, but he didn't go home," Joe said.

"But, we didn't actually *see* him set fire to the barn," Mandie spoke up. "We couldn't say for sure that he was the one who did it unless we actually saw him, right?"

"You are absolutely right, my dear," Uncle John agreed. "We are jumping to conclusions. Just because Joe and Dimar saw him near the barn last night doesn't mean he was the one who started the fire."

"But what other reason would he have for lying about not being able to walk and then showing up at Uncle Ned's barn the night of the fire?" Joe argued. "If he were just curious, he wouldn't have taken off like the wind when he saw us."

" 'Judge not, lest ye be judged,' " Mandie quoted. "Do you remember our Sunday school lesson not long ago, Joe?"

Elizabeth gazed admiringly at her daughter and smiled.

"I don't understand why you are always defending him, Mandie, after all the things he has done to us." Joe shook his head.

Uncle Ned pushed a plate of food toward Uncle Wirt. "Sit. Eat. We go get message in cave."

Uncle Wirt sat down and began eating.

"I would like to talk to Tsa'ni if anybody sees him," Uncle John said.

"No one is going to be seeing him around for a while. I'm sure of that!" Joe was emphatic.

"You boys better get some sleep," Uncle John told them.

"Sleep? We want to help fix the barn!" Joe said between mouthfuls.

"Sure thing," Dimar added.

"All right, but you must both be terribly tired—or did you sleep some last night?" He looked at the boys with a knowing grin.

They both dropped their heads. Joe told him, "I guess I dozed off a little after we lost Tsa'ni."

"So did I," Dimar admitted.

Uncle Ned got his tools from the barn, harnessed up the horses to the wagon, and he and Uncle Wirt set out for the cave.

The boys went out to work on the barn with Uncle John.

Mandie and Sallie helped Morning Star and Elizabeth with chores around the house. Everyone was occupied for the day, though constantly on the alert. But just as Joe predicted, the day passed peacefully with no sign of Tsa'ni.

Inside the cave Uncle Ned and Uncle Wirt began hammering away at the stone wall. After hours and hours of work, they had made a continuous crack around the carved message and stood back to survey their work. Then there was a soft rumble. The two men held their breath listening. The rumble became louder and louder until the whole cave seemed to tremble.

"Rockslide!" gasped Uncle Ned, snatching his lantern and tools as he stumbled backward to the other side of the cavern.

The two men were temporarily stunned, and then suddenly the whole wall broke into pieces and a portion of the ceiling came crashing down. They ran for their lives. The noise was deafening. They had barely reached the entrance when the whole cave seemed to collapse. They ran without stopping until they were safely on the road. When they gazed back, it seemed the entire mountainside had changed in appearance. Huge boulders had slid down the side, dragging trees and brush with them into the waterfall. Everything in view was in shambles.

"Cave—gone!" Uncle Ned gasped.

"Gone!" echoed Uncle Wirt.

"Tsali message gone!" Uncle Ned wiped tears from his eyes as he thought about the great Indian hero who had remembered his people even in death.

Uncle Wirt could not speak. He simply turned toward the wagon on the road. Uncle Ned followed him and together they rode silently back to tell the others the news.

It was late afternoon when Mandie and Sallie saw them coming and ran to meet them. The girls could tell immediately that something was wrong.

"Uncle Ned, what happened?" Mandie asked as he stopped the wagon in front of the barn and stepped down. John and the boys came out at once.

"Cave gone. Tsali message gone," Uncle Ned shook his head in sorrow.

"Gone? How could it be gone?" Mandie asked.

"Rockslide. Cave gone. Message buried," Uncle Ned replied.

"A rockslide? Are you all right?" Uncle John asked, checking them over. "How did you manage to get out?"

"Run. God with us," Uncle Ned explained.

"Cave gone," Uncle Wirt repeated, shaking his head in bewilderment.

"That message Tsali left would have meant so much to our people," Sallie stated sadly.

"Now no one will ever believe us when we tell them about it," Joe said dejectedly.

"Part of our history has been lost," Dimar added.

"But we still have the gold," Mandie reminded them.

"Yes, and we still must decide what to do with it," Uncle John said.

As they sat around the table for the evening meal, they discussed the matter at length.

"I'll watch the barn again tonight," Joe offered after a lull in the discussion.

"So will I," Dimar said.

"You boys need a good night's rest," Uncle John told them.

"We can take our blankets and roll up in them on the grass outside. If anyone comes around, we will surely wake up," Joe insisted. Dimar nodded in agreement.

"Well, I certainly hope so," Elizabeth said. "It could be dangerous."

"Gold bad luck," Uncle Ned muttered.

"Not the gold, Uncle Ned. It's the greedy people," Mandie said.

Elizabeth spoke up. "What *are* we going to do about the gold? We can't keep it here forever."

"I know," Uncle John replied. "We'll have to decide what to do very soon."

"Why can't we put the gold in the bank?" Mandie asked.

"Good idea! Have you ever heard of bank robbers, Mandie?" Joe protested sarcastically.

"Bank robbers don't ever come to Bryson City." Mandie was sure of herself.

"I suppose the bank *is* a possible solution," John said. Turning to Wirt and Ned, he asked, "Do you think we could get it to the bank early tomorrow morning before the town is stirring?"

Both the old men nodded affirmatively.

"Well, if the people decide to storm the bank and take it, it belongs to them anyway," Joe conceded.

"No. Gold bad luck to Cherokee," Uncle Ned insisted. "Cherokee not steal gold."

"But what about Tsa'ni?" Dimar asked. "He wanted the gold."

"Tsa'ni!" Uncle Wirt spat out. "Bad Cherokee!" He rose to leave.

"Don't be too hard on him, Uncle Wirt," Elizabeth told him. "We don't know for sure who set fire to the barn."

But Uncle Wirt was angry, it was plain to see.

"He lied about not being able to walk and he should be punished for that," John said. "Will you be back tomorrow to help us move the gold to the bank?"

"Early tomorrow," the old man nodded as he waved good-bye.

As darkness began to fall, the two boys took their blankets to spread on the grass by the barn. The girls went up the ladder to their room and watched from the window until they were too sleepy to stay awake any longer. Snowball curled up contentedly at Mandie's feet.

It was long after midnight and both boys were sleeping soundly. The figure of a man appeared out of the brush and came stealthily toward the barn. He stopped at the corner of the building and lowered the flame of his lantern to the grass against the wall.

Joe stirred uneasily in his sleep, unseen by the intruder. Then his subconscious registered the distinct odor of burning grass mixed with the stench of liquor. He was awake in a flash, taxing his brain to orient himself to the situation. Then he saw the blaze not ten feet away, and he lunged to his feet. The figure, still not aware of Joe, darted around the corner. Joe headed the other way to alert Dimar who was already awake.

"He's on that side of the barn," Joe whispered softly, pointing to the north side.

They crept around the building in opposite directions and were both surprised to find themselves face to face with Snuff and Rennie Lou. With one fell swoop Joe had Snuff on the ground. Dimar kept his eyes on Rennie Lou, who stood there in a daze.

"We got you this time!" Joe shouted as he held him to the ground.

"Hey, wait a minute. I ain't done nothin'," the man protested, his speech slurred.

Dimar took a deep breath and gave his loud Indian call for help. Within seconds Uncle John and Uncle Ned came rushing out of the cabin.

Noise of the scuffling woke the girls and they slid down the ladder and watched at the door.

"Why, it's the man and woman who captured us on the mountain," Mandie said, as she watched Uncle John "handcuff" Snuff with his belt.

Morning Star slipped past the girls without a word and joined the others outside. Rennie Lou had come out of her stupor and saw a chance for escape while Dimar and Joe went to stomp out the fire. But she was no match for the strong Indian woman, who subdued her after a short struggle.

"I ain't done nothin'!" the woman was yelling. "Leave me alone, squaw!"

Morning Star ignored her threats and kept a firm grip on her arm.

"Hey, you're a white man," she directed to Uncle John. "You gonna let this Injun woman bully me?"

"Anything she wants to do to you will be all right with me," Uncle John replied. "Don't you realize these young people are the ones you kidnapped on the mountain? You two are going to jail as soon as we can get the law to take over."

"Take palefaces to Bryson City," Uncle Ned said as he went to hitch the wagon.

"This time of night, Uncle Ned?" Elizabeth asked as she joined John.

"Yes," the old man nodded.

"He's right, Elizabeth. We can't keep them here, and they should have been behind bars before now," John told her.

"Please, mister, don't do that," Snuff begged.

Uncle John ignored him as he called to the girls, "Mandie, can you bring us some rope? We need to secure these two for the trip to town."

Sallie and Mandie came out with several coils of rope. The boys helped Uncle John tie the couple up and get them into the wagon.

"Could we go along, Uncle John?" Joe asked.

"Oh, yes, please!" Dimar joined in.

Uncle John hesitated but then added, "Well, I suppose we do need you two as witnesses of the kidnapping and the arson."

"Right!" the boys exclaimed together.

"What about us?" Mandie protested.

"This is man's work, child," Uncle John told her. And they were off.

"Mmm, so it wasn't Tsa'ni after all," Mandie said as they walked back to the house.

"No, I do not think he was the one, Mandie, and I am glad it was not a Cherokee," Sallie said.

"But he was prowling around here for some reason—probably knew we had the gold." Mandie continued. "Tsa'ni really is strange, pretending to be hurt when he isn't. I wonder if he ever went back home."

Tsa'ni had never reached home. He was at that moment caught in an abandoned hunter's trap in the woods. This time he was really hurt.

CHAPTER ELEVEN

SPREADING THE WORD

"Well, we might as well all go back to bed," Elizabeth told the girls. "It'll take them a long time to get through in town and get back here."

The girls reluctantly went back upstairs, but soon were fast asleep. Snowball curled up close to Mandie. It seemed no time before the rooster was crowing and they could hear Morning Star in the kitchen. The girls quickly got dressed and went downstairs. Elizabeth was setting the table.

"I hope they got to town all right." Mandie stretched and yawned. "Those people are awfully mean and rough."

"I'm sure they got there all right. They tied those two with enough rope to wrap around the house," Elizabeth said.

"Eat." Morning Star smiled, pointing to the table.

The girls laughed and at that moment Uncle Wirt came through the door. He glanced around for the men.

"Where are Ned and John?" He looked puzzled.

"Joe and Dimar captured the people who set fire to the barn last night," Mandie said matter-of-factly, "and they've all gone to Bryson City to turn them over to the authorities."

Uncle Wirt stood there listening in amazement while they explained what had happened the night before. He breathed a loud sigh of relief and sat down at the table.

"Not Tsa'ni!" He could hardly believe it.

"Did he ever come home, Uncle Wirt?" Mandie asked.

"No," the old man replied. "Never come home."

Everyone looked at one another, wondering where the boy could have gone. Mandie thought, *He must be ashamed for what he has done and is staying away long enough to get the nerve to face his family.*

Uncle John, Uncle Ned, and the boys arrived back from town before they had finished eating and sat down at the table to join them. Joe and Dimar began eating as though they were starving.

"I'm glad you are all back safely," Elizabeth said. "Aren't you going to tell us about your trip?"

"Yes, yes, the law was mighty glad to get our hoodlums. Seems they were wanted in quite a few counties for several different offenses," John related. "Now we can all breathe a sigh of relief."

"We take gold to bank," Uncle Wirt reminded them.

"As soon as we can eat and get it loaded, Uncle Wirt," Uncle John replied.

"Hurry, take away gold," Uncle Ned said.

"Once it's safe in the bank, we'll inform the Cherokees of its existence," Uncle John stated.

"How do you plan to do that?" Mandie asked.

"Council pow-wow," Uncle Ned told her. "They tell people."

"How will all the people decide what they want to do with the gold?" she asked.

"They will take a vote. A place will be set up in the council house on the Cherokee reservation," Uncle John explained

Joe finally laid down his fork. "Boy! That sure was good! Now I have the strength to help load that gold."

Uncle Ned rose and took a rifle from the wall. Uncle Wirt examined his own gun, and John picked up his from the other end of the room.

"Guns?" Elizabeth looked alarmed.

"We need all the protection we can get to get this load in to town. You never know what kind of trouble we might run into," John assured her.

"I know how to use one of those rifles," Joe spoke up. "Can I carry one, too?"

"I do have one more. You and Dimar can decide between you which one will carry it," John said as he reached for the other gun standing by the bed.

Joe took it and then looked at Dimar. "Here, you carry it the first half of the way to town and I'll carry it the second half."

"Fair enough," the Indian boy said, taking the gun.

"Careful, now. The guns are already loaded," John cautioned them.

The girls wanted to help, of course, but were waved aside as the men and boys loaded the gold into the wagon. It didn't take long. Morning Star brought out several quilts to cover the sacks scattered on the floor of the wagon. Joe and Dimar perched on top of them, while the three men climbed onto the driver's seat.

"Please don't be too long. We'll be worried," Elizabeth called to them.

"We'll hurry back," John promised, waving to her. Then he instructed everyone to keep his gun out of sight. "We don't want to appear too well-armed. It could look mighty suspicious."

Mandie stood watching them pull into the road. Then she lifted her face to the sky. "Please, God, get them there and back safely."

"I trust God to take care of them, too," Sallie said, touching Mandie's shoulder. "I have asked Him into my heart."

"Oh, how wonderful, Sallie!" Mandie hugged her. "Isn't it good to be able to pray and trust God for everything?"

"It sure is, Mandie," she answered, smiling happily.

The men arrived at the bank in Bryson City just as Mr. Frady, the banker, was opening up for the day. He was a short, fat, nervous little man and he jerked around to look at the wagon pulling up at the door. *Three men and two bogs—that could mean trouble,* he thought, but then he spotted a familiar face under a wide-brimmed hat.

"John Shaw!" Me hurried down the steps to greet him. "It's been a long time!"

"Wilbur, it's good to see you, old man," John returned his greeting. "We are in desperate need of your bank right now." He lowered his voice. "We have about a bushel of gold under these quilts, and we need a safe place to keep it."

Wilbur's gray eyes grew round behind his spectacles. *"A bushel of gold?* Are you joshin' me, John?"

"No, sir, it's real gold," John replied, chuckling at the banker's reaction.

"If I didn't know you, John Shaw, I'd say you had just pulled off a big robbery," Wilbur told him. "Come on in." He opened the door and the two of them stepped inside.

"Let me open the safe before you bring it in," the banker said, stepping to a large heavy door at the back.

"How about if we drive around to the back door? It won't be so public that way," John suggested.

"Of course. That's the safest way," Wilbur agreed.

They swung the wagon around to the back door and hastily unloaded the gold into the bank's safe. No one was about and Wilbur kept the front door locked until they were finished.

"Now that we have it all in here, tell me, where in the world did it come from and what are you planning to do with it?" Wilbur asked John, as the others returned to the wagon.

"It's very confidential right now, Wilbur, but we'll have it off your hands in a few days. We want to keep it quiet so there won't be a robbery."

Wilbur wiped the sweat from his furrowed brow. "Well, I should hope not! How many people know about it?"

"Just Uncle Ned and Uncle Wirt and the rest of my family—and Dimar, the Indian boy with us," John told him. "I have promised not to discuss our plans right now, but if you do hear anything about a mysterious pile of gold, pretend you never saw it. Is it a deal'?"

"You bet!" Wilbur agreed. "But please don't leave it here too long. I would like to sleep at night."

"We'll see you in a few days then," John waved as he left by the back door and joined the others in the wagon.

"Glad job done," Uncle Ned said, with a sigh of relief, as he picked up the reins and they moved through the alley and into the main street.

"Well, it's up to you and Uncle Wirt now to get the word out," John reminded them. "But don't tell anyone where it's being kept."

The two Indians left John and the boys back at Uncle Ned's cabin and went directly on their mission to tell the Cherokees about the gold.

"Shucks, we didn't even get to use the rifle," Joe complained as he handed the gun back to John inside the cabin.

John hesitated and then said, "Go ahead and try it out. You and Dimar can go back into the woods. You'll find more ammunition in the box over there. Just be careful."

The boys were overjoyed. "Thank you, Uncle John," Joe beamed, taking the rifle back.

"Thank you," Dimar added as the two headed for the door.

Mandie called after them. "You be careful, Joe Woodard, and don't go shooting somebody, you hear?" Joe stopped and turned, laughing at her outburst. "Mandie, you know I have my own rifle at home. This won't be the first time I've used one."

"Yes, but this is a strange place and that's Uncle John's rifle—I know you have never used that one before," the girl answered seriously.

Joe's face turned red as everyone smiled.

"If I didn't like you so much, Amanda Shaw, I'd say something mean!" With that he and Dimar hurried out the door.

Little did Mandie know how close the two boys would come to shooting someone. They walked on through the woods for a while, looking for an appropriate place for target practice. The trees were dense and it was hard to see very far ahead. Then they came to a small clearing.

"How about here?" asked Joe.

"Good," the Indian boy agreed.

Joe shot at a broken limb, and suddenly there was a loud clanging noise. The boys froze in silence, listening. Then it came again.

"What's *that?*" Joe whispered.

"Sounds like an animal caught in a trap." Dimar returned the whisper. "Careful, it could be dangerous." He slowly crept forward, Joe following. The clanging sound became louder, as if to beckon them on. "I think it's behind that bush over there," Dimar said softly, pointing ahead.

They cautiously moved toward the bush. Then suddenly they caught a glimpse through the leaves of what lay on the other side of the bush and they stopped in shock. There, completely helpless in an abandoned trap, was Tsa'ni, his foot tightly secured by the metal spring. He looked at them with a guilty stare as they came into view. The clanging had stopped.

"Not *you* again!" Joe slapped his hand to his forehead in exasperation.

"It seems all we do is get this boy out of trouble!" Dimar remarked.

"Would you please get this thing off my foot?" Tsa'ni sounded demanding. "That's all I want you to do."

The boys looked at each other and then at Tsa'ni's foot. It had been bleeding and was very swollen. Evidently the boy was in a lot of pain.

Joe stepped aside with Dimar so they could talk.

"I don't see how we can get that thing off his foot," Joe whispered. "We don't have tools, and besides, his foot is all swollen. Let's go for help. He'll think we are just leaving him alone."

Dimar nodded.

They walked back to Tsa'ni and shook their heads.

"I don't think we can help you. If we turn you loose, you'll just get into more trouble," Joe said to him. "This way we know where you are."

"You do not deserve any help," Dimar added.

Tsa'ni looked at them in shock. "Please! Just release my foot. I'll get home somehow by myself."

"No, we cannot help you, Tsa'ni," Joe insisted. "We don't have any tools to release that spring."

Joe and Dimar turned and walked away. When Tsa'ni realized they were not going to help him, he called and called after them, "Please! Please!"

Once out of sight, Joe and Dimar started running toward Uncle Ned's cabin. They were almost breathless when they finally got there. Uncle John was chopping wood by the barn and saw the boys coming. He dropped the axe and hurried to meet them.

"Uncle John, we've found Tsa'ni," Joe told him, handing him the rifle. "He's caught in a trap in the woods."

"We told him we would not help him," Dimar said.

"We didn't want him to know we had gone for help. Let him worry a little after all his meanness," Joe added.

"Let me get some tools and we'll go see what we can do," Uncle John said, shaking his head. "He certainly gets into more trouble than anyone I've ever known."

"We'll need a blanket or something to carry him back. His foot is in pretty bad shape, and I don't think he can walk this time," Joe told him, as John went toward the barn for tools.

"Ask Morning Star for one while I get the tools," John replied.

Morning Star got a blanket, some bottles and a cloth from the shelf, and rolled it all up together inside the blanket.

"I go too," she declared. "Special medicine."

Elizabeth understood. "She wants to go with you to doctor him with her medicine. That's what's in the bottles."

Mandie was thinking aloud. "You see, you should never tell a lie. He said he couldn't walk before and it was a lie. Now he really can't walk. I think it happened to him because he lied."

"Yes, he is a bad Cherokee," Sallie agreed.

"You should see his foot. I know he can't walk this time. He must have been caught in the trap ever since we chased him night before last. We lost him in that direction," Joe told them.

"Go." Morning Star went outside to join John as he came from the barn. The boys followed.

It was quite a job prying the trap from Tsa'ni's foot because it was so tightly secured in the swollen flesh. The foot was extremely painful to the touch, but John tried to be careful as he gently but steadily freed the flesh from the prongs of the spring. When the foot was finally free, Morning Star washed it with liquid from one of the bottles. Tsa'ni winced and bit his lip in pain. Then Morning Star gently wrapped it in a clean piece of cloth and stood up.

"Take him," she said, pointing to the boy.

John and the two boys laid Tsa'ni on the blanket and, rolling the edges of it, made a swing to carry him. Since Uncle Ned's house was much closer than Tsa'ni's, they carried him there and laid him on a bed downstairs. Morning Star administered more of her medicine.

"You boys go tell his mother he is here, and when Uncle Ned and Uncle Wirt come back with the wagon, we'll take him home," Uncle John told them. "I'll be outside."

He went out the door, and Joe and Dimar left on their errand.

The two girls had been watching the whole thing from a distance. Tsa'ni had ignored everyone until now and had not spoken a word.

Mandie came over to his bed now. "I'm sorry you are injured, Tsa'ni, but the Bible says you reap what you sow and you sure have sowed some wild lies. I think you had better pray about it. We'll all pray for you."

Tsa'ni looked at her sullenly. "What I do is my business, not yours!"

"You have been messing in our business, Tsa'ni; that's how you got hurt!" she reminded him, standing up and straightening her skirt. "Now that you are really hurt maybe you won't be able to mess in our business anymore."

Elizabeth stepped in. "Amanda, why don't you and Sallie go outside? Let Tsa'ni rest until his grandfather gets back."

"Yes, Mother," Mandie answered as she scooped up Snowball and turned to Sallie. "Come on. We'll see what Uncle John is doing."

Elizabeth did not uphold the things Tsa'ni had done, but she could see how weak he was and she didn't think it was the right time for him to be reprimanded.

Morning Star brought him a bowl of soup, and cradling the boy's head in her lap, she fed him with a spoon. He didn't say a word but greedily swallowed the broth.

Joe and Dimar came back, bringing Tsa'ni's mother with them. She ran to her son, fell to his side and started weeping. Joe and Dimar looked at each other and went back outside.

When Uncle Ned and Uncle Wirt finally came home with the wagon, John stopped them.

"No use to unhitch the wagon, Uncle Ned," John told them. "We'll be needing it. Uncle Wirt, the boys found Tsa'ni in the woods. He's inside. He has really been hurt this time, I'm afraid."

The two Indians went inside and came back out shortly, carrying Tsa'ni in the blanket. They put him into the wagon, and helped his mother climb in beside him.

"Please hurry back," John said as they pulled away in the wagon. "I want to hear what you've accomplished today concerning the gold."

"Soon," Uncle Ned called back.

As they all sat around Uncle Ned's table later that night, the old man told his news.

"Pow-wow tomorrow, council house," he said. "Told Cherokee Papoose found gold. Cherokee no want gold."

"But you did get all the chiefs to agree to let the Cherokee people vote on what to do with the gold, didn't you, Uncle Ned?" John asked.

"Cherokee vote pow-wow tomorrow, council house," the old man answered.

"You mean you can get all the people together to vote on something that fast?" John asked in amazement.

Uncle Wirt spoke up, "Tell one Cherokee. Cherokee tell another Cherokee. News travel fast."

Mandie smiled at the way he put it. "You mean when you tell one Cherokee something, he will tell another and so on, until they all know?"

Uncle Wirt nodded.

"It sure has been a busy day for the Cherokees," Joe whistled. "Imagine passing the word to over one thousand people in one day!"

"Approximately thirteen hundred to be exact," John said. "Of course, the families are large in most cases, and they live in large family groups together."

"That's still a lot of people," Mandie agreed.

"So now all the Cherokee people know about the gold?" John asked again.

"Yes, all know," Uncle Ned nodded.

"Did you tell them to come to the council house tomorrow and vote on what they thought should be done with the gold?" John continued. He wanted to be sure they understood each other.

"Yes," Ned said.

Mandie, Sallie and Joe looked at one another.

"Just think, we are the cause of all this," Joe laughed. "I feel kinda good about it when I think of all the good it will do them."

"I'm glad to be a part of it," Sallie said. "I hope the people decide on a good use for the gold."

"Well, I guess we'll know tomorrow," Mandie said, and then turning to Uncle John, she asked, "Can we go over to the council house to watch tomorrow?"

Her uncle hesitated, looking at Ned and Wirt.

"Papoose go. Papoose Cherokee. Papoose vote," Uncle Ned told her.

"You mean I can vote, too, Uncle Ned?" Mandie was excited.

"Mmm," the old man nodded.

"Can I go along for the ride even though I am not Cherokee and can't vote?" Joe asked wistfully.

Uncle Ned and Uncle Wirt both nodded. "Go."

The four youngsters discussed the matter long into the night after they had gone up to bed.

The next day would hold more excitement for them. It would be a day long to be remembered.

CHAPTER TWELVE

THE CHEROKEES' DECISION

Jerusha, Dimar's mother, came riding up on a pony early the next morning just as Morning Star was putting on the coffee. She walked in through the open doorway, smiling, as she said, "Vote." She put her arms around Mandie, Sallie and Joe and tried to tell them how happy she was that they had found a fortune for the Cherokees.

"Gold," she said, hugging the three. "Find gold. Make Cherokee feel good. People need things."

The three laughed. "Oh, Jerusha, we are so happy for all the Cherokee people. Uncle John says there is enough gold to do a lot of good," Mandie told her. "Maybe you could build a new church, or a hospital, or even a new school."

Jerusha nodded her head. "Vote." Evidently it was a new English word for her and she kept trying it out. She turned to her son and embraced him. "Vote."

"Yes, I will vote," Dimar said, embarrassed by his mother's display of affection.

Morning Star stepped forward. "Sit. Eat." Jerusha sat down and everyone else joined her.

Elizabeth sat next to Dimar's mother. "I'm so glad you could come down to vote. This is such an important thing for the Cherokees. I know you will all agree on something you need."

The woman nodded her head. "We agree what to do with gold."

At that moment more guests arrived. Everyone turned to stare as Tsa'ni was carried into the house by a huge man, who turned out to be his father. His mother, Meli, came in behind them.

"We vote," the man said as he put Tsa'ni on a chair and turned to Uncle Ned. "We vote." Meli took a place at the table.

Uncle John got up from the table and came across the room to shake hands with the man. "Good morning, Jessan. I'm glad to see you."

Jessan replied, "John, long time since we met."

"Where have you been, Jessan?" John asked.

"I take corn to Asheville to sell. Come back to vote," he said.

John turned to Mandie who was listening to their conversation. "This is Jim's daughter, Amanda. Mandie, we call her. Mandie, this is your cousin, Jessan, Uncle Wirt's son."

Mandie got up and smiled at him. "I'm so glad to meet you. I want to get to know all my Cherokee kinpeople."

Jessan laughed, showing perfect white teeth. "Lots of Cherokee kinpeople."

"How is Tsa'ni's foot?" she asked.

"Better," Jessan replied. "Well soon."

Mandie liked her cousin, Jessan, immediately. He seemed too nice to have such a miserable son as Tsa'ni. She was thinking of the many people she would meet when she went with the others to the council house to vote.

Uncle Ned's cabin was practically running over with people, and they soon began loading up for the journey to the council house. Everyone was in a happy mood except Tsa'ni, who never said a word and tried to ignore what the others were saying.

Mandie was glad she didn't have to ride in the same wagon with Tsa'ni. There seemed to be an air of contempt and sulkiness wherever he was. Uncle Wirt and Jerusha rode with him and his parents.

Joe and Dimar sat on either side of Mandie. Joe was aware again of Dimar's interest in Mandie. She never seemed to notice. Joe was determined Mandie would be his wife when they grew up, and he didn't want anyone else making eyes at her. He liked Dimar, but not when he stared at Mandie.

As they arrived at the reservation center the seven-sided, dome-roofed council house came into view. There must have been several hundred Cherokees milling about it. Every Cherokee in North Carolina must have come to vote. They laughed and talked happily with each other. Almost all the women had red kerchiefs tied around their heads. The young girls looked as if they were wearing their best dresses as they shyly chatted with the young Indian men. It seemed to be a great big party.

When Uncle Ned found a place to leave the wagon and unhitch the horses, they all got down and walked to the council house. All the people turned to look at the group. Mandie smiled at them.

Elizabeth turned to Joe. "Well, I guess we're the only white people around, so we'll have to wait outside," she said, laughing. "Let's stand in the shade here by the doorway."

"Sure, Mrs. Shaw," Joe agreed. Turning to Mandie who was going ahead with Uncle John, he called to her. "Don't forget. Vote for a church, a hospital, or a school. Maybe a hospital would be best, the way Tsa'ni keeps getting himself hurt," he laughed.

Mandie called back to him. "Maybe that would be the best anyhow."

She followed the crowd inside. The Indians moved back to make way for her. She gazed at the inside of the huge building. There were bleachers to sit on. Stout log poles held up the dome-shaped thatched roof and the symbols of the clans adorned the posts. The place of the sacred fire was directly ahead as they entered. Behind the fire sat men with stacks of papers and books.

Uncle Ned was watching her, proud to show off his people's council house. He pointed to the men. "Vote," he said and led them across the room. He explained in Cherokee who Mandie was. Most of the Cherokees knew Uncle John from his visits.

The six men sitting behind the papers got up and smiled at her.

"Jim Shaw's papoose vote," one spoke, indicating the papers.

The second man said, "Papoose find Cherokee gold."

Between Uncle John and Uncle Ned they called the men's names as they spoke to the girl, but Mandie was too fascinated with everything to remember who they were. However, she knew they must be important people to occupy the place behind the fire.

The first man handed Mandie a piece of paper. "Vote," he said.

She took the paper, looked at it, saw that it was completely blank, and turned to Uncle John. "What do I do? Just write down what I think should be done with the gold?"

"That's right. Just write down whatever idea you have about using the gold." Uncle John turned to the first man and took a piece of paper for himself. "Have all these people already voted?"

"Yes," the man answered.

"We must be late, Uncle Ned," John whispered to the old man.

Uncle Ned had a sly smile on his face. He moved away from the others and wrote on his piece of paper and handed it back to the man who was giving them out. The man carefully recorded it in his book.

Mandie sat down on a bleacher and wrote the word *hospital* on her slip of paper and returned it to the man, as Uncle John, Morning Star, Dimar, and Sallie all gave their papers back to the Indian in charge.

"We wait," Uncle Ned told them, pointing to seats nearby.

Mandie turned and saw Tsa'ni being brought in by his father, Jessan. Meli, Jerusha, and Uncle Wirt followed. They took pieces of paper from the men, wrote, and returned them. They turned around and looked at Mandie and her group.

Mandie quickly turned to Dimar and Sallie. "I hope they don't come over here with Tsa'ni."

Before they could reply, the other group headed their way and sat down on the bleachers in front of them. She pulled her long skirt back and moved her feet to keep from touching them. No one spoke. Everyone seemed to be waiting.

The men with the papers began gathering up all their things. The first one, who had spoken to Mandie, stood up. He beat on a drum a couple of times. Silence fell over the crowd.

"Vote is done. We have counted all votes," he said in a loud, booming voice. "I will read the decision of our people on what to do with the gold found in the cave." He picked up one of the open books and began reading from it. "We, the Eastern Band of Cherokee Indians of North Carolina, do not wish to accept the gold found in the cave." He paused and looked up.

Mandie couldn't believe her ears.

He continued, "Even though it was purported to have belonged to our great warrior Tsali and to be left by him for our people, gold has always brought bad luck to our people. Therefore, we hereby designate as the holder of the gold with complete authority to use it as she wishes, the daughter of our beloved Jim Shaw, who has gone on to the happy hunting ground. We leave it in the hands of Amanda Elizabeth Shaw, who found the gold, to do whatever she deems best with it. Signed—The Eastern Band of Cherokee Indians of North Carolina."

Mandie was really in a daze now. She couldn't even think straight. The gold belonged to her Cherokee kinpeople and was worth a fortune, according to Uncle John, but here they were refusing to accept it and were giving it entirely over to her. She didn't know what to do.

The man was still talking. "This decision was made unanimously. There was not a dissenting vote."

Mandie heard that all right. That meant Tsa'ni had voted in her favor also. She just couldn't believe it was happening. She must be dreaming. She pinched herself to see if she was awake.

"Amanda Shaw, would you please come up here and accept the decision of our people?" He was looking straight at her, waiting.

Mandie turned to Uncle John. "Uncle John, I can't walk up there. I'm too scared. Why did they do such a crazy thing?"

Uncle John smiled, got up and took her hand, pulling her to her feet. "Come on. I'll go with you." He walked over to the man, practically dragging Mandie with him. The man extended the sheet of paper to Mandie.

"This is your authorization from the Cherokee people," he said.

Mandie trembled as she took the paper and turned to face the hundreds of Cherokees. "Oh, I love you, my Cherokee kinpeople. I love you." Tears came into her blue eyes. She held the paper against her heart. "I'll do my best, with Uncle John's and Uncle Ned's and Uncle Wirt's help, to use the gold wisely."

Something that sounded like a war whoop went up from the hundreds of Cherokees as they showed their gratitude. Mandie just stood there, unable to move. The first thing she knew Joe was tugging at her hand.

"Mandie, let's get out of here," he whispered.

The crowd started moving. The people passed by to speak to her, some in English, some in Cherokee.

She lifted her face as she moved along toward the others. "Thank you, God. Thank you. My people do love me."

She and Uncle John sat back down. Joe and her mother had taken seats next to them, now that the voting was over. Everyone was saying nice things to her, but she couldn't understand a thing they were saying. She was still in a daze.

She was staring directly into Tsa'ni's face as he turned to look at her. He managed to get up on his good foot and extend his hand to her as he turned around.

"Love, my cousin, love," he said, his face lit up by a big smile. "Please, forgive me!"

"Oh, Tsa'ni, my cousin, love." She smiled and put her arms around his neck and kissed him on the cheek. "My Cherokee kinpeople."

She turned and smiled at the people surrounding her. "I think we will build a hospital for my people!"

The crowd cheered.

She was sure she had made the right decision.

But now she felt that something even greater had been accomplished. She had gained her cousin's love and acceptance as a Cherokee. God had overruled. After having struggled so long with negative thoughts toward her cousin, the battle was won. She was proud to be part Cherokee, and even prouder to be a Christian.

MANDIE
AND THE
GHOST BANDITS

CONTENTS

"It is more blessed to give than to receive."
(Acts 30:35)

CHAPTER ONE

JOURNEY ON A TRAIN

In the dark alley behind Bryson City Bank, Mandie Shaw stood on tiptoe to peer over the side of the wagon. Her heart beat faster at the sight of the small leather traveling bags full of gold nuggets.

Mandie's Uncle John and two Cherokee Indian friends loaded bag after bag of gold nuggets into the wagon while Mr. Frady, the short, round banker, watched nervously.

Uncle Ned, Mandie's old Indian friend, plopped two bags of nuggets into the wagon. "Gold bad for Cherokee," he mumbled.

Mandie, with her white kitten, Snowball, on her shoulder, took Uncle Ned's hand and returned with him to the vault for more. "But Uncle Ned," she said, "just think what a wonderful thing we are going to do for the Cherokees with all this gold. Something that could never be done without it. We should be thankful for finding it in the cave."

"Humph! Gold not good for Cherokee," Uncle Ned insisted. "Better left in cave."

"But you know the great Cherokee warrior, Tsali, left a message with the gold where we found it," Mandie argued. "Remember? He said the gold was for the Cherokees after the white man made peace. In fact, the inscription said it was a curse on the *white* man, not the Indian."

Uncle Ned frowned at her. "Then curse on Jim Shaw's Papoose. And I promise Jim Shaw I watch over Papoose when he go to happy hunting ground."

"My father would not believe in any old curse, Uncle Ned," Mandie assured him. "And neither do I. It's all a bunch of malarkey. God watches over us, remember?"

"Big God not watch over Cherokee when white man take land away," he said, picking up two more bags of nuggets.

Mandie shook her blonde head. "I can't explain that. God sometimes does things that seem bad to us—like taking my father to heaven. But it's to teach us a lesson—how to be better Christians. I don't know what it was, but He must have had a reason for the terrible suffering the Cherokees went through back then." She looked pleadingly at the old man. "Please, Uncle Ned, you believe in God. I know that."

The tall, old Indian set down the bags and hugged the small twelve-year-old. "Papoose right. Must believe in Big God. Now we take gold to Asheville. Build hospital for Cherokees," he relented.

Mandie kissed his dry, withered cheek as he straightened up. Uncle Ned smiled, patted her on the head, and picked up the bags again.

Mandie followed Uncle Ned outside. "And we have to trust God to help us get it there safely," she reminded him.

Tsa'ni, Mandie's Cherokee cousin, sat in the driver's seat of the wagon. "How many more?" he called. "There must be a large amount of gold in there."

Uncle Wirt, Tsa'ni's grandfather, passed a bag to Uncle John at the back door. "You just watch wagon. We load bags," he yelled at Tsa'ni.

Mandie looked startled at the harsh tone of Uncle Wirt's voice. She knew he was still angry with his grandson Tsa'ni for the many bad deeds he had done. But Mandie thought the boy had changed since the time he tried to beat them to the gold. She believed he should be given a chance to prove himself.

Walking to the side of the wagon, Mandie spoke quietly. "There's a little more, Tsa'ni," she told him. "But it's awfully heavy. That's why it's in such small bags. They think it will look more like luggage that way, too."

"Are we taking this gold to the train?" Tsa'ni asked.

"Yes, it's all been kept secret because of the danger involved, but we're going directly from here to the depot. Then we'll take the train to Asheville," Mandie explained in a low voice.

"What happens when we get to Asheville?" Tsa'ni asked.

"We'll put the gold in a bigger bank so it'll be safe. Then we're going to start building the hospital for the Cherokees on some land between Deep Creek and Bird-town," Mandie explained.

"So, it has all been planned," the Indian boy said, "and no one has told me a thing."

Just then Uncle John called to Mandie from the doorway. "Hop in, Mandie. That's all."

Mandie, with Snowball clinging to her shoulder, climbed into the back of the wagon and made a place for herself among the bags of gold. Tsa'ni followed. Uncle John shook hands with Mr. Frady, the banker. "Well, Wilbur, thank you. We've finally got it off your hands," he said.

"Thank goodness!" the short, round man replied. Nervously, he wiped the sweat from his brow. "Maybe I can get some sleep now. That was just a little bit too much for me to worry over, John."

Uncle John turned to the two Indians. "Let's get going," he said. "My wife should be waiting at the depot with the others by now." The three men climbed into the wagon.

"I wish you Godspeed," Mr. Frady called from the doorway.

Uncle John tipped his wide-brimmed hat at Mr. Frady as Uncle Ned shook the reins, and the horses pulled the wagon down the alley past an old drunk and onto the dark, deserted street. It was time for everyone in Bryson City to be at home eating supper.

The train would be in shortly. The whole operation was going smoothly. Their secret seemed well kept.

Snowball nosed around the quilts covering the gold in the bottom of the wagon bed and disappeared underneath in his inspection of the leather bags.

Tsa'ni suddenly made a quick movement and pulled the kitten out from its hiding place, tossing him to Mandie.

"That animal friend of yours knows how to bite," he said, rubbing his leg. Under the quilt his hand touched something. Pulling it out he found an old half-burned candle. He looked at it for a few seconds, then put it in his pocket.

"I'm sorry, Tsa'ni," Mandie apologized. She shook the kitten lightly. "Snowball, you know you aren't supposed to behave like that. Now curl up in my lap and be still," she scolded.

"Where did you get such a cat?" Tsa'ni asked.

"Oh, I've had Snowball since I lived in my father's house at Charley Gap. He goes with me everywhere I go," Mandie said, softly rubbing the kitten's white fur. Snowball purred contentedly. "He's a smart cat. He helped my friends and me escape from the bootleggers who kidnapped us when we got lost in the mountains."

"Now, how did he do that?"

"Well, they tied our hands, and Snowball played with the ends of the rope until it was loose enough for us to get away," Mandie explained. "Snowball also knows when it's time to eat and time to go to bed."

"That is nothing. Most animals know that," Tsa'ni retorted.

A train whistle sounded in the distance and soon the depot came into view.

Uncle John turned around in the front seat. "Remember, Mandie, when we stop, I want you and Tsa'ni to go directly to your mother. She should be right inside. Uncle Ned and Uncle Wirt and I will unload the gold into one of the train cars. We don't want to draw any unnecessary attention."

"Yes, sir, I understand," Mandie answered.

When Uncle Ned stopped the wagon by the depot platform, Mandie stood. "Come on, Tsa'ni. Let's go," she said quietly.

Clutching Snowball, she jumped down. Tsa'ni followed, and they both hurried inside the wooden building where her mother and friends waited.

When Elizabeth, Mandie's mother, saw the two through the doorway, she stood up from the long bench where she and the other young people were sitting.

Mandie looked around the large room. *This place looks like a church with all these benches like pews*, she thought. There was even a wood stove standing in the middle of the floor, just like the one in their church back home in Franklin.

Elizabeth met her daughter with a hug. "I already have all the tickets, so we can get right on the train," she said as the train came puffing up and stopped by the platform.

"Sallie, Joe, Dimar, get your things. Here are yours, Amanda." She gave Mandie a small bag. They were only carrying the essentials for overnight because they planned to go home to Franklin from Asheville.

Together they boarded the first passenger car and sat down to wait for the men.

Since Mandie had been on a train only once before, her excitement was hard to contain. She wanted to see and feel everything. Sitting on a long cross seat at the end of the car and beside the other young people, she rubbed the soft, dark upholstery and looked around in the dim lamplight. There were only a few other passengers.

Sallie, Uncle Ned's granddaughter, straightened her long, dark dress, which had been made especially for this journey. "I have never been to Asheville," she said. "I am excited about going there." She pulled her bright red shawl around her shoulders.

"I've been to Asheville several times with my father," said Joe, Dr. Woodard's son. "It's a beautiful town but it's full of hills. And, boy, does it get cold at night in that place."

"I look forward to seeing the great home of Mr. Vanderbilt," said Dimar, the Cherokee boy who was with them when they found the gold.

"Oh, Dimar," Mandie laughed, as she rubbed Snowball's fur. "We aren't going to visit Mr. Vanderbilt. Are we, Mother?"

Elizabeth smiled at the conversation and said, "I doubt it, but I do know the man."

Mandie sat up straight and the others leaned forward. "Really, Mother?" Mandie asked.

"Well, actually, my father knew him," her mother replied. "Don't forget that I lived in Asheville a long time before I married your Uncle John."

"Why, yes, I hadn't thought of that," Mandie said. She turned to Dimar. "I don't know whether you understand or not, Dimar," she said. "You see, my grandmother had my mother's marriage to my father annulled when I was born."

Dimar looked puzzled but continued to listen. "She told Mother I had died. Then Grandmother gave me to my father and told him that my mother didn't ever want to see him again. So he took me and moved to Swain County where he married another woman. I always thought *she* was my mother until my father died and I found my Uncle John in Franklin. He's my father's brother. Uncle John knew where my real mother was in Asheville, and he asked her, and my grandmother to come to his house so we could see each other. Then my mother and Uncle John got married. See?" She took a deep breath.

Elizabeth smiled at Mandie's long explanation.

"I knew some of that by listening," Dimar said. "That is interesting, like a storybook. Are we going to visit your grandmother in Asheville?"

Mandie turned to her mother for an answer. She knew her grandmother didn't like the fact that Uncle John had exposed her long-kept secret. And she wasn't very happy that Elizabeth had married John. "Are we, Mother?" Mandie asked.

"My mother is away visiting relatives in Charleston, and I'm not sure what your Uncle John has planned for us," Elizabeth told her.

Just then Uncle John came up the aisle with Uncle Wirt right behind him. "I've made plans for us to stay at the hotel," he said, sitting beside his wife.

"A hotel? What is a hotel?" Mandie asked.

The other youngsters were wide-eyed with interest. In 1900 few young people in western North Carolina had traveled very far from home.

Sallie and Dimar waited for an explanation, too. With a knowing grin, Joe crossed his arms and leaned back in his seat.

"A hotel is a place where you pay to spend the night," Uncle John explained. "It has bedrooms to sleep in that they rent out by the night and a dining room where you can buy your meals. It's for travelers."

Sallie looked confused. "We are going to buy a bedroom to sleep in?"

Joe laughed. "No, silly, you don't buy a bedroom. You only pay so much money per night to be allowed to sleep in the room."

"And how do you happen to know so much about it, Mister Doctor's Son?" Mandie asked, sarcastically.

Joe straightened his shoulders. "Because I *am* a doctor's son," he said, "and a doctor travels a lot. I have often stayed in a hotel with my father when he allowed me to travel with him."

"You have?" Dimar asked.

"Sure," Joe said. "But it's not that exciting. It's just a room with a bed in it. You just go in the room and go to sleep like you do at home, only the hotel rooms are real fancy, and there are lots and lots of bedrooms in one big building. And there are all kinds of people sleeping in the same building." Joe enjoyed being the center of attention. "When you're hungry," he explained, "you go into this huge room with lots of tables and you tell the lady what you want to eat, and she brings you the food. That's all there is to it, except you have to pay money for it."

Uncle John smiled. "You sound like a well-seasoned traveler, Joe."

Mandie frowned. "Well, who sleeps in the same room with you?" she asked.

"No one, silly, unless you want them to." Joe laughed. "When you pay money for the room, you tell them who is to sleep in the room. That's all," he explained.

"Then we are all going to sleep in one room?" Sallie asked.

"No, Sallie," Uncle John told her. "You see, each room has only one big bed, so we will need at least four rooms—one for you and Mandie, one for Uncle Wirt and Uncle Ned, another for Mandie's mother and me, and we'll see if all three of the boys can manage in one room."

Sallie was shocked. "Oh, but that is so many rooms, and you have to pay money for each room. Could we not all sleep in one room? It would not cost so much money that way," the Indian girl reasoned.

"That's not the way hotels do business, Sallie," Uncle John replied. "Usually only two people can sleep in a room. But don't worry about the money. It has all been taken care of."

"It sounds like fun, Sallie." Mandie giggled. "You and I get a whole room all by ourselves."

"You must promise not to talk all night, though," Elizabeth cautioned them.

"Uncle John"—Mandie changed the subject—"where is Uncle Ned?"

"He stayed with the cargo back in the baggage car," Uncle John said in a low voice. "After a while Uncle Wirt and I will take our turns looking after it. We thought it would be better if we didn't let it completely out of our sight."

The train gave a lurch and the couplings between the cars clanged as it began pulling out of the station. The sudden movement caught the young people unaware and they fell against each other, laughing.

"Away we go!" shouted Mandie above the noise.

The whistle blew, and the train picked up speed as it rounded the bend, leaving town and safety behind. None of them knew what danger lurked ahead in the dark night.

CHAPTER TWO

GHOST BANDITS IN THE DARK

After a while the journey became monotonous. In the dark there was nothing to look at through the windows, and the train crept slowly around the mountain.

Bored, Mandie came up with an idea. "Why don't we go back and see Uncle Ned for a little while?" she suggested. "He's all alone back there. Want to?"

"Yes!" cried her equally bored friends.

"Could we, Mother?" Mandie asked.

Elizabeth looked at John. "What do you think?"

"Well, I suppose it'd be all right," John answered. "Just don't stay too long," he told them. "And Sallie, tell your grandfather I'll be back in a little while to relieve him."

"Yes, sir," Sallie replied, as they stood up and started down the aisle of the train car.

"And please be careful when you go from one car to the other," Elizabeth called. "It could be dangerous if you don't watch your step."

"We will," they promised as they went out the door at the end of the car. When they stepped onto the platform between the cars, the cold mountain wind whipped around them and the noise of the train was deafening. They hurried into the next car.

Joe quickly shut the door behind them and stood there shivering for a moment. "I thought it was supposed to be summertime," he laughed.

"Yes, but the wind is always cold at night in the mountains," Dimar told him.

"A breath of cold air is good for us," Tsa'ni added.

There were a few passengers in the car they had just entered, but when they moved to the next car they found it completely empty.

Sallie looked around the dimly-lit car. "There certainly aren't many people on this train," she remarked.

Mandie stopped to look out a window. She leaned against the glass. "Look!" she cried, pointing outside. "Horsemen!"

The group crowded in front of the window.

"In the moonlight they look like ghosts," Mandie joked.

Joe cupped his hand against the window to see better. "What are they wearing over their clothes?" he asked.

"I do not know, but they are keeping pace with the train," Tsa'ni answered.

"It is too dark to see their faces," Dimar said.

"Oh, they see us!" Mandie said, waving her hand.

Joe looked away from the window. "I think they're trying to get on the train," he warned.

Suddenly, the train jerked to a stop. All five young people staggered and grabbed for anything to keep from falling. The train had stopped on a hill, and they found it difficult to stand upright. They all looked at each other questioningly.

"Why are we stopping here?" Sallie asked.

"I don't know," Joe answered, "but something is wrong."

Just then, a loud clang came from the direction of the baggage car. Dimar led the way as they rushed to the back door of the car to see what had happened. Dimar tried to open the door. It was stuck. He peered out the window. "The baggage car," he cried. "It has come apart from the rest of the train! It is rolling back down the track!"

"Oh, no!" Mandie yelled. "Uncle Ned . . ."

"Grandfather!" Sallie screamed.

Joe pushed his way to the window to look. At that moment there was a deafening crash. He turned slowly. Both girls were in tears, and a sick look of realization covered the faces of Dimar and Tsa'ni.

Mandie ran for the front door of the train car and threw it open. Joe hurried after her and the others followed.

Outside, Mandie hopped off the train and blindly started in the direction of the baggage car. Snowball clung to her shoulder in fright. Joe and the others stepped off the train more cautiously.

"Mandie! Wait!" Joe called. "Look! We're right on the edge of a steep ridge."

Mandie stopped. In the dim moonlight she could see the sharp drop-off just a few feet away. Her heart thumped louder as she realized the danger she was in.

Joe rushed to her side and took her hand. "Come on, all of you," he commanded. "Let's get back to the others on the train. We can't find that baggage car by ourselves."

But just as they turned to get back on, there was a loud noise and the train started up again.

They all froze in panic. By the time they could think clearly enough to run, it was too late. The train was going too fast and all five of them could never get on board without someone getting hurt.

Mandie hid her face in her hands and cried.

Sallie began to shake all over. "Grandfather!" she wailed. "Now, how will we get help for my grandfather?"

Tsa'ni put his arm around her shoulders. "Do not cry, Sallie. We will, somehow," he said.

Sallie pulled away and bumped into Dimar. Dimar grabbed her arm to keep her from falling.

"Do not move. It is steep here," Dimar told her.

"Doo-oo not moo-oove at a-a-all-ll," said a spooky voice behind them.

The young people whirled to see one of the horsemen seemingly float toward them. As he drew nearer they could see he was wearing a flowing, ground-length, light-colored cape and a light wide-brimmed hat. A tiger mask covered his face, and he carried a dimly-lit lantern. He looked huge.

The young people stood speechless with fright. They huddled together as he approached.

The ghostly man swung the lantern up to light their faces and spoke in an angry, eerie voice. "Wha-a-at are you-oo do-oo-inng he-e-ere?" he asked.

Dimar, with a protective arm around Sallie, looked him boldly in the face. "We were on the train when the baggage car wrecked," he answered. "And when we came out to see what happened, the train pulled away. But who are you and what do you want?" Dimar asked.

The creature spat tobacco juice on the ground and held the lantern closer to Dimar's face. "We-ell-ll-ll, what da ya kn-now-w, ah In-n-n-ju-u-un!" he taunted in his spooky voice. He swung the lantern in front of the other faces. "Thr-ree-ee In-n-ju-u-uns! Well-ll now-ow, wha-a-at air you-oo two-oo whi-i-ite young-un-ns do-oo-in-n' with the-e-ese hyar In-n-ju-u-uns?"

Mandie stepped forward, angry about the insinuation. "The three Indians happen to be our friends. Not only that, I am one-fourth Cherokee myself," she retorted, flipping her blonde hair.

At Mandie's sudden movement, Snowball dug his claws into her shoulder. Mandie winced and took the kitten into her arms.

"Too-oo ba-a-ad you-oo got offuh that trai-ain-n."

Just then, two other ghostlike figures materialized out of the darkness. They were both dressed exactly like the first.

One of them cleared his throat. "Watcha got hyar?" he asked. "By grannies, we're agonna hafta do sump-umm with these hyar younguns."

The third creature pulled a rope from under his long, flowing costume. "Better tie their hands behind 'em, and git 'em on the wagon and take 'em so fur away they cain't innerfear."

He grabbed Dimar's hands and tied them behind him as the first creature tied Tsa'ni's and Joe's. The other one tied the girls' hands behind them. Afraid to fight back or run away, the young people shivered on the edge of the mountain in the semi-darkness. They had no idea whether or not the men were armed.

The first creature spoke again, dropping his spooky voice disguise. "Tiger number two, you and Tiger number three take 'em away. I'll git back to work. Hurry up and git goin'."

Joe spoke up. "Mister, if you'll just let us go, we'll find our way home and won't bother you."

"No, we won't bother you," Mandie agreed. "We only want to find my family and Sallie's grandfather. Whatever your work is, we won't interfere."

"I say you won't innerfear," the first creature replied. "Git goin'."

He disappeared into the darkness. The second creature motioned with his lantern for the young people to follow him. The third creature brought up the rear.

Silently, they walked single file along the railroad track for a few yards. Then Mandie stopped suddenly, turned her face to the sky, and spoke, "What time we are afraid," she paused and Joe joined her in the last part, "we will put our trust in thee, dear God," they said.

The creature bringing up the rear overheard them and gave Joe a shove.

"Git a move on!" he muttered. "Ain't no God up thar gonna hyar you."

"Oh, but God does hear us, and He does answer our prayers," Mandie insisted.

The creature leading the way walked back to "take care of" Mandie when Joe stepped between them.

"You leave her alone, mister," Joe demanded.

"Well, then, you'd better tell her to shet up. And keep yourself quiet, too," the creature replied. "Else all of ya gonna git whut's comin' to ya."

Mandie whispered in Joe's ear. "Sorry. I'll be quiet, but I'll still pray."

Joe smiled at her.

"Up this trail! Git!" the creature ordered as he led the way.

The group stumbled silently among the brush and rocks as they climbed the mountainside. They stayed close to one another, having no idea what their fate would be, and worried about what had happened to the others.

After a short time they came to what looked like an old wagon trail. There, all alone, stood an old wagon with two horses hitched to it.

"In the wagon!" yelled the creature leading them.

The young people looked at one another silently. With their hands still tied, they managed to climb into the back of the wagon. The two creatures sat on the seat—one sitting backwards to watch them; the other, whipping the horses into a run. The trail was terribly rough. The wagon lurched over rocks and bumps and holes in the darkness, jostling the youngsters from side to side.

Snowball, still clinging to Mandie, protested loudly. Mandie tried her best to hold onto him by turning her head sidewise and raising her shoulder.

The wagon finally came to a halt in front of a deserted hut with a low, steeply-slanted roof. In the woods, Mandie had lost all sense of direction and wondered how they would ever find their way back.

The driver stepped down from the wagon. "Out and inside!" he ordered.

They could do nothing but obey. Inside the dark hut the first creature swung his lantern around, inspecting the interior. The other one stayed outside. The dim light showed no windows and only one door. The hut was just one big room with a huge rock fireplace. The young people looked around in dismay, afraid to speak. A nearby shelf held an old coffeepot, tin plates, and utensils. A pile of dirty, ragged quilts lay in one corner on the floor. That was all they could see.

The creature turned to go. "Now we're gonna put an iron padlock and chains on the door outside so thar ain't no way ya kin git out of hyar, and thar ain't no use yer tryin'," he sneered. "That'll teach ya to poke into other people's business."

"Please, mister, if you'd just let us go, we'll go straight home," Mandie begged.

"Yeh, go home by way of the wrecked train to see what happened to thet gold, eh? Ain't no way we gonna let ya go. We gonna git thet gold and be gone 'fore ya ever git out of hyar, *if ever.*" He gave an evil laugh. "Ya may never git out of hyar. This is a deserted part of the mountains. Ain't no one ever comes this way. So we done got y'all tuck care of." He laughed again, stepped outside, and closed the heavy log door.

With the sound of a metal padlock and chains fastening on the outside, Mandie and her friends became prisoners with little hope of ever being rescued.

CHAPTER THREE

THE LITTLE BIRD

With the lantern gone, the hut became dark as pitch. The group huddled together in the center of the floor and helped one another untie their hands.

"If we only had a light," Sallie wished out loud.

With that reminder, Tsa'ni thrust his hands into his pockets and triumphantly produced the candle he had found in Uncle Ned's wagon. "Wish granted," he said smartly, although no one could see what he had. He stood up and felt his way to the huge fireplace on the back wall.

Sallie heard him moving about. "What do you mean?" she asked.

"Tsa'ni, where are you going?" Joe stood up, trying to find him.

"I am going to make a light for Sallie," the Indian boy said from near the fireplace. "If I can only find something to strike a flame."

"Are you going to build a fire in the fireplace?" Dimar asked.

"No. It might smoke and suffocate us because there is no ventilation in here," Tsa'ni replied.

The others could hear him striking stones. Suddenly a spark caught a piece of straw in the fireplace and flamed. They gathered around him and then saw the candle in his hand.

"Where did you get the candle?" Dimar asked.

"That's the candle you found in Uncle Ned's wagon!" Mandie cried. "He found it in the wagon after we loaded the gold at the bank," she explained.

"Yes," Tsa'ni said. He lit the candle, stomped on the burning straw, and set the candle in one of the tin plates on the hearth. "See what I did for you, Sallie?"

"Thank you, Tsa'ni," Sallie answered gratefully.

The flame threw a dim light around the room. They all gathered near the candle and sat down once more. Snowball curled up on Mandie's lap for a nap.

Sallie sighed. "Oh, my poor grandfather!" she said sorrowfully. "I wonder where he is!"

"And I wish I knew where my mother and Uncle John are right now," Mandie added. "How did all this happen, anyway?"

"Somehow those ghost creatures must have known about the gold on the train and caused the wreck," Dimar mused.

"I'm sure your folks are all right, Mandie," Joe comforted. "Don't worry."

There was a long silence. Tears came into Sallie's eyes as she envisioned her grandfather at the bottom of the ravine.

Mandie reached over to take Sallie's dark hand in her own small white one. "We have to trust God to take care of all of them, Sallie," Mandie said, "and figure out a way to get us out of this place." She glanced around the cabin, hoping to find some way to escape.

Snowball stirred and jumped out of Mandie's lap. Prowling around the cabin, he uncovered an old rope among the dirty quilts and played with it, scooting the end across the floor.

"Look what Snowball found!" Mandie cried.

"What good is a rope to us?" Joe asked.

"Maybe we could think of some plan to use the rope to escape," Dimar suggested. "Let us all try."

The young people grew silent again, trying to think of possible uses for the rope. Suddenly there was a twittering noise and a small bird flew down from the rafters. Snowball, at once alert, began chasing it.

"A bird! Snowball, come back here and leave that little bird alone!" Mandie scolded.

But Snowball had other plans. He chased the bewildered little bird around the room until it finally beat its wings against the huge fireplace and found the chimney opening. The bird disappeared. Mandie tried to grab the kitten, but she was a few seconds too late. Hungry for the little bird, Snowball clawed his way right up the inside chimney wall.

Mandie stood at the fireplace trying to see up the chimney. Soon the scratching noises stopped, and the frightened meowing began.

"Snowball! Come back down here, you silly cat!" Mandie called. "Kitty, kitty! Snowball!"

"He must have thought the chimney was a tree!" Joe laughed.

Mandie cocked her head in an effort to see where the kitten was. "Joe, it's not funny! How in the world will I ever be able to get him down?" Mandie wailed.

Dimar came and stood beside her. "I will go up and get him!" he offered.

"Go up the chimney?" Sallie frowned.

"Yes, it is quite wide. I think I can manage," Dimar insisted. "Snowball must be holding onto the rocks inside the chimney." Dimar stooped to pick up the candle and tried to shine the light up the chimney.

"I think he has gone too far up, Dimar. You can't reach him," Mandie moaned, clenching her fists.

"Dimar can climb the chimney," Tsa'ni said. "I know how, too."

"Climb the chimney?" Mandie questioned. "Dimar, you might fall!"

"I will not fall," Dimar told her. "You see, by bracing my toes on one side of the chimney and my backside on the other, I can push myself up and reach Snowball. I will not fall."

"If you can do that," Mandie reasoned, "maybe we could all climb the chimney and get out of here.—What do you think, Sallie?"

"I think we should try it," the Indian girl agreed.

Mandie picked up the rope Snowball had been playing with. "What if we tied the rope up on the roof like we did in the cave when we rescued Tsa'ni from that pit?" she asked.

Tsa'ni examined the rope. "It might work if the rope is long enough," he said.

Joe grabbed one end and stretched the rope across the room. "It's a lot longer than this room is wide," he said.

Dimar took the rope from Joe. "Yes, it looks long enough," he said. "I will take the rope with me and climb all the way to the top. After I secure it there, I will throw the end back down the chimney for you to use in climbing," he told them.

The others anxiously watched as Dimar, with the rope coiled around his shoulder, disappeared into the black recesses of the chimney.

Snowball continued to meow for help.

"Let us know when you find Snowball *and* when you get to the top, please!" Mandie called.

After a few moments Dimar yelled down to them. "I now have Snowball on my shoulder," he said.

"Oh, thank you!" Mandie said gratefully.

They all waited around the fireplace in silence. Then there was a loud clattering noise, and the girls cried out in fear.

"Dimar! What was that?" Joe called up the chimney.

"It is just me on the roof. It is made of tin." Dimar's voice came faintly down the chimney. "I have Snowball out, too. I am fastening the rope around the top of the chimney and will throw the end down to you. Here it comes!"

There was a swishing sound and the end of the rope appeared in the dim candlelight in the fireplace. Joe lunged forward and grabbed it.

"We have it, Dimar," he called. He turned to the others. "Girls first. Sallie or Mandie?"

"Sallie, you go first," Mandie told her Indian friend.

"All right, but, Mandie, please be careful when you come up. It looks rather frightening," Sallie told her. She took the end of the rope, stooped to put her head up the chimney, and then stood up. Grasping the rope tightly, she swung herself off the stone floor. As her feet touched the side of the chimney she kept moving her hands up the rope. The rope was rough and her hands burned as she climbed. Her arms felt as though they were going to pull out of their sockets, but with determination she made her way up.

At the top Dimar helped Sallie climb out of the chimney onto the steep, tin roof. Her legs trembled as she stood, but she breathed a sigh of relief. She smelled the soot on her skin and clothes and tried to brush it off with her hands. "I made it, Dimar, but I must be rather dirty," she said.

Dimar laughed. "It does not matter. We will all be dirty," the Indian boy said. Leaning over the top of the chimney, he called, "Who is next?"

Stooping carefully on the slick roof, Sallie picked up Mandie's kitten from where he sat licking himself. "Snowball doesn't like the dirt either," she said.

Inside the hut, Mandie grasped the end of the rope and worked her way up the chimney as Sallie had done. Soot, loosened by the rubbing of the rope, fell into her face and hair, and she squinted to keep it out of her eyes. Suddenly, she felt her skirt catch on something. She tried to wriggle free, but it tore. *Mother will*—She stopped mid-thought. *Mother will be glad I'm alive*, she decided, *if I ever get out of this chimney.*

When she finally got to the top, Mandie felt Dimar's strong hands lift her out of the chimney and onto the roof next to Sallie.

"Do not move!" Sallie warned, handing the kitten to Mandie. "The roof is very steep."

Mandie tried to stand still as she smoothed Snowball's dirty, white fur.

Dimar called for one of the boys to come up.

Joe offered the rope to Tsa'ni. "You go next."

"I will wait. I must put out the candle before I leave," Tsa'ni replied. "I will go after you."

"Well, if you insist," Joe said, grasping the end of the rope.

When Joe arrived safely at the top, Dimar called for Tsa'ni.

Tsa'ni blew out the candle, rolled it in some old ashes for it to cool, and then put it in his pocket. Taking hold of the rope, he pushed himself up and began the climb easily. Suddenly, about halfway up, he felt something give.

"The rope is about to break!" he called to the others on the roof.

Mandie bit her lip. "Please, dear God, don't let it break now!" she cried.

Dimar called down to him, "Try to hurry. Maybe you can get up before it breaks."

But it was too late. At that moment the rope snapped. Tsa'ni braced his feet against one wall and his backside against the wall behind him. He was going to have to work his way up without the rope. It was a miracle he hadn't fallen.

The young people waited fearfully on the roof. Hearing nothing more, Dimar leaned over the top of the chimney. "Tsa'ni, are you all right?" he called.

"Yes, I am all right," Tsa'ni answered. "The rope broke, but I can work my way up."

They could hear the scuffling noise as the Indian boy moved on up the chimney.

Dimar pulled on the remaining piece of rope. Excited, he called down to Tsa'ni. "There is quite a long piece of rope left. If you can manage to get far enough to reach it, you can use it the rest of the way," he said as he tossed it back down the chimney.

"I will try," Tsa'ni replied.

"Poor Tsa'ni. He is always getting into trouble," Mandie moaned.

"Usually through his own doings, though," Joe added.

"But this is not his fault," Sallie defended him.

"I guess not. In fact, it could have been me on the broken rope. He wanted to be last so he could put out the candle and bring it with him," Joe explained.

Just then Tsa'ni called from inside the chimney. "I have the rope!" he said.

Dimar checked to see that it was secure. "It seems to be all right at this end," he answered.

In a few moments a scratched and bruised Tsa'ni appeared at the top of the chimney. He, too, was covered with soot. Dimar and Joe helped him out onto the tin roof.

"Good exercise!" Tsa'ni laughed, rubbing his scratched back.

"Now all we have to do is slide down this roof and jump to the ground," Dimar told them. "Thank goodness the cabin has a low roof. It will not be so far to jump."

"Sounds like fun when we can't see what we're jumping into," Joe laughed.

"I will go first and see what is beneath," Dimar told them. "Listen for me. I will look all the way around the cabin and pick the best side for you to jump."

"I do not mind going first," Tsa'ni offered.

"Neither do I," Joe chimed in.

"No, you two stay with the girls and help them slide down when I call to you," Dimar said, lying down on his stomach. Pushing himself off with his hands, he started sliding down backwards. It was too dark to see much, but the others heard the thud when Dimar landed on the ground.

"I am down!" Dimar yelled.

He walked all around the cabin. "I think the best place is where I came down. There is more grass and weeds here. Not so many thorny bushes."

"All right, we'll send Sallie first," Joe called to Dimar.

Sallie looked at the steep roof and took a deep breath. Twisting her heavy skirt around her, she lay on her stomach and gave herself a backward push as she had seen Dimar do. Before she could plop onto the ground, Dimar broke her fall.

"Mandie coming next," Joe called to Dimar.

"What will I do with Snowball?" Mandie protested. "How will I get him down?"

"Here," said Tsa'ni, pulling the rope off the chimney. "We will tie this around him and you hold onto the end of the rope as you slide down. He will have to come with you whether he likes it or not."

"It won't hurt him?"

"No, it will not hurt him," Tsa'ni replied. "Hold him still while I roll this rope around him."

Snowball did not like the idea, but Tsa'ni rolled the rope around and around the kitten until he couldn't get loose. He gave the end of the rope to Mandie.

"Snowball, be still!" Mandie ordered. "We have to slide down to the ground." She rubbed his head, and he purred. But he would not be still.

Lying down on the roof as she had seen Sallie do, she grasped the rope and slid down, pulling the protesting kitten with her. Sallie caught him as he came off the roof and Dimar broke the fall for Mandie.

Mandie took the howling kitten in her arms and untied the rope. "You shouldn't carry on so, Snowball. Remember, this was all your idea," she told him as she stroked his ruffled fur. He was soon purring softly.

Tsa'ni came down next, with Joe following.

At last the young people, grimy with soot, were safely on the ground outside the cabin. They stood close together in the dark.

"Now what do we do?" Sallie asked.

"We have to find everybody, so we'll just start walking, I guess," Mandie replied.

"But my grandfather is probably in one direction and your mother and the others in the opposite direction. Remember?" Sallie said, trying to brush more of the dirt from her dress.

"I think we should find our way back to the wrecked train," Dimar suggested. "When your mother and Uncle John and Tsa'ni's grandfather can get off the train, I think they would head back toward the wreck to find us."

"Yes, you're right, Dimar," Joe agreed, adjusting the suspenders on his trousers. "That sounds sensible."

"I know my grandfather would come back to find us," Tsa'ni said.

"And *my* grandfather may still be in that wrecked baggage car!" Sallie cried.

Poor Uncle Ned, Mandie thought, *he may have been killed when the baggage car wrecked. Please, God, let him be all right.*

"Then it is agreed. We will try to find our way back to where the train wrecked," Dimar said.

"Yes," the others answered.

"I will walk in front," Dimar declared, "and Tsa'ni, you and Joe walk behind the girls. That way they will be protected." He turned to go.

"Protected?" Mandie asked shakily.

"Yes, from anyone or any *thing* we might meet on our way," Dimar explained.

Mandie shivered as she remembered the panther she had encountered on her first visit to her Cherokee kinpeople. "Thank you, Dimar," she replied and took Sallie's hand. Her other hand clutched Snowball to her shoulder.

So the group went down the vague trail with only a little moonlight to illumine their way. Worry showed on their faces as they hastened their steps to find the others. They didn't know what they would find, but they had to get back to the wrecked train car.

CHAPTER FOUR

RUNAWAY TRAIN

When the train stopped, the adults heard the noise of the wrecked car but didn't know what was happening. Then the train started up again and began picking up speed. Uncle John went back to look for the young people and found the baggage car missing and no sign of Mandie and her friends. The other passengers were frightened, too. They said they had seen the youngsters go on into the next car but they hadn't returned.

Terror gripped Elizabeth. She didn't know whether Mandie and Uncle Ned and the other youngsters had been in the wrecked car or not. Uncle Wirt and Uncle John tried to comfort her, but the engine was going so fast around the curves it was all they could do to stay on their seats. The train was so noisy they couldn't even talk.

Elizabeth practically screamed in her husband's ear. "John, we've got to get off this train and go back to see what happened to Amanda, and Uncle Ned, and the other children!" she cried.

John, with his arm tightly around her, nodded his head in agreement. He was too worried to talk.

Uncle Wirt sat opposite them with a furious expression on his old face. He, too, was worried.

The train came to a sudden, screeching halt and almost threw them to the floor. They looked out the windows. It was so dark outside they couldn't see a thing. Everything became still. Everyone was waiting to see what was going to happen next. There was the sound of a horse galloping away into the distance.

The engineer opened the door at the end of the car and came inside. "I am very sorry, ladies and gentlemen," he began, as he wiped the sweat from his round, red face. "A bandit left his horse and climbed on board when they stopped the train a ways back, and he forced me to open up, full-throttle. Then, a little while ago, he jumped off."

"Why?" Elizabeth managed to ask, shakily.

"I don't rightly know, ma'am," he replied. "You see, they uncoupled the baggage car when they stopped the train back yonder and it went down into the gorge—"

"—Amanda, Uncle Ned, the children!" Elizabeth cried, unable to stop shaking.

John held her tightly against him. "Is that the only car that went off the track?" he asked the man.

"Yes, sir, far as I could tell in the dark," the engineer replied.

"Maybe the children got off when the train stopped," John suggested. "You know how curious and adventuresome they are."

Uncle Wirt clasped his hands together. "But we not sure, and Ned in baggage car, and baggage car in gorge for sure," he reminded them.

"I'm afraid he was. But maybe he managed to get out," John said, grasping for hope.

"What are we going to do?" Elizabeth asked the engineer.

"We're almost in Asheville, so we'll go into the station," the man replied. "If you'll all be patient, I'll go back up front and get this train—what's left of it—into the depot."

He turned and went back out the door.

"We must remember not to mention the gold to anyone," Uncle John cautioned Elizabeth and Uncle Wirt.

"Of course, John," Elizabeth replied, still in tears. "If this train can't go back, how are we going to get back to where the car went off the track?"

John still tried to comfort her. "We'll get some horses in Asheville and head toward Franklin. From there we'll go up the mountain. It's too steep and dangerous to ride back in from Asheville. Besides, I'm hoping the youngsters and Uncle Ned will head for our house in Franklin if they are able to."

Uncle Wirt leaned forward. "We get help, find lost ones. Find bad men, too," he told Elizabeth.

She managed a weak smile through her tears and put her hand over the old man's. "Thank you, Uncle Wirt," she said.

The train slowed as it came into Asheville. John, Elizabeth, and Uncle Wirt picked up their belongings and prepared to leave the train.

There was no one around except the baggage boy and the stationmaster. When the stationmaster heard what had happened, he was very upset. "There won't be another train going back that direction until tomorrow," he said.

John asked him about the local livery stables. "We need a light wagon or buggy to take up to Franklin," he said.

Elizabeth interrupted, "No, John, get three horses. You know I can ride astride as well as anyone. It'll be much faster."

"The trip will be awfully rough for you," John warned.

"Don't worry about that," she said. "All I want right now is speed. We must hurry."

"All right, if you say so." John disappeared with the baggage boy and soon returned with three horses from the livery stables.

Uncle Wirt led the way through shortcuts he knew in the woods. Some of the trails were so overgrown they didn't look like trails anymore, but the old Indian knew every step of the way.

Well into the morning they arrived in Franklin. Tired and dirty, they tethered the horses in front of the house. John helped Elizabeth dismount.

Jason Bond, the caretaker, came to the front door when they rode up. He couldn't believe what he was seeing. They were supposed to be in Asheville. "Mr. Shaw, what has happened?" he inquired, hurrying down the walkway.

While John explained, Elizabeth stood by the horses, trying to adjust her heavy skirts that had become twisted and wrinkled during the hard ride. She was a little shaky, but proud to have kept up with the men.

"We only need a bite to eat, Jason, and fresh horses and we'll be off," John told him, as they all walked to the front porch.

"Let me get a horse and go with you, Mr. Shaw," Jason begged.

"No, Jason, we need you here in case they come home," John told him. "Uncle Wirt and I will go."

Elizabeth stopped and touched John's arm. "You aren't going anywhere without me," she said.

"But there's nothing you can do. You're all worn out, darling. Let Uncle Wirt and me take care of things," John replied.

"Absolutely not! I am going with you!" Elizabeth was adamant.

"Dr. Woodard, Joe's father, is in town," Jason said. "He came by last night. Said he wouldn't go back home until tomorrow. He'll probably want to go with you."

"If he's not here on a life-and-death case, I hope he *can* go with us. We might need a doctor," John told him. "While we're eating, see if you can find him, or get word to him to come over at once."

Aunt Lou, the housekeeper, heard the commotion and was waiting for them at the front door. Elizabeth told her the news, and the large black woman wiped tears from her round cheeks with her apron.

"Lawsy mercy, my chile, she done got lost!" Aunt Lou cried, "and all them other 'lil ones, and that pore old Mister Ned." She put her arm around Elizabeth. "And Miz 'Lizbeth, you looks like you gonna drop any minute."

"I'll be fine as soon as I eat," Elizabeth told her. "I'll run upstairs and change into some riding clothes. You get Jenny to set out some food for us."

Uncle Wirt stood silently at the door. He, like the others, was worried about what they might find when they got back to the wrecked train car.

A short time later, while they were hastily eating, Liza ushered Dr. Woodard into the dining room. "Well, John, what brings you back so soon? I thought you all were going on to Asheville," he said.

John rose to pull out a chair at the table. "Sit down, sit down," he invited. "Liza, bring Dr. Woodard a plate."

As they informed Dr. Woodard of the situation, he assured them that he would go with them. His son, Joe, was among those who discovered the gold. Dr. Woodard was the only other person who knew about the transfer.

Within minutes the four adults left on horseback. They were well equipped with extra blankets, ropes, lanterns, and food, and Uncle Wirt guided them through the trails he knew.

Some time later they came upon an old cabin by a stream in the woods. Uncle Wirt slowed his horse to dismount. "I send word to Bird-town," he said.

"That's a good idea, Uncle Wirt, and Deep Creek, too," John suggested.

A young Indian man who evidently knew Uncle Wirt came from behind the house. They exchanged Cherokee greetings, and Uncle Wirt explained where they were going.

"You go Deep Creek and Bird-town. Need braves at train," the old man ordered.

"I go like lightning," the young man replied. Instantly he ran to the pony tied by the side of the house and was on his way.

"Braves find bad men," Uncle Wirt told his three companions.

All four were silent as they traveled on. What would they find when they got to the wrecked train?

CHAPTER FIVE

TSA'NI IN TROUBLE

"Won't we ever get there?" Joe complained, as he stumbled over the exposed root of a huge tree in the darkness.

"The railroad track is not very far now." Dimar spoke from the front of the group. "When we find it, we will walk down the tracks until we come to the place where the train wrecked."

"Dimar, are you serious?" Mandie asked. "You know part of the track is high up in the air. We could fall off in the dark."

"We will hold hands. Then if one slips, the others can keep him from falling," Dimar explained as they continued through the woods.

"But if we hold hands we will have to walk sideways," Sallie informed him.

Tsa'ni spoke up. "I still have the piece of rope," he said. "We could hold onto the rope together."

"Hey! Remember that time we got lost in the mountains and those bootleggers tied us up? We could tie all of us together the way they did," Joe suggested.

"That sounds like a good way to do it," Sallie agreed. She held her dark, full skirt above her ankles in an effort to avoid the briars in the underbrush.

"Yes, that's the best idea yet," Mandie said, holding tightly to her kitten.

"Well, we must begin using the rope then, because there is the railroad track. Up the hill there," Dimar told them, motioning in the darkness.

"I can't see a thing," Mandie said.

"Neither can I," Joe added.

"Dimar, how do you see that far?" Sallie asked.

"Now I see the tracks," Mandie said, excitedly.

"Yes, they were there all the time," Tsa'ni said sarcastically.

When the young people reached the tracks, as Joe had suggested, they began working with the rope. Dimar fastened one end around his waist and gave the free end to Sallie. She, in turn, wrapped it around her waist and passed it on to Mandie, who did likewise, then Joe, and then Tsa'ni.

"It is just barely long enough," Tsa'ni said, securing the rope around his waist. "Now if one falls, we all fall."

"Oh, no, Tsa'ni," Mandie disagreed. "You see, there would be four of us left standing to pull the other one back up."

"Then we had better be quick if one of us falls," Tsa'ni replied.

Dimar carefully stepped onto the tracks and the others lined up behind him. But before Dimar could give the word to start, Mandie spoke up.

"I think we should ask God to protect us," she said. "I'm scared."

"The rope will protect us," Tsa'ni retorted.

"Tsa'ni!" Sallie rebuked. "Of course the rope will help us, but we need God to watch over us."

"I do not believe in the white people's God," Tsa'ni said vehemently.

Dimar was shocked. "But you go to church with your father and your grandfather," he said.

"Yes, but that is only because they make me go. When I am grown I will not go to church anymore. They will not be able to force me," Tsa'ni answered.

Mandie's heart cried out in pain. *Tsa'ni did not believe in God!* What could she say to him to convince him he was wrong? She knew he was quite stubborn and sometimes quite mean, so she would have to be very careful with whatever she said.

"Tsa'ni, just say our little verse with us. We always say it to God when we're afraid, and then we just leave everything in His hands. He takes care of us, no matter what happens," Mandie tried to convince him.

"But I am not afraid," Tsa'ni rebelled.

"I'm not afraid either, really," Joe spoke up. "But I always say the verse with Mandie and the others, just to tell God I'm depending on Him."

Mandie tried to turn around and look directly at Tsa'ni at the end of the line, but the rope was too tight.

"Please, my Cherokee cousin, believe that God will protect us from harm if we ask," Mandie begged.

"No, I will not say it!" Tsa'ni snapped.

"Then we will say it without you," Dimar told him, reaching behind to take Sallie's hand. Sallie took Mandie's, and Mandie put Snowball on her shoulder to reach for Joe's hand.

The four spoke together. "What time we are afraid, we will put our trust in thee, dear God."

In a whisper Mandie added, "And dear God, please help Tsa'ni."

"Are we ready to go now?" Tsa'ni asked angrily.

"Yes, we are ready to go," Dimar answered. "Please, be careful and go very slowly. If we come to one of those places where the tracks go over a gorge, we will have to walk on the crossties."

After what seemed like hours of little progress, Dimar spotted a dangerous place ahead. "Here is one of those places," Dimar called over his shoulder. "We will have to go very slowly."

They all stopped. The tracks spanned the deep gorge in midair. And as he had said, there were only the crossties to walk on. The track was open. There was no dirt beneath it and nothing alongside it—just the width of the track supported by a bridge framework.

As they started across, Mandie made the mistake of looking down. The ground beneath dropped clear out of sight in the darkness. Her stomach turned over, and she shivered in the chilly night air. *Suppose someone's foot slipped, could the others save him—or her? It would be horrible to fall through the tracks.* She could almost feel the pain. Then she silently rebuked herself. *I told God I would trust Him and here I am worrying about what might happen. Please, dear God, forgive me. I do put my trust in you.*

"This is nerve-racking work," Mandie said, trying to fit her steps to the distance between the crossties without pulling or pushing the others. Everyone seemed to be holding his breath and concentrating on his feet. Snowball clung to Mandie's shoulder.

"I have done this before, lots of times," Tsa'ni bragged.

"Well, I don't think I ever want to do it again," Joe said.

"It is exhilarating up here in the air," Tsa'ni replied, throwing his hands over his head.

Mandie glanced quickly over her shoulder. "Tsa'ni!" she cried. "Please be careful!"

At that moment the Indian boy lost his footing and slipped between the crossties. Thrown off balance, he dangled in the air, trying to grasp the framework beneath the tracks.

The sudden fall jerked the others. Joe, being next to Tsa'ni, had to sit down on the crossties to keep from being pulled down with him. Mandie frantically clutched Snowball and swayed as she tried to keep from falling. Sallie and Dimar, ahead of her, did not feel the jolt quite as badly.

Dimar immediately took over. "Please sit down!" he told Sallie and Mandie. He unfastened the rope from his waist. "Hold on, Tsa'ni, hold on. I will help you."

The girls carefully sat down on the crossties next to Joe.

"Why does Tsa'ni always have to make trouble?" Joe muttered.

"Because he is a bad Cherokee," Sallie replied.

"Pray for him," Mandie urged, "so that he doesn't fall."

Dimar gingerly stepped past the other three to get to Tsa'ni.

Sallie hung her head in shame, then raised her face toward the sky. "Please, God, do not let him fall."

Mandie was looking heavenward, too. "Please take care of him, dear God," she prayed.

As Dimar knelt on the tracks and tried to reach Tsa'ni's hand below, Joe knew he had to help, too, even though he didn't like Tsa'ni.

"Untie the rope from around y'all," Joe told the girls.

"But we might fall, too," Sallie protested.

"You won't if you sit perfectly still," Joe answered. "I need the rope for Tsa'ni."

"Of course," Mandie answered, as Sallie quickly untied the rope from her waist and passed the end to Mandie, who immediately pulled it loose from herself and passed it on back to Joe.

Dimar changed positions. "I still cannot reach you, Tsa'ni," he said.

"Wait. I'm getting the rope free," Joe told Dimar. "Then we can pull him up." He rolled up the rope and crawled back to where Dimar was stooping, trying to reach Tsa'ni.

The other end of the rope was still around Tsa'ni's waist, but it wasn't doing any good because he was hanging onto the bottom of the track with his hands, and his feet were kicking at the huge wooden post supporting the track. He kept trying to catch his toes on the post to take some of the pressure off his hands. So far he had not said a word.

Dimar helped Joe tie the rope around a crosstie and then called down to Tsa'ni.

"We have the rope secured up here and we are going to throw the end down to you. Watch for it," Dimar called to him.

Tsa'ni did not answer except to call out, "Hurry up!"

The first streaks of light began to brighten the sky. The two boys could see Tsa'ni hanging below and they threw the rope down over the side of the tracks, but it didn't go anywhere near Tsa'ni. They tried again and again but it wouldn't fall near enough for him to grab it.

"I cannot hold much longer," Tsa'ni finally said in a hoarse voice.

Mandie and Sallie sat holding hands, helplessly watching as the boys kept throwing the rope toward Tsa'ni. They silently prayed that he would be able to reach the rope.

Suddenly, Tsa'ni's hands gave way and he fell. The rope, too, broke, and the others watched in terror as he disappeared into the gorge below.

"Tsa'ni!" the boys yelled in terror.

Mandie and Sallie burst into tears, holding onto one another for comfort. Dimar and Joe looked at the dangling piece of rope. Dimar silently pulled it up and unfastened it from the crosstie.

Joe took command. "We've got to get across this thing," he said. "Then when the track is back on the ground again, we can get off and climb down there and see if we can find Tsa'ni."

"That is exactly what I was thinking," Dimar replied.

Mandie wiped her tears on her apron with one hand and held tightly to Snowball with the other. "Are Sallie and I going down after Tsa'ni, too?" Mandie asked.

Dimar looked at Joe. "Joe and I will search for him as soon as the track gets back on the ground," he answered.

"If you and Joe are going, then so am I," Mandie insisted.

"Me, too," Sallie added. "I do not wish to be left alone."

Joe looked at Dimar. "I suppose it wouldn't be safe to leave them alone, would it?"

"I guess not. They will have to go with us," Dimar agreed. "However, it will probably be very steep and rough down there."

"I'll be all right," Mandie assured them.

The sky had begun to lighten and in the growing daylight they could see that they were about halfway across the gorge. The crossties were more visible now, but the young people could also see how far below the land was.

The remaining piece of rope was not long enough to tie around them again, so they held onto it between them as they carefully walked single file down the tracks. It was a slow, scary process, but they were even more afraid of what they would find in the ravine.

CHAPTER SIX

SEARCHING

As the young people neared the end of the railroad bridge, the ground gradually came up to meet them, and they breathed a little easier. The awesome trek in open space was over.

Dimar stepped from the tracks onto the ground and led the others to safety.

"Whew!" Mandie blew out her breath. "Dimar, is there any more of that kind of tracks between here and where the baggage car wrecked?"

"I do not think so," Dimar assured her with a smile. "It will get steep down the side instead." Now that it was daylight he looked at her with admiration. *She is beautiful, in spite of her grimy, tear-streaked face,* he thought.

Dimar had often looked at Mandie that way, and Joe was jealous. He spoke up quickly. "Well, suppose we try to find Tsa'ni now," he suggested.

Suddenly there was a noise on the gravel. They all turned to see Tsa'ni climbing up the hill through the thick brush.

"That will not be necessary," he said, coming toward them. He was swinging the piece of rope that had been tied around his waist when he fell.

Everyone stared at him, unable to speak. Was that really Tsa'ni?

"I told you the rope would protect me," he laughed.

"Oh, Tsa'ni, what do you mean?" Mandie asked.

"When my hands slipped, the rope broke and I fell a great distance. But luckily, I landed in the top branches of a tree. All I had to do was get untangled and climb down," he explained, still swinging the piece of rope. "I escaped with hardly a scratch."

"And here we've been mourning for you all the time," Joe complained. "What a waste of tears!"

"You see, God did protect you," Sallie told him.

"I didn't need God. The tree broke my fall," Tsa'ni tossed back at her.

"No, Tsa'ni. God protected you. He used the tree to save you," Mandie explained.

"The *tree* saved me," the Indian boy insisted.

Joe began to walk ahead on the tracks. "There's no use in arguing with the ignorant dumbhead," he said. "We've got more important things to do, like finding Uncle Ned and the gold. Besides, I'm hungry. Let's go."

Dimar agreed. "Yes, we must hurry."

The girls followed Joe and Dimar, trying to keep up with their rapid pace. Tsa'ni lagged slightly behind the others.

"I wonder if my mother and Uncle John and Uncle Wirt got to Asheville all right," Mandie said.

"I don't imagine they stayed in Asheville if they got there," Joe told her. "They'll be out looking for us and Uncle Ned."

"I pray that my grandfather is all right," Sallie said, her voice shaking.

"Do you think he was still in the baggage car when it went off the tracks, or do you think the bandits captured him?" Dimar asked.

"I do not know what to think. It was all so sudden," Sallie answered. "But either way is bad. If my grandfather was still in the baggage car when it derailed, he may have been badly injured." She swallowed hard. "But if the bandits captured him, they may have harmed him."

"Especially since he is an Indian," Tsa'ni said bitterly.

"I can't understand why people are so prejudiced against certain other people. God made us all, and in His sight we are all equal," Mandie reasoned as they hurried along the railroad tracks.

"There are lots of people who think they are living as Christians, but they commit that sin," Dimar joined in.

"I do not claim to be a Christian, so I can say that I think the Indians are much *better* than the white people," Tsa'ni declared.

The other four were shocked.

"How can you say such a thing, Tsa'ni?" Dimar questioned.

"I am ashamed of you, Tsa'ni—as one Indian to another," Sallie told him.

"Why did you come with us in the first place?" Joe asked.

Tsa'ni did not answer.

After several moments of awkward silence, Mandie spoke. "I think the best thing we can do is to quit talking until we get to where we're going. That way, there won't be any hard feelings," she suggested.

The others agreed. Tsa'ni remained silent and trailed along behind.

At last the sun came up and the air grew warmer as the young people trudged along. Birds sang their greetings as they flew hither and yon among the trees. Now and then a butterfly flitted across their path, and once in a while a colorful wildflower peeked out of the underbrush. It was a beautiful day, but the youngsters were tired, hungry, and worried.

After a while the river and the railroad tracks came together and traveled side by side. The rushing water invited the young people to soak their tired feet, but they could not relax.

Ignoring their blisters, scratches, bruises, and sore limbs, they marched forward. At last they came around a curve where the tracks turned away from the river. And there, in the ravine below, lay the wrecked baggage car, splintered against the mountainside.

"There it is!" Mandie cried.

As exhausted as they were, they all broke into a run.

Sallie ran ahead of the others. "Grandfather!" she exclaimed, racing to the edge of the ravine.

Mandie was right behind her. When Mandie's father died, Uncle Ned had promised that he would look out for "Jim Shaw's Papoose," and now it was her turn to look out for Uncle Ned. "Please, dear God, let him be all right. Please let Uncle Ned be all right," she prayed silently.

Dimar and Joe came up behind the girls as they paused to look.

"We must go down together," Dimar told them.

"Yes," agreed Joe. "It looks kind of steep."

Tsa'ni stood alone on the tracks and watched as the others descended into the ravine. They slipped and slid until they finally reached the train car. The car lay on its side. It looked as though it had rolled over several times.

"It's so broken up I don't see how we can get inside to look for Uncle Ned," Mandie said.

"Simple," said Joe. "Dimar and I will crawl in through that hole in the side."

"But, Joe, suppose it turns over while you're in there. It's just hanging on the side of the mountain," Mandie cautioned them.

"Let it turn over," Joe answered. "It won't hurt us. We'll just tumble with it."

"May I go with you? My grandfather may be in there," Sallie begged.

"No, it is too dangerous," Dimar said. "If we find him inside we will bring him out."

The girls waited and watched while the two boys went through the hole in the train car. As the boys disappeared inside, Mandie, with Snowball on her shoulder, reached for Sallie's hand and held it tightly.

After what seemed like hours, the two boys reappeared, empty-handed. They shook their heads as they approached.

"Grandfather!" Sallie began to cry.

"Uncle Ned, where are you?" Mandie moaned.

Joe stepped forward and took Mandie's hand in his.

"I'm sorry, Mandie. He isn't there," he said to her softly. "And neither is the gold. Everything inside is completely smashed. Uncle Ned must have managed to get out somehow. Either the bandits took him or he got out on his own."

Tsa'ni, listening from where he stood, came forward to join the group. "I suggest we search immediately. If the old man is injured, he cannot be very far. That is, *if* he is still alive," he added.

At Tsa'ni's cruel remark, Sallie began to cry louder.

"Let us separate and search the surroundings," Dimar said.

"Immediately, please," Sallie begged through her tears, still holding Mandie's hand.

"Dimar, suppose you take Sallie with you, and Joe and I will go with Tsa'ni," Mandie suggested.

"Fine," Dimar replied. "If you find anything, Tsa'ni, give me a call. I will do the same. And please do not forget to watch for the bags of gold, also. They may be hard to find since they are so small."

"I would think the bandits took the gold," Joe said. "That is probably why they wrecked the train. But it wouldn't hurt to keep our eyes open."

"I will give you a whistle, Dimar, if we find anything," Tsa'ni agreed. "We will go to the left of the car and you and Sallie go right. We will meet back here when we have covered all the ground," he said.

The group separated. Mandie, with Snowball on her shoulder, followed Joe and Tsa'ni down the incline, through bramble bushes and rocks. She didn't mind the pricks and scratches. She was set on finding her dear friend, Uncle Ned.

Tsa'ni walked bent over to watch the ground for footprints or other clues. Joe and Mandie watched the bushes and trees for any sign of a trail. In the dense forest the trees grew so close together it took time to look at all of them.

"No one has come this way," Tsa'ni called over his shoulder. "But maybe we will find a trail ahead."

Mandie turned to Joe, who was walking behind her. "Then Uncle Ned could not have come this way," she said.

"What Tsa'ni means is that no one came directly down the path we're taking," Joe explained. "Uncle Ned could have taken a path even two feet from where we are. We just have to keep walking up and down in order to cover all the area around the wrecked car. Don't give up yet."

"I won't give up. God will help us find him," Mandie said as they walked slowly forward.

"Don't say that too loudly, or we'll get a few smart remarks from Tsa'ni," Joe warned her.

"We'll have to see what we can do about Tsa'ni," Mandie said.

"I think he's hopeless," Joe replied.

"No one is hopeless, Joe. There is always hope," Mandie argued.

As they neared the river, the ground was steep and covered with slippery green moss. Mandie, trying to look all around for any sign, was not watching her step. Suddenly, her feet went out from under her and she sat down hard. Snowball, frightened by the jolt, jumped free and ran into the weeds nearby.

Joe helped her to her feet. "Are you all right?"

Mandie laughed nervously. "I'm all right," she said. "I should have been paying more attention to where I was walking. Oh, goodness, where did Snowball go?" she asked, brushing off the back of her skirt.

The two looked around quickly, but there was no sign of the white kitten. Tsa'ni did not notice their predicament and went on ahead.

Mandie searched the tall weeds. "Snowball! Kitty, kitty, kitty!" she called. "Come here, Snowball!"

The kitten meowed loudly. Joe and Mandie stood still to listen.

"He sounds either angry or hurt," Joe remarked.

"This way, Joe," Mandie said, turning to the left. "Sounds like he's over this way—toward the river."

She went on through the bushes, looking for the kitten, with Joe right behind her. The meow grew louder.

Then Snowball hopped out of the weeds in front of them. With his fur up, he meowed loudly.

"Snowball, you shouldn't run off like that," Mandie scolded. She stooped to pick him up, but he was too quick for her. He bounded into the bushes. Mandie and Joe followed. But as they came through the underbrush into the open area by the river, a terrible sight greeted them.

There on the sandy riverbank lay Uncle Ned on his back. His head was covered with blood. His bow and arrows were by his side.

Mandie, blinded with tears, rushed forward. She dropped to her knees at his side.

"Uncle Ned! Uncle Ned!" she cried, touching the still face. "Please, Uncle Ned, don't be dead! Please speak to me, Uncle Ned! Oh, dear God, please don't let him be dead!"

Joe knelt by her side and tried to find a pulse in the old man's wrist. He held his hand over Uncle Ned's mouth to see if he was breathing. He couldn't feel a thing. Jumping up, he yelled for Tsa'ni.

"Tsa'ni! Quick! Here by the river!" Joe called.

In seconds the Indian boy came rushing through the bushes.

Mandie cried as she held Uncle Ned's wrinkled hand in hers.

"Move, woman!" Tsa'ni ordered. He pushed Mandie aside to kneel by the old man. He, too, felt for a pulse and breathing with no results. "I am afraid he is very near death."

Tsa'ni stood up and gave a loud Indian call for help. Dimar and Sallie quickly joined them. When Sallie saw the condition of her grandfather, she sobbed uncontrollably.

"We must get him out of here at once!" Dimar ordered.

"Oh, dear God, how? Show us how!" Mandie said through her tears.

At that instant a faint Indian call answered Tsa'ni's. Speechless, the five young people looked at one another.

"God has sent help!" Mandie cried.

Tsa'ni gave a shrill whistle and again received an answer.

"Keep it up. Whoever it is will find us," Dimar told him.

They all waited silently, listening for the response. Each time it grew louder.

Then suddenly, Uncle Wirt burst through the bushes, followed by Uncle John, Elizabeth, Dr. Woodard, and four young Indian braves from Deep Creek and Bird-town.

Mandie rushed to Dr. Woodard, grasped his hand and pulled him down beside Uncle Ned. "Dr. Woodard, quick!" she cried.

The others gathered around as the doctor carefully examined the old Indian. Dr. Woodard looked up. "He's not dead, but he's close to it," he said gravely. "I cannot help him here, but if we don't treat him immediately, he probably will not live."

"We take him home," Uncle Wirt told them.

"It would be better if we could get him to John's house in Franklin," Dr. Woodard said. "We could care for him better there."

"Then we'll take him to my house," Uncle John declared.

Elizabeth put her arms around her daughter and tried to comfort her. But Mandie's whole body shook as she sobbed. Uncle Wirt put his arm around Sallie. It was a sad moment, always to be remembered—Uncle Ned, the dear old man, lying there helpless, and close to death.

Uncle Wirt turned to the braves and spoke rapidly in Cherokee. The young Indians immediately unrolled the blankets they carried and prepared a hammock-type bed to carry the old man over the mountain. Gently lifting him, they placed him on the blankets. Each brave took hold of a corner and lifted him from the ground. The old man did not move or utter a sound.

"Speed is the important thing," Dr. Woodard cautioned them. "We must get him to Franklin as quickly as we can."

The braves nodded in understanding.

"Braves, run!" Uncle Wirt ordered. "Quick!"

Without hesitating a second, the braves took off through the bushes, carrying the old man. Mandie and Sallie tried to follow, but Uncle John held them back.

"Wait! We have horses up at the tracks," Uncle John told them. "Since the braves left their horses, we'll have enough for all of us to ride back home."

"Braves run faster through woods than horses," Uncle Wirt said.

"Yes, they'll be there by the time we arrive," Uncle John agreed. "Thank goodness Aunt Lou and Jason Bond can help."

Mandie looked up at her mother. "Ever since we found the gold, Uncle Ned has said the gold was bad luck to the Cherokees, and now he may die because of it," she said shakily. "Oh, how could we have been so greedy that we ignored his beliefs?"

Elizabeth held her daughter tightly. "Now, don't blame yourself, dear," she said. "The gold will eventually be a good thing for the Cherokees when we get the hospital built."

"The gold is nowhere to be found," Joe informed them as they all climbed the steep side of the ravine.

The adults stopped and stared.

"So the bandits got away with it!" Uncle John said angrily.

"Cherokee catch bad men," Uncle Wirt vowed as the group hurried on up the mountainside.

Sally looked up at Uncle Wirt. "Please catch the bad men who hurt my grandfather," she said.

Uncle Wirt took her hand in his and squeezed it gently in reply.

Riding double on some of the horses, the group galloped off toward Franklin.

Mandie fought back the tears. "Please, God, don't let him die!" she implored.

CHAPTER SEVEN

MANDIE KEEPS WATCH

Uncle Ned, bathed and dressed in a clean nightshirt, lay very still in a bedroom across the hall from Mandie's room. Dr. Woodard tried everything he knew, but there was no improvement in the old man's condition. Finally, he sent the braves to Deep Creek to bring back Uncle Ned's squaw, Morning Star.

Everyone hovered around Uncle Ned's doorway, waiting for some word.

"I have an idea he was thrown out of the train car and landed on his head," Dr. Woodard told them. "I can't find any broken bones, though. Now that his head has been washed, you can see that there are several large cuts in the scalp."

Mandie tugged at the doctor's hand. "Dr. Woodard, will—will he—live?" she asked.

"Will he, Doctor?" Sallie echoed.

"I don't know," Dr. Woodard replied. "Only the Lord knows that. I have done all I can. I'd say it's up to the Lord now."

Mandie noticed that Sallie was crying and gave her Indian friend a hug. Their tears mingled in love for the old man.

Sallie pulled Mandie across the room with her to the bed where her grandfather lay. "We will stay with him," she managed to say.

"Yes, and we will pray." Mandie said. "I know God will heal him." She held her friend's hand and they knelt by the bed.

"I think we should all pray. Come on," Elizabeth told the others. She led the way into the room and knelt behind the girls. Only Tsa'ni remained outside in the hallway. Aunt Lou, Liza, Jason Bond, and Jenny joined the others. The room was soon full of people on their knees, praying for Uncle Ned to be healed, and thanking the Lord that he had lived so far.

As the group became silent and got to their feet, Dr. Woodard spoke. "We must arrange a schedule now. He shouldn't be left alone, and I have other patients I must see now."

"I am not leaving Uncle Ned, not for one second," Mandie declared.

"Neither am I!" Sallie told them.

"But you were up all of last night, and you only ate a snack while Dr. Woodard was working with Uncle Ned," Elizabeth objected. "You two girls didn't even take a good bath when you changed clothes. You'll be Dr. Woodard's patients next if you don't take care of yourselves."

Mandie shook her head angrily. "No, no, no! I won't leave him! He would never leave me! I love him!"

"I know. I know, dear," Elizabeth said. She tried to put her arm around Mandie, but the girl pulled away. "Let's go take a nap and then you can come right back," her mother suggested.

Mandie stomped her foot. "No! I am not leaving this room!" she cried.

Elizabeth looked at her husband in despair.

"Mandie," Uncle John said firmly. "I know how much you have grown to love Uncle Ned since your father died and how Uncle Ned has been watching over you—"

Mandie wiped at her tears with her apron.

"—but we cannot permit you to throw a temper tantrum like this."

Mandie felt badly for the way she had acted and began to cry softly. Dr. Woodard understood the situation and stepped forward. "John, may I make a suggestion? Why don't you let Mandie and Sallie rest in here tonight?" He pulled one of the big, plush armchairs to the side of the bed. "That way, they can keep watch and still rest a little, too."

John thought for a moment. "Well, I suppose that would be all right. Elizabeth?" His wife nodded.

Dr. Woodard pulled a second big chair to the other side of the bed, and the girls scrambled into them. Snowball hopped up beside Mandie and curled up in a corner of the big seat. Joe took his place behind the big chair as if watching over both Uncle Ned *and* Mandie.

Elizabeth looked at John again. Mandie was her daughter, but she didn't know how to discipline her. They had never even met each other until a few months ago. She hardly knew how to be a mother. John, sensing how Elizabeth felt, and knowing Mandie didn't normally act like this, put his arm around Elizabeth and moved her toward the door.

"All right, girls," Uncle John told them. "We are going to get some sleep, but we'll be back. If you get too sleepy, Aunt Lou or Liza will take over for you."

Mandie jumped up from the chair and ran to put her arms around her mother, wiping tears from her face.

"Mother, I'm sorry." Her voice was trembling. "I love you. I do. It's just that I love Uncle Ned, too, and I have to stay here and wait. I want to be here when God heals him," she said.

Elizabeth squeezed her tightly. "I understand, dear. You and Sallie get comfortable in the chairs. We'll be back later."

As Mandie went back to her chair, John turned to Uncle Wirt, Joe, Dimar, and Tsa'ni, who was watching them from the doorway. "Come on, Uncle Wirt, boys," he said. "Aunt Lou will show you some rooms where you can rest."

Joe started to leave with the others, but quickly returned to Mandie's side.

"Do you want me to stay with you?" he asked in a low voice. "I can lie down on the rug there."

"Thank you, Joe," Mandie told him. "I appreciate your offer, but why don't you come back after you sleep?"

Joe squeezed her hand and started to go. "I'll be back soon," he promised.

Out in the hallway, Dr. Woodard gave John a slip of paper. "Here are the names of the patients I'll be seeing," he said. "If there is any change in him at all, send for me immediately. Otherwise, I'll be back as soon as I can. I'll plan on spending the night here."

"You don't really think there is any hope for him, do you?" John asked.

"Well, as I said in there, it's up to the Lord now," the doctor replied. "He does still work miracles."

"I know. We'll all be praying for him."

After everyone was settled, Aunt Lou and Liza went down to the kitchen.

"We'se gotta git my chile somethin' to eat, Liza," Aunt Lou told the young black girl.

"Think that Injun man gonna live?" Liza asked.

Aunt Lou whirled on her heels. "Liza, don't you let me hear you talk like that agin," the old housekeeper said firmly. "That man is Mister Ned what loves my chile and watches over her. And you don't go callin' him Injun man no more. You hear that?"

"Yessum," Liza replied, looking down at the floor.

Aunt Lou pushed through the kitchen door. Jenny, the cook, was stirring something on the big iron cookstove.

"Jenny, I wants two trays loaded with some of everything you got in this kitchen," the big woman ordered.

"Two of everything, Aunt Lou?" Jenny frowned.

"Yep, two of everything you'se got cooked already, that is," Aunt Lou said. "Right now!"

"Yessum!" Jenny answered. Taking two trays from the shelf over the stove, she placed dishes on them and called for Liza. "Here, Liza, help me fill these up."

Aunt Lou supervised as Jenny and Liza opened each pot on the stove and dished up its contents.

"Now, I wants a pitcher of sweet milk," the big woman told Jenny.

"Who all's gonna eat all dis stuff?" Jenny asked, filling the milk pitcher as ordered.

"Jest my chile, and that other poor li'l girl and that smart little cat," Aunt Lou said. "He's the one what found Mister Ned. You oughta heerd what kind of troubles they done gone through."

"Yessum. Miss Amanda done told me 'bout them creatures what wrecked the train—look like ghosts," Liza told her.

"Well, shake a leg, girl. Them chillen's hungry." Aunt Lou picked up one tray and Liza got the other one.

"I don't 'member them sayin' they'se hungry," Liza answered as she followed Aunt Lou through the doorway. "They done et one time since they got home."

"Et? They ain't et enough to keep a bird alive. I knows when my chile is hungry. She don't hafta tell me," Aunt Lou said, climbing the winding stairway to the second floor.

As they entered Uncle Ned's room with the trays, the two girls looked up.

"We'se brought my chile and her li'l friend some food," Aunt Lou said quietly. Setting the tray on a table by Mandie, she motioned for Liza to take the other tray to Sallie. Aunt Lou filled two glasses with milk and set the pitcher aside.

"Now here's enough milk for y'all and the cat," Aunt Lou said, putting the glasses on each tray.

"But, Aunt Lou, we just ate not long ago," Mandie protested.

"See what I done said? They jest et 'while ago," Liza chimed in.

Aunt Lou scowled at Liza. "Liza, you jest hesh your mouth. These chillen's gonna eat what we done brought 'em," she said.

Mandie inhaled the tempting aroma of the food. "We'll try, Aunt Lou," she said.

"Liza, go git two pillows for these chillen so's they kin curl up in dese big chairs and rest after they done et," the old woman said.

"I be right back," Liza promised, dancing quietly out of the room.

Sallie took a bite of fried okra. "The food tastes delicious, Aunt Lou," she said.

"Jenny be a good cook," Aunt Lou replied.

"Jenny is the best cook in the whole world," Mandie added.

Liza danced back into the room with two frilly pillows. As the girls sat in the big chairs eating, Liza plumped up the pillows behind them. Snowball, for once too tired to eat, stayed curled up sound asleep in the corner of Mandie's chair.

"Now, you chillen eat. We'se got work to do, but we'll be back," Aunt Lou said, waving Liza to the door.

Mandie set her tray aside and got up to give the big woman a hug. "Thank you, Aunt Lou. I love you."

The old woman bent to hug her. "I loves my chile, too, and we'se all aprayin' the good Lord spares Mister Ned's life," she said.

"Thank you, Aunt Lou," Sallie replied.

"You go finish eatin' now, Mandie," Aunt Lou ordered. "We'll be back." She closed the door quietly behind them.

When Mandie and Sallie could eat no more, they pushed their trays aside and curled up in the chairs. In spite of their determination to stay awake, before long, both of them were sound asleep. Aunt Lou, knowing this would happen, slipped back inside the room and sat down near the foot of the bed to keep watch.

CHAPTER EIGHT

PRAYER CHANGES THINGS

When Morning Star arrived during the night, she fell weeping upon her husband's bed. Only Mandie and Sallie could calm her.

Mandie knelt with the old squaw and Sallie by the bed. "Morning Star, Uncle Ned is not going to die," she said. "God is going to heal him."

Morning Star couldn't understand everything Mandie was saying, so Sallie translated it into Cherokee.

"God is testing our faith, Morning Star. We must put our faith in God to heal Uncle Ned," Mandie continued. "I believe He will answer our prayers."

As Morning Star calmed down, she took her husband's hand and began to pray in the Cherokee language. Refusing to leave the room to eat or sleep, she stayed with Mandie and Sallie as they watched and waited.

Every day Dr. Woodard came to examine Uncle Ned. But on the third day he sadly shook his head. He turned to John Shaw who was standing nearby.

"I'm afraid we're going to lose him," the doctor said.

Hearing his words, Mandie ran to the bedside and began to cry. She grabbed the old man's hands in hers and shook him.

"Uncle Ned! Uncle Ned! Come back to me. Please don't die!" she cried hysterically, tears streaming down her cheeks.

Sallie knelt beside her grandmother to explain in Cherokee what the doctor had just said.

Morning Star looked up at Dr. Woodard. "God heal. No die," she said firmly.

Uncle John tried to settle Mandie down. But as he reached to pull her hands away from the old man's, Mandie cried out in joy.

"Uncle Ned! Uncle Ned, I knew you wouldn't leave me," she exclaimed.

They all hovered closely around the bed, astonished to see his eyes open. Uncle Ned looked directly at Mandie, then curled his fingers around her hand.

Dr. Woodard reached for the old Indian's wrist, waited silently for a moment, then smiled. "His pulse is normal," he announced. "God still works miracles."

"Grandfather, I love you," Sallie whispered.

Morning Star gently rubbed his forehead. "God heal," she muttered.

Uncle Ned managed a slight smile for his wife and grandaughter. "Eat," he said softly.

Everyone laughed and began to praise God. Aunt Lou hurried Jenny into making some hot broth for the old man. Before long Morning Star was holding his head and feeding him with a spoon.

Uncle Ned continued to improve a little bit each day. As soon as he was able, he told them what had happened to him. Propped up on his pillows, and with everyone gathered around him in great anticipation, he began his story.

"Ghosts ride horses," he said. "Train stop. They unhook train. Baggage car roll backward. Go off track. I jump out. Hurt head. Get water. No more remember."

There were lots of questions, and the young people told him what they had been through. But no one knew what happened to the gold.

Several days later, when Uncle Ned was well enough to sit up in a chair, Mandie waited until everyone else was out of the room, and then came to sit on the rug at his feet. Leaning her head against his knee, she said, "Uncle Ned, I need to talk to you. Are you well enough to talk?"

He nodded and smiled. "Well enough to get up and go," he said.

"I've been thinking a lot since you got hurt," the girl began. "You know, the gold is all gone. I guess the bandits stole it. But you know what I think?" She looked up at him very seriously. "I think God took it all away from us because we forgot to tithe. We forgot to give Him ten percent of it."

Uncle Ned was startled with her thinking. "No, no, no, Papoose!" he said anxiously. "Big Book say Big God throw blessings out window to people if people tithe."

"But we didn't tithe," Mandie said.

"Then we no get blessings," the old man replied. "But Big God not punish. Papoose find gold, but bad men take it away—not Big God."

"Do you really think so? I've been so worried about it," she said.

"So. Bad men take gold—not Big God," the old Indian repeated. "Cherokee find bad men, get gold back for Papoose."

"Oh, I hope we can get it back. I want so much to build that hospital for the Cherokees," Mandie told him. "And if we get it back, we will most certainly give ten percent of it to the Lord."

The old man smiled and patted her blonde head. "Then we must watch so we catch. Blessings fall down on us from window up there." Uncle Ned pointed upward.

Mandie felt better after her conversation with her dear friend. She knew Uncle Ned was right. And now that he was so much better she had time for her friends.

During those first trying days, Joe had more or less been her shadow, and of course, Sallie was always with Mandie and Uncle Ned. But it seemed that Dimar and Tsa'ni had done nothing but sit around and eat. Leaving Morning Star with Uncle Ned, Mandie decided to round up her friends. She found them all together in the parlor.

As Mandie entered the room, Polly Cornwallis, her friend from next door, rushed up and put her arms around her.

"Mandie, I was so sorry to hear about everything," she said, shaking her black curls out of her eyes. "Mother and I have been in Nashville. We just got back this afternoon."

"I'm glad you came, Polly," Mandie told her. "Have you met all my friends?"

Whirling about to smile at Joe, Polly replied, "Yes, Joe just finished introducing all of us."

"Well, then, since Uncle Ned is so much better, and Morning Star is staying with him for a while," Mandie explained, "I thought you might all like to see the secret tunnel Joe and I have told you about."

The others were on their feet immediately.

"Yes, yes," Dimar answered.

"Oh, please," Sallie chimed in.

"It would be interesting," Tsa'ni said.

Joe came to Mandie's side. "I'll be the guide for you," he laughed as he led the way into the hall. "Hadn't we better get the key from your Uncle John?"

Sticking her hand in her apron pocket, Mandie withdrew a large key and held it up. "I already have."

Snowball bounced along under their feet as Joe led the way up the stairs to the third floor and into Uncle John's library. The young Indians were fascinated with the beautiful house. They had never seen such a large mansion before.

Joe walked over to the heavy draperies in the corner of the room and pulled them aside, revealing a door. Mandie inserted the key and swung it open. Behind the door was a paneled wall. Pushing a latch, she waited for the panel to swing aside and then showed them steps going down.

Dimar was impressed. "That is very clever," he said.

"I think so, too," Mandie said with pride. "Uncle John said my great-grandfather built this house when the Cherokees were being moved out of North Carolina. He didn't like the way they were being treated, so he had this tunnel built just for them. He hid as many Cherokees as he could in this tunnel until things became peaceful. It was about 1842 when the Indians moved out and set up their own living quarters," Mandie explained. She turned to Tsa'ni. "That's how my grandfather and my grandmother met," she said. "He was twenty-eight, and she was a beautiful eighteen-year-old Indian girl. So you see, my family not only married Indians, they helped them survive when no one else would."

Tsa'ni only tightened his lips and said nothing.

Sallie sighed. "What a beautiful romance!"

"Yes," Mandie agreed. "My grandmother was Uncle Wirt's sister, you know. So he is really my great-uncle."

"Let's go," Tsa'ni complained.

Joe led them through the door to the steps. "It's kind of dark in places," he cautioned, "so be sure to watch your step."

Snowball meowed at Joe's feet. Joe picked up the cat and handed him to Mandie.

As they made their way through, Sallie and Dimar were thrilled, knowing the tunnel had once protected their people. When they finally emerged in the woods, almost out of sight of the house, they were really excited.

"What an adventure!" Dimar exclaimed, looking back to the exit door concealed by bushes.

Sallie turned to Mandie. "You know that my grandfather and my grandmother lived here at one time, don't you?"

Mandie set Snowball down and the kitten rubbed around her ankles. "Yes, Uncle John told me. Morning Star and Uncle Ned came to live with them after my grandfather died. He said my father was only five years old then," Mandie replied.

"My grandfather has never mentioned this tunnel to me," Sallie said. "He lived here, so he must have known about it."

"Your grandfather is the world's greatest keeper of secrets!" Mandie laughed.

"The old people do not like to talk about the Cherokee removal, or anything that reminds them of it," Dimar volunteered.

Tsa'ni changed the subject. "When are they going to look for the gold?" he asked.

Everyone stared at him.

"Who is going to look for the gold?" Joe asked.

"My grandfather and Mandie's uncle are planning to," Tsa'ni answered.

Mandie stood up straighter. "The Cherokees put me in charge of the gold, so I will go with them to hunt for it," she told them.

"So will I," Joe put in.

"And I," Sallie said.

Dimar was again admiring Mandie's pretty blue eyes. "I also would like to go with you," he said.

"Could I go, too?" Polly asked. "I'd just love to look for those creatures that stole it."

"Oh, Polly!" Mandie replied. "It won't be fun. They were awfully dangerous looking."

"Joe already told me about them," Polly said. "Do you think I could go with you?"

"I suppose. You'd have to ask your mother and also my Uncle John," Mandie said.

"Then let's go find out," Polly said, turning to go up the hill to the house.

The young people found Uncle John with Uncle Wirt and Elizabeth in the parlor. Not waiting for any greeting or explanation, Polly walked straight to Uncle John and asked, "Could I please go with y'all to search for the gold?"

Uncle John looked at her and then at the other youngsters.

"Do what?" he asked.

"You are making plans to hunt the gold, and everyone else is going, so I'd like to go, too," Polly explained.

"Now wait a minute," Uncle John said, addressing the anxious young people. "This business about the gold must be kept absolutely secret. No one is to know about it outside of our immediate group here. If it got to be public knowledge, we'd have half the country out here looking for it. We'd never find it. Do you all understand?"

They nodded in agreement.

Mandie sat down on a low stool near her uncle. "But, are we going to look for it?" Mandie asked.

"Uncle Wirt and I will," John answered.

"But, Uncle John, I am responsible for the gold. My Cherokee kinpeople put me in charge of it, so I must go, too," Mandie pleaded.

"It's too dangerous," Uncle John told her.

"I'm not afraid," Mandie protested. "I have to find it so I can give ten percent of it to the Lord, and we can receive His blessings."

"You can give the ten percent after Uncle Wirt and I find it," he reasoned.

Just then Snowball came into the room and jumped into Mandie's lap. That gave Mandie an idea. "I have to go so Snowball can go," she said. "Remember, he was the one who found Uncle Ned. Maybe he can help us find the bandits."

No one dared to laugh.

"Amanda, darling," Elizabeth said gently, "I want you to stay here with me to help take care of Uncle Ned. Please."

"But, Mother, Uncle Ned said we must find the gold so we can tithe," Mandie told her. "And he can't go, so I have to."

Uncle John finally relented. "All right, you youngsters can go with us to the wrecked train car, but I don't make any promises after that," he told them. Turning to Joe, he added, "If we get that far we'll stop at your father's house, Joe. He must be home by now."

"John, are you going to permit this?" Elizabeth asked in disbelief. "You know I don't want Amanda to go."

"I never could resist blue eyes!" he laughed. "Especially when they're so much like yours."

The young people dashed out of the room and ran over to Polly's house to ask her mother's permission. After a lot of talking, they finally convinced her that it was not dangerous, and that they were only going to the wrecked train car. Polly went home with Mandie to spend the night so they could start out early the next morning.

Mandie was excited about the trip to the wrecked baggage car, but would they ever really find the gold again?

CHAPTER NINE

OFF TO FIND THE GOLD

Before sunrise the young people quietly slipped out of bed and gathered in the kitchen. Jenny was busy preparing breakfast and food for the journey. Since Elizabeth was not going, Uncle John had told Liza she could go along to look after the three girls. Liza was so excited she danced around in circles among them while their conversation grew louder and louder.

Aunt Lou heard the commotion and came into the kitchen. "You best be quietenin' down or Mr. John'll be in here to see what's goin' on! Liza, 'member youse jest goin' to take care of my chile and these heah other li'l girls."

"Yessum," Liza calmed down. "I behave. I see to Miss Amanda and Miss Sallie and Miss Polly. I see they behave, too."

Mandie laughed. She knew the trip would be more fun with Liza along. "And I'll see that Liza behaves," she said mischievously.

"Lawsy, Missy," Liza said. "I ain't got nobody sweet on me to go smoochin' with."

Everyone broke into laughter.

"Git outa heah," Aunt Lou said, shooing the young people out through the door. "Git yo' breakfast in the dinin' room. Liza be bringin' it in a minute."

Mandie was the last one out of the kitchen. "Can Liza eat with us, Aunt Lou?" she asked.

"Hesh yo' mouth, chile. Liza don't belong in the dinin' room," the big woman told her.

"But, Aunt Lou, Liza's going to eat with us on the trip. She has to, or eat somewhere by herself," Mandie insisted.

"Well, that won't be under the roof of Mr. John's house," Aunt Lou told her. "While she under Mr. John's roof, she gonna act like the servant girl she be. Now, git on in there wid yo' friends."

"I just don't understand it, Aunt Lou," Mandie argued. "Why can't she eat with us? When I lived at my father's house in Swain County everyone ate at the same table."

"You'll understand some day, my chile. Now git!" the old woman said.

Mandie sat down at the big dining room table with her friends. Before long her mother and Uncle John and Uncle Wirt joined them.

"Uncle John, why can't Liza eat breakfast with us?" Mandie asked, as soon as her uncle was seated. "After all, she'll have to eat with us on the trip."

Liza came through the doorway with huge platters of scrambled eggs, bacon, ham, and grits. "Oh, you want Liza to eat with us?" Uncle John asked. Looking up at the young servant girl, he said, "Liza, you get a plate and sit down over there next to Mandie. We're all in this thing together beginning today."

Liza almost dropped the platters as she set them down. "What, Mister John?" she gasped.

"Mandie wants you to eat with us since you're going on the journey too. So get yourself a plate and sit down," Uncle John told her.

"Yes, Liza, sit right here next to me." Mandie used her foot to push out the chair next to her.

"Missy, I can't do that. Aunt Lou, she git all over me," Liza protested.

"But Uncle John is the boss here. You heard what he said. Get your plate," Mandie insisted.

Liza gave up. "Yes, Missy, I git me a plate and be right back," the black girl said, returning to the kitchen.

Elizabeth looked at John.

"I told you I just can't resist those blue eyes, especially when they look so much like yours," John told her.

"First thing you know, you'll have all the servants in an uproar," Elizabeth protested. "The other servants won't like the idea at all."

"Leave it to me. I'll take care of it if and when that time comes," John told her. "After all, I'm half Indian. I'm not expected to act in the usual 'white people' fashion," he laughed.

"Oh, John, you can be funny!" Elizabeth smiled.

Polly was sitting next to Mandie and gave her a nudge. "Mandie, you have some great parents!" she said.

"One parent," corrected Mandie. "Uncle John is still my uncle, even though he is married to my mother."

"They are very much in love," Dimar said, helping himself to more eggs and bacon.

She missed her father so much, it was hard to sort out her feelings about all that happened.

Uncle John was the "richest man this side of Richmond," according to Liza. Why hadn't he shared his wealth with her father who was desperately poor? She would always wonder about that.

Liza came back through the door with a plate in one hand and a platter of hot biscuits in the other. After putting the biscuits in the middle of the long table, she sat down next to Mandie.

"Here," Mandie said. She reached for the platter of eggs and passed it to Liza.

Joe passed the bacon and ham.

Dimar watched in amusement from the other end of the table. "Eat," he said.

"That's one word that's good in any language—eat," Joe laughed.

Liza nervously helped herself to the food, and then sat there pushing the food around with her fork. She cast a sheltered glance now and then at the others at the table.

"Liza, eat," Uncle John's voice boomed from the other end of the table. "We've got to get going."

"Yes, sir. Yes, sir, Mister John," Liza answered and quickly shoved her mouth full of food.

Sallie looked across the table at Liza and felt sorry for her. *Poor Liza!* she thought. *She's so nervous sitting at the big table that she can't eat.* She almost choked on the food and hurried to wash it down with coffee that was too hot.

"Please do not worry. We are all on your side," Sallie told her. "I felt the same way the first time I sat at this great table in this fancy house. You see, I live in a log cabin with my grandfather and grandmother."

"I ain't never lived in a log cabin, Miss Sallie," Liza replied. "I wouldn't know how to act in a log cabin."

All the young people laughed.

"I also live in a log cabin," Dimar told her.

"And so do I," Tsa'ni added.

Turning to Mandie, Liza asked, "Where all these log cabins at?"

"Liza, haven't you ever seen a log cabin?" Mandie asked. "You know I lived in a log cabin with my father, too. That's how people live out in the country away from town. Log cabins are scattered all over the woods and fields."

"I ain't never lived in de country either. I be born right heah in this house," Liza told them.

"You were?" Mandie said. "Where are your mother and father?"

"They be done dead with de new-moanie, long time ago, when I was a li'l tyke. Aunt Lou, she tuck care of me after that," Liza told them.

"My father died from the same thing," Mandie said.

Uncle John's voice boomed out again. "Eat up, everyone! Whoever is going with me, be ready in fifteen minutes."

He got up and left the table, with Elizabeth and Uncle Wirt following.

"You heard him. Eat," Joe said. "Let's hurry and get done!"

Liza tried her best to swallow the food. She *was* hungry, but to have to sit here with "Miss Amanda" and her friends was too much for her. She pushed her plate away and stood up.

"I'se done," she said. "Let's git our things and go."

Mandie looked at the girl's plate. "But, Liza, you hardly ate anything at all," Mandie objected.

Liza turned to her and spoke softly. "To be honest 'bout it, Miss Amanda, I jest didn't wanta eat in here with all these people. It'd be like you eatin' with Mr. McKinley in the White House."

"You really mean that, don't you, Liza?" Mandie replied. "I'm sorry if I spoiled your breakfast. I won't do it again."

"That's all right, Missy. Next time I eat in the kitchen where I belongs," Liza replied.

When they got outside, Uncle John had horses and ponies tethered at the front gate, loaded with blankets, rope, lanterns, and food. The adults stood waiting on the front porch. Elizabeth caught Mandie by the arm.

"Amanda, you haven't put on your riding outfit," she reprimanded.

"But, Mother. Sallie doesn't have one on, and neither do Polly and Liza," Mandie protested.

"I told my mother we were riding in a wagon," Polly explained. "I didn't know we were going to ride ponies. But it's all right. She won't mind."

Elizabeth frowned at her husband. "John, we need to teach Amanda some proper manners for young ladies," she said.

John laughed. "Why don't we let it go this time? It'll be quicker and safer in that rough mountain terrain if they all ride astride. Seems like I remember *you* saying the same thing not too long ago." He kissed Elizabeth on the cheek.

Elizabeth gave in. "It seems like I always come out on the losing end," she said with a little laugh.

Mandie took her mother by the hand. "Please tell Uncle Ned we'll be back soon," she said. "I didn't want to wake him this early in the morning to tell him good-bye."

"Of course, dear," Elizabeth answered. She gave her daughter a squeeze. "Be a good girl."

"Everybody ready?" Uncle John asked. "Run and find yourselves a pony."

Mandie picked up Snowball and rushed out to the road with the others to claim her pony. Mandie knew she had to help Liza feel comfortable with them. "Liza! Here! Get this pony next to mine!" she called.

Liza gratefully did as Mandie said.

Waving good-bye to Elizabeth, Aunt Lou, and Jenny, the group took off down the road.

A long time later, they approached the place in the railroad tracks where they knew the wrecked baggage car would be. As they drew rein and looked down the ravine, they spotted the wrecked baggage car still hanging onto the side of the mountain.

"We walk from here," Uncle Wirt told them.

Dismounting, they followed him carefully down the slope.

"Watch for trail marking," he said.

"Here is where we went down to the wrecked car," Dimar said, pointing to the spot. "Then we split up, and Sallie and I went over this way," he continued. "Tsa'ni took Mandie and Joe over that way and we all met at the river where we found Uncle Ned."

"When we came in answer to your call, we must have taken almost the same path then, Dimar," Uncle John replied. "That's a lot of shoes making prints in the dirt."

Suddenly, Uncle Wirt stooped to examine the ground. "Boot make this mark," he said, pointing to a firm print in the dirt. "We no wear boot!"

Uncle John bent to look at it. "You're right. That's the print of a hard heel and pointed toe, like riding boots."

"Him go this way." Uncle Wirt walked closer to the baggage car. "Then on. All way to train car."

"Great!" Joe said.

Mandie started looking around, holding Snowball tightly in her arms. "Now if we can find the same prints going *away* from the car . . ."

The group fanned out and soon Dimar called, "Here is the same print going toward the river."

Uncle Wirt found more. "Horses been here. Go up riverbank," he said.

"Yes," Mandie told him. "There were three of them. They came from all different directions."

"Do you want to look inside the baggage car in case we missed something?" Joe asked.

"It looks like it might roll away," Uncle John speculated.

"We went inside, and it did not move," Dimar told him. "It is leaning against big bushes on the other side."

Uncle Wirt headed for the broken place in the side of the car where the young people had entered before. He tried to shake the car, but it wouldn't move. He climbed up and went inside. Uncle John, Dimar, and Joe followed right behind him, but Tsa'ni stayed outside with the girls.

Liza surveyed the wreck. "Lawsy mercy, Missy. Thank the Lawd youse didn't go down the mountain wid dat car," she said.

"Yes, we have plenty to be thankful for," Mandie replied.

"Did you see it fall down the mountain like that?" Polly asked.

"No, but we heard the crash. This is the car my grandfather was in," Sallie told her.

"Oh, dat pore man!" Liza moaned. "So now we's gonna find the bad men what wrecked the train and hurt your grandfather?"

"We will *try* to find them," the Indian girl said.

"Won't you be afraid if we do?" Polly asked.

"No, I will not be afraid. We have all these big, strong men with us now," Sallie replied.

"I'd just like to catch up with them, for all the trouble they've caused," Mandie said.

Tsa'ni clenched his fists. "But they were white men and we are Indians," he said to Sallie. "We cannot do anything to them."

"That's what you think," Mandie told him. "You just wait and see what happens if we find them. Uncle John will see to that."

"Well, since he is living as a white man and not like an Indian, he can prosecute them, I suppose," the Indian boy replied.

"You know he is half Cherokee, but he can live as he chooses. So can you and all the other Cherokees," Mandie informed him.

"You certainly do not know much about it, do you?" the boy told her. "Someday you will find out what it means to be Indian by white people's standards."

When the men and the other boys came out of the wrecked car, the girls stared in amazement. Joe ran toward them wearing a tiger face mask like the bandits had worn.

"Joe, stop that!" Mandie gasped. "Was that mask in there?"

He nodded.

"It does not look so scary in the daylight," Sallie told them.

"Well, I'd sure hate to meet that thing in the dark," Polly declared.

"I'd be done passed out if that thing come toward me in de dark," Liza told them, moving away from Joe.

Joe took another step toward her and raised his arms.

"Liza, there were three of them. And it was dark. And they wore long, flowing cloaks and big hats," he teased.

Liza backed off. "Git 'way from heah!" she squealed.

Dimar came up and took the mask from Joe. "We did not find this mask when we went inside last time, because everything was broken and thrown around. But the railroad must have come since then and taken all the broken baggage out. All that is left is trash," he told the girls.

Uncle John and Uncle Wirt joined them in their discussion.

"That mask proves the bandits were in the baggage car," Uncle John reasoned.

Uncle Wirt nodded. "We trace hoof prints," he said.

Uncle John started for the horses. "We're going to see if we can follow their trail," he told the young people. "Coming?"

No one had to be asked twice. Back at the riverbank, they began the tedious job of tracking the bandits' horses.

The closer they got to the gold, the more danger awaited them.

CHAPTER TEN

A VISIT TO CHARLEY GAP

Uncle Wirt managed to pick up enough tracks in the dirt to follow the bandits' trail. Slowly and carefully, he led the way over the mountain.

The trail ride was fun for the young people. And, as Mandie had expected, Liza turned out to be the life of the search party.

"I ain't never been outside Franklin," Liza told them. "I thought the whole world was a city with lots of houses and people, but we ain't seen a soul 'cept us since we left the road. I wouldn't wanta live out heah." Her eyes opened wide. "I'd be askeered them bears and panthers and things would come and git me."

"When we see one, we'll let you know, Liza," Joe teased.

The black girl looked startled. "You mean we might come close to some of them things?"

"We might see anything in a forest like this," Dimar answered. "But I brought my bow and arrows. So did Tsa'ni and his grandfather. You are well protected. We will not let anything harm you."

Joe patted the rifle slung over his pony. "And Mr. Shaw and I are carrying rifles," he assured her.

Tsa'ni sat up taller in his saddle. "I also have a rifle, as well as my bow and arrows," he said.

"So you double smart," Liza told him. She turned to Mandie. "Missy, don't you think we oughta brought us a gun, too?"

Mandie laughed. "No, Liza, we might shoot somebody."

"But we could shoot the bandits," Liza said.

"No, no," Sallie protested. "We only want to capture them and turn them over to the law."

Polly gradually maneuvered her pony through the group until she was riding ahead next to Joe.

Seeing this, Liza leaned over to Mandie and whispered, "You better watch Miss Sweet Thing. She be after your Mister Joe."

Mandie laughed and then strained her neck to watch the two ahead. They seemed to be joking and talking as they rode along together. A pang of jealousy cut through her, but she could not let Liza know it.

"Oh, Liza, he's not my Mister Joe," Mandie told her. "He can talk to anybody he wants to."

"It ain't him, Missy, that I'm a'talkin' 'bout. It's that Miss Sweet Thing. She shore is tryin' to latch onto him," Liza warned.

"Polly is my friend, and she's also Joe's friend," Mandie replied.

"You jest watch what I'm a'sayin'," Liza insisted. "She layin' it on so thick the bees git drownded in it."

Mandie smiled but did not answer. Adjusting Snowball to a higher position on her shoulder, she petted the kitten thoughtfully. She knew Polly was interested in Joe, but she wasn't worried. She had known Joe all her life. Of course, Mandie was jealous when Polly flirted with Joe, but she tried not to let it bother her. She was sure Polly would eventually find someone else to "latch onto," as Liza called it.

Up ahead, the men stopped, and the young people hurried to catch up. John and Uncle Wirt dismounted and stood in a grassy spot, by a sparkling spring where the horses could drink.

"Eat now!" Uncle Wirt announced. "Must water ponies."

Taking their food bags from their ponies, the young people tethered the animals where they could graze near the water. Sitting on the rocks by the spring, they enjoyed the ham and biscuits, boiled eggs, and apples that Jenny had packed for them.

Uncle John came to sit by Mandie. "Uncle Wirt has tracked them this far, but we thought we'd better stop to rest and eat." He paused, then looked directly at her. "Do you know where we are?" he asked.

Mandie glanced at him and then around the forest, trying to find a familiar landmark.

"Uncle John!" she cried, grabbing his big hand. A tear trickled down her cheek.

Her uncle took out a big handkerchief. "Don't cry, dear," he said, wiping her tears. "You do know where we are, don't you?"

"Yes, yes, Uncle John." Mandie's voice trembled. "My father's grave is right over the hill up there and—and—his—house is not far away."

"I wanted you to know before we got there. I didn't want it to be a sudden shock," Uncle John said. "We'll stop when we get there, and I'll help you find some flowers to put on his grave."

Mandie buried her face on his chest as he hugged her to him.

Joe overheard the conversation, but had already realized where they were. He passed the word to the others, and they all became silent.

Uncle John got up and spoke to Joe. "We're planning to spend the night at your father's house tonight."

"Great!" Joe exclaimed.

When the others began to talk among themselves, Joe slipped away from the crowd and went to Mandie, who was sitting alone now, except for Snowball. He took her hand in his and squeezed it.

"Mind if I ride beside you?" he asked. "I know you've been trying to stay with Liza to make her feel comfortable. But if you don't mind, I'd like to be with you when we ride up over that hill," he said gently.

Mandie leaned forward and took his other hand in hers. "Of course, Joe. I want you to," she said with a smile.

After they mounted again, Joe and Mandie rode directly behind Uncle John. At the top of the hill, when the cemetery came into sight, the others stopped and waited. They knew Mandie wanted to be alone.

Mandie slid down from her pony, handed Snowball to Uncle Wirt, and took Joe and Uncle John by the hand. Together they walked among the graves until they came to the one with a home-made marker reading: "James Alexander Shaw; Born April 3, 1863; Died April 13, 1900." The mound had flattened some, and it was covered with grass. A handful of wilted flowers stuck out of a clay pot next to the marker.

Mandie let go of their hands and fell on her knees by her father's grave. Tears blurred her vision.

"Daddy, I still love you. I haven't forgotten you. I never will!" she cried softly.

Uncle John knelt by her side and put his arm around her. "Just remember that he's in heaven, darling. And one day you can see him there," he assured her.

"I know, I know! But I miss him! I loved him so much!" she said between sobs.

"I loved him, too, dear. He was the only brother I had." Uncle John stood up to pull a handkerchief from his pocket and wiped his eyes.

Joe squatted next to Mandie. "I'm sorry those flowers are dead," he apologized. "I know I promised you I would keep flowers on the grave, but I haven't been home for a long time. Want to look for some now?"

Mandie nodded, wiping her tears on her apron as Joe helped her up. "Yes, let's find some pretty flowers," she said, taking their hands.

Strolling around the edge of the cemetery, they picked several bunches of Indian Paintbrush and carried them back to replenish the clay pot.

Uncle John stared at the grave with its crude marker. "Mandie, we're going to have a real tombstone put on your father's grave, a granite one," he said.

Mandie smiled up at her uncle with tears glistening in her eyes. "One with a flower pot attached, so we can keep lots of flowers here?"

"Anything you want, darling. As soon as we can get time we'll go to Asheville and look at some," he promised. "Now I think we'd better go back and join the others. We have to pass awfully close to your father's house in order to get to Dr. Woodard's."

"We do?" She looked surprised and then added, "I suppose you do have to go down that road to get to Dr. Woodard's house."

"Yes," Uncle John replied. "But I know how much trouble your stepmother has caused. We're going to try to stay out of sight."

Joe helped Mandie mount her pony. "I haven't forgotten, Mandie," he said. "I'll get your father's house back for you when we grow up. Remember, I promised I would?"

"Oh, I hope you can, Joe," the girl answered.

Joe stayed close to Mandie from then on.

In her mind, Mandie relived the day their old horse, Molly, had pulled the wagon bearing her father's coffin up the hill to the cemetery. She also painfully remembered the empty ride back down. Silently, she thanked God for sending Uncle Ned to her. He had promised her father to watch over her and he kept his promise. He always turned up just when she needed him. Mandie wished he could have come with them, but Uncle John had insisted he was not well enough for the rough journey.

"Ps-s-st!" Joe leaned over and pointed. Her father's house was barely visible through the trees. They stopped their ponies and those behind them waited. The men looked back and slowed down.

"Just think," Mandie sighed, "all my life, I grew up believing that woman living there was my mother. Then my father died, and Uncle John showed me the truth. But I will always wonder why my father didn't tell me," she said sadly.

Joe's pony snickered and bumped into Mandie's pony, giving it a jolt. Snowball didn't like being jostled around on Mandie's shoulder, and he jumped down.

"Snowball! Come back here!" Mandie called. She slid down from the pony and tried to catch him. Joe quickly dismounted to help. But the kitten wanted to play games. Snowball ran and stopped until he thought they were going to try to pick him up. Then he ran again, too quick for them to catch him.

Everyone watched silently. Uncle Wirt had warned them that they must not be seen or heard by anyone at the log cabin in the hollow below.

"Snowball, come here!" Mandie tried to coax him. "Here, kitty, kitty, kitty!"

But Snowball had a mind of his own. He turned to look at her, meowed loudly, and then bounded through the trees toward the house below. Mandie and Joe started after him, but stopped in the shelter of the bushes at the edge of the clearing. The kitten went on.

As they watched from the bushes, they could see and hear someone talking. Moving to get a better view, Mandie's heart beat wildly. Her stepsister, Irene, and her boyfriend, Nimrod, sat on a stump by the side of the house.

"Nimrod, quit holdin' onto me so tight. It hurts," Irene protested.

"I jest wanna be near you," Nimrod answered.

Mandie looked around in despair. How would she ever get her kitten back? Snowball was roaming the yard below. Glancing up the hill, she noticed Uncle John motioning for her to come.

"We'll get Polly to go down and get Snowball," he said. "They've never seen her, so they won't know who she is."

"Maybe she can slip down there and get him before they see her," Mandie suggested.

"She can try, and we'll watch from here," Uncle John said.

Polly gladly consented, and cautiously made her way down the hill into the yard. The two on the stump had not seen the kitten. Snowball was nosing around a flower bed nearby. Polly eased up to him, but when she reached to pick him up, he let out a yowl. She quickly squeezed him in her arms so he couldn't get down. Irene and Nimrod immediately turned around and saw Polly with the kitten.

Irene jumped up. "Who are you? What you doin' here?"

"I just lost my cat," Polly mumbled as Nimrod towered over her. She turned to go, but Irene grabbed her by her black braid.

"Not so fast. This jest don't sound right to me," Irene told her.

The group on the hill watched breathlessly. Mandie was about to go down and rescue Polly when a loud yell startled her.

"Irene! Irene, where you at?" Irene's mother called from the back door. "Irene!"

Irene immediately let go of Polly. "Quick, Nimrod! Behind the barn!" she whispered. "Don't let Mama see you! I'll be back out soon as I kin git away from Mama. Wait fer me." Her mother continued yelling as Irene ran to the house.

Quick as lightning, Polly ran up the hill and disappeared into the trees. She didn't stop running until she reached Mandie and handed her the kitten.

Polly laughed. "Whew! That was a close call!" she said, trying to catch her breath.

Mandie put her arm around her friend. "Thank you, Polly. You don't know how much I appreciate that," she told her.

"That woman is your stepmother?" Polly asked.

"Yes, and that's her daughter, Irene," Mandie replied. "I lived in that house with them most of my life."

The weary group continued on. By the time they passed through Charley Gap and stopped in back of Dr. Woodard's house, the sun had disappeared beyond the mountains. When the doctor and Mrs. Woodard heard the commotion outside, they came into the yard to greet them.

"Light and come in!" Dr. Woodard called.

"Oh, Joe!" Mrs. Woodard cried, "it's so good to have you home."

Joe gave his mother a hug as his dog, Samantha, and her four puppies excitedly ran rings around him. Mandie had to back away from them and hold her kitten. Snowball didn't like the dogs at all, so Mandie hurried inside.

Dr. Woodard's house was made of logs like the others in the area, but it had two stories. Upstairs, there were four bedrooms, crammed full of huge beds with headboards that almost reached the ceiling. Mr. and Mrs. Miller, who lived in a cabin down the hill on the Woodards' property, helped out around the house.

Before long, Mrs. Woodard and Mrs. Miller had a delicious supper cooked and on the table. The young people ate as though they hadn't had a bite to eat for a month. Liza was still uncomfortable eating with the others, and offered to clean up the kitchen.

But Mrs. Woodard shooed all of them out.

"No, we don't need any help," she told them. "You young people just go out on the porch, or make yourselves comfortable somewhere, and rest. I know what you've been through today."

Mandie wandered outside to sit on the porch steps in the bright moonlight. Liza sat down beside her.

"Lawsy, Missy, if Aunt Lou knowed whut I be doin', sittin' at other people's tables and eatin' and then not even cleanin' up the dishes, she'd wring my neck. I could've at least put the vittles up instead of lollygaggin' around here doin' nothin'," Liza told her.

Sallie and Dimar came out and sat in the porch swing while Tsa'ni walked into the yard to play with the dogs.

"You see, Liza, I told you everybody sits at the same table to eat where I come from," Mandie said happily.

"Well, that ain't my style, I guess," Liza replied. "I think dat woman oughta let me do sumpin'."

Just then, Joe came out the door, overhearing what Liza said. "Liza," he said, "my mother considers you a guest in our house same as all these other people, and you sure don't go letting guests wash dishes."

Polly stood at the doorway. "Hey, Joe, how about showing me your horse that you told me about?"

"All right," he said. "Mandie? Liza? Y'all want to go, too?"

Before Mandie could answer, Uncle John called to her from inside. "Mandie, will you come inside for a minute?"

"Of course, Uncle John," Mandie answered. "I'll catch up with you later, Joe."

Mandie glanced at Liza, who made a face. Mandie sighed and then went inside. Joe and Polly were off to the barn. She felt that pang of jealousy again, and wished Liza would go with them.

Inside, Mandie looked around the finely-furnished living room.

Mrs. Woodard motioned toward the settee between her and Uncle John. "Sit down, dear. I won't keep you but a minute," she said. "I just wanted to give you some information for your mother."

"Yes, ma'am," Mandie replied as she sat down by the gentle, attractive woman who looked just a little older than her mother.

Mrs. Woodard handed her some papers. "This is information about the school your mother asked me to look into when I went to Nashville last week."

Mandie took the papers, noting the bold letters across the top. "Miss Tatum's Finishing School for Young Ladies," she read aloud. "Why, what is this for?" Her heart fluttered in fear of what it might mean.

"The school, dear, that your mother is thinking about sending you to," Mrs. Woodard replied.

Mandie sat there in shock.

Mrs. Woodard looked embarrassed. "Did you not know?" she asked.

Mandie shook her head, fighting the tears in her eyes that threatened to spill down her cheeks. "Leave home and all my friends, and go away to a strange school?" she whispered.

Uncle John walked over to Mandie and knelt beside her. "I'm sorry, Mandie. I thought your mother had discussed it with you," he said. "We've been trying to decide what's the best way for you to get your education since you live with us now."

Mandie's voice trembled. "Please, Uncle John, don't send me away," she begged. "I can go to school in Franklin."

"We talked about that, but they don't seem to teach everything your mother thinks you ought to learn," he replied.

Mrs. Woodard put her hand on Mandie's shoulder. "This school— Miss Tatum's—is one of the best schools in the southeast," she said.

"Several of my friends have sent their daughters there. They all liked it, and they seemed to learn all the necessaries."

Mandie squeezed her eyes shut and swallowed hard to keep from crying.

"Put the papers with your things, Mandie, and go on back to your friends," said Uncle John, giving her a little hug. "We'll discuss this with your mother when we get back home."

"Yes, sir," was all Mandie could manage to say. She took the papers upstairs and put them in her bag, then rushed back downstairs and out onto the porch.

Liza sat alone on the steps, while Sallie and Dimar talked together on the swing and Tsa'ni played with the dogs. That meant Polly was still with Joe in the barn. But now, the sinking feeling in her stomach made her lose all interest in joining them. She flopped down on the steps beside Liza.

"Better ya git down to dat barn and see whut's goin' on," the black girl warned her.

Mandie didn't answer. She was fighting tears.

Liza frowned. "Missy, what de matter?" she asked. "You done give up on dat Mister Joe? Dat Miss Sweet Thing might jest be spreadin' some of that syrup on him."

Mandie tried to smile and took a deep breath.

"I guess they'll be back soon," Mandie replied.

"Sound like you done wore plumb out," Liza said. "Ain't got enough fight left in you to do battle."

"Liza, why did I have to ask Polly to come along anyway?" Mandie fussed.

"Yeh, I'd like to know that m'self," Liza said.

"She is my friend, but I don't like everything she does," Mandie complained. "She's such a pest. I wish I hadn't asked her to come."

But Mandie would soon regret her unkind words.

CHAPTER ELEVEN

POOR POLLY!

At daybreak the next morning, Joe was in the kitchen starting a fire in the big iron cookstove when he was startled by heavy pounding at the back door. Rushing to answer it, he found Morning Star and two braves standing there.

"Ned send message for John Shaw," one of the men announced.

Joe opened the door wide and asked them to come in. "Sit down. I'll get Mr. Shaw," Joe told them. He pointed to the chairs by the cookstove.

The heat felt good to the Indians. Even in the summertime the mornings were chilly.

Joe darted upstairs, but met John Shaw coming down. Uncle John had heard the pounding and came to see what was happening. Uncle Wirt and Dr. Woodard were right behind him.

"Morning Star is here with two of Uncle Ned's Indian friends. They have a message for you," Joe explained.

As John came into the kitchen, one of the Indians rose, pulled an envelope from his belt and handed it to him.

Opening it, John recognized Elizabeth's handwriting. Silently, he read:

I am writing this for Uncle Ned. Uncle Wirt's son, Jessan, has brought him word that the bandits were seen in the woods near Asheville. There are several abandoned huts near Mr. Vanderbilt's property, and they are believed to be hiding out in one of these. Jessan said that someone found one of the long cloaks the bandits were wearing hidden in a woodpile near there. The braves and Morning Star will give you the exact directions. Uncle Ned is much better and insists on going out. Please take care of yourself, and Amanda and the others, of course.

I love you. God keep you for me.

> Your wife,
> Elizabeth

"Look at this," John said, handing the note to Dr. Woodard. Realizing Uncle Wirt could not read English, he gave him the details.

"Must go at once," Uncle Wirt said.

Joe sprang into action. "I'll wake the girls and Dimar and Tsa'ni."

Racing up the stairs, he pounded on the door where the four girls were sleeping. Then he burst into the room where the other boys were.

"Hey, everybody, get up! We gotta go! Uncle Ned knows where the bandits are!" Joe yelled.

Dimar and Tsa'ni, already dressed, rushed downstairs.

Mandie stuck her head out of the room. "We'll be right down!" she called.

Hearing the noise, Joe's mother came out of her room and hurried to investigate. Joe followed her down the steps.

Mandie pulled her dress over her head. "Just think, we've almost caught up with them. It won't be long now," she said.

"I wonder how my grandfather knew where they are," Sallie said.

"Yo' grandfather know everything, Miss Sallie," Liza told her. "He got eyes in de back of his haid."

The four girls laughed, and hurriedly finished dressing.

"This is getting exciting," Polly squealed. She turned her back for Liza to button her dress. "Let's hurry."

"Bring your bags," Mandie told them. "Joe said we had to go." She snatched Snowball from the bed, grabbed her bag and rushed out of the room. The others followed.

Mandie led the way as the girls raced down the stairs. Then suddenly there was a scream and Polly tumbled down on top of the others. Mandie, Sallie, and Liza managed to catch themselves, but Polly fell several steps before she could stop.

The pain showed on her face. "Oh, I must've broken something!" she wailed, rubbing her ankle.

Dr. Woodard rushed to the stairway and examined the girl's foot.

He shook his head. "It looks like you've got a nasty sprain in that ankle," he said.

"Oh, no!" Polly moaned.

The doctor picked her up, carried her down the steps, past the anxious faces below, and set her on a chair by Morning Star.

"Sprained ankle," he said to John. "Let me get my bag."

The doctor quickly bathed Polly's foot in a strong-smelling liniment. As he began to bandage her ankle, the girl winced with pain.

"You won't be able to walk on that for a few days," he told her.

"Of all the luck! What will I do?" Polly asked.

Morning Star patted her hand and said, "I take home."

"Home? But I don't want to go home. I want to see those bandits when we catch them!" Polly protested.

"I'm afraid you'll have to go home, or else stay here a few days 'till it heals," the doctor told her. "It will be a miserable trip back over the mountain."

"I am sorry, Polly," Sallie told her. "My grandmother will help you to get home."

"But I don't want to go home," Polly argued. She turned to Uncle John and asked, "Can't I go on with y'all?"

"Polly, I'm sorry but I don't think that would be a good idea. Your ankle will be painful for a few days, and we may be going into a rough part of the woods," he answered. "Morning Star will be going back to my house and you can go with her. I'll send Liza back with you, if you like."

When Liza heard this, her mouth dropped open. Here they were, getting near the bandits, and now she would have to give up the excitement to go home with Miss Sweet Thing. Like Miss Amanda said, why did they ever bring her in the first place?

After a quick breakfast, Mandie and Liza talked out in the yard.

"I jest don't like dat girl," Liza grumbled, throwing her blanket over the pony. "And now here she breaks up my tea party."

Mandie grinned at her friend. "I'm glad she has to go home. You'll be doing me a favor, getting her out of my way," she said.

Liza tossed her head and laughed. "Yeh, I guess you be right, Missy. I'll take dat Miss Sweet Thing right back home so she can't chase yo' Mister Joe no mo'. But she oughta not acome in the first place. She ain't nothin' but trouble."

Mandie avoided Polly until the Indians were ready to leave. Then she waved good-bye as Polly rode off with Morning Star, Liza, and the two braves. She stared after them for a long time, relieved to see Polly go. She knew she was jealous and shouldn't be happy over her friend's misfortune, but she kept telling herself it was better this way. After all, Polly had her own accident. Mandie had nothing to do with it.

Some time later, loaded with food and good wishes from the Woodards, the group, led by Uncle Wirt and Uncle John, once again continued their journey. Joe stayed close to Mandie, with Snowball on her shoulder, and Sallie and Dimar rode right behind them. Tsa'ni brought up the rear as usual. *There is something wrong with that boy,* Mandie thought. *He always stays far behind the rest of us. He doesn't talk much and what he does say is argumentative. Why did he even come along?*

Uncle Wirt took a shortcut he knew—up mountainsides, down inclines, across rivers, and through thick underbrush. Mandie began to wonder if they'd ever get there. Suddenly an Indian on horseback appeared out of nowhere and waited on the trail ahead of them.

Mandie squinted in the bright sunshine. Instantly, a big smile spread across her face. Digging her heels into the sides of her pony, she raced around the men ahead of her. She ignored their yells to slow down. Nothing could stop her. Catching up with the

Indian rider, she got close enough to grab one of his wrinkled old hands.

"Uncle Ned! Uncle Ned!" she cried. "What are you doing out here? We left you in bed."

The old man smiled at her and said, "Gold bad luck. Come see gold not make bad luck for Jim Shaw's Papoose. I promise him."

Just then Sallie rode up, looking very concerned. The other men and boys gathered around too, demanding to know why the old Indian had left his sickbed and come riding through the mountains like this.

"No more sick," Uncle Ned insisted. "Go find bad men." He patted his bow and arrows slung over his shoulder, and slipped down from his horse. "But now, time to eat," he said, finding a place to sit by the cool, tinkling stream.

Mandie sat down by him with her food, while Snowball curled up in the grass at her feet. "I've been thinking about what you told me, Uncle Ned—about tithing," Mandie told him. "God must be giving us blessings in advance. So much has happened. Tsa'ni was not killed when he fell off the railroad tracks. And you didn't die when the baggage car crashed. We have a lot to be thankful for already. Can there possibly be more?"

"Big God love Papoose," the old man said. "She ask. He answer."

"Yes, I'm thankful for all the prayers He has answered," Mandie said. "And I pray that this chase will soon be over. We have to get the gold back so we can make our tithe."

Mandie sat staring at the clear, sparkling stream as Joe came up to join them. "Did Polly get home all right, Uncle Ned?" he asked.

"Yes, foot big," the old Indian answered, holding up his hands to illustrate. "Sore."

"I imagine it had swelled pretty badly by the time she got home," said Joe. "Too bad she got hurt and couldn't go the rest of the way with us."

Mandie fought the jealousy that rose inside of her. "I don't think Polly should have come in the first place," she said. "She's not used to this kind of life. She has been brought up in town as a lady. She can't take the rough ordeals we get into sometimes."

"Oh, give her a chance," Joe argued. "She has to learn."

"Well, this was too long a trip for her to learn on. Let her learn something somewhere else," Mandie retorted.

"Mandie!" Joe exclaimed. "You ought to be ashamed of yourself talking about your friend like that."

"She's no friend of mine!" Mandie shot back.

"Mandie!" scolded Joe.

Uncle Ned smiled, looked at the two of them, and said, "Papoose got jealous streak for Joe."

Mandie's face turned red as Joe whirled to look at her. Grinning, he said, "Is that so, Mandie? Then you must think more of me than I thought you did."

Mandie jumped up and headed toward her pony. "It's time to go," she called back, picking up Snowball on her way.

Joe ran to catch up with her. Putting his hands on her shoulders, he turned her around to face him.

"Mandie, you don't have to be jealous of Polly," he said. "She's just a friend, that's all."

Mandie shook free from his grasp. "Oh, yeh," she replied sarcastically. She mounted her pony.

As the others got ready to move, Sallie rode up beside Mandie. Having witnessed the scene between Joe and Mandie, she tried to relieve the tension. "I would like to ride beside you, Mandie, so we can talk," she said.

"Of course, Sallie. Come on."

Riding off behind the men, the two girls talked back and forth about nothing in particular, but carefully avoided the topic of Joe. Finally Mandie decided to tell Sallie about the school in Nashville. She hadn't said a word about it to anyone else. She was hoping that somehow she wouldn't have to go.

"Sallie, do you know what my mother is planning?" she asked. "She is planning to send me away to school—far away from home."

"Oh, Mandie!" Sallie cried. "You will have to leave all your friends and your nice home?"

"Right. Mrs. Woodard gave me some papers for Mother," Mandie explained. "Mother had asked her to find out about a place called Miss Tatum's Finishing School, way out in Nashville."

"Do you have to go?" the Indian girl asked.

Mandie brushed a branch out of her way. "I don't know," she replied. "I told Uncle John I didn't want to. He said we'd talk about it with Mother when we got home. I don't want to leave all my friends and family to live at some school where I don't know anyone. That name sounds silly anyway. Imagine going to a 'finishing' school. Everyone would laugh at me."

"I would not laugh at you. I would feel sorry for you," Sallie told her. "Why can you not go to school in Franklin where you live now?"

"That's what I asked Uncle John, but he said they didn't teach some things my mother wants me to learn. I can't imagine what things they are, but I know I'd rather go to school at home where my friends are," Mandie said.

"I have heard that some of the girls enjoy going to these schools away off," Sallie told her. "They make new friends."

"I don't want to leave my mother and Uncle John and Liza and Aunt Lou and everybody. I'd even have to leave Uncle Ned. He couldn't come to a girls' school to watch over me," Mandie said.

"You do not know my grandfather," Sallie laughed. "He promised to watch over you, and nothing will keep him from doing that."

"It would be a hardship on him. He'd have to find a place to stay in Nashville. He couldn't very well stay at the school, and it'd be too far away for him to go back and forth," Mandie replied. She looked at her friend pleadingly. "Please hope and pray that I won't have to go."

"I will," Sallie promised. "Now I understand why you have been so upset since we got to Doctor Woodard's house."

"Upset? You mean you could tell it?" Mandie asked.

"Yes, you have not been as cheerful as usual," Sallie answered. "I believe you hurt Joe's feelings back there, but I understand now."

Mandie's eyes widened. "Hurt *Joe's* feelings? *He* got mad at *me*!" she said defensively.

"Did he? I think *you* caused the problem by criticizing your friend, Polly," Sallie told her bluntly. "Of course, it's none of my business, but I hate to see my friends angry with each other."

"You think I caused it?" Mandie asked, trying to remember exactly what she and Joe had said.

"Yes," Sallie replied. "I heard my grandfather say you were jealous, and I agree with him. Think about it, Mandie. You and Joe have been close friends all your lives. Suddenly Polly meets Joe and decides she likes him, too. That is enough to make anyone jealous."

Mandie frowned in bewilderment. "Then, what should I have said or done?" she asked.

"Just ignore Polly's attitude toward Joe," Sallie advised. "She will become disenchanted sooner or later. I think she is only flitting about. She is not serious about anyone or anything. That is just her personality. Some people are like that."

Mandie knew her friend was right. "Thanks for your advice, Sallie," she said. "I guess I have been mean, and I'm really sorry. I'll have to do something about it."

At the next rest stop, when they dismounted, Mandie walked over to Joe, smiled apologetically, and reached for his hand. "Joe, could we take a little walk?" she asked.

Joe was happy to see his friend smile. "Sure, Mandie," he replied with a big grin. "Let's walk down the stream a little ways."

They strolled silently for several minutes, then stopped to watch the tiny cricket frogs hopping along the edge of the stream.

As they stood close together, Mandie faced Joe and swallowed with difficulty. "Joe, please forgive me for acting like I did about Polly," she said. "I'm really sorry. I won't do it again."

Joe turned to face her, and smiled. "It's all forgiven, Mandie. I understand," he told her. "I've been riding next to your Uncle John.

He told me that you were upset because they were thinking about sending you away to school. I don't blame you. I'd be upset, too. In fact, *I'd* just plain rebel."

"Oh, Joe, it would be awful to leave everyone and go away by myself to some strange place with strange people," she told him, petting Snowball on her shoulder. "I just couldn't stand it."

"I'm sorry, Mandie. If I can do anything to help you out, I will," Joe promised. "I don't want you to go away either. I'd hardly ever get to see you."

"I know. I'd probably only get to come home for holidays, and there aren't many of them," Mandie said. Tears glistened in her blue eyes. "I just don't know what to do."

Joe pulled the bandana from around his neck and wiped away her tears.

"Don't cry, Mandie. We'll think up some way to get out of it," he said. "Maybe when your mother sees how you feel, she won't make you go."

"Maybe," Mandie said. "But she really wants me to learn how to be a proper lady."

"A proper lady?" Joe laughed. "That's funny. I thought you were a proper lady already."

Mandie giggled. "You know what she means. She wants me to learn how to put on the social airs."

"I'm not so sure I want my future wife to learn all that nonsense," Joe told her. "You might get so you think you're better than I am."

Mandie jerked his hand. "Don't ever say that! That will never happen! You know that!"

"Let's hope it doesn't!" Joe said.

Rejoining the rest of the group, Joe and Mandie continued on their gold-recovery mission. But, somehow, they had to find a way for Mandie to get out of going to Miss Tatum's Finishing School.

CHAPTER TWELVE

THE CREATURES IN THE WOODS

As the group got a glimpse of the wealthy Mr. Vanderbilt's mansion in the distance, Uncle Ned held his hand up signaling them to halt.

"Must be quiet. Go slow now," he told them. "Into woods." He pointed to a faint trail leading off to the left from the main road.

They followed him into the dark woods. The sun sank lower in the sky, and thick trees blocked out most of the remaining daylight.

The old Indian stopped in the thick underbrush and dismounted. "Leave horses here," he said. "Bring rope, bow, arrows."

"Joe, we must be awfully close now," Mandie whispered excitedly.

"Yes, and you stay back," he whispered, slinging his rifle over his shoulder. "I'll go ahead with the men."

Mandie took Snowball in her arms as she and Joe joined the group around Uncle Ned. Dimar stood ready with one hand on his bow and arrows and the other on his rifle. Tsa'ni trailed along behind.

Uncle John spoke in a loud whisper. "We will move forward slowly," he explained. "And when we spot the cabin, you young people stay back out of sight."

"I would like to go with you," Dimar volunteered.

"We'll probably need you boys later, but let us men handle things first," Uncle John answered. "We'll let you know what we're going to do."

They crept quietly through the woods until they came within sight of an old rickety cabin. Uncle Wirt pointed to the woodpile nearby. Running over to it, he held up one of the long cloaks the bandits had worn. It was just as Uncle Wirt's son, Jessan, had said.

There were three horses tied behind the hut, and an old wagon stood in front. The strong odor of fish cooking filled the air, and a faint sound of voices came from inside the hut. There were no windows in the hut—only one door, and it was standing open.

Uncle Ned slipped behind a tree on one side of the cabin, and Uncle Wirt moved into position on the other side. Uncle John hid behind a tree between the other two. The young people huddled together where they were, waiting breathlessly.

Suddenly Snowball jumped down from Mandie's shoulder and darted for the door of the hut. Mandie caught her breath and froze. When the kitten stepped into the clearing around the cabin, they all watched and waited anxiously.

Snowball walked straight through the doorway of the cabin. Immediately, there was a big commotion inside. The cat meowed loudly. "Hey, come hyar, you cat!" a gruff voice hollered.

Snowball ran out the door with a big, burly man close behind. He stooped and grabbed the kitten. Snowball started biting and scratching. The man shook him violently.

"You dumb cat! Bite, will you? I'll kill you for that!" he yelled.

The kitten managed to get loose, but instead of returning to Mandie, he ran in circles around the clearing. The man grabbed an axe from the woodpile and chased the cat furiously.

Mandie could stand it no more. She had to save her kitten. Breaking quickly through the underbrush before anyone could stop her, she ran into the clearing, intent on rescuing Snowball.

When the bandit saw her, he whirled and started in her direction. "How did you git hyar?" he bellowed. "Hey, you're that gal on the train with that cat, ain't you?" he said as he got closer.

Mandie began to chase Snowball, and the man chased her. Then, all of a sudden, a sharp arrow whizzed across the clearing and grazed the bandit's leg. He screamed and fell to the ground, clasping his bleeding leg.

A second man edged out of the hut to see what was going on. Uncle Ned and Uncle John rushed forward and knocked him down. With Uncle Wirt's help they tied him and the wounded man to a tree away from the clearing.

The third man, still inside the hut, called out. "What's goin' on out there?" There was no answer. He came to the doorway. But when he saw the others in the yard, he slammed and barred the door.

Mandie hurried with Snowball to the shelter of the trees. "Snowball, why do you always have to cause trouble?" she scolded.

Uncle John summoned the boys. "All right, come on if you want to help," he said.

The boys followed quickly.

"How are we going to get that man out of the cabin?" Joe asked.

"We can shoot him out," Uncle John suggested. "The cabin has enough holes in it to shoot through. Or we can just wait for him to come out. He has to, sooner or later," he said as the two old Indians joined them.

"Why do we not burn him out?" Tsa'ni asked.

"Burn him out? Suppose the gold is in that cabin and it burns up," Dimar protested.

"Gold wouldn't burn up," Uncle John informed him.

"Fire dangerous!" Uncle Wirt added.

"I agree," said Uncle John. "He doesn't really have a chance. We're all armed. The odds are in our favor. Everyone get your weapons ready. I think we can get him to surrender."

As soon as the bows and arrows and rifles were aimed and ready, Uncle John called to the man inside. "Come out!" he said. "We've got you completely surrounded, and we are armed."

There was no answer. Everyone waited silently, their weapons pointed at the only door of the old shack.

Mandie and Sallie remained at a distance, watching and biting their fingernails, afraid someone would get hurt.

Slowly, the door to the cabin opened, and the last bandit, seeing all their weapons, hurried out into the yard.

"Don't shoot! I give up!" he called as the men and boys advanced.

Quickly, Uncle Ned threw his rope around the bandit, and Uncle Wirt helped tie him up. After leaving him with the other two, Uncle Ned and Uncle Wirt joined the others.

"All right, let's go find the gold," Joe said, leading the way into the cabin.

The girls started to come forward and follow, but Uncle Ned waved them back.

"Stay!" he called to them, as he, too, entered the hut.

Mandie took the rope she was carrying and let one end dangle so that Snowball could play with it. Worry clouded her face. "What if they don't find the gold in there, Sallie?" she asked. "Those men might've spent it."

Sallie laughed. "I do not think they could spend that much gold so soon."

Snowball scratched around at Sallie's feet, throwing dirt everywhere.

The Indian girl looked down. "Why does Snowball keep scratching in the dirt?"

"I don't know," Mandie answered. "Snowball, please be still."

Then she saw what the kitten was playing with. It looked like a string, but when she stooped to pick it up, it wouldn't come all the way out. Part of it was buried under the ground. The more Mandie pulled at it, the more excited she became.

"Sallie, look!" she cried. "This string is attached to something underground!"

Sallie knelt beside her. "Do you think it could be one of the drawstrings on the bags of gold?" she asked.

"Oh, I hope so," Mandie replied as both girls started digging with their hands.

They were right. Within minutes they had uncovered one of the bags of gold. And from the looks of the tangled web of strings, it appeared that the other bags were there, too.

Mandie picked up Snowball and the bag of gold. "Let's get Uncle Ned!" she exclaimed, heading for the cabin. Sallie stayed right behind her.

As they got to the doorway, Mandie shouted. "Uncle Ned, we've found it!" They all stopped their searching and gathered around her. "It's buried out there where we've been standing all this time," she said, laughing.

With everyone helping it didn't take long to uncover the rest of the gold. After loading it into the old wagon in front of the cabin, they hitched up two of the bandits' horses. Then they brought the bandits back into the clearing and made them get into the wagon.

Uncle John looked at them with great satisfaction. "We're taking you into town and turning you over to the authorities," he said.

"Mister, please don't do that," one of them begged. "You've got yer gold back. Jest let us go."

Uncle John climbed in beside them. "How did you happen to know about the gold anyway?" he asked.

"Well, it's sorta like this. We got some friends you'ins knows. Rennie Lou and Snuff. They still in that thar jail but we'ins got out. They was the ones what told us about the gold," one of the bandits replied.

"Then we just hung around 'til we found out what you was gonna do with it. I acted like an ol' drunken bum and laid in that thar alley behind the bank in Bryson City while you'ins were loadin' it up," he said proudly. "I heard the whole plan."

"Oh, hesh up!" yelled one of the other bandits.

"Rennie Lou and Snuff," Uncle John repeated. "The man and woman who kidnapped Mandie, Joe, and Sallie in the mountains and then tried to burn down your barn, Uncle Ned. Remember, we took them into town and turned them over to the law."

"Bad people," Uncle Ned said. "These bad people, too."

"Take to jail," Uncle Wirt told him.

So that's what they did. On the way into town, the young people rode their ponies behind the men, while Uncle Ned drove the wagon full of gold and bandits.

When they turned the bandits over to the jailor, he said he would summon the local doctor for the wounded man.

Then Uncle Ned headed the wagon in the direction of the huge bank in downtown Asheville.

Uncle John knew the banker, and it didn't take long to unload the gold and place it in the bank's vault. It would be safe there until they could start building the hospital for the Cherokees.

Since it was getting late and they had missed their hotel stay, thanks to the bandits, Uncle John checked them into the hotel in Asheville for the night. Early next morning they began the trip back to Franklin. Elizabeth and Morning Star would be waiting for them.

It was exciting to stay in the hotel, but Mandie was anxious to get home and tell her mother all the wonderful news. Yet on the other hand, she dreaded any further discussion of the school in Nashville.

CHAPTER THIRTEEN

GETTING THINGS SETTLED

When the tired travelers finally reached Franklin, they found Elizabeth and Morning Star waiting for them in the parlor. "Oh, John, I'm so glad you're home," Elizabeth said, greeting her husband with a hug.

John kissed her. "We're all dirty, tired, and hungry," he replied, "but very happy to be here."

Elizabeth looked over the entire group. "You young people had better get cleaned up," she said. "Then go out in the kitchen and get a bite to eat. But after that, into bed, every one of you. You all need a nap—and no arguing."

There was no protest. Mandie's eyes sparkled. "Oh, Mother! Isn't it wonderful?" she bubbled. "The gold is safe. We finally found it. The bandits are in jail, and the gold is in the bank at Asheville!"

"I'm glad, dear." Elizabeth smiled. "We'll discuss your trip more after a while. Now go along with the others." She waved Mandie on through the doorway to clean up.

Jenny and Liza weren't around at the moment, but Aunt Lou waited for the youngsters in the kitchen. The old woman smiled and put her arms around Mandie. "My chile!" she said. "I knowed de good Lawd gonna send you back safe!"

"Aunt Lou, we found the bandits and the gold," Mandie said excitedly.

"I knowed you would." The old woman grinned. "Now, y'all jest get your food waitin' there on the stove and then git on upstairs to rest. I'se got to take some of this out to Mister John, and Mister Ned, and Mister Wirt and Miz Lizbeth."

The hungry young people gathered around the cookstove and began filling their plates, while Aunt Lou piled a large tray full of food for the adults.

Mandie and her friends could hardly hold their heads up as they ate at the kitchen table. They were too tired to talk—almost too tired to eat. They might have fallen asleep at the table had it not been for Aunt Lou's bustling in and out to wait on the adults. Aunt Lou finally sent them to bed, and they readily obeyed.

After that much-needed nap, as soon as Mandie could get away from the others, she hurried over to Polly's house. She had to make things right with her friend.

Polly sat on her front porch with her foot propped up on a stool. "Hello, Mandie," Polly greeted her. "Aunt Lou told our cook that y'all had got home. Do sit down and tell me what happened."

Mandie related the details of their trip to her friend and then fell silent.

"There's something you aren't telling me, Mandie," Polly said.

"Yes, there is," Mandie replied, twisting around in her chair. Her heart pounded as she tried to find the right words. "I don't know how to explain it, but I've had some bad feelings toward you, and I want to ask your forgiveness for being rude."

"Bad feelings toward me? When?" Polly asked in surprise. "And how can I forgive something that I don't even know about?"

"I suppose—I got a little jealous of, uh, of you and Joe," Mandie faltered.

"Me and Joe? That's funny." Polly laughed.

"And then when you hurt your foot, I was glad you had to go home," Mandie confessed. "Will you forgive me?"

Polly looked as though she couldn't believe it. "You were glad I had to go home? But then, why did you ask me to go along in the first place?" she asked.

"Because you're my friend," Mandie told her. "It probably doesn't make sense to you, but will you please forgive me?"

"Sure, Mandie," she said. "I know I talked like I was brave, but I have to confess I was getting tired of all that running around all over the mountain. And I sure didn't want to come face to face with those bandits. So you see, I was glad to come home, but I didn't want anyone to know it."

Mandie giggled. "Oh, Polly, I'm sorry," she said. "I am so glad for your friendship, and I wouldn't want to do anything to spoil it."

Polly changed the subject. "Guess what? My mother is sending me away to school," she told Mandie.

"No!" Mandie couldn't believe it. "Where?"

"All the way to Nashville," Polly replied.

"Not Miss Tatum's Finishing School for Young Ladies?" Mandie gasped.

"How did you know?" Polly asked.

"Because my mother has the same idea, but Uncle John said we'd talk it over," Mandie told her.

"You don't want to go?"

"No, I don't," Mandie said. "Don't tell me *you* really want to go."

"Oh, yes," Polly assured her. "I think that would be great fun to live at a school that far away from home."

"Well, I don't," Mandie stated flatly. "And I hope I can talk my mother out of it. I don't want to go so far away and not be able to see my friends and my family."

"My mother doesn't know that I know it, but she had other motives. You see, if I go away to school, she'll be free to travel all she wants to," Polly said. "I'll be more or less on my own, and that suits me fine. I wish you'd go, too, Mandie. We could have lots of fun together way out there away from everybody."

"Sorry, Polly, but I don't want to go. I may have to, but I'm not going without a fight," Mandie told her.

When Mandie got home, she found Uncle Ned alone on the front porch, and sat down beside him. Another matter still troubled her.

"Uncle Ned, I've been trying to figure out how we can give ten percent of the gold to the Lord," she said, leaning back on her hands.

"Cherokees make Papoose boss of gold," he said. "Papoose give tithe."

"But I mean, what can we actually do with the ten percent? Should we just give it to your church at Bird-town, or should we do something else with it?"

The old Indian thought for a moment, and then a big grin came over his wrinkled face. "Church no have music box," he told her.

Mandie smiled broadly. "Then that's what we'll do. We'll buy the biggest, most expensive organ we can find to put in your church," she said excitedly. "Do you think the other Cherokees will agree?"

"Cherokees give gold to Papoose," Uncle Ned told her.

"Yes, but I have to use it for the good of the Cherokees," she replied. "It really belongs to them. I'm only going to spend it for their good."

"Get music box for church," the old man said, nodding his head. "That be tithe. Then watch window open and Big God throw blessings out to people."

"We have already received many blessings," Mandie said gratefully.

"More to come," Uncle Ned assured her.

Mandie leaned forward and lowered her voice. "Uncle Ned, did you know that my mother is planning to send me all the way to Nashville to a finishing school?"

"No!" he exclaimed.

"Yes, and I will have to leave all my friends and family, and go to this strange school where there are all strange people and I won't know anyone," she complained. "And worst of all, you can't go with me, or even come to visit. What will I do, Uncle Ned?"

"Not good," her old friend muttered. "Must not send Papoose so far away."

Mandie stood up. "I'm going to talk to my mother and Uncle John about it right now. I'll let you know what happens."

Mandie found her mother and Uncle John in the small sitting room adjoining their bedroom. Entering, she sat down on a footstool near her uncle.

"Uncle John, have you talked to Mother about the school yet?" she asked, holding her breath. She feared his answer.

"That's what we've just been talking about," he replied.

"Well, what did you decide?" Mandie asked.

"That you won't be going to Nashville to school," Elizabeth answered. "However—"

"—That's good news," Mandie interrupted. "I'm so glad I don't have to leave my friends and go all the way to that strange town."

"Amanda, wait until I've finished," her mother reprimanded. "You won't be going to Nashville, because we've decided to send you to the school I attended in Asheville. It will be much closer. Also, your grandmother lives in Asheville. Remember?"

Mandie took several deep breaths to steady her voice. "But, Mother," she protested, "why do I have to go anywhere out of town? Why can't I go to school right here in Franklin?"

"The school here in Franklin doesn't teach everything you need to learn, and their standards aren't as high," Elizabeth explained. "You must be prepared for society."

"Once you get settled in and make some new friends, you'll like Asheville, dear," Uncle John tried to comfort her. "It's not very far away, and you can come home whenever you like—on weekends and holidays."

"Oh, phooey!" Mandie said in a defeated voice. "I want to live at home all the time, with you and Mother."

"But, Amanda, all girls have to be educated," her mother said. "Just be thankful that we can afford a private school."

Mandie didn't answer.

Uncle John made an attempt to smooth things over. "Let's try it for a little while, and if you don't like it, we'll bring you home. But I really think you'll make new friends there. And you'll be able to get better acquainted with your grandmother. You know, you've only seen her once."

Mandie remembered when she met the heavyset woman in the expensive clothes. Her grandmother had not been very friendly. Mandie wondered if she could ever break through that cold wall between them.

She stood up. "I guess I have to go if you say so," she said, managing a reluctant smile. "But at least I don't have to go to Nashville."

Elizabeth looked at John as Mandie left the room. "She doesn't realize how much we'd like to have her stay home where we can be with her every day, but there are things you have to sacrifice sometimes," she told him.

"I really meant that, Elizabeth, when I told her we'd bring her home if she doesn't like the school," John reminded her.

"Yes, I agree," Elizabeth replied.

Mandie rushed back downstairs to Uncle Ned on the front porch. "Uncle Ned, I don't have to go to Nashville to school after all," she told him, excitedly.

"Papoose stay home?" he asked, smiling.

"No, not exactly," she answered. "I have to go to a school in Asheville where my mother went."

"But that not far," the old man assured her. "I go see Papoose in Asheville."

"Will you, Uncle Ned?" she asked eagerly. "I won't know anyone there and it'll be awfully lonesome."

"I promise Jim Shaw I watch over Papoose. Keep promise," the old Indian told her.

Mandie looked at him suddenly, surprise dawning on her face. "You know what? We just planned the tithe, and I've already got a blessing. I don't have to go all the way to Nashville to school," she said excitedly.

"Blessing number one," Uncle Ned agreed. "More to come. We thank Big God."

"Oh, yes, Uncle Ned," she said, reaching to take his old hand in hers. The two of them looked up toward the morning sun.

"Thank you, God. Oh, thank you," she whispered.

"Thank you, Big God," the old man echoed, quickly wiping a tear from his eye.

Mandie knew God's blessings were beginning to shower down upon her.

MANDIE

AND THE
FORBIDDEN
ATTIC

To My Very Special Cousins,
H. D. "Jack" Wilson
and
Mary Ellen Mundy Wilson,

With Love and Thanks
for their
Encouragement Over the Years

CONTENTS

MANDIE AND THE FORBIDDEN ATTIC

"Train up a child in the way he should go;
and when he is old, he will not depart from it."
(Proverbs 22:6)

CHAPTER ONE

A STRANGE NEW SCHOOL

Mandie's heart did flipflops as the train came to a halt beside the depot in Asheville, North Carolina.

"Well, here we are," Uncle John said. "I see the rig from the school is out there."

Mandie could not speak. She knew the dreaded time for parting had come. She would be left at the school alone while her mother and Uncle John returned home to the city of Franklin where they lived. She couldn't stand the thought of leaving them.

It seemed like only yesterday that her father had died and she went to live with Uncle John. Mandie didn't know her real mother, Elizabeth, until Uncle John brought them together. Then before long Uncle John and Mandie's mother were married, and Mandie was delighted. But now, they were making her go to the boarding school her mother had attended.

"Come along, Amanda," her mother urged.

As though in a daze, Mandie trudged down the aisle. She felt numb and detached from the scene as she stepped off the train.

Elizabeth hurried over to the waiting surrey, and the old Negro driver came forward to greet her.

"Uncle Cal!" Elizabeth said as the family joined her. "This is my daughter, Amanda, and my husband, John Shaw."

Uncle Cal tipped his hat.

"John is my first husband's brother," she explained. "You probably remember Jim. I left the school to marry him. He was Amanda's father."

"Yessum, I sho' do 'member Mr. Shaw," the old man replied. "Pleased to meet you, Mr. John Shaw," he said, shaking hands.

Mandie held out her small gloved hand. "How do you do, Uncle Cal," she said.

"I'se jes' fine, Missy." The old man squeezed her hand warmly. "You sho' de spittin' image of yo' mama when she be 'bout yo' age," he said, surveying the little blue-eyed blonde. "Jes' wait 'til Phoebe see you. She gonna think Miz Lizbeth done come back to school agin."

Mandie smiled. "Thank you, Uncle Cal." Instantly, she knew she had a friend.

Uncle John began helping the old man load Mandie's trunk and bags onto the surrey. As Mandie watched them, pains of protest gripped her stomach. But she had promised her mother and Uncle John that she would give the school a try. They promised her that if she couldn't be happy there, they would bring her back home, and she could go to school in Franklin.

Mandie was determined to fight the sadness and loneliness of being separated from her mother and Uncle John. She would trust God to give her the strength.

As they drove the short distance from the train station to the school, Mandie rode in silence. She did not hear the horses clip-clopping down the cobblestone streets, nor her mother's conversation with Uncle Cal. She saw nothing of the town as they passed through. She was trying to be brave, but it wasn't easy.

As Uncle Cal turned the surrey up a half-circle graveled driveway, Mandie stared at the huge white clapboard house surrounded by magnolia trees at the top of a hill.

The surrey stopped in front of the long two-story porch supported by six huge white pillars. A small sign to the left of the heavy double doors read "The Misses Heathwood's School for Girls." Tall narrow windows trimmed with colorful stained glass flanked each side of the doors. Above the doors, matching stained glass edged a fan-shaped transom of glass panes.

Behind the bannisters along the veranda were white rocking chairs with green, flowered cushions. Over to the left, a wooden swing hung by chains attached to the ceiling. At the corner, the porch turned and went around the left side of the house.

Mandie's attention returned to the doorway as a short, thin, elderly lady, wearing a simple black dress, came out to welcome them. Leaving the surrey, John, Elizabeth, and Mandie started across the lawn.

"My, my, Elizabeth, dear. I'm so glad to see you," the schoolmistress said, smoothing her jet black hair with her hand. "This must be your husband and Amanda, of course."

"Yes, Miss Prudence, this is my husband, John Shaw," Elizabeth replied.

John removed his hat and nodded his head slightly. "How do you do, ma'am," he said.

Miss Prudence nodded in acknowledgment.

"And, Amanda," Elizabeth continued, resting her neatly-gloved hand on Mandie's shoulder. She pushed her daughter a little forward. "Amanda, this is Miss Prudence Heathwood."

Not knowing what else to say, Mandie echoed her uncle's greeting. "How do you do, ma'am."

"Welcome, Amanda. I know you're going to like it here," Miss Prudence told her.

Mandie wished she could be that sure.

Miss Prudence called to the Negro who waited by the surrey. "Uncle Cal, please take Miss Amanda's things to the third floor, room three."

"Yessum," Uncle Cal replied.

Miss Prudence turned back to Elizabeth. "Do come in, Elizabeth—all of you," she said, leading the way.

They followed the woman through the doorway into a large center hallway. Mandie stared upward. Delicate plaster-of-Paris angels and roses decorated the high white ceiling. Across the hall a huge chandelier, which seemed to hold a hundred candles, hung near the curved staircase leading to a second-story balcony. Dark wooden wainscoting covered the lower third of the wallpapered walls.

Miss Prudence led them off to the right into an alcove furnished with huge tapestry-covered chairs. A large flower arrangement sat on a marble-topped table.

They sat down in big, comfortable chairs.

Elizabeth leaned forward. "John and I will be taking the train home this afternoon," she said.

"Oh? You aren't staying at your mother's?" Miss Prudence asked.

"No, she's out of town," Elizabeth answered.

She's always out of town when we come to Asheville, Mandie thought. *Maybe she is still angry with Uncle John for reuniting Mother and me after she went to so much trouble to separate us.*

Mandie hardly looked up when a maid came in to serve cold lemonade. Mandie's mother and Miss Prudence continued their conversation, but Mandie didn't hear it. She was deep in her own thoughts.

She still couldn't understand why her father hadn't revealed the truth about her mother and stepmother. Her stepmother had been so unkind. Without Uncle Ned, her father's old Cherokee friend, Mandie wouldn't have found her Uncle John and her real mother. *Maybe Grandmother doesn't want me because my father was half Cherokee*, she thought.

Suddenly Mandie realized that someone was talking to her. "I'm sorry, Mother, I didn't understand what you said," she apologized.

"Miss Prudence was saying that we may use the guest room on this floor to freshen up. It'll soon be time to go to the dining room," her mother explained.

Mandie quickly rose. "Yes, ma'am. That would be a good idea."

Miss Prudence led the way down the hallway. "Right this way," she said. "Of course, Elizabeth, you know where it is. I don't think we've changed a thing since you were a student here. We haven't even installed those new electric lights everyone is talking about."

She stopped at the guest-room doorway. "I'll meet you in the dining room at twelve sharp. The other girls have already arrived. We can accommodate only twenty at the table at a time, so we have two sittings."

"Then you have twice as many girls now as you did when I was here." Elizabeth smiled. "We'll be prompt."

The guest room was beautifully decorated. A handsome four-poster bed stood in the middle of the floor. Clean towels and a large ceramic bowl and pitcher of water waited on a washstand in the corner. But going to a door in the far wall by the fireplace, Elizabeth found a bathroom, complete with water tank high on the wall, and a chain to pull for flushing the commode. There was a bathtub standing on four feet that looked like claws, and an enormous marble lavatory with cut glass handles on the faucets.

"This is lovely. I should be out shortly," Elizabeth said, closing the bathroom door behind her.

Uncle John sat down in a velvet-covered chair near the bed. "I'll rest here," he said.

"Me too," Mandie added. Plopping down onto a footstool, she removed her bonnet and gloves, and discarded her small purse on the floor. She was wearing a very proper traveling dress of brown silk and matching buttoned shoes, white silk stockings under the long, full skirt, and white gloves with tiny pearl buttons. The outfit was only one of many that her mother had a seamstress make for Mandie's school term. Mandie was already tired of the fancy clothes. She sighed, propped her elbow on her knee, and rested her chin in her hand.

"Tired?" Uncle John asked.

"I'm so tired and disgusted already!" Mandie told him in a shaky voice. She fought back the tears.

"Come now, dear," he said, reaching to pat her blonde head. "You promised us you would at least try it."

"I know, Uncle John. It's just all so strange." She took a deep breath to steady her voice. "I've never been in a place like this before."

"It'll take time. But before you know it you'll be home for a holiday and telling us how much you like the school."

"I'll try. But please tell Uncle Ned not to forget his promise to visit me on the first full moon. That will be Thursday of next week."

"I will, Mandie. We all love that old Indian. I'm sure he'll keep his word to your father when he died to watch over you. He'll be here. You can depend on him."

The sound of laughter and talking drifted down the hall.

Uncle John looked at his pocket watch.

"Wash up, Mandie, and get your mother. It's time to eat."

A few minutes later, Elizabeth led the way to the huge dining room where several girls stood behind chairs around the long table. Sparkling red glass dishes lay on the crisp white tablecloth, ready for the meal. The Shaws hesitated just inside the French doors. Miss Prudence entered from the opposite side of the room and motioned for them to sit near her at the head of the table.

Mandie reluctantly took her place behind the chair next to Uncle John. On the other side of her, a tall girl with black hair and deep black eyes stared at her without speaking, or even smiling.

Miss Prudence shook a little silver bell as she stood at the head of the table. "Young ladies," she announced, "we will return our thanks." Miss Prudence watched to see that every head was bowed and then spoke, "Our Gracious Heavenly Father, we thank Thee for this food of which we are about to partake, and ask Thy blessings on it and on all who are present. Amen. Please be seated."

There was a scraping of chairs as they all sat down.

"Since everyone has arrived now," Miss Prudence continued, "we would like you to get acquainted. Please introduce yourselves and tell us where you are from. We will begin with Etrulia and go around the table."

The introductions began, but Mandie was too tense to remember the names.

Then the girl next to her spoke. "I'm April Snow," the black-haired girl said in a rebellious tone, "and I'm from Nashville, Tennessee."

There was silence and Mandie realized they were waiting for her to speak.

"My name is Amanda Shaw, Mandie for short, and I'm from Franklin," she said, twisting her fingers together.

"And, young ladies," Miss Prudence added, "these are Amanda's parents, Mr. and Mrs. John Shaw."

John and Elizabeth smiled, but Mandie caught her breath. These were not her parents, plural. She had only one real parent—her mother. Miss Prudence knew that Uncle John was not Mandie's father. How could she say such a thing? Mandie wanted all the world to know that her dear father was Jim Shaw and that he was in heaven now. Mandie didn't dare speak up, but she realized it would be difficult to untangle Miss Prudence's remark.

At the end of the meal Miss Prudence stood again and rang the bell.

"Since classes don't begin until tomorrow," she announced, "you may have the rest of the day to unpack and get to know one another."

Everyone left quickly so that the table could be cleared and reset for the second seating. Miss Prudence took the opportunity to show the Shaws around.

On the main floor, they toured the dining room, kitchen, parlor, music room, library, and two classrooms. Miss Prudence's and Miss Hope's rooms were on this floor. A connecting room also served as the school office.

On the second floor, there were more classrooms, two huge bedrooms and two baths. Each bedroom had four double beds to accommodate eight girls. Mandie's room was on the third floor where the new students lived. There were three bedrooms with four double beds, two bathrooms, and more classrooms.

When they entered the last bedroom, Mandie was alarmed to find her trunk and bags standing at the foot of a huge bed.

"This is the room you will live in, Amanda," Miss Prudence informed her. "You will share this bed with April Snow, and there will be six others rooming with you."

Mandie cringed. *There's no privacy,* she thought, *not even to say my prayers!*

Minutes later, in the alcove downstairs, Mandie tearfully kissed her mother and Uncle John good-bye. Then Uncle Cal took them back to the train station.

Mandie sat alone in the alcove for a long time, trying to compose herself before encountering any of the other girls. She whispered a prayer asking God to see her mother and Uncle John safely home, and to give her the strength to live up to her mother's wishes.

Finally she slipped down the hall and into the guest bathroom to bathe her face. Still not wanting to talk to anyone, she went out onto the veranda and sat in the swing. But April Snow found her anyway.

Standing squarely in front of Mandie, she said, "I would suggest that you get busy and unpack your things, or do something with them. They are in the way. Everyone else has finished unpacking."

Mandie stood up quickly. "Oh, I'm sorry. I didn't stop to think—"

"There's no time to stop and think around here," April interrupted. She sauntered off to the other side of the porch.

Mandie took a deep breath to control her anger and headed for her new sleeping quarters. She met some of the girls coming down the stairs, and when she got to the bedroom she realized that the others had indeed finished.

At the evening meal everyone seemed to be talking to everyone else. No one spoke to Mandie. She silently pushed the food around on her plate until Miss Prudence rang the bell and stood to recite the rules.

"Young ladies," the schoolmistress began. "All lamps will be extinguished at ten o'clock each night. No one is allowed out of the room after that. Aunt Phoebe, Uncle Cal's wife, will knock on your doors at seven in the morning to wake you. First breakfast sitting will be at seven-thirty. You are dismissed for the day now."

Mandie spent the evening by herself in a rocker at the end of the veranda. No one approached her for conversation, and she was glad to be left alone in her misery.

When bedtime came, April informed Mandie which side of the bed she could have and demanded that Mandie not wriggle around, snore, or talk in her sleep. Mandie numbly agreed and crawled into her side of the bed—next to the wall.

Unable to sleep, Mandie lay very still, not wanting to disturb April. She wondered what her mother and Uncle John were doing. She missed her friends back home. The girl next door, Polly Corn-wallis, had been sent to a school in Nashville. Mandie wondered if Polly liked her school. *I can't wait until next week*, she thought. *Then Uncle Ned will be here.* He truly cared about her. And he would give her a report on her other Indian friends and relatives. She hoped he would also have news from her special friend, Joe, Dr. Woodard's son.

Mandie turned her head on the pillow. She was worried about her kitten, Snowball, too. She had never left him before.

After what seemed like hours, Mandie could hear the girls' slow, even breathing around the room, and she decided that everyone else was asleep. Slowly and quietly, she crept out of the end of the bed. She slipped out into the hallway, barefooted and in her nightgown. She remembered seeing a window seat at the other end of the hall. On tiptoe she made her way there where she could sit, and look at the stars, and talk to God.

There was not one minute of privacy in this place.

Near the window seat Mandie noticed a small bedroom with only one bed. The room was right next to the stairs to the attic and the servants' stairway going down. Mandie wished she could have that room.

She thought of when she lived with her father and stepmother on the farm at Charley Gap. Everything was fine until her father died and her stepmother quickly remarried. She couldn't get rid of Mandie soon enough. Uncle Ned had helped her find her Uncle John. She didn't even know about him until then. Mandie remembered the first time she met her mother. And then when Uncle John and her mother married, Mandie was excited to be part of a real family again.

Suddenly Mandie heard a sound of metal clanging and boards squeaking. The noise seemed to be coming from the attic above her. She froze, holding her breath and listening. But nothing else happened.

Maybe one of the servants sleeps in an attic room, she thought. But then she remembered that Miss Prudence had said Uncle Cal and Aunt Phoebe had their own little cottage in the backyard. The other servants lived in town and came in during the day. *Oh, well, maybe it was a rat*. She took a deep breath, trying to dismiss her concern.

There! It did it again! The same noise. It couldn't be a rat. Mandie wasn't going to wait to hear the noise again. She ran quietly back to her room.

Slipping into bed she lay awake, listening. Would she hear the noise again, or was her room too far away? The only sound was the deep breathing of the other girls.

With her thoughts still on the noise, she finally drifted off to sleep. Someday she would have to sneak up to the attic and investigate.

CHAPTER TWO

SILLY LESSONS

The next morning, Mandie dressed and appeared for breakfast. The other girls ignored her, but Mandie was content to be left alone.

The morning was spent in the classrooms with two young lady teachers who lived in town. When Mandie heard about the so-called social graces the girls were expected to learn, she silently rebelled.

"Each girl will practice walking up and down the hallway, balancing a book on her head," Miss Cameron instructed. "This will correct your posture and develop that dainty step that all ladies have."

The girls laughed.

Miss Cameron tapped her pencil on her desk. "That is not conduct becoming to a lady. You will show proper courtesy toward adults," she said sternly. "And I assure you that carrying a book on your head without its falling is not easy, however frivolous it may sound."

At first Mandie thought the task was impossible. Then she learned to go very slowly and hold her breath.

The next lesson was how to stoop properly to pick up something from the floor.

"A lady never bends forward with her posterior in the air," Miss Cameron informed them. "You must always bend your knees and slowly lower your body until your hand can reach the desired object. Then you slowly straighten up, smoothing your skirts as you stand."

This exercise made Mandie feel like an old lady too feeble to bend.

And then Miss Cameron offered instructions on how a lady controls her voice. "A lady never, never shouts," she said. "Even when she is angry, she keeps her voice under control. A lady never talks loudly to someone too far away to hear normal conversation. She walks over to the person to talk to them, rather than yelling from a distance."

Such silly stuff, Mandie thought. She was thoroughly disgusted with the school. *How could I ever endure it without God's help?* she wondered.

At the noon meal Miss Prudence introduced a new girl who had just arrived. She sat on the other side of Mandie.

"Young ladies, this is Celia Hamilton from Richmond," Miss Prudence told them. "She will occupy the small vacant room on the third floor."

Mandie turned to the tall, slender girl with thick, curly auburn hair and looked into the saddest eyes she had ever seen.

Mandie's heart went out to her. She smiled and said, "Welcome."

"Thank you," Celia answered with a faraway look in her green eyes.

Neither said anything more, and when Miss Prudence dismissed them after the meal, Mandie had to go on to the next class on her list.

Celia didn't show up for supper. Miss Prudence announced that the new girl was tired from her trip and was excused from the evening meal so that she could retire early.

After the dining room had been cleared, Mandie and the others went out onto the veranda. Mandie sat alone while the other girls talked in small groups. After a while, Mandie went to the kitchen to get a drink of water.

As she pushed open the swinging door, Mandie almost collided with an old Negro woman who was tidying up the kitchen.

"I'm sorry," she quickly apologized.

The woman stopped working and stared at her. "Lawsy mercy, if you ain't Miz Lizbeth all over agin."

Mandie smiled and held out her hand.

"You must be Aunt Phoebe, Uncle Cal's wife. He said you'd say that when you saw me." Mandie giggled. "I'm Amanda Shaw, Elizabeth Shaw's daughter. They call me Mandie."

"And why ain't dat man tole me Miz Lizbeth's got a daughter and dat she be right heah under my nose." Aunt Phoebe put her arm around the girl and gave her a big squeeze. "Lawsy mercy, Missy Manda. I sho' am proud to have you heah."

"I'm not so glad to be here, Aunt Phoebe," Mandie confided.

"Heah, lemme git you a glass of dis heah milk I'se puttin' 'way and you set right down theah and tell old Phoebe what be wrong."

The woman quickly poured a glass of milk from the pitcher on the sideboard and handed it to Mandie. She motioned to the table in the corner. They sat down, and soon Mandie was opening her heart to Aunt Phoebe and telling her all her troubles.

"So, you see, Aunt Phoebe, I really don't want to be here," Mandie admitted. "I think it's a prissy school. I don't care about learning all those silly things they've been teaching us today. I'm not that kind of person. I love to live the way God intended we should—walk, chase butterflies, watch birds, and maybe even climb trees," she added with a big grin.

"Missy Manda, you sho' not like yo' mother when she yo' age. She liked to dress up and act like a lady."

"But my mother was brought up that way. I wasn't. I lived in the mountains in a log cabin almost all my life, and my friends are not society people. Why, my best friends are Indians and country people who would make fun of these put-on airs." Mandie whirled the empty glass on the table.

"But now you live wid yo' mother. You got to live de way she do," Aunt Phoebe reminded her. "Her pa was a rich man. And now she be married to Mistuh John Shaw. He be de richest man dis side o' Richmon'."

Mandie laughed. "That's exactly what Liza said about Uncle John."

"And who be Liza?"

"Liza is my friend. She works at Uncle John's house in Franklin." Mandie smiled. "She's always getting into trouble with Aunt Lou. Aunt Lou is the boss. She runs the house for Uncle John."

"Dey be my kind o' people? Dark skinned?"

"Yes, Aunt Phoebe. Why, you even remind me of Aunt Lou, except that she is much fatter," Mandie teased.

"Well, you say Aunt Lou be de boss theah, den I be de boss heah," the old woman said, rising from the table. "It be time fo' you to go to yo' room. It soon be ten o'clock and you don't wanta git in bad wid Miz Prudence, leastways not whilst you still new."

"I didn't realize it was so late." Mandie quickly embraced the old woman. "Good night. I'll see you tomorrow."

"Young ladies not 'llowed in de kitchen, and I don't go in de dinin' room. I does de cookin'. Millie does de waitin' on de table."

"But you have a house in the backyard, don't you? I'll come back there to visit you."

"I don' know 'bout dat. Ain't nobody ever done dat 'fore. It might not be 'llowed."

"Well, I won't ask." Mandie grinned. "I'll see you as soon as I can find a chance."

Hurrying up the stairs to her room, Mandie found the other girls in their nightgowns, talking or reading in bed. April lay reading, propped up with both pillows. She looked up. Mandie quickly entered the room, took her nightgown from her designated drawer in the huge bureau, and ran for the bathroom to undress.

When Mandie returned in her nightgown, carrying her clothes, April looked up again.

"What's the matter? You afraid to undress in front of the other girls?" April asked.

"Of course not," Mandie replied, hanging her dress on the hook assigned to her. "I took a quick bath."

"Bath? You have to get a time on the schedule to do that. The rest of us have already made up a list," April informed her.

"A list?" Mandie went to the side of the bed to get in. "What do you mean?"

"With eight girls to a bathroom, we had to decide who was going to take a bath when. So, four of us will be taking baths at night and four in the morning," April explained. "Each girl will have just ten minutes in the bathroom. The only ten minutes left is from six-twenty to six-thirty in the morning. No one wanted to get up that early." April grinned. "And since you weren't here when we made up the schedule, you'll have to take your bath then."

Silence fell over the room. The other girls watched for Mandie's reaction.

"That's fine with me." Mandie gave a little laugh as she slid between the sheets. "I like to get up early. I've been doing that all my life."

"You'll get tired of it," April said.

Mandie reached for a pillow behind April and gave it a yank. "I believe you have my pillow. There's only one pillow for each girl."

April pressed backward, trying to prevent her from pulling it away, but Mandie succeeded. She plumped up the pillow and lay down.

"Humph!" April said, rearranging the pillow that was left.

Suddenly a loud bell rang from somewhere nearby. The girls looked startled. Mandie sat up in bed.

April laughed. "That's the huge bell in the backyard. It's ten o'clock. They want to be sure we know it." She stuck the book she was reading under the mattress and blew out the oil lamp by the bed. The other girls quickly extinguished their lights, and the room became dark.

Mandie lay very still, not wishing to disturb the haughty girl sharing her bed. But the other girls continued whispering and giggling.

After a while April raised her voice to them. "All right, maybe you aren't sleepy but I am, and I want quiet in this room," she ordered. "Remember, they will wake us up at the ungodly hour of seven o'clock and those taking morning baths have to be up before that. So stop the noise and go to sleep," she commanded.

Although they quit talking immediately, for a long time there was the sound of restless tossing and turning in the other beds. Finally April dozed off and soon the only sound was the quiet breathing of the sleeping girls.

Mandie was not sleepy, and she hadn't had a chance to say her prayers, so she slipped out of bed and walked softly to the window seat at the end of the hall.

As she sat there looking at the moonlight among the trees and the stars twinkling in the sky, she heard a muffled sob. Tiptoeing to the stairway leading to the attic, she stopped and listened. No, it wasn't coming from the attic. It must be in the small bedroom. She eased up to the door and listened. Someone was definitely crying. She couldn't decide whether to open the door or not. Then she remembered the new girl, Celia. She was in that room because the other rooms were all full.

Mandie turned the doorknob and pushed the door slightly. In the dim moonlight from the windows she could see a sobbing figure on the bed. She stepped inside and softly shut the door behind her.

"Celia, is that you?" she whispered loudly.

The sobs immediately stopped, and Celia turned to see who was in her room.

"Celia, it's Mandie. What's wrong?" she asked, approaching the bed.

The other girl sat up. "Oh, they'll catch you out of your room!" she cried in a shaky voice.

Mandie sat on the side of the bed. "Everyone else is asleep," she said. "Now tell me what's wrong."

"Oh, Mandie, I'm just lonely and—and—" She began to sob.

"I'm lonely, too," Mandie replied. "But there's something else wrong, isn't there?"

"Y-Yes," the girl sobbed, pushing the pillows up against the headboard.

"What is it, Celia? Tell me. Maybe I can help."

"No one can bring my father back," Celia cried.

"Your father? He's dead?"

"That's why I was late coming to school," Celia explained.

"He died recently?"

"He—he was thrown from a horse last week. He was just— just buried the day before yesterday. Oh, Mandie, I loved him so much!"

Tears came into Mandie's blue eyes. She put her hand on the other girl's shoulder. "I know how you feel. My father . . . died, too. And I loved him very much. I miss him, and I think about him every day, remembering all the wonderful times we had together."

Celia dried her eyes. "Did he die suddenly?"

"Yes, he wasn't sick very long," Mandie told her. "I know how you feel, Celia. I loved my father more than anyone else on this earth. But, you know, he's up there in heaven now, waiting for me. Someday I'll be with him again."

"Do you really believe that, Mandie?"

"Believe it? Of course I believe it. Please don't tell me you don't."

"I know it's all in the Bible, and I go to church and pray, but it's so hard to give him up." She broke into sobs again.

Mandie put her arm around the shaking girl. "Celia, please don't cry. It won't help at all. I know because I've been through it. You just have to throw your shoulders back, hold your head high, and believe in God," she said. "Celia, you have a mother, don't you?"

"Yes, my mother couldn't bring me to school. She was deep in shock over my father's death. I didn't want to leave her like that, but she made me come."

"She was probably right. I think it would be better to be here with other girls—to keep occupied. When I lost my father I didn't have anyone to turn to. My stepmother, who I thought was my real mother, got married again right after my father went to heaven. She sent me away to work for another family. If it hadn't been for Uncle Ned, I wouldn't have had anyone to talk to."

"Who is Uncle Ned? And how did you get here if you were sent away to work?"

"Celia, you wouldn't believe what happened to me. You see, Uncle Ned promised my father that he would watch over me when he died. Uncle Ned is a very old Indian, and he really keeps his promise to my father. He helped me find my father's brother." Mandie took a quick breath. "I didn't even know my father had a brother. And when I found Uncle John, he got in touch with my real mother and got us together. And then he married my mother."

"That's quite a story, Mandie, but I think I get it. Do you really have an Indian friend?"

"Sure, lots of them. In fact, my father's mother was a full-blooded Cherokee."

"Oh, Mandie! It doesn't make any difference to me, but if I were you I wouldn't tell that to the other girls in this school. They're all so uppity they would probably give you a rough time about it."

"I don't care if they know. I'm proud of my Indian blood. But since they haven't tried to make friends with me, I won't volunteer the information. Everyone seems to know everyone else, but I don't know anyone." Mandie sighed. "I didn't want to come to this silly school anyway."

"But, Mandie, you know me. I'm your friend."

"Thank you, Celia. I liked you from the minute I saw you. You didn't put on airs like the other girls."

Celia smiled. Mandie was glad to be able to take her friend's mind off her sadness.

Suddenly they heard the noise that Mandie had heard the night before. The sound of metal clanging and boards squeaking seemed to come from the attic. The two girls froze. The dimness of the room made it all the more eerie.

"Did you hear that?" Celia whispered.

"Yes, and I heard it last night, too. It sounds like something in the attic."

The noise stopped. The girls remained still, waiting for it to begin again. But it didn't.

"I don't like being way down here in this room alone," Celia told her.

"Maybe I could move in here with you," Mandie offered. "I sure wouldn't mind getting away from April."

"Would you want to, really?"

"I'd love to. Let's ask Miss Prudence tomorrow."

"Yes, let's do."

"If I move in here, maybe we could investigate the attic together, and find out what's making that noise."

"You mean actually go up there?" Celia stared at her with her mouth open.

"Sure. We could sneak out after everyone else is asleep," Mandie said. "You're not afraid to go up there, are you?"

"No, no, no. But what if we got caught?"

"Nobody's going to catch us. This room is far away from the others, and we'll be real quiet."

"But there's no telling what's up there."

"If we find anything awful we can scream our heads off. We'd get caught, but at least someone would rescue us." Mandie got up and started for the door. "Right now, though, I'd better get back to my bed before someone misses me."

"But I'm afraid to be left alone, especially with those noises up there."

Mandie reached for the doorknob and her hand touched a key sticking out. "Hey, there's a key in the door. As soon as I leave, you lock the door. Then no one can come in and bother you."

Celia jumped up and hurried over to examine the key.

"Thank goodness!" she exclaimed.

"I'll catch up with you tomorrow, and we can ask Miss Prudence if I can move in here with you," Mandie told her. "Now lock the door. Good night."

Mandie softly opened the door and stepped out into the hall. Hearing the lock click behind her, she hurried down the hallway and slipped back into her own bed. She hoped she could persuade Miss Prudence to let her move in with Celia. Then the two of them could find out what that noise was.

CHAPTER THREE

MANDIE'S ENEMY

Mandie and Celia met outside the dining room at breakfast and stopped to talk.

"Did you hear anything else last night?" Mandie whispered.

Celia shook her auburn curls. "Not a sound. I locked my door and went to sleep right away. Are we still going to ask Miss Prudence if you can move in with me?"

"Oh, yes—that is, if you want me to."

"Please do, Mandie. I'm afraid to be alone in that room. It's so isolated."

Miss Prudence came up behind them and Mandie turned around.

"May Celia and I speak to you for a few minutes after we eat?"

The schoolmistress looked from one girl to the other. "Of course, Amanda. I'll see you in my office."

Miss Prudence stepped into the dining room and stood at the head of the table. The girls took their places behind their chairs. Mandie and Celia smiled at each other.

The schoolmistress kept glancing at Mandie and Celia during the entire meal, as if wondering what they wanted to talk about. Mandie had not made friends with the other girls, and Celia seemed to be living in a world all her own. Aware of Celia's sad circumstances,

Miss Prudence had placed the girls together at the table, hoping they would develop a friendship.

After the meal, the two girls hurried out of the dining room, getting to the office ahead of Miss Prudence. They waited in the hallway.

The assistant schoolmistress, Miss Hope, was just leaving the office. She supervised the second sitting in the dining room.

"Did you girls want something?" she asked.

"We're waiting for Miss Prudence," Mandie told her.

Miss Prudence hurried toward them down the hallway.

"Well, here she is now," Miss Hope said. "Oh, dear, I almost forgot to take my announcements with me." She turned back into the office.

Miss Hope was shifting papers on the nearby desk when her sister, Miss Prudence, invited the girls into the office.

"Now," Miss Prudence began, "sit down and tell me what you wanted to see me about." The girls sat down in the armchairs in front of the desk.

Mandie looked at her friend and then at Miss Hope. Celia seemed frightened of the old schoolmistresses. Miss Hope appeared preoccupied with hunting for her papers.

Mandie took a deep breath. "I would like permission to move into Celia's room with her," she began. "She's all alone and so far away from the others."

Miss Prudence looked from one girl to the other. "It's not our policy to shift girls around once they are settled in a room," she began. "It would create quite a commotion if everyone requested to move."

"But I'm afraid to stay by myself in that room," Celia ventured. "Last night I just happened to find the key in the lock and I locked the door."

"No doors are to be locked. You may bring me the key at supper," Miss Prudence replied. "This place is new to you. You will get used to it after a while. Now, if that is all you two wanted, I have other things to do."

Miss Hope stood at the door, listening.

Mandie looked at her friend and began to protest. "But, Miss Prudence, Celia and I have so much in common."

"What Mandie means," Celia said, "is that we have both lost our fathers. She came to talk to me last night when she heard me crying."

The schoolmistress bristled. "She went to your room? What time was this?"

Mandie decided there was no point in lying. Celia had unintentionally given her away. "It was after ten o'clock," Mandie admitted. "I couldn't sleep, and I walked down the hallway. I heard Celia crying, so I went into her room to see if I could do anything. As we talked we found out we had both lost our fathers," Mandie explained.

"Young lady," Miss Prudence said sternly, "you know that it is against the rules to go outside your room after ten o'clock at night, much less visit in another room. Did you not hear me recite the rules yesterday?"

The two girls trembled at hearing her firm tone.

"Miss Prudence, I'm sorry I—" Mandie apologized.

"Sister," Miss Hope interrupted, "I see no harm in what Amanda has done. Quite the contrary. One of us should have checked on Celia to see that she was all right. We knew about her father's tragedy."

"Sister, I am handling this matter," Miss Prudence cut her short. "Now you two will obey rules here without any exceptions. Is that understood?"

"Yes, ma'am," Celia meekly replied.

"Yes, Miss Prudence," Mandie echoed. "I'm sorry I broke the rules, but Celia was all by herself in that room, and she was terribly sad and lonely. Could I please move in with her? Please?"

Miss Prudence looked at her sharply. Amanda didn't give up easily.

Neither did Miss Hope. "Sister, I see no harm in allowing Amanda to move into the room with Celia," she said. "In fact, I think it would be a good idea. That room is too isolated for one girl alone. Of course, I know you are handling the matter, but that is my opinion."

Miss Prudence was silent for a long moment, looking from her sister to the two girls. Mandie and Celia held their breath, waiting.

Concern clouded Miss Prudence's eyes. "And suppose some of the other girls hear about this and decide they want to move around also?" she asked her sister.

"Let's say there has to be a good reason to move. In this case I think we have a very good reason," Miss Hope replied. "And if there should be a good reason for some other girl to move, then we will allow that, too."

Miss Prudence cleared her throat before speaking. "All right, Sister, if you want to be held responsible for any other requests to move, then we will get Uncle Cal to move Amanda's things into the room with Celia," Miss Prudence agreed. She looked at the girls sternly, "And you two young ladies, just remember this. There will be no more violations of the school rules. Next time, Amanda, it will be much more serious."

"Yes, ma'am. Thank you, Miss Prudence," Mandie replied.

Celia added her thanks, and the girls smiled at Miss Hope.

Miss Hope left the office quickly with her papers in her hand. "I almost forgot it's time for me to go to the dining room," she said.

That afternoon, while the other students spent their free period on the veranda, Mandie and Celia helped Uncle Cal move Mandie's belongings.

The two girls, with their arms full of clothes, followed Uncle Cal out of Mandie's old room and walked straight into April's path.

"So, you just can't take it, huh?" April said, blocking their way. "I know the other girls have told you that my mother is a Yankee and my grandfather was a Union soldier, but I didn't think you would move out on account of that."

Mandie frowned. "But I didn't know that, April," she protested. "Besides, that doesn't make any difference to me, none at all."

"I don't believe you. Why else would you move out?"

"Really, April, I didn't know anything at all about you," Mandie insisted. "And what difference does it make which side your family was on? The War of Northern Aggression has been over for many, many years now."

"Mandie is moving into my room because I was afraid to stay there by myself," Celia told her.

"Afraid, huh?" April scoffed. "What're you afraid of?"

Mandie pushed past April. "Oh, come on, Celia. We don't have time to waste."

"You'll be sorry," April called as the two hurried down the hallway.

"I see now why you wanted to get away from that girl," Celia whispered.

Mandie soon realized another advantage of staying in the isolated room. The time would soon arrive for Uncle Ned to visit her, and it would be much easier to slip out of this room to meet him.

On the night of the full moon, the two girls sat talking in the dark, waiting for everyone else to go to sleep. Mandie couldn't wait to meet Uncle Ned in the yard. The ten o'clock bell had already rung and all the lamps were out.

Mandie told Celia her plan. "As soon as I get down the steps and into the yard, I'll come around to where I can watch this window. If you hear anyone coming, just close the window. I'll hurry back in," she said.

"I'll keep watch, Mandie, but I want to meet Uncle Ned."

"If he sees anyone besides me, he'll leave. Maybe the next time he comes you can meet him."

"Please ask him. Don't forget," Celia begged.

Mandie, still dressed, picked up a dark shawl to put over her head so that her blonde hair wouldn't shine in the moonlight.

"I won't forget." She crept out into the hallway. She had already planned her way out of the house in preparation for Uncle Ned's visit.

Hurrying down the servants' stairway in the dark, she ended up in the kitchen. The moon shone through the windows, so she could see the bolt on the outside door. Sliding the bolt over, she opened the door. Outside, she kept close to the shrubbery around the house and made her way to the side yard. She glanced up at the open window. Everything was all right so far.

Mandie didn't know where Uncle Ned would wait for her. Cautiously, she stepped out into the open, hoping he would see her and come on out. Her heart beat wildly, and she kept turning to watch for him. As she waited, her hopes began to fade. She was afraid he would forget to come or that circumstances beyond his control might prevent his visit.

Then she heard his familiar bird whistle nearby. She turned to see him standing in the shadows of a huge magnolia tree. She ran and threw her arms around him. Tears of joy streamed down her cheeks.

"Uncle Ned! Uncle Ned! I knew you would come!" she cried as he embraced her.

"Sit, Papoose," he said, pointing to a white bench by the walkway. "Must hurry. Not want someone see Papoose. Make trouble."

They sat down and Mandie held his old, wrinkled hand.

"Oh, I'm so glad to see you," she said. "This is a miserable place, Uncle Ned, and they expect you to learn such silly things!"

"But Papoose must get book learning. I promise Jim Shaw," the old man replied. "Everything in this earth life not happy. Must do unhappy things, too."

"I know. I'll have to stay here and learn all these silly things. But how I wish I were home and could see all my friends. How is everybody?" she asked.

"All friends fine," he said with a smile. "Send much love." Uncle Ned looked at her closely. "Papoose make friends here?"

"I have one good friend. Celia Hamilton. She's my roommate. The other girls are too snobbish," Mandie told him. "Celia is keeping watch for me in that window right up there." She pointed. "She will let me know if anyone comes. Uncle Ned, she wants to meet you."

"Next time, Papoose." The old man stood up, pulled an envelope out of his belt, and handed it to Mandie. "Friends write Papoose letters."

Mandie gave a muffled squeal. "Oh, thank you!" She felt the envelope. *It must have quite a few letters in it,* she thought.

The old man looked toward the sky. "Must go now," he said. "I ask Big God watch over Papoose." He squeezed her small hand, then leaned over to embrace her.

"Thank you, Uncle Ned. And I'll ask God to watch over you and all my friends until I can return. Please come back as soon as you can. Please!"

"Next time moon changes I come," he told her. "Go back in house now. I watch."

Mandie kissed his wrinkled cheek and ran for the back door. At the doorway she stopped and waved good-bye. Even though she couldn't see him in the darkness, she knew he was watching.

Inside the kitchen she carefully wrapped the shawl around the envelope. Then she went to the sink and got a drink of water.

The narrow servants' stairs were so dark Mandie couldn't see April blocking the way. Caught up in her thoughts, Mandie almost ran into her.

"Well, well, well! Where have you been?" April asked.

Mandie jumped. "I got a drink of water in the kitchen," she said quickly. She hoped April wouldn't see the shawl she held behind her.

"And what's wrong with the water in our bathroom upstairs?"

"I don't drink water out of bathrooms," Mandie said, imitating the snobbish tone of some of the other girls. "Now move out of my way, or I'll scream and the whole school will come running."

"You wouldn't dare!"

"Just stand there and see." Mandie tried to nudge her aside.

April stared at her a moment and then moved slightly.

"All right, you get through this time, but just remember, I know you were out of your room well after ten o'clock."

"And so were you," Mandie taunted, running up the stairs.

Celia was waiting at the door. "Is everything all right?"

"Fine, except I met April Snow as I was coming up the stairs. I have an idea she'll try to cause trouble," Mandie said. "But look!" She held up the envelope in the dim light. "Uncle Ned brought me letters from everybody."

Mandie draped her shawl over the back of a chair and sat down in the moonlight by the window. She tore open the envelope and excitedly shared her letters with her friend. Everyone was well, and everyone hoped Mandie was enjoying the school. They all said they missed her and hoped she'd soon come home, at least for a visit.

But April wasn't through with Mandie.

CHAPTER FOUR

YOUNG GENTLEMEN CALLERS

The next morning, Mandie's shawl was missing. She had hung it across the back of a chair while she read her letters, but now it wasn't there! Both girls looked all around the room, but they couldn't find it anywhere.

"Thank goodness I put my letters under my pillow!" Mandie exclaimed. "Otherwise they might have disappeared, too."

"Do you think April took your shawl?" Celia asked.

"I don't know. I can't imagine why she would do a thing like that. I sure wish Miss Prudence hadn't made us give her our key."

"Are you going to tell Miss Prudence about the shawl?"

"Not yet. Maybe whoever took it will bring it back," Mandie replied.

After making their bed, the girls laid their nightgowns across the foot of the bed, according to the school rule, and went downstairs.

Later, the girls didn't have time to think about the shawl. The students from Mr. Chadwick's School for Boys came across town to call on all the new girls for afternoon tea.

Miss Prudence told them it would be an opportunity for them to practice their social graces. "You will be graded on how you conduct yourselves," she reminded them.

Mandie wore her pale blue voile dress with white sprigs of baby's breath scattered among its folds. Around her neck, she clasped the strand of tiny pearls Uncle John had given her as a going away present. She let her blonde curls hang free around her shoulders.

Celia sat beside her friend in the parlor, dressed in a bright green muslin dress with a matching hair ribbon. She twisted her handkerchief and blushed at even the thought of a boy speaking to her. She wanted to hide in a corner by herself.

"You stay right here with me, Celia," Mandie told her. "We need each other's support. This is just something we have to do."

"But Miss Prudence said each boy had drawn one of our names. There's no telling what kind of boys we'll end up with," Celia protested.

"If we don't like them, we just won't talk," Mandie said.

The girls heard the sound of horses outside, and in a few minutes Miss Prudence entered the parlor with a tall, thin man wearing spectacles.

"Young ladies, this is Mr. Chadwick," she told the girls. "His young men have arrived. Now, when they appear at the doorway and call your name, please rise and go outside. We will serve tea on the veranda as soon as all names have been called. Now, Mr. Chadwick, I believe we're ready."

"Thank you, Miss Heathwood," the man answered. "Excuse me, ladies." Stepping back to the doorway, he beckoned to the first boy in line in the hall.

The boy stood in the doorway, introduced himself as William Massey, and called, "Miss Etrulia Batson."

Etrulia, shy and quiet, stood up shakily. "I'm Etrulia Batson," she said.

William stepped forward, offered her his arm, and escorted her out of the parlor.

The line continued. Mandie and Celia clutched each other's hands as the tension mounted.

A boy of medium height, with a shy smile and unruly brown curls, stepped to the doorway. "I'm Robert Rogers, and I'm looking for Miss Celia Hamilton," he announced.

Mandie nudged her friend, but Celia froze. "Get up," Mandie whispered. "He called your name. Isn't he cute?"

Celia managed to get to her feet. She nervously smoothed the folds of her long skirt and took a deep breath. In a soft voice she replied, "I'm Celia Hamilton."

Robert strode forward, smiling. "I was afraid of what I'd get, and here I got the prettiest girl in the school," he told her.

Celia blushed. As they left the room, she saw Mandie smile at her.

With the line dwindling, Mandie began to think that maybe they would run out of boys, and she wouldn't have to bother being nice to someone. But the very last boy in line was hers.

A tall, handsome young lad with brown hair and dark brown eyes stepped to the doorway. Seeing Mandie was the only girl left in the room, he laughed.

"My name is Thomas Patton and I'm looking for Miss Amanda Shaw," he said, bowing slightly. "This was worth waiting for."

Mandie rose, straightened her skirts, and lifted her chin. "I'm Amanda Shaw," she replied. Then with a nervous giggle she added, "My friends call me Mandie, but they don't like nicknames at this school."

"My friends call me Tommy," the boy whispered loudly, "but nicknames aren't permitted at our school either. They want us to learn how to be real gentlemen, and they say real gentlemen don't go by nicknames." He offered his arm and Mandie tucked her hand in the crook of his elbow. "Just between you and me, I don't think they'll ever make a real gentleman out of me."

Mandie laughed as they went out onto the veranda. "And I know they won't ever make a real lady out of me. It's impossible."

The other girls turned to look as Mandie and Tommy sat down near April and her escort. Mandie looked around for Celia, and saw her at the other end of the porch. She was listening attentively to her new friend.

"Where are you from, Mandie?" Tommy asked.

"Franklin, North Carolina," she replied. "And you?"

"I'm from Charleston, South Carolina," he said.

Mandie's eyes widened. "Charleston? Where the beaches are? I've never seen the ocean. Tell me about it, please. What is it like?"

"It's the biggest body of water I have ever seen," he teased. Then more seriously he added, "You know that already, of course. But when the tide comes in, it brings huge waves that splash water way up onto the beach. And then when the tide goes back out, and takes all the extra water with it, it leaves all kinds of shells and tiny ocean creatures that have washed up from the sea. I have a collection of shells and sand dollars."

"Sand dollars?" she asked.

"Sand dollars are little flat circular urchins with a star pattern in the middle. They live on the bottom of the sea and the tide washes them ashore. Of course they're dead then, and can't bite," he teased. "Seriously, they look like they're made out of the same thing shells are. They don't look like they were ever alive."

"And you collect these things and put them in your house?"

"Sure. Next time I go home I'll get you one."

"Oh, thanks, I'd love that. I want to see the ocean someday." Mandie's blue eyes twinkled.

"You and your parents will have to come to visit us. I'll show you the beaches and the whole town. Charleston has lots of historical places to see, you know."

"Yes, I've read about it. I'd love to visit sometime."

Mandie became aware that April continually stared at Tommy and paid little attention to her escort. April leaned toward them to hear their conversation.

Seeing some seats vacated near Celia, Mandie stood up quickly. "My friend is at the other end of the porch, and I see two empty seats," she said.

As they walked away, April kept her eyes on Tommy. Even after they had sat down, she was still staring at them.

The maids came out and served tea while Miss Prudence and Miss Hope watched the girls.

Mandie was so nervous she was afraid she would drop something. She looked around to see what the others were doing. Most of them seemed to know exactly how to behave at afternoon tea.

Celia's hand shook so much that she didn't dare lift the cup to her lips for fear of spilling the tea.

Robert noticed that she was not drinking it. "Is something wrong with your tea?" he asked.

Celia blushed and said the first thing she could think of. "Oh, no, I—uh—just don't like tea."

"Well, don't drink it then," Robert said.

"Celia, you should try," Mandie urged. "Miss Prudence might notice that you didn't drink it."

Robert reached over and quickly exchanged cups with Celia. He had already finished his tea. "Here, I'll drink it for you. Then you'll have an empty cup," Robert said with a laugh.

"Thanks," Celia said. "Here comes Miss Prudence now. I hope she didn't see what we just did."

"She didn't," Mandie assured her. "I was watching. She was walking the other way when you swapped cups."

"What if she did see us," said Tommy. "Not everyone likes tea. People shouldn't be forced to drink it just to learn the social graces, as these teachers call it."

Miss Prudence strolled by with Mr. Chadwick and surveyed the various students.

Tommy waited until they had passed, then said, "You know our school is coming over for the dinner party next weekend. Mandie, would you consider being my partner?"

"Aren't we drawing names again?" Mandie asked.

"No, I don't think so. That was just for this first visit. After this we're supposed to know everyone," said Tommy.

"How can they suppose such a thing?" Robert asked. "I certainly don't know everyone." He smiled at Celia. "But then I don't want to know everyone. Celia, will you do me the honor of being my partner?"

"Well, I—yes, if that's the way we're doing it," Celia answered.

"You didn't answer my question, Mandie," Tommy protested.

"Thank you, Tommy, I'd enjoy being your partner," Mandie responded.

Mr. Chadwick stood in the center of the porch. "All right, gentlemen, it's time for us to go home," he announced. "I hope you remembered to ask a partner for the dinner party next week."

Excited conversation broke out among the students as the boys prepared to depart. After saying good-bye to Robert and Tommy, Mandie and Celia walked down the long hallway.

Suddenly, April rushed up behind them. "Tommy Patton is mine for the party," she told Mandie.

Mandie stopped and stared up at the tall girl. "Just what do you mean by that?" she asked.

"Just what I said. Tommy Patton is my partner for the party."

"What did you do, April? Ask him? I'm afraid he has already asked me."

"I don't care who he asked. He's going to be my partner," April fumed.

"He does have a mind of his own, you know," Mandie said. She flashed an amused look to Celia, who stood by listening. "And he asked *me*, so he is going to be *my* partner."

"Let me tell you one thing," April growled at her. "You'd better forget that he asked you, or I'll just conveniently remember that I caught you coming up the backstairs last night after ten o'clock."

"Oh, mind your own business," Mandie said angrily.

April hurried on down the hallway. "I'm warning you," she called back over her shoulder. Then she ran upstairs.

Mandie and Celia just stood there, puzzled by the girl's behavior.

"Well!" Mandie said. "What do you suppose that was all about?"

Celia shrugged her shoulders, and the two girls returned to their room for a rest period before the evening meal. As soon as they opened the door, Mandie noticed that her nightgown was missing. She knew that she had laid it across the foot of the bed. Celia's was there but Mandie's was not.

"It looks like someone took my nightgown," Mandie said, glancing about the room. "If they don't quit taking things, I'm going to run out of clothes pretty soon. My shawl this morning and now my nightgown."

"I'll bet it was that April Snow," Celia accused.

"But she was downstairs on the porch with us," Mandie replied.

"Yes, but she came flying up the steps ahead of us after she threatened you in the hall."

"I suppose it's possible, but why would she do that?"

"I don't know. Are you going to report it to Miss Prudence?"

"No. I can't prove anything. I think I'll just do some detective work on my own. Maybe I can find out for sure who's doing this," Mandie said, as she took another nightgown from the bureau drawer.

Mandie certainly didn't want to get the wrong person in trouble. She wasn't certain that April was taking these things. She would just have to watch April carefully from now on. Although Mandie wasn't a tattletale, she also wasn't going to be threatened, nor was she going to put up with her clothes disappearing.

At supper, April didn't say anything to Mandie, and when they were dismissed from the table, she hurried out to the veranda. Mandie and Celia went to their room to write letters.

Long after the ten o'clock bell had rung and the lights were out, Mandie and Celia lay awake. They talked quietly about the disappearance of Mandie's clothes. Suddenly they heard the clanging metal and squeaking boards again. They looked at each other, and their bodies stiffened in fright.

"There's that noise!" Celia whispered.

"It sounds like it's in the attic," Mandie whispered back.

"It does seem close."

Mandie sat up on the side of the bed. "Let's go see what it is," she said in a low voice.

"No!" Celia objected.

"We don't have to let *it* see *us*. We'll just find out what or who is making that noise," Mandie told her. "Come on!" She started for the door.

"Aren't you going to take a light?" Celia asked.

"Here, we can take this one," Mandie said, lighting the lamp by the bed. She picked it up, and Celia joined her near the door.

All of a sudden, the noise stopped. The girls stood still.

"It went away," Celia whispered.

Mandie set the lamp back down and blew out the light. "We should still look out in the hall," she said, opening the door. Celia was right behind her.

As they stepped into the hallway, someone laughed softly and asked, "And where are you young ladies going?"

Mandie instantly recognized April's voice.

"None of your business, April Snow. And what are you doing out in the hall after ten o'clock?" Mandie asked.

"I'd say that's none of *your* business." April sauntered down the hall toward her room and disappeared around the corner.

The two girls looked at each other.

"April must have been making that noise," Celia said in disgust.

"Maybe and maybe not," Mandie replied, "but we'd better wait for another night to investigate the attic. April may be on her way to tell Miss Prudence that she caught us out of our room. Let's go back to bed."

The girls were really puzzled now. Was April making the noises in the attic? Had April taken Mandie's shawl and then her nightgown? April was always making threats but there still wasn't any proof of wrong-doing. They would have to investigate the attic at their first opportunity and see what was really there.

CHAPTER FIVE

LOCKED OUT IN THE NIGHT

The next morning, when Mandie started to get dressed, she reached for her blue dress which she had hung on the chifferobe door.

"My dress!" She gasped. "It's gone, hanger and all."

Celia turned to look. "Oh, Mandie, you've got to tell Miss Prudence now. Do you want someone to take all your clothes?"

"I don't understand how anyone could come in here while we're asleep and not wake us," Mandie replied. "I'll talk to Uncle Ned about it. He's coming to see me tonight."

"May I go down there with you to meet him?"

"I'll have to ask first," Mandie replied. "You can stay at the window, and I'll signal if he says it's all right." She pulled out a bright red dress from the chifferobe and took a strand of multicolored beads from a little box on the bureau.

"Those beads are beautiful. Where did you get them?" Celia asked.

"Sallie Sweetwater gave them to me before I left. She's my Indian friend. She's also Uncle Ned's granddaughter." Mandie fingered the necklace tenderly. "These beads are very old," she explained. "Sallie's great-grandmother made them. They're one of my most treasured possessions." Mandie reached for her robe. "Well, if I don't get to that bathroom on time, I won't get a bath," she said.

Later, on their way down to breakfast, the girls met April coming up the steps. They all looked at each other, but no one spoke.

As soon as April was out of hearing range, Celia turned to her friend. "There she goes!" Celia accused. "She should be going the same direction we are for breakfast. I think she is the culprit. And I also think you ought to talk to Miss Prudence, or maybe to Miss Hope."

"I suppose I will, as soon as I get a chance."

At the table, Miss Prudence had already returned thanks and was about to ask the girls to be seated when April rushed in and took her place.

Miss Prudence frowned. "April, I will see you in my office as soon as we finish breakfast," she said sternly.

April nodded without saying a word.

After breakfast, as the two girls walked down the hallway, Celia said, "So April is in trouble with Miss Prudence for being late to the table."

"I'd hate to be in her shoes," Mandie replied. She couldn't wait to tell the whole story to Uncle Ned. He would help her know what to do.

That night when the old Indian came, he and Mandie sat on the bench under the magnolia tree. Mandie kept an eye on Celia at the bedroom window.

"Uncle Ned, I have a problem," Mandie began. "You see, there's a girl here, named April Snow. She and I shared a bed in the other bedroom. She got furious with me because I moved into the room with Celia. You know that Celia and I are good friends. But April said I was moving because her mother was a Yankee." Mandie threw her hands up in the air. "I didn't even know about her mother. Yet April has been nasty to me ever since."

"What she do, Papoose?" the old man asked.

"She watches me all the time. When I was going to my room after your last visit, April met me on the steps. She asked me where I'd been. I didn't tell her, of course. Then yesterday the boys from Mr. Chadwick's School came for tea and April decided she liked the boy I was with. Tommy asked me to go to the dinner party Saturday night, but April says she wants him for her partner. She keeps saying things like, 'I'm warning you' and 'You'll be sorry.' "

"All talk? Not do anything to Papoose?"

"I don't know," Mandie said. She told him about the missing clothes. "I'm not sure whether or not she was the one who took them."

"Papoose tell Miss Head Lady?" he asked.

Mandie smiled at his name for Miss Prudence. "I wanted to ask you if I should mention this to Miss Prudence. The Bible tells us to do good for evil, and if someone smites you on one cheek, turn the other. Uncle Ned, do you think that means I shouldn't do anything to cause April trouble?"

"Papoose not make trouble for girl. Good for girl if Papoose go when sun rises and tell Miss Head Lady," said the Indian. "Must not lose fine clothes. Mother of Papoose not like that."

"I guess my mother would be upset to know I had lost those things."

The old man stood up. "Must go now," he said.

Mandie jumped up and looked at the window above. "Uncle Ned, I promised Celia I'd signal to her if she could come down and meet you. Can she, Uncle Ned, please?"

"Make sign quick. Must hurry," he said, looking up.

Mandie waved to Celia and the girl quickly disappeared. In a few minutes she was running toward them across the yard.

"Celia, this is Uncle Ned," Mandie said. "And, Uncle Ned, this is my friend Celia Hamilton."

Celia curtsied briefly. Uncle Ned smiled and put his hand on her auburn curls.

"No, no, Papoose Celia. Not bow down to me. I only old Indian, not Big God. He only one to bow down to."

Both girls smiled.

"They teach us these things here at school," Celia explained. "A lady never shakes hands. She either nods her head or curtsies, and I thought I should curtsy, from all that Mandie has told me about you. I think you are a great man."

"I only old Indian watching over Papoose," Uncle Ned replied. "Must go now. Come next moon." He turned to Mandie. "Papoose not forget. Go see Miss Head Lady when sun rises."

"I will, if you say so," Mandie promised. She pulled him down for a quick kiss on the cheek.

"Go," he told them.

The girls ran across the backyard and stopped to wave as they entered the screened-in back porch. The old man disappeared into the trees.

Mandie grasped the doorknob and pushed, but the door wouldn't open.

"Celia! The door's locked!" she whispered in the darkness.

"Somebody locked us out?" Celia asked.

"They must have. It couldn't have locked by itself. There's a bolt on the door, remember?"

"April was probably watching us!" Celia accused.

"We'll have to find some other way to get inside the house. There's no way to move the bolt from out here."

"Mandie, please do something about April," Celia complained.

"I intend to, first thing in the morning. But right now, let's look around. Maybe we can find a window open or something. We've got to get back in before someone misses us. I'll bet whoever locked us out is waiting to see what we'll do. Let's go."

Celia followed her friend. They walked all the way around the house without finding any way to get in. Finally, they sat down on the back steps.

"It looks like we'll be caught this time. There's no way in," Celia sighed.

"There's a solution to every problem if you think about it long enough," Mandie told her. She propped her elbows on her knees and rested her chin in her hands. *Uncle Ned has already gone*, she thought. *Of course there probably isn't anything he could do to help us anyway.* Mandie didn't have a friend at the school besides Celia. *Oh, yes, I do*, she thought. *Aunt Phoebe! Maybe she is still up. Aunt Phoebe must have a key to the house*, Mandie reasoned. *She's the first one up. She comes to wake us every morning.*

Mandie jumped up. "Celia, what about Aunt Phoebe? She must have some way to get inside the house every morning. Let's see if she'll help us."

"Won't she tell on us?" Celia asked.

"No. Aunt Phoebe is my friend. Come on."

As the girls walked toward the little cottage, they noticed a faint light behind the drawn curtains. Evidently someone was still awake.

When they stepped onto the small front porch in the darkness, they were suddenly startled to find Aunt Phoebe and Uncle Cal sitting in the rockers on the porch.

"My chillun cain't git in de house?" the old woman asked.

Mandie's eyes widened. "How did you know, Aunt Phoebe?" she asked.

"We sits heah. See lots o' things," Aunt Phoebe replied. She rose from the chair and stood in front of her husband. "Cal, gimme de key."

The old man pulled a door key from his pocket and handed it to her. "Jes' be sho' you don't wake dem two wimmens," he warned his wife. "If you does, we git no sleep tonight."

"We knows how to be quiet. My chillun heah too skeerd not to be quiet. Mistuh Injun Man done gone. Dey got no hep 'cept us."

"You saw Uncle Ned?" Mandie gasped.

"We sees, but we not tell. We knows who Mistuh Injun Man be. C'mon," she beckoned. "We'se gotta go to de front do' wid dis key." Aunt Phoebe led the way around the house.

She quietly slipped the key into the front door lock, turned the tumbler, and slowly pushed the door open. Putting her finger over her lips, she motioned for them to be quiet. Aunt Phoebe pushed them inside, closed the door, and locked it behind them.

The girls stealthily made their way up the main stairway in the darkness. They didn't see or hear anyone along the way. And when they finally closed their bedroom door, they both sighed with relief.

"Whew! That was a close call!" Mandie exclaimed.

"Too close, Mandie."

Just then, the clanging, squeaking noise began again in the attic. They looked at each other in silence. Hadn't they had enough adventure for one night?

With sudden decision, Mandie whirled and opened their door. "Quick! Let's see what it is!"

She started up the attic steps in the darkness. Celia followed, too afraid to speak. The noise grew louder. Slowly and carefully, they tiptoed up the steps until they reached the door at the top of the stairs. A small window by the door gave a dim light. They held their breath.

Mandie rested her hand on the doorknob, trying to decide whether or not to open the door. After a few moments, she gently turned the knob and swung the creaking door open. The room was pitch black. Suddenly there was a sound like a hundred rats scampering across the floor.

The girls panicked and flew back down the stairs, not stopping until they were safe in their room.

"Mandie, I'm afraid!" Celia whispered. "Let's put something in front of our door, so if somebody tries to come in, we'll hear them."

"Yes!" Mandie agreed. She looked around.

The room was small. There was a fireplace on one wall. The bed stood against another. A bureau, chifferobe, and two overstuffed chairs occupied most of the remaining space. A floor-length mirror on a gilt stand stood in a corner.

Mandie made her decision quickly. With Celia's help she succeeded in moving both of the heavy chairs in front of the door.

She stood back and surveyed their work. "That ought to discourage anyone from pushing their way in here."

Feeling a little safer, the girls quickly undressed and hopped into bed.

They soon fell asleep, secure in the knowledge that the chairs were guarding their door. But would the chairs keep out someone who really wanted to get in?

CHAPTER SIX

APRIL'S TROUBLE

Next morning, Mandie swung her feet out of bed, plopped them on the floor and quickly withdrew them. What had she stepped on? Leaning over the edge of the bed for a look, she let out a sharp cry. The precious beads Sallie had given her were all over the floor.

Awakened by the cry, Celia crawled over to see what Mandie was looking at. "Oh, Mandie! What happened?"

Mandie climbed out of bed and stooped to recover the beads that were scattered everywhere. "Somebody broke my beads, the beads that Sallie gave me." Her voice quivered.

Celia bent to help. "Don't cry, Mandie. I'll help you restring the beads. Let's just be sure we find all of them."

"How could anyone get in here?" Mandie asked, looking toward the door. "The chairs are moved!" she exclaimed. "I see how they did it. We put the chairs on that throw rug. It would slide easily on the hardwood floor. We went to all that trouble for nothing."

When Miss Prudence arrived at the dining room door for breakfast, the two girls were waiting for her.

Mandie spoke quickly. "Miss Prudence, may I see you a minute as soon as we're finished eating?"

The woman looked at her in surprise. "Why, yes, of course, Amanda. In fact, I was going to ask you and Celia to come to my office anyway."

The girls glanced at each other, sure that the schoolmistress knew they had been out of the house the night before. They ate very little. After breakfast, they followed Miss Prudence to her office.

Miss Prudence stood behind her desk and scowled at the two girls sitting before her. She cleared her throat. "I would like to know what you two were doing out of the house after ten o'clock last night," she said, pausing to indicate the seriousness of the matter. "You know you are not supposed to be out of your room, much less prowling around the yard. Now, I want an explanation."

Mandie decided she had to tell the truth and face the consequences. "Miss Prudence," she began shakily. "We went outside, and then someone locked the back door so we couldn't get back in."

"And what time was that?" Miss Prudence wouldn't give up easily. "Were you outside before or after ten o'clock?" she probed.

Celia tried to help. "Miss Prudence, we—"

Suddenly Aunt Phoebe appeared in the doorway, smiling at the girls. "Miz Prudence," she interrupted, "dese heah chillun come to see me last night, and somebody lock dat back do'." Aunt Phoebe fiddled with her apron. "It was aftuh ten o'clock 'fo' we got Cal roused up and got de key to open de front do'. Dese two was skeerd to death."

The girls couldn't believe their ears.

"Aunt Phoebe, are you telling the truth?" Miss Prudence asked.

"Whut I say is de truth, Miz Prudence. Dey come see me, and somebody lock dat do', and it be aftuh ten o'clock 'fo' we gits dat front do' open."

Mandie realized Aunt Phoebe was telling the truth in a somewhat twisted fashion. For some reason she was trying to keep them out of trouble, but Mandie felt guilty about it.

The old woman stood in the doorway, smiling. She didn't move to go or try to explain why she was there in the first place. She just stood there.

The schoolmistress didn't know what to say.

Then April appeared behind Aunt Phoebe.

Miss Prudence stood up straight and cleared her throat again. "All right, young ladies, I do not believe it's proper to visit Aunt Phoebe so late at night, but go on now to your classes. I do not want to hear of any more doings of this nature." She turned to the Negro woman. "Aunt Phoebe, what did you want?"

The girls got up to leave. Mandie decided not to mention the disappearance of her clothes. She would tell Miss Prudence later when things calmed down. The schoolmistress didn't seem to remember that the girls had asked to talk to her. Mandie and Celia took their time leaving the office, hoping to hear Aunt Phoebe's reply.

"I jes' wanted to know whut you wants from de mahket today," the old woman replied.

"Aunt Phobe, I'll have to see you later about the market," said Miss Prudence. She nodded to the tall girl in the hall. "Come on in, April."

Aunt Phoebe moved quickly down the hallway in the opposite direction from the girls. Then Miss Hope scurried into the office.

Mandie frowned at Celia. "Things are really popping this morning," she said.

"Yes, and Aunt Phoebe sure popped us out of that one," Celia added.

"I wonder why," Mandie said as the girls walked to their classroom.

April sat in Miss Prudence's office, drumming her fingers on the arm of the chair.

Miss Prudence sat behind her desk and Miss Hope dropped into a chair at the side. "April, we asked you to come in here this morning because I wanted Miss Hope to hear what you told me about Amanda and Celia being out late last night." She nodded to her sister. "It seems, however, that it was not their fault. Aunt Phoebe said that they were visiting her before ten o'clock and were locked out. They couldn't get back in until she unlocked the front door. Evidently that was *after* ten o'clock."

Miss Hope leaned forward. "Is that what happened, Sister?"

"Yes," Miss Prudence replied. "Aunt Phoebe stood right there and told me all about it, just now."

"But that isn't so, Miss Prudence," April argued. "I saw them with my own eyes. Mandie went outside first, and then Celia followed in a few minutes. It was after the ten o'clock bell."

"Come now, April, we don't doubt Aunt Phoebe's word," Miss Prudence told her. "You must be mistaken about the time."

"No, ma'am. I was standing by the window in my bedroom, looking out. When I saw Mandie go outside I looked at the clock. It was ten-thirty. In a few minutes Celia followed."

"Then your clock was wrong," Miss Prudence said with finality. "You may go now so you won't be late for your class."

April stood and shrugged her shoulders. "All right. If you don't believe me—" She left the room.

April got as far as the stairway and then turned back, tiptoeing next to the wall. She wanted to eavesdrop on the two schoolmistresses. There was definitely something going on here. She was positive she had seen the two girls go out after ten o'clock, and she intended to hear what the two women had to say about it.

"Sister, do you really believe Aunt Phoebe?" Miss Hope asked.

"Well, I hope she's telling the truth," Miss Prudence replied. "I'd hate to think she was lying for the two girls."

"According to April, Amanda seems to be a born trouble maker."

"I know her mother is a lady," Miss Prudence mused. "But her father had savage blood. I do hope that wild streak is not going to assert itself in Amanda."

April's ears perked up. She grinned to herself. So Mandie was a half-breed. None of the girls in the school would have anything to do with her if they knew she was part Indian. April would spread the word. This was her chance to get even.

She hurried to her classroom. Since class had already begun, April slipped quietly into a seat near Mandie and watched her.

Mandie always felt uncomfortable when April stared at her. When Miss Cameron asked Mandie a question, she didn't answer.

April leaned over and whispered just loud enough for Mandie to hear. "Hey, half-breed, teacher is asking you a question!"

Mandie's face burned when she realized the girl was talking to her. She crossed her fingers to control her anger.

Looking up at the teacher, she apologized. "I'm sorry, Miss Cameron, I didn't understand the question."

"Please, Amanda, keep your attention on the lesson or you'll never learn anything," the teacher rebuked. "Now I asked you, who became president when Abraham Lincoln was assassinated?"

"Why, the vice-president, Miss Cameron," Mandie said.

All the girls laughed.

"Class, please remember your manners," the teacher scolded, tapping the desk with her pencil. "Now, Amanda, of course the vice-president became president, but what was his name?"

"Oh, Andrew Johnson, ma'am. That was the only way he could ever get to be president." Mandie saw her chance to get back at April for calling her a half-breed. "He was from Tennessee but he was a traitor. I guess the North would take anybody—even a traitor." Mandie hoped April got the slur at her Yankee mother.

She did. In a louder whisper, April repeated her accusation. "I know your father had savage blood."

The girls within hearing distance gasped.

Miss Cameron dismissed the class, and the girls filled the hallway. Mandie waited in the hall for April to come out of the room. She was the last one out.

Forgetting all her resolutions to not argue with April, she walked up to the tall girl, put her hands on her hips, and announced, "My grandmother was a full-blooded Cherokee, and I'm proud of it. I'm part Cherokee because that's the way God made me."

A hushed whisper ran through the crowd.

April turned to the other girls and spoke. "Did you hear what she said? She admits to having Indian blood. What do you think of that?"

Just then Miss Prudence came down the hallway. She couldn't hear the conversation, but April and Mandie seemed to be arguing about something. She walked up and stood between them.

"Into my office, both of you. Immediately!" she commanded.

Everyone gasped and moved away.

But Celia, who had heard everything, came to Mandie's side. "I'll go with you, Mandie," she offered.

"Thank you, Celia, but this is between April and me," she told her friend. Mandie silently followed Miss Prudence and the tall girl to the office.

Taking her place behind her desk, Miss Prudence sighed in exasperation. "Now sit down like two ladies and explain what you were yelling about in the hallway," the schoolmistress demanded.

The girls sat down but neither said a word. April stared at Mandie, hoping to scare her into silence. Mandie didn't want to be a tattletale.

After several minutes Miss Prudence spoke again.

"I asked both of you a question and I expect an answer. What were you yelling about?"

Mandie fidgeted in her chair but did not answer. April kept staring at her, ignoring the question.

"Speak! Now! If I have to call in the girls who overheard this argument, you will both be expelled from school," Miss Prudence warned them.

Mandie was worried. She either had to tattle on April, thereby getting her into trouble, or else not tell and get expelled from school.

Mother would be too hurt, she thought. *I have to explain the situation. I'm sure April won't.*

Mandie sat up straight. "Miss Prudence," she began, "it all started when April called me a half-breed. She said, 'I know your father had savage blood,' and then—" Mandie stopped abruptly.

Miss Prudence's face had turned beet red, and she was gasping for breath. She realized that April had overheard her conversation! Miss Prudence sputtered, trying to think of something to say. She certainly couldn't admit her part in this. Mandie's mother would come to take her daughter home, and the school's reputation would be ruined.

Mandie anxiously leaned forward. "Miss Prudence, are you all right?"

April sat back in her chair, enjoying the scene.

"What? Oh, yes, yes. I'm fine," Miss Prudence replied. She didn't dare look at April.

"Didn't you know that I'm part Cherokee?" Mandie asked.

"Of course I did, Amanda. I knew your father." The schoolmistress regained her composure and then spoke to the other girl. "April, you will apologize to Amanda, and you are immediately suspended from school for ten days. I will send for your mother."

"Send me home if you like, but I will not apologize to Amanda," April sneered. "It's all true. My mother might not even be at home. She was supposed to visit her family in New York after she left me here."

Mandie was sorry that April had to be suspended, but hadn't she brought it upon herself?

"We'll find your mother," Miss Prudence told her. "In the meantime, all your social privileges are cancelled. You will be allowed out of your room only to attend classes and for meals. Remember, you must remain in your room at all other times."

"But the party is tomorrow night," April objected.

Mandie realized how disappointed the girl must be, but she couldn't help feeling some satisfaction that April was being punished.

Miss Prudence stood. "You will not attend the social under any circumstances," she said. "You will be confined to your room." She paused for a moment. "You may go to your classes now. I will let you know when we have contacted your mother, April. And Amanda, I will do my best to restore order after that terribly unfortunate incident," she said.

"Thank you, Miss Prudence," Mandie replied.

At the noon meal the schoolmistress stood before all the girls in the dining room and rang the tinkling silver bell next to her plate.

"Young ladies," she began, "the unladylike conduct of one of our students has come to my attention. I am sure some of you heard April Snow call Amanda Shaw an unladylike name." Miss Prudence cleared her throat and continued. "This is a serious offense, and therefore, April has been suspended for ten days."

The students gasped and loud whispering instantly filled the dining room.

Miss Prudence rang the bell again. "As soon as April's mother can be contacted," she continued, "April will be forced to leave the school for ten days. At the end of that time we will decide whether we would like to have her back. Meanwhile, she is confined to her room except for classes and meals."

All the girls turned to gaze at April, but she didn't seem to notice. April was staring into space, ignoring the whole scene.

Miss Prudence went on. "I want to state here and now that there will be no more of this type of behavior. Everyone is to forget what was said. If I hear of any of you even discussing the matter, you will be liable for suspension, also."

Mandie and Celia looked at each other in shock. Mandie was confused. She felt relief that April was leaving, but she hadn't meant to cause her so much trouble. Still, she did have to tell the truth. There was no way around that.

But now April really had a reason to be angry with Mandie. What if they couldn't reach her mother for a few days? April could have plenty of opportunities to get even.

CHAPTER SEVEN

MORE NOISES IN THE NIGHT

The girls had worked hard decorating the huge barn in the backyard for the party.

They made paper lanterns to hang across the lawn and inside the building. Bright, twisted streamers stretched overhead. Long boards lying across two sawhorses became tables with white bedsheets serving as tablecloths. Dozens of chairs, stored in the loft, were brought down and cleaned. At one end of the barn was a stage used for school plays. For the evening's event, the girls decorated it with magnolia leaves and flowers from the garden. Oil lamps hung in safe places to be lit when needed, and a three-piece minstrel show had been engaged to perform.

Each girl daintily lettered two place cards for the table—one with her name and one for the boy who would be her partner. There were gallons of lemonade in the kitchen and the hand-cranked ice cream churn stood ready. The girls had been helping prepare the food all week. They were even allowed to do a little experimenting. There was more food than they could possibly eat, but anything left would be taken to the local orphanage.

On the evening of the party, Mandie and Celia dressed nervously in their room. Celia wore a pale lavender muslin dress with green lace and ribbons. She arranged her auburn hair in curls and tied them back with a matching green ribbon. Around her neck hung a delicate cameo on a thin gold chain.

Mandie had chosen her pale pink chiffon dress accented with deeper pink rose petals. Her blonde hair hung loosely in ringlets around her shoulders. She wore a tiny silver locket that contained pictures of her father and mother.

Twirling in front of the long mirror in the corner, she laughed. "Hey, is that really Amanda Elizabeth Shaw? I look so old."

Celia came to stand by her. "So do I. I suppose we have to grow up some time, but I don't think I'm going to like it."

"You will by the time you get there," Mandie assured her. "Just think, we won't have to go to school anymore. We can stay home with our families."

"No, you're wrong there," Celia said. "I don't have any brothers and sisters, and neither do you. We'll both be expected to get married and have babies so the family won't run out."

"No, you're the one who's wrong," Mandie replied. "Once we're grown we'll have minds of our own. If we want to get married, we will. And if we don't, we won't."

"I suppose you'll marry that boy Joe you told me about."

"Joe and I—" Suddenly the bell interrupted her reply. "That means it's time for us to go downstairs."

Celia gulped. "Do I have everything on that I'm supposed to? Is it all arranged properly?" she asked.

"You look fine, Celia. Let's go."

By the time all the girls assembled on the veranda, the three surreys full of boys had arrived. Uncle Cal hurried out to help with the rigs and horses.

The schoolmaster left the first surrey and made sure the boys met their partners in an orderly fashion.

Tommy and Robert immediately spotted Mandie and Celia as they approached the porch steps.

Tommy teasingly bowed to Mandie. "Miss Amanda!"

Robert imitated him. "Miss Celia!" he said.

The girls held back a giggle as they greeted them.

"My, my!" Mandie exclaimed, eyeing their fine dark suits. "You look like real gentlemen tonight."

Tommy pulled at his collar. "These things are terribly uncomfortable," he complained.

"I'm not sure I can eat very much with all this on, either," Robert added. He sat down beside Celia on the veranda.

Celia smiled at him. "I'm not sure I can eat at all."

"Me either," Mandie said. "The girls cooked all the food and it may not be fit to eat."

"We'll manage," Tommy assured her.

Mandie found herself comparing Tommy with her lifetime friend, Joe. Tommy and Joe both had that happy, carefree spirit, but Tommy was taller and looked a little older. She wondered what Joe would look like dressed up in an expensive suit like Tommy's. Joe never wore a suit except to church. And he did wear one to her mother's wedding. But the suits he wore were not finely tailored like these. Still, Joe was her kind of people. And he had told her he wanted to marry her when they grew up.

Miss Prudence cleared her throat loudly. "It is time to go to the barn in the backyard," she announced.

"The barn?" Tommy shrieked. "You mean we're going to have a dinner in a *barn*?" He looked down at his fancy clothes.

Mandie laughed. "It's not what you think," she explained. "The barn isn't used for animals. They've made it into a theater for the school's dramatics class."

As the two girls and their partners entered the building, the boys whistled in appreciation of what they found inside.

"You girls have really been busy," Tommy remarked.

"Thank you for noticing," Mandie said with a giggle. "Now, we're supposed to find our places. We're at the second table next to Celia and Robert."

The four of them walked down the side of the table directly under the loft opening. Celia stopped. "Here are mine and yours, Robert," she said. "Mandie and Tommy are supposed to be next to us."

They all looked, but Mandie's and Tommy's place cards were not there.

Mandie was puzzled. "I know they're supposed to be here. Some-one must have switched them."

At that instant, a small piece of straw dropped from the loft above. Mandie looked up. There was a flash of red as someone moved out of sight. April! It had to be! Since she couldn't come to the party because of Mandie, April was determined to make more trouble for her.

Celia saw Mandie looking up. They exchanged knowing glances.

"I think we have an uninvited guest," Mandie whispered to Celia.

By then everyone had found a place and was standing behind a chair waiting to be seated. Mandie and her friends felt embarrassed as Miss Prudence frowned at the four of them standing behind only two chairs.

When the schoolmistress realized what the situation was, she came and asked everyone to move down a little so that two places could be added at the table. While Mandie and Miss Prudence discussed the matter, Robert and Tommy found two chairs across the room and brought them over.

"We'll get to the bottom of this later," Miss Prudence promised. "I'll have Aunt Phoebe bring more silver and china."

Mandie risked a question. "Miss Prudence, is April Snow in her room?"

The woman looked sharply at Mandie. "She had better be."

"There's someone in the loft," Mandie said quietly without look-ing up.

"I'll take care of it," Miss Prudence answered. She returned quickly to her place at the head of the table and asked everyone to be seated.

A few minutes later, as Uncle Cal passed by Miss Prudence, she stopped him and spoke to him. The old man glanced upward, then walked to the back of the barn and climbed the ladder to the loft. Mandie watched as he disappeared upstairs. In a moment he came back down the ladder and shook his head at the schoolmistress. Miss Prudence turned her gaze upon Mandie.

Tommy had been watching the whole thing. "What was that all about?" he asked.

"I told Miss Prudence I saw someone in the loft, so I guess she sent Uncle Cal to look. Evidently he didn't find anyone, but there's another way out. There's a ladder at the window on the outside," Mandie told him.

"And how do you know?" he teased.

"Because I've used it," Mandie answered. "We had to take things out of the loft for this party, and I helped."

Tommy grinned at her. "You're quite a girl—or young lady—I guess I'm supposed to say," he corrected himself.

There wasn't a lot of conversation during dinner. The boys were too busy devouring everything in sight. Evidently the girls' cooking experiments were a success.

After the meal, the minstrel show began. The enthusiastic applause was followed by encore after encore. Eventually Miss Prudence shook her tinkling silver bell and announced that it was time to say good night.

Later in their room, Mandie and Celia chattered about the evening.

Celia plopped down on the bed. "Robert is really nice," she said, beginning to get ready for bed.

"Yes, he is," Mandie agreed, "and so is Tommy. He's going to write me a letter."

"Robert said he wanted to call on me one day soon, but I said I didn't think we were old enough for that."

Mandie nodded and picked up her nightgown. "You're right. Besides, we've got other things to do. We have to learn everything this school wants to teach us so we can get out of here," she said, pulling her nightgown over her head.

Mandie sighed deeply, picked up her Bible from the table by the bed, and sat down. "Tomorrow is Sunday. I need to read my Sunday school lesson before I go to bed," she said. Celia took her

Bible and sat on her side of the bed. "We still have ten minutes before we have to put out the light," she replied.

"Our lesson is on the Beatitudes in Matthew," Mandie said. "I sure need to learn all this. It's so hard to love your enemies. I don't think I've been doing a very good job with April."

"Mandie, nobody's perfect. I'm sure God will forgive you for telling Miss Prudence your suspicions about April in the loft. She deserved that."

"But, Celia, it doesn't matter whether or not the other person deserves it. We aren't supposed to do bad things to people when they do bad things to us."

"That's all right up to a certain point. But you had to tell on April. This whole thing is getting out of hand."

"Listen to this," Mandie told her. "Read chapter five, verse forty-four. 'But I say unto you, love your enemies, bless them that curse you, do good to them that hate you, and pray for them which despitefully use you, and persecute you.' " Mandie looked up from reading. "You see, we're even supposed to love people who are mean to us."

"But how can you love someone who acts like April? She's impossible!"

"Celia, I don't know what—" The ten o'clock bell interrupted Mandie's answer. "I guess we'll have to blow out the light, now."

They closed their Bibles, placed them on the table, and Mandie extinguished the lamp.

The girls crawled into bed and were soon dozing.

Suddenly, the clanging, squeaking noise startled them awake. They sat up in bed. The noise overhead sounded even louder this time. Celia grabbed for Mandie in fright.

"Let's go up there," Mandie said. She jumped out of bed. "Only this time we'll take a lamp with us."

"But what if we get caught?"

"Nobody's going to catch us. Come on," Mandie urged. She lit the lamp and picked it up.

Celia stayed close behind Mandie as they tiptoed out to the hallway. Suddenly the house was completely quiet.

"The noise stopped. Let's go back," Celia begged, pulling at Mandie's nightgown.

"No, Celia. We only need one trip up to the attic to see what's making the noise," Mandie said with determination. She started up the dark steps. "I'm going."

Celia gave in and followed. As the two girls approached the attic, they could see that the door at the top of the stairway was closed. Mandie reached forward and pushed the door open slowly. She held the lamp inside the doorway and looked around. The lamp threw only a small amount of light in the dark attic.

Mandie stepped forward. "Look at all the old furniture in here," she whispered. "I don't see a thing that could have been making the noise."

Celia stayed close to her friend. "Let's go, Mandie," she begged. "There's nothing here."

Mandie stumbled over something. The glass chimney on the lamp crashed to the floor. Mandie blew out the light. She couldn't let the flame burn unprotected.

Then, in the darkness, from the other side of the attic, came the clanging metal and the squeaking board noises. The girls turned and ran, stumbling down the dark stairs as fast as they could go. When they reached the last step, they saw a light coming toward them. Before they could find a place to hide, Miss Prudence appeared in her long trailing nightgown at the bottom of the stairway.

She held her lamp up to see the girls' faces. "Aha! So you two *do* prowl around after ten o'clock," she accused. "What have you been doing up in the attic?" Glancing down, she noticed the lamp base in Mandie's hand. "And where is the shade to that lamp?"

Mandie bit her lip. "I'm sorry, Miss Prudence. I broke it. I tripped and it fell off," she explained. "I'll pay for it."

"Yes, you'll pay for it. And you'll also pay for being out of your room. You two will be confined there for ten days except for church, and classes, and meals. And if you don't abide by the rules, it will be much more serious than that. Do you both understand?"

Mandie hung her head. "Yes, ma'am, Miss Prudence," she replied.

"Yes, ma'am," Celia echoed.

"Now, what were you two doing up in that attic at this time of night?" the schoolmistress demanded.

"We've been hearing noises in the attic," Mandie answered. "And tonight the noises seemed to be louder, so we went to investigate."

"Noises? What kind of noises?"

"It sounds like metal banging, and we could hear boards squeaking like someone walking around up there," Mandie told her.

"Metal banging and someone walking in the attic? How far-fetched can you get?" She turned the girls around and ushered them down the hallway toward their room.

"But, Miss Prudence, we're serious," Mandie protested. "We've been hearing noises like that ever since we came to school."

"We have, Miss Prudence, several times," Celia added.

The woman stopped and looked doubtfully at the two girls. "All right," she conceded. "I'll get Uncle Cal to look in the attic tomorrow. He'll have to go up there anyway to clean up the broken glass. Now, not another word out of either of you." She pointed the girls to their door. "Get in that room and don't come out until breakfast time tomorrow."

The girls quickly obeyed and closed the door behind them. They listened for Miss Prudence to go down the hallway, then began whispering in the darkness of their room.

"What a bad break!" Mandie exclaimed. "If I hadn't broken that lamp shade, we might have found something up there."

"Well, I guess the fun is over." Celia sighed and crawled into bed.

"Oh, no, it isn't." Mandie slipped under the covers on her side. "I still plan to see what's up there."

"Mandie, you don't dare!"

"Oh, yes, I do! And don't tell me you're afraid to go with me."

"But, Mandie, there's no telling what will happen to us if we're caught again."

"We won't be caught again."

"But you always say that," Celia complained.

"Next time we'll be more careful," Mandie promised. "But, Celia, you don't have to go with me if you don't want to."

"No, I don't have to. But I suppose I will," Celia replied. "I just wish I could understand why you're so determined to go up there."

"I can't explain it," Mandie answered, "but something tells me I should keep looking."

"Well, I sure hope it's worth getting into trouble for," Celia said.

CHAPTER EIGHT

CAUGHT!

Even though all the girls were required to attend Sunday school and services, they were not all in the same classroom at church. Therefore, Mandie and Celia did not see April until they filed into the pews across the aisle from Mr. Chadwick's boys.

April sat at the end of the pew directly across from Tommy. She tried her best to attract his attention, but Tommy didn't seem to notice her. He looked straight ahead.

Celia poked Mandie and motioned for her to look. Mandie smiled as she and her friend sat down in the pew directly behind April.

During the entire service April kept looking at Tommy. When the audience stood to sing a hymn, she deliberately reached out and dropped her handkerchief in the aisle.

When Tommy didn't respond, she tried other tactics. Quickly replacing her hymn book in the rack, she leaned across the aisle and spoke loudly above the music. "Tommy, do you have an extra hymnal? We seem to be short one over here," she said.

All the girls held their breath and looked to see if Miss Prudence had heard. But the schoolmistress kept singing heartily.

Without missing a note, Tommy handed April his hymnal and turned to share Robert's.

April took the book but did not sing a word. She just stood there holding the open hymnal and watching Tommy. At the end of the song, as everyone sat down, April leaned across the aisle and handed Tommy the hymn book.

"Here, would you put this back where it belongs?" she said loudly.

Everyone nearby turned to look, including Miss Prudence. She frowned at April, then turned her attention to the pastor's sermon.

When the service was over, Miss Prudence guided April out of the church. "This way, April, with the other girls," she said.

The boys left by the other aisle, but April had to go with Miss Prudence. After shaking hands with the pastor at the door, the girls began their short walk back to the school.

Celia nudged Mandie. "Imagine carrying on like that in church," she said softly so no one else could hear.

"I suppose it's her last chance, for a while at least. I heard Miss Prudence tell her that her mother would be here to get her after the noon meal," Mandie said.

"Hallelujah!" Celia laughed.

"Celia, didn't the Sunday school lesson do you any good at all?" Mandie scolded.

"We'll discuss that later."

Mandie sighed. "I guess we'll have plenty of time. Remember, we have to stay in our room except for meals and classes."

"Oh, well, at least that's better than being suspended like April," Celia replied.

Reaching the school, the girls hurried to their room to leave their bonnets, gloves, purses, and Bibles. They would have to move quickly to get to the dining table on time.

As Mandie and Celia entered their room, Mandie immediately sensed something wrong. Looking about, she discovered that her pink chiffon dress was missing. She had hung it on the hook next to Celia's lavender dress the night before.

"Oh, no! Not again!" she exclaimed.

Celia understood immediately. "April!" she accused.

"I'm not sure, but April is going home today. We'll see what happens while she's gone," Mandie said. "Come on. We don't want to be late to the table. We're in enough trouble already."

In the dining room, a tall, arrogant-looking woman stood behind the chair next to Miss Prudence.

The schoolmistress rang her little silver bell. "Young ladies, this is Mrs. Snow, April's mother. April will be going home today, and we are not sure when she will return."

There was no doubt that April went home that afternoon. So when they heard the noises in the attic that evening, they knew it couldn't possibly be April.

Immediately after supper, Mandie and Celia went straight to their room. The sun still shone brightly, and the two girls sat on the window seat, silently watching the other girls stroll around the lawn below.

The noise was barely discernible at first. Gradually it grew louder. The girls looked at each other. A moment later, the noise stopped.

"It can't be April this time," Mandie reasoned.

"No," Celia replied.

"Are we going to see what it is or not?"

"That depends."

"Depends on what?"

"On what you decide," Celia answered. "I always go along with you."

"All right. Let's go." Mandie led the way to the door, and they stopped to listen. "I can't hear anybody in the hall," Mandie whispered. Slowly, she opened the door.

"Quick! Let's get out of this hall!" Celia told her.

They quietly ran for the attic staircase and hurried up the steps. The window let in plenty of light this time, so they could see that the door at the top was closed.

"The door!" Mandie whispered. "I didn't close it last night."

Celia thought for a moment.

"But Miss Prudence was going to send Uncle Cal to clean up the glass, remember? He probably closed it."

"Right," Mandie agreed. She put her finger to her lips, then slowly turned the doorknob and swung the door inward.

The two girls stood at the doorway and looked around. There was enough light to distinguish most of the discarded objects of furniture around the attic: tables, chairs, chests, trunks, and boxes.

"There's nothing here," Celia whispered.

"No, I guess not," Mandie answered. Still looking around, she moved her foot. Crunch. She looked down. The glass chimney she had broken had not been cleaned up. She pointed to it, motioning to Celia.

"Uncle Cal didn't come up here. Who closed the door?" she whispered.

At that moment a huge rat ran across Celia's foot. She screamed. "Let's go!" she cried. Running out of the room, she stumbled down the stairs with Mandie following.

But just as they turned the corner to go to their room, they saw Miss Prudence.

The woman put her hands on her hips and advanced toward them with a stern expression on her face. "This is it!" she exclaimed. "You have broken my orders to stay in your room. You are both suspended from school for ten days. Celia, I will contact your mother immediately, and Mandie, I will send word for your grandmother to come and get you, since she lives here in town."

Terrible thoughts revolved in Mandie's head. Going to her grandmother's house would be more dreadful than being suspended.

"My grandmother?" she protested. "But, Miss Prudence, I don't really know my grandmother. I don't think she'd want me to come to her house. I've never been there. I've only seen her once in my whole life."

Miss Prudence looked at her in surprise. "And what is wrong between you and your grandmother?" the schoolmistress asked.

"She didn't like my father," Mandie replied, "because he was half Cherokee. She didn't want him to marry her daughter."

"I know all about that," Miss Prudence said with impatience. "But she is your grandmother whether she likes it or not, and she shall hear from me."

Celia hung her head. "My mother is ill, Miss Prudence, because of my father's death. Do I have to go home? It would worry her so much."

Mandie spoke up quickly. "My grandmother's house is huge, so I know she has plenty of room. Couldn't Celia go with me to my grandmother's house?"

"Oh, yes, please, Miss Prudence," Celia begged.

The schoolmistress relaxed her stern expression. "I suppose it doesn't matter where you go, as long as I know you are in responsible hands. But the decision will remain with Mandie's grandmother, of course," she said. "I suppose you girls were in the attic?"

Mandie nodded. "We heard the noise again."

"It certainly is strange that no one else has ever heard these noises," said Miss Prudence.

Mandie swallowed and looked her straight in the eye. "We're not lying about it, Miss Prudence. We really have been hearing noises up there."

"Probably rats. Now get your things together, and do not—I re- peat—do not leave that room again tonight. I will send a message to your grandmother as soon as I can find Uncle Cal." Miss Prudence stood watching while Mandie and Celia returned to their room.

The girls began picking up their belongings and piling them on the bed.

"Thank you, Mandie, for asking me to your grandmother's," Celia said.

"Never mind thanking me," Mandie teased. "I'm afraid to face my grandmother alone. But I didn't want your mother to be upset, either. This way, maybe she won't ever find out."

"Then I'm glad I'm going with you."

"Oh, Celia, I just thought of something!" Mandie exclaimed. "Uncle Ned is supposed to visit me tomorrow night. How will he know where I am?"

Celia thought for a moment. "Ask Uncle Cal to watch for him. He and Aunt Phoebe said they saw him when he was here before."

"Smart!" Mandie replied. "I'm glad you're going with me, too."

Later, the two girls stood on the veranda watching, while Uncle Cal loaded their belongings into the surrey.

As they began the drive to her grandmother's house, Mandie spoke her concern to Uncle Cal. "You will watch out for Uncle Ned, won't you, Uncle Cal, and tell him where I am?"

"I sho' will, Missy. I be lookin' fo' 'im," the old Negro assured her. "Phoebe see bettuh in de dahk. I gits huh to watch. Don't you worry none, Missy. We looks fo' 'im."

"I appreciate that, Uncle Cal," Mandie told him. "You know why we're going to my grandmother's house, don't you?"

"Missy, I don' ax. Miz Taft, she tell me y'all gits ten days outa school to spend wid huh."

"Ten days out of school because we've been bad," Mandie said, explaining about the noises in the attic.

"Ain't ne'er been nobody in de attic since years ago, Missy, when I tuck some things up dah fo' Miz Prudence. Ain't nobody e'er goes up dah."

"But we really did hear something—several times," Celia insisted.

"Mought be de rats."

"No, we saw some rats up there, but rats couldn't bang on metal and make the boards squeak, could they?" Mandie asked.

"Reckon not, Missy. Reckon we oughta find out whut's up dah, but I reckon Miz Prudence ain't gonna do it."

"You're right, Uncle Cal," Mandie agreed. "She didn't believe us at all about the noises."

Uncle Cal turned the surrey off onto a driveway leading to a huge mansion.

Celia's eyes grew wide. "Mandie, is this where your grandmother lives?" she asked.

"I'm afraid it is," Mandie replied. "But I've never been inside. My grandmother was never at home when we were in Asheville."

The closer they got, the bigger the mansion looked.

"She sure has a big house!" Celia exclaimed.

Suddenly, Mandie's stomach felt like it was tied in knots. "Uncle Cal, are you sure she said it was all right for Celia and me to come and stay awhile?"

"Missy, she say, 'You go back right now and git dem girls, tonight. Don't wait 'til tomorruh. Go now.' And dat's whut I done." Uncle Cal stopped the surrey in the driveway near the front door.

A Negro man in butler's uniform appeared at the doorway and came forward, greeting them with a smile. "Evenin', Missy Manda and Missy Celia. Y'all jes' go right in. I bring yo' things."

Mandie and Celia said good-bye to Uncle Cal and walked slowly toward the ornate front door.

At the door, a black maid greeted them. "Evenin', Missies," she said. "Miz Taft, she say 'bring y'all right in.' Dis way, please."

The maid led them down a huge center hallway and through double doors into the most elegant parlor either girl had ever seen. Mandie had thought her Uncle John's house was a mansion, but it couldn't compare with this one. The one time Mandie talked to her grandmother, she had learned that her grandmother was well off. But Mandie hadn't dreamed of anything this beautiful.

Her grandmother sat reading by a window that overlooked a bright, lush flower garden. She put down her book. "Come in, come in," she said, motioning for them to sit in the plush, high-backed chairs near hers."Sit down. Take off your bonnets and gloves and get comfortable."

The girls sat down, and Mrs. Taft studied Celia carefully.

"So this is Jane's little girl, Celia," she said.

The girls looked at her in surprise.

"You girls don't know it, but, Amanda, your mother went to school with Celia's mother."

The girls turned toward each other and grinned.

"No wonder we're such good friends." Mandie laughed.

"It's almost like we're kinpeople," Celia added.

"I'm so glad to invite you to my home, Celia. I hope you enjoy your stay here," Mrs. Taft said kindly. "Now, they tell me you two kept insisting you heard noises in the attic, and that you kept breaking rules in order to investigate. Is that right?"

Mandie looked down and fidgeted with her gloves. "Yes, ma'am." She lifted her chin. "But we *did* hear noises in the attic. And Miss Prudence wouldn't believe us. So we *did* break the rules, I guess," she admitted.

Mandie's grandmother laughed. "Exactly what I would have done under the circumstances. I have a mischievous streak in me, myself," she said with a twinkle in her eye.

The girls stared at her in amazement.

"Oh, I'm far too old for such tomfoolery now, but when I was young, nothing could have stopped me," she assured them. "You see, Amanda, that is something you have inherited from me."

Mandie smiled. "Yes, Grandmother, I guess we are pretty much alike. I imagine you were a lot of fun when you were my age. And here I was bracing myself for a good scolding from you."

The woman laughed again. "I wouldn't scold you for having a natural curiosity. However, you must remember the old saying: 'Curiosity killed the cat.' "

Mandie sat forward on her chair. "I intend to investigate again when we go back to school," she confided. "That is, if we hear the noises again."

"Oh, no, Mandie," Celia protested. "Next time we'd probably be sent home for good."

"Don't worry about that, Celia," Mrs. Taft said. "They wouldn't dare expel my granddaughter and her friend. That could ruin their reputation in certain circles. I am surprised that Miss Prudence had the audacity to go this far. Actually I rather imagine that she is already regretting her action."

Back at the school office Miss Prudence paced up and down in front of her sister.

"I suppose I shouldn't have been so harsh as to suspend the girls for ten days. I really should have just tried to scare them with the idea. But that Amanda is quite uncontrollable. Rules don't seem to mean a thing to her," Miss Prudence complained.

"But, Sister, Amanda seems to be such a sweet girl," Miss Hope replied. "She was raised in a log cabin, remember? She probably doesn't know any better. I don't think Amanda would deliberately do something wrong."

"But she did. She broke the rules twice, two nights in a row," Miss Prudence reminded her. "I trust Mrs. Taft is not too upset about our sending the girls to her. If she wanted to, she could really make trouble for the school. You know that."

"Yes, Mrs. Taft has a great deal of influence," Miss Hope agreed. "I wouldn't want to get on the wrong side of that lady."

"Well I have decided that when the girls come back to school, I shall try to ignore their curiosity excursions," Miss Prudence declared. "If they want to run around in that spooky attic at all hours, I'll let them—as long as the other girls don't find out."

Miss Hope shuddered. "I can't even imagine having the nerve to prowl around in the attic in the middle of the night," she said. "I wonder if there really is something up there."

That night as Mandie and Celia went to sleep in a huge guest room at Mrs. Taft's, Mandie couldn't get her mind off the noises in the attic. How could she wait ten days to find out what was making those strange sounds?

CHAPTER NINE

VISITORS AT GRANDMOTHER'S HOUSE

The next morning, the two girls ate breakfast with Mandie's grandmother in the cheery sun room.

"You young ladies will have to find something to entertain yourselves this evening," Mrs. Taft told them. "I'm sorry, but I had already planned to go to the theater with my friends tonight. I inquired about more tickets, but they are sold out."

"That's all right, Grandmother. We can find lots to do around here," Mandie assured her.

"Lots to do?" her grandmother questioned.

"Yes, ma'am. Like exploring your house. It's fascinating," Mandie replied. Then with a mischievous look in her eye she added, "Or we could investigate the attic."

"I don't think you'll find anything interesting there," her grandmother replied. "I keep my attic clean and orderly, not unkempt like you described Miss Prudence's." She added, smiling, "However, you may give it a try."

The day passed quickly for the girls. They walked around the grounds exploring every nook and cranny. In the stables they found the beautiful thoroughbred horses. They climbed up on an ornate carriage that would be a museum piece someday, and pretended they were grand ladies riding to the theater. Outside, they met

Gabriel, the gardener. Gabriel was a tall, stoop-shouldered man who delighted in having a captive audience for a tour of his magnificent gardens.

After a very proper evening meal, Mrs. Taft left for the theater and the girls went to their room. During the afternoon, they had made plans for an exciting night.

"Your grandmother is nice, Mandie," Celia said.

"She seems to be," Mandie replied. "And it was awfully considerate of her to go out and give us time to slip back to school and explore the attic."

Both girls began to change into dark clothes.

"Yes. We'll have to wait until after ten o'clock, but since she said she wouldn't be back till about midnight we've got plenty of time," Celia agreed. She hesitated. "Mandie, do you think we are doing anything wrong?"

"Yes and no," Mandie said thoughtfully. "But I keep feeling that I have to go back. I prayed about it, and I just think I should find out what's going on in that attic."

"Do you really believe God answers prayer?" Celia asked.

"Of course," Mandie replied. "Haven't you ever had your prayers answered?"

"No," Celia answered. "Sometimes I pray and pray, but then I don't know if God answered my prayers or it just happened by itself."

"Oh, Celia, nothing can happen by itself. God makes things happen," Mandie told her. "If something happened after you prayed, God was answering your prayers."

Celia thought about that for a minute. "I wish I had your kind of faith, Mandie," she said.

Before they knew it, the china clock on the mantlepiece was chiming ten times.

Mandie jumped up. "It's ten o'clock!" She grabbed a dark scarf to tie over her blonde hair. Celia did likewise.

Mandie tucked some matches in her pocket. "I just hope there's a lamp in our bedroom at school that we can use," Mandie said.

"First we have to get inside," Celia reminded her. "They lock all the windows and doors at night, remember?"

"We'll get in somehow. Ready?" Mandie inspected her friend's appearance.

Celia adjusted the scarf over her curls. "Ready," she replied.

Keeping an eye out for the servants, the girls tiptoed down the huge circular staircase and hurried out the front door unnoticed. Earlier, they had unlocked one of the French doors in the downstairs library so they could get back in without alerting anyone.

As they hurried down the dark streets, they saw only an occasional passerby. They went out of their way to avoid the train depot. They knew people might notice them there. A sharp train whistle blew in the distance. It grew louder as a train came into town, and the girls were glad they had stayed away.

When Mandie and Celia reached the school, they began searching for some way to get inside. Cautiously, they pushed and shook various windows and doors, but to no avail. After what seemed like hours, the two were tired and disheartened. They sat down on the back steps to think the matter over.

After a moment Mandie stood and looked up at the second story. "Celia," she whispered. "Look! There's a window up there that's open. I'm pretty sure it's a bathroom."

Celia joined Mandie and looked upward.

"If we could climb up on the porch roof, I think we could get in that window," Mandie said.

"But how are we going to get up there?"

Mandie looked around the walls of the screen porch. She inspected the posts holding up the roof and the cross boards that supported the screen wire.

"I think we could climb this corner post," Mandie suggested. "See the cross boards there?" Mandie was just about to put her foot up on one of the boards when she heard a low bird whistle. Mandie whirled around. "Uncle Ned!" she whispered to her friend.

Celia followed as Mandie ran around the corner of the house to the magnolia tree where Uncle Ned always waited.

"Oh, Uncle Ned!" she whispered as she took the old man's hand in hers. "I forgot. Did Uncle Cal find you and tell you that we're staying at my grandmother's house?" she asked.

"Cal tell me, but I see Papoose come from road. I wait to see what Papoose do," he told her.

"We're trying to get inside so we can go up to the attic," Mandie said.

"But Papoose already caught for going to attic. Sent away from school. Must not go back inside," the Indian advised.

"But I have to, Uncle Ned. I have to find out what's making that noise in the attic. My grandmother is not home tonight so we came back."

"No, no, no!" the old man admonished her. "Must not do this. Papoose hear train whistle?"

Mandie looked at him, not understanding. "Why, yes, we heard the train coming, but we stayed away from the depot."

"Mother of Papoose and Uncle John on that train. They come see Grandmother," he told her.

Mandie's face lit up. She tugged at his hand. "Come on then. Let's go back to my grandmother's," she said.

"No, cannot go. Next moon will visit Papoose. Go now. You, too, Papoose Celia."

Mandie pulled him down to plant a kiss on his wrinkled cheek. Then grabbing Celia's hand, and holding her skirts high with her other hand, she raced back to her grandmother's house.

Even though they ran every step of the way, when they reached the mansion, four visitors were walking the floor of the library. The maid couldn't find the girls anywhere, and she told them that Mrs. Taft had left Mandie and Celia alone while she went to the theater.

The girls burst into the room through the French doors. There was a big commotion. Mandie spotted Snowball sitting on top of the mahogany desk. She was so glad to see him, she ignored everyone else, grabbed her white kitten and nearly squeezed the breath out of him.

"Oh, Snowball!" she cried, rubbing his white fur. He purred and licked her face with his little rough tongue.

Suddenly embarrassed that she hadn't spoken to her visitors, Mandie quickly went to her mother and Uncle John. Snowball clung to the shoulder of her dress.

"Oh, this is so nice!" she cried. "Mother! Uncle John!" Tears of joy slid down her cheeks. Then all of a sudden she realized she had two more visitors. She whirled around. "Dr. Woodard! And Joe!" She planted a kiss on the doctor's chubby cheek and grabbed Joe's hand. "It's so wonderful to see all of you."

Mandie then remembered her manners. "Oh, Mother, this is Celia. She's the daughter of your friend, Jane Willis Hamilton."

Elizabeth walked over and put an arm around Celia. "I can't believe it!" she exclaimed. "My daughter making friends with Jane's daughter, and neither one of us knowing it. Celia, I'm so glad to meet you, dear."

Celia smiled. "I can't wait to tell my mother who Mandie is," she said.

When all the introductions were over, everyone sat down and Mandie's mother took on a serious tone. "Now, Mandie, I want you to tell us just where you two have been," she demanded.

Mandie looked at Celia. "We were out taking a walk."

"A walk? At this time of night?" her mother asked.

"Grandmother was gone, and we didn't have anything else to do," Mandie said weakly.

"Amanda, young ladies do not go out this time of night unescorted," her mother scolded.

Mandie stroked her kitten's fur. "I'm sorry, Mother. We won't do it again," she promised.

"You had better not do it again. Something might have happened to you two. What would Celia's mother have thought? Celia's under *my* mother's supervision. Amanda, stop to think once in a while before you do these wild things," Elizabeth lectured.

That completely silenced Mandie. Celia hung her head.

Dr. Woodard tried to lighten the conversation. "We came with your mother and Uncle John to tell you how things are going with the hospital," he said.

Mandie and Celia leaned forward with excitement. Mandie had told Celia how she and her friends had found bags and bags of gold. The gold had belonged to the Cherokees, but Mandie was their heroine, and they put her in charge of it. Now that gold was being used to build a hospital for the Cherokees.

"Oh, please tell us all about it, Dr. Woodard," Mandie said. Snowball snuggled up closer.

"Well, we've got the excavation done and the stakes are up," the doctor said. "It won't take long to lay the foundation and get the walls up. We ought to have it mostly done before cold weather."

Mandie jumped up and danced around the room. She grabbed Joe's hand and pulled him with her. "I'm so glad!" she exclaimed.

Elizabeth watched her daughter, then looked at her husband, and shook her head. Evidently the lessons at the school had had no effect on her.

Joe grasped Mandie's hand tightly to stop her dancing. "We're saving most of the trees," he said. "I told them you didn't want the trees cut down."

"No, don't let them cut down the trees. There wouldn't be any shade, and the birds wouldn't have any place to rest," Mandie said. She walked over to her mother. "When can I go see it, Mother?"

"We need to talk, Amanda," Elizabeth answered. "You and Celia come with me to the parlor." Turning to the others she said, "Excuse us. We'll be right back."

The two girls exchanged glances. Mandie handed Snowball to Joe, and she and Celia followed Elizabeth down the hall. When they reached the parlor, Elizabeth sat on the red velvet sofa while the girls took the chairs.

"Now, young ladies," Elizabeth began, "I want this understood once and for all. If you don't behave yourselves at school, Amanda, you will be brought home to Franklin where I can have you under my own twenty-four-hour watch." And turning to Celia, she said sternly, "Celia, I will talk to your mother, as well. There's no excuse for what you two have been doing. We are sending you to school to learn, not to go traipsing around in dark attics."

The girls' eyes widened.

"Yes, I know about it," Elizabeth continued. "Miss Prudence also sent me word. That's why I'm here tonight."

The girls sat silently.

How can I get her to understand? Mandie wondered. *Something is urging me to keep investigating until I solve the mystery of the noise in the attic. Until I do, I don't think I'll have any peace.*

Her mother broke into her thoughts. "As far as your being allowed to see the work on the hospital, that is out of the question right now, Amanda. Until you settle down and apply yourself to your school-work, there will be no extra activities. Is that understood?"

Mandie stared at her mother. Elizabeth had never talked to her like that before. *Have I really been so bad that Mother has to lecture me?* Mandie wondered. She blinked repeatedly to keep her blue eyes from filling with tears. It hurt to have her mother scold her so harshly.

Finally, she nodded. "Yes, Mother. I'm sorry," she managed.

Then she really burst into tears and flew into her mother's arms, sobbing uncontrollably. "I'm sorry, I'm sorry," she kept repeating.

Celia silently wiped a tear from her own eyes. Mandie was her dearest friend, and it hurt to see her so distressed.

Elizabeth smoothed her daughter's blonde hair and held her tightly. "All right, Amanda, I love you. That's why I had to make you see the wrong you are doing."

Mandie knew she couldn't make her mother understand how important that noise in the attic had become to her, so she decided not to say any more about it.

Celia finally spoke. "Mrs. Shaw, please don't let my mother know. She's still sick with grief over my father's death. What I have done would hurt her so much. I should have stopped and thought about the consequences before I got into this. I'm more sorry that I can express."

"All right, Celia. I will spare your mother under the circumstances, but remember, this reprimand applies to you, too. You need to settle down and get your mind on your schoolwork," Elizabeth said. "I want you to know I was very sorry to hear about your father. He was a nice man. I knew him years ago."

"You did?" Celia replied.

Elizabeth stood. "Yes, and you look more like him than you do your mother," she said. "Now, both of you go wash your faces, and then come back to the library. I'm sure you'd like to spend some time with Joe, Amanda."

The two girls did as they were told and found a bathroom down the hall. Mandie closed the door behind them. "You know I'd much rather be at home in Franklin than in that silly school. But that's what Mother wants, so I'll try to get through it somehow."

Celia turned on the crystal-handled faucet. "My mother feels the same way, so I suppose I'll have to endure it as well. But it isn't going to be easy." She splashed cold water all over her face, then turned to get a towel.

Mandie looked in the mirror. Her eyes were red and her hair was a mess. She washed her face and tried to smooth her hair.

As they opened the door to return to the library, they heard Mrs. Taft greeting Elizabeth down the hallway.

"What brings you here this time of the night, Elizabeth?" she asked.

"You know what brings me here, Mother. Miss Prudence contacted me."

"You didn't come all the way from Franklin just because Amanda got suspended from school for a few days, did you?"

"Of course, Mother."

Mrs. Taft smiled. "I thought it sounded exciting, poking around in dark old attics, looking for noises." She laughed.

"Mother, it might have been exciting, but it was disgraceful to get suspended from school."

"Oh, come now, Elizabeth. I always wanted you to have that kind of spunk when you were growing up, but you were always meek as a mouse, just like your father."

"Oh, Mother, really!"

"Now, Honey, settle down. Who came with you?" she asked, changing the subject.

"They're all in the library. John is here, and Dr. Woodard and Joe, and Snowball."

"That cat? You brought him on the train?" Mrs. Taft's laughter floated down the hallway.

The two girls slowly made their way back to the library. They both knew it would be fun having Mandie's grandmother on their side. Mandie had prayed so often for her grandmother to like her. Now, for the first time, she was beginning to feel like a granddaughter.

CHAPTER TEN

SNOWBALL DISAPPEARS

After breakfast the next morning, Celia decided to let Mandie have some time alone with Joe.

"If you don't mind, Mandie, I think I'd better wash my hair this morning," she told her friends. "It'll take a while to get dry."

"Oh, sure, Celia. Go ahead," Mandie replied. "We'll catch up with you later."

Mandie led Joe outside. "Let's go to the garden," she suggested. "I want you to see my grandmother's beautiful flowers. And her gardener, Gabriel, is absolutely unbelievable!"

Clutching Snowball, Mandie walked with Joe down the pathway through the flowers, smelling, touching, and admiring. Then they came to a bench by a water fountain.

"Would you like to sit down a minute, Mandie?" Joe asked.

"Sure, Joe," Mandie replied. She sat on the bench and Joe joined her. Snowball curled up on her lap. "Isn't it beautiful here?" Mandie asked.

"Yeh, but I'd much rather be back home. I don't like so much finery."

"Neither do I," Mandie admitted. "I admire this place, but I wouldn't want to live here. I'll be glad when I get through with that silly school and can go home." She stroked Snowball thoughtfully. "You know Celia and I got suspended for ten days, don't you?"

"Yeh, I know. That was a dumb thing to do."

"I suppose it was dumb, but there's something compelling about that noise in the attic. I feel I just have to find out what it is before it's too late."

"Too late for what?" Joe asked.

"I don't even know," Mandie answered.

"Well, why can't you do it and get it over with, instead of getting caught every time?"

"That's what I intend to do. As soon as I get back to school I'm going to find out once and for all what that noise is."

"Didn't you promise your mother you'd behave at school and not go chasing that noise anymore?"

"No, she didn't ask me to promise. She just said if I didn't settle down and study, she'd bring me home where she could watch me. I didn't make any promises."

"But, Mandie, that was understood. Your mother took it for granted that you had promised."

"I'll try real hard not to get caught again."

"Mandie, that's not being honest. I don't understand what's come over you." He looked closely at her. "You and Celia weren't out just taking a walk last night, either, were you?"

Mandie's cheeks felt suddenly warm. Joe had caught her in a lie.

"We really did take a walk—all the way back to school. We were going to try to get in and search the attic, but Uncle Ned was waiting. It was his night to visit me. And he told us y'all were here."

"Mandie! You had better straighten up and start telling people the whole truth. And you've got to learn something at that school."

Mandie frowned at him. Her face flushed at the tone of his voice.

"You've got to learn something at school," he repeated, " 'cause I don't want a dumb wife," he teased, taking her hand in his.

Mandie's heart beat a little faster. She would never forget the first time he told her he wanted to marry her when they grew up. She took a deep breath. "All right, I'll try to do better. But I do have to find out what's in the attic."

"All right," Joe said, "but hurry up and get it over with. Remember, you can't have everything just the way you want it. Life isn't like that. There's good and there's bad. And there are some things that we think are unbearable."

"I know I have to get an education," Mandie conceded.

"I'm sure your mother would rather have you at home with her every day," Joe reasoned. "But she knows you have to be educated, so she is willing to give you up for a while. Have you ever stopped to think about that, Mandie?"

"I've thought about it," Mandie answered. "But I haven't talked to her about it."

"Well, maybe you should," Joe suggested, and then added, "End of lecture. Now, let's find that gardener you were talking about." He stood up and Mandie followed him. Snowball jumped to the ground.

That evening Mandie talked to her mother as they sat on the sun porch.

"Mother, I have to ask you to forgive me," Mandie began.

"Oh?" her mother replied.

"I'm afraid I told you a lie last night," Mandie confessed. "Celia and I weren't just out for a walk. That was only part of it. We walked back to school to try to get inside and go up to the attic."

Elizabeth studied her daughter for a minute before speaking. "That's what I thought," she said. "I was waiting to see if you would tell me the truth. I knew you wouldn't just take a walk that time of the night."

"I'm sorry, Mother. Please forgive me," Mandie pleaded.

Elizabeth drew a deep breath. "You are forgiven this time but, Amanda, please don't let it happen again. I am not trying to be unkind. I want you to know that I'm only interested in your well-being," she assured her daughter. "Above all, however, please don't ever lie to me again. Whatever you do or get into, I'd rather be told the truth. You should trust me enough to know you can tell me anything. Real love depends on trust." Her voice quivered slightly. "Oh, Amanda, you just can't imagine how much I love you."

Mandie slipped out of her chair and sat next to her mother on the settee. She took her mother's hand in hers and squeezed it hard. "And I love you more than I can ever tell you, Mother. I thank God every day for bringing us together."

After a few minutes of silence Elizabeth wiped a tear from the corner of her eye. "We have to go home tomorrow, Amanda," she said. "Dr. Woodard has patients to see, and your Uncle John has business to look after. I want to leave with the assurance that you will do your very best at school. I shouldn't have to worry about what you might be doing while we are separated."

"I'll learn everything I can," the girl promised. "But, Mother, what good will it do me to learn all those social things? I need to learn more mathematics so I can keep track of the Cherokees' gold."

Elizabeth laughed. "That's what we've got your Uncle John doing. He knows all about money. That's a man's work."

"But, Mother, the Cherokees put the gold in my hands to use for them, and I'd like to keep up with it."

"Don't worry about that. Your Uncle John will sit down with you when you come home and go over every penny."

"And when am I coming home?"

"We'll come and get you for Thanksgiving week. Your Uncle John was planning to keep it a secret, but we're going to visit your Cherokee kinpeople that week."

"Oh, Mother! Thank you!" Mandie hugged her. She couldn't wait to see all her father's relatives at Bird-town and Deep Creek.

"You won't let your Uncle John know that I told you?"

"No, Mother, I won't. Thank you for sharing the secret," Mandie said with a twinkle in her eye. "Since you know Celia's mother, do you think we could invite them to our house for Thanksgiving?"

"We'll decide that later. It would be better if you don't ask Celia until we're sure what plans your Uncle John has for that week."

That night Mandie slept better, knowing that she would be able to see her Cherokee kinpeople at Thanksgiving.

The next day when everyone prepared to go to the train station, they couldn't find Snowball. He had been around Mandie's feet all morning, but at the last minute the kitten disappeared. It was as though he knew they were going to take him away from Mandie.

Mrs. Taft had told the girls that when they returned to school, they could plan to visit her on weekends. So Mandie secretly hoped they wouldn't find Snowball before they had to leave. Then she would be able to see her kitten every weekend.

Finally, they had to quit looking for Snowball. They didn't want to miss their train. At the depot when everyone kissed and waved good-bye, Mandie didn't even shed a tear. She knew she would soon be going home to visit.

Just before Joe boarded the train, he squeezed Mandie's hand.

She whispered in his ear. "Don't let anyone know I told you, but I'm coming home for a whole week at Thanksgiving."

A big smile broke across Joe's face. "I'm glad, Mandie. I really do miss you. Please don't get into any more trouble."

Mandie smiled back at him. "I'll do my best not to."

Later, when Mandie, Celia, and Mrs. Taft returned home, Snowball sat on the front porch waiting for them.

Mandie picked him up and stroked his fur. "You're a smart kitten!" she laughed.

Mandie and Celia enjoyed playing with Snowball during the rest of their stay at Mrs. Taft's. It hadn't turned out to be so bad after all.

The day the girls returned to school, they were packed and dressed, waiting in the parlor for Mrs. Taft to join them. She was going with them to have a little talk with Miss Prudence, she said.

Uncle Cal came from the school to pick them up. After loading their belongings, he waited in the surrey outside.

Snowball rubbed around Mandie's ankles as the girls waited impatiently for Mrs. Taft. They were excited about going back to school. Mandie picked up her kitten and gave him stern instructions. "Snowball, you be a good kitten for Grandmother, and I'll see you soon," she said, smoothing the fur on his head.

The kitten purred in response.

"Come, Amanda and Celia," Mrs. Taft called from the doorway. "We're ready."

Mandie put Snowball down. She and Celia quickly joined her grandmother in the hallway, then walked out to the waiting surrey. As Celia closed the front door behind them, she didn't notice the white flash of fur darting outside.

When the surrey arrived at the school, Miss Prudence welcomed them. "Please come in," she said, leading the way into the house. She called over her shoulder to Uncle Cal, "You know where to take their things—to their old room."

Mrs. Taft stopped Uncle Cal and said, "When you finish unloading, would you wait for me, please? I will only be a few minutes, but I need a ride back home."

"Yessum, I sho' will," Uncle Cal replied with a smile.

The schoolmistress led them into the little alcove where she had taken them on Mandie's first day at school. The girls sat down with the two women.

"Miss Heathwood, I have come to say a few things that I think ought to be made clear," Mrs. Taft said emphatically.

Miss Prudence glanced nervously at the girls. "Maybe the young ladies would like to go on up to their room," she suggested.

Mrs. Taft raised a gloved hand. "No, Miss Heathwood, I want them to hear what I have to say. I think it is very possible that the school made a serious mistake in suspending these two girls. They are now ten days behind their classmates in their studies because of a silly rule. And I don't think it would be to the school's advantage to engage in such punishment again."

The girls looked at each other in astonishment.

Miss Prudence straightened her skirts. The worry lines in her face deepened. "That's what I was expecting from you," she said. "However, the girl's mother put her in this school, and she is the one who should consult me. Not you." She paused for a moment, then continued. "I'm very sorry they are behind with their schoolwork, but it's their own fault. I must have my rules obeyed, no matter who is breaking them."

Mrs. Taft stood to her feet. "We'll see about that!" she exclaimed. "I'd say you'd better remember who your patrons are." She turned to Mandie and Celia. "Study hard and catch up, girls, and I'll see you next Sunday for dinner."

"Good-bye, Grandmother, and thank you for everything." Mandie almost felt like giving her a hug, but she didn't know how her grandmother would react.

"Thank you for letting me stay in your beautiful home, Mrs. Taft," Celia said.

"You're both welcome," Mandie's grandmother replied. "Now go up to your room and get on with your lessons." In a moment she was gone.

Mandie and Celia stood in the hallway, staring after her.

Miss Prudence came up behind them. "Get your things unpacked, young ladies, and be in the dining room in time for dinner," she said. Without saying anything more, she walked away.

Mandie took a deep breath. "Well, I guess that's that," she said.

"Let's go," Celia urged.

As they unpacked in their room, Mandie bent down to push an extra box under the bed. "I can't imagine why Grandmother did that," she said. Then she did a double take. What was that white thing she saw under there? *Oh, no. It couldn't be*, she thought. Lying on her stomach, she gave it a pull. Out came a ruffled, protesting Snowball. The girls burst into laughter.

"Snowball, how could you do this? You're going to get us into more trouble!" she giggled. "I know Miss Prudence won't allow you here." Mandie shook the kitten gently and looked into his blue eyes. He tried to lick her fingers.

Celia sat down on the floor, rolling with laughter. "He must have hidden in our baggage," she said.

"Maybe we can hide him here in the room. Then on Sunday we could take him back to Grandmother's," Mandie said.

That plan only lasted part of the day. When the girls left the room to go down to supper that night, Snowball made a beeline through the open doorway and disappeared down the hall toward the main staircase. The girls ran after him, but they couldn't find him.

"I guess we'd better forget about Snowball until after we eat," Mandie said. "If we're late for dinner, we'll really be in trouble."

"We can come back up and look for him as soon as Miss Prudence dismisses us," Celia suggested.

In the dining room the girls looked to see if April Snow had returned, but her place was vacant.

After supper, some of the girls who had never been friendly before, welcomed Mandie and Celia back. The pair must have seemed abrupt in their conversations, but they were anxious to hunt for the kitten.

When Mandie and Celia reached the upstairs hallway they ran into Aunt Phoebe.

"Lawsy mercy, Missies! Y'all sho' in a hurry," the old woman said. "I put food for dat white cat in yo' room."

Mandie looked puzzled. "Aunt Phoebe, how did you know about my kitten?"

"Cal, he say cat sittin' theah 'tween boxes when he unload de surrey. He know cat belong to Missy, so he tuk it up wid de rest, an' shut him up in de room. I lef' milk and food fo' de cat."

"But he isn't in our room. When we came out for supper, he ran out and disappeared," Mandie told her.

"Den we hafta hunt him. Miz Prudence she kill dat cat if she find him in dis house."

They searched everywhere but still couldn't find Snowball.

Mandie and Celia went to their room. It looked as though the kitten had really disappeared this time.

"Let's leave the door open just a crack in case he comes back this way. Maybe he'll come in," Mandie said.

But at that moment, Snowball had plans of his own. He wasn't about to give up the nice lap he was curled up in, or the soft hand rubbing his fur. He was completely happy.

CHAPTER ELEVEN

THE MYSTERY SOLVED

Even though Snowball hadn't been found by bedtime, the girls had to close their door. Mandie knelt by the bed to say her nightly prayers.

"Dear Lord, please send Snowball back to me," she prayed aloud through her tears. "I love him, and I don't want anything to happen to him," she said, raising her face toward the ceiling. "I thank you for your help, dear Lord. Amen."

Celia joined her. "Yes, dear God, please send Snowball back to Mandie. He's such a good little kitten. Please send him back," she prayed.

Instead of getting into bed, the girls put out the lamp and went to sit in the window seat. Even after the ten o'clock bell rang, they still sat there.

"You know, in a way I'm glad to be back at school," Mandie told her friend. "I want the time to hurry up and pass. At Thanksgiving, my mother is coming to take me home for a whole week!"

"You're going home for Thanksgiving?" Celia was surprised.

"Aren't you going home then, too?"

"I don't know. My mother hasn't said anything about it in her letters," Celia replied.

"Don't forget to write and tell her that my mother went to school with her. And be sure and ask her if you're going home for Thanksgiving week."

"All right," Celia agreed. "I'll write her a letter tomorrow."

Suddenly they heard the noise. The metal clanged and the boards squeaked. Both girls jumped up.

"Now!" Mandie exclaimed. She reached for their new lamp and the matches. Quickly lighting the lamp, she rushed to the door. Celia stayed right behind her. The noise continued as they cautiously climbed the stairway to the attic.

At the top of the steps, Mandie held the lamp in one hand, slowly turned the doorknob with the other, and pushed the door open.

This time the lamplight illuminated an unbelievable sight. A young girl with big brown eyes and long, tangled brown hair, and wearing Mandie's pink chiffon dress, was sitting on the floor with an iron poker in her hand. She was hammering at the lock on an old trunk.

When the girl saw Mandie and Celia, she froze in fear. Dropping the poker, she backed into a corner. And as the poker hit the floor, Snowball came bounding out of the darkness. Mandie quickly handed the lamp to Celia and picked up the kitten.

For a few minutes all three girls stood there, silently eyeing each other.

Then Mandie stepped forward in anger. "Why are you wearing my dress?" she asked.

The girl merely whined and cowered in the corner.

"I suppose you took my other dress, and my shawl, and my nightgown and broke my beads, too, didn't you?" Mandie accused. "What are you doing up here, anyway? You don't go to this school."

The girl did not speak but watched them fearfully.

All of a sudden Mandie realized that the girl looked sick and hungry. She felt sorry for her. "Are you hungry?" Mandie asked.

The girl still would not speak. Mandie turned to Celia. "Come on. We can get the food Aunt Phoebe left for Snowball and bring it up here. I think she looks hungry."

They hurried back down the steps with Snowball and gave him the bowl of milk Aunt Phoebe had left. Then they took the plate with a piece of meat on it back up to the attic.

When they returned the girl was still in the corner. Mandie advanced toward her and held out the plate of meat. The girl looked at it, then at them, then grabbed the meat from the plate and devoured it. Mandie and Celia watched in amazement.

The poor girl must be starved, Mandie thought. "Do you want to come down to our room with us?" she asked.

The girl ignored the question and kept eating.

"What do we do now?" Celia asked.

"I don't know," said Mandie. "Let's go downstairs and talk. Maybe we can figure out something." She waved to the girl. "We have to go now, but we'll be back," she promised.

When they got to their room, they sat down on the window seat again, and Snowball jumped up between them.

Suddenly Celia gasped. "God answered our prayers," she said. "He sent Snowball back to you!"

Mandie hugged her kitten and looked up at the dark sky outside.

"Thank you, dear God. Thank you," she whispered.

"That poor girl up there!" Celia exclaimed. "There's something wrong with her."

"I wonder why she won't talk," Mandie said. "Who is she? And how did she get up there in the first place? I'd also like to know what's in that trunk she's trying to open. Might be something real interesting. But that will just have to wait."

"Mandie, we've got to tell someone about her," Celia reminded her friend.

Mandie stood up and paced the floor. "I know we can't let her stay up there and starve. But if we bring her downstairs, then Miss Prudence will know we've broken the school rules again. This time she might dismiss us for good."

"But we can't leave her up there like that just to save our own skins. I really think she's sick, don't you, Mandie?"

"I'll send for Dr. Woodard. He'll know what's wrong with her," Mandie said.

"Too bad we didn't find her that night we came over here from your grandmother's. Dr. Woodard was already in town then."

"I know," Mandie agreed. "And now if we ask him to come, then everyone will know everything."

Mandie continued to argue with herself. "But why should she suffer for our sins? We would get into trouble, but she needs help." Mandie paused to think. "Oh, I have an idea! I'll ask Aunt Phoebe if the girl can stay in her house until Dr. Woodard can get here and see what's wrong with her."

"Aunt Phoebe might not agree to that. She might get into trouble, too."

"If I know Aunt Phoebe, she just might be willing to help." Mandie's eyes sparkled. "I'll ask her first thing in the morning."

At five-thirty the next morning, the girls shut Snowball in their room and made their way downstairs. Unbolting the back door, they went outside and hurried across the yard to the little cottage.

Aunt Phoebe, already up and dressed, came to the door. "Lawsy mercy, Missies! What y'all doin' up and dressed dis early in de mawnin'? Git in dis heah house 'fo' Miz Prudence sees y'all." She swung the door open and pulled them inside.

"Aunt Phoebe, we've got a problem," Mandie began, and then explained about the girl in the attic and their idea of bringing her to Aunt Phoebe's house.

"There's something wrong with her," Celia said. "She won't talk."

Aunt Phoebe put her hands on her hips and tapped her foot. "Y'all's a-fixin' to git yo'selves in mo' trouble," she said.

"We thought of that, Aunt Phoebe, but our troubles are not important compared to that girl's. She needs help," Mandie pleaded. "Please, Aunt Phoebe. We'll get her over here without anyone seeing her. No one will know about it."

"And tell me whut gonna happen if Miz Prudence find out 'bout dis?"

"I don't know, but we have to help the girl, even though it may cause trouble for us. We can't just ignore her," Mandie told the woman.

"She's almost starved to death," Celia said with concern.

Aunt Phoebe wasn't convinced. "Best y'all jes' march right up to dat Miz Prudence and tells huh. Let huh take care o' things."

"There's no telling what Miss Prudence might do," Mandie argued. "But if you'll let her stay here until Dr. Woodard comes, he can take her to the hospital or see that she gets medical attention. Please, Aunt Phoebe."

At that moment a loud voice called from the next room. "Phoebe, you do whut dem girls want. I send a message today to dat doctuh," Uncle Cal told her as he came into the room.

Phoebe turned to grin at her husband. "Lawsy mercy, Cal. Dat whut you want done? Heah I'se 'fraid to take de girl fo' fear you don't like it," she said.

"Now you knows we gotta hep Miz Lizbeth's girl," he told her.

The girls smiled broadly.

"Best y'all gits huh right now 'fo' anybody gits up!"

Mandie and Celia ran back to the house and hurried up to the attic. The girl was asleep on a pile of old quilts in a corner. Mandie noticed her other missing clothes lying on the floor nearby. Mandie touched the girl on the shoulder, and she sat up with a start. She stared at them in fear.

"Come on, we're going to eat," Mandie told her.

The girl stood up quickly and backed away.

"We're going to get food," Celia said.

But the girl refused to come near them.

"I have an idea," Mandie suggested. "She likes my clothes. I'll go get a dress and offer it to her."

Mandie and Celia ran downstairs to their room, and Mandie pulled a bright red gingham dress from the hanger. Being careful not to let Snowball out, they rushed back upstairs.

Mandie approached the girl, holding out the red dress in front of her.

The girl's eyes lit up. She advanced toward Mandie with her hand out to grab the dress. Mandie kept moving backward just out of the girl's reach, and the girl followed. They managed to get her all the way down the attic stairs, down the servants' steps, and out into the backyard.

Then Mandie ran ahead waving the dress at the girl. "Hurry!" she called.

The girl followed Mandie right through the front door of Aunt Phoebe's house.

Once inside the house, Mandie handed her the dress and pulled her gently into a rocking chair. The girl rubbed the folds of the dress and made little moaning noises as she rocked back and forth.

Aunt Phoebe studied the girl carefully. "I say she look sick. Sick in de haid," the old woman said. "Now, how do we keep huh in dis house?"

"When you and Uncle Cal leave," Mandie suggested, "just lock the outside doors so she can't get out. I'll bring her some pretty ribbons and things that will keep her entertained until Dr. Woodard can get here," she said.

Uncle Cal put his hands on his wife's shoulders. "Best we feeds huh fust. She sho' look mighty hungry," he said.

Aunt Phoebe pulled a little table near the rocking chair. "I don't know how you gits dat kind of sick people to eat, but I'll try."

She went into her kitchen and after a few minutes returned with a bowl of hot mush and a glass of milk. She set them in front of the girl.

Immediately the girl grabbed the bowl and started eating. But the whole time she was eating, her keen brown eyes watched everyone else in the room.

Aunt Phoebe smiled and patted the girl's thin shoulder. The girl looked up at her and smiled faintly. Everyone was delighted with her reaction.

Mandie approached the girl and stooped down in front of her, smiling. "We all really care about you. We want to be your friends. Can you tell me your name?"

The girl smiled back but did not utter a word.

"My name is Mandie. What's your name?" she asked.

The girl's only answer was a big smile.

"I thinks dat girl don't hear a word we'se a-sayin'," Phoebe said.

"You mean you think she's deaf?" Mandie asked.

Aunt Phoebe nodded. "Dat or she don' know how to talk."

Mandie got up and slipped around behind the rocking chair. Right behind the girl's head she yelled, "Tell me your name!"

The girl jumped out of the chair and whirled to stare at Mandie.

"Oh, I'm sorry!" Mandie cried. "You *can* hear. I didn't mean to scare you. Sit back down and eat."

The girl just stood there, looking at her. Mandie rested her hand on the girl's shoulder to turn her around and gently pushed her back into the chair. Mandie kept smiling at her. Finally the girl smiled back and picked up her spoon to resume eating.

"Den she don' know how to talk," Aunt Phoebe said.

"Maybe she's just scared—afraid to talk to us," Celia suggested. "She might have had some kind of shock before we found her."

"Well, best you girls gits back in dat house 'fo' Miz Prudence git up and see you, or we's all gonna git a shock," Aunt Phoebe warned.

"Will you get a message to Dr. Woodard for me, Uncle Cal?" Mandie asked.

"I sho' will, Missy. Jes' you write it out and I sees it gits to 'im," he promised.

"We have to go to classes today and I may not get a chance to see you. I'll write a note to Dr. Woodard and leave it under my pillow for Aunt Phoebe to bring to you," Mandie told Uncle Cal.

As Mandie and Celia left, they looked back. The girl was eating and not paying attention to anyone else. They shrugged their shoulders and headed for the schoolhouse.

"So far so good," Mandie whispered as they slipped back into their room. She took a piece of paper from her notebook and sat down. "I don't think I'll tell him the whole story. I'm just going to say a friend needs his help real bad, immediately."

A heavy feeling lifted from her shoulders when she signed the note and tucked it into an envelope addressed to the doctor. She slipped it under her pillow.

At last she knew why she was compelled to investigate the attic. She still might get into trouble over it, but she was glad she had persisted. Now maybe she could help.

Mandie paused for a moment to pray that God would heal the girl, making her well, and strong, and happy again.

"Oh, Celia," Mandie said to her friend. "I'm so glad it wasn't April who took my things."

"And *I'm* glad you didn't tell Miss Prudence about it like I kept telling you to do," Celia admitted. "It would have been awful if April had been blamed for something she didn't do. She gets into enough trouble on her own."

Mandie agreed.

CHAPTER TWELVE

GRANDMOTHER TO THE RESCUE

When Mandie and Celia arrived at their first class, Miss Cameron greeted them at the door. "We're so glad you are back," she said.

The other girls echoed her welcome.

Miss Cameron's eyes sparkled as she tapped her pencil, calling the class to order. "Amanda, while you and Celia were gone, we made plans for our first play," she said. "And the girls voted on the actresses for it. By a two-third's vote you have been selected for the leading role in the play."

Mandie stared at her teacher, completely speechless. How could she get all those votes? She hardly knew anyone except Celia. *How can I act in a play in front of an audience?* she thought. *I've never done anything like that!*

Celia nudged her. "Say something, Mandie. They're waiting."

Mandie rose in a daze and opened her mouth to speak. Nothing came out. She tried again. "Thank you. I appreciate your confidence in me." Her legs melted and she plopped down in her seat.

The class applauded.

Preparation for the play began immediately and took so much time that Mandie had very few opportunities to see the girl in Aunt Phoebe's cottage. Celia visited as often as possible and kept her up-to-date.

The next few days crept by, and Mandie didn't hear anything from Dr. Woodard. She worried that he might not have received her letter. Maybe it got lost, or maybe he was out of town when it came. She knew he traveled a lot.

Aunt Phoebe and Uncle Cal took good care of the girl from the attic. They gave her food and a bed to sleep in, but they kept the doors locked when they were out of the house. The girl seemed content but still did not say a word.

When Mandie learned that the girl loved Snowball, Aunt Phoebe said she could bring him over to the cottage for the girl to play with. Both Snowball and the girl were happy to have someone to play with, and Mandie was relieved that she wouldn't have to worry about getting caught with her kitten at school.

Everything seemed to be going fine. Then one afternoon during rest period, while Mandie and Celia were visiting, Miss Prudence made an unexpected appearance at Aunt Phoebe's house.

"Aunt Phoebe, I was wondering if—" She stopped short. Miss Prudence came into the room and closed the door. "Amanda, Celia, what are you two doing here?" Miss Prudence asked. "And who is that other girl? Where did she get that cat?"

"Miz Prudence, I kin explain," the old woman began.

The girl from the attic sat still, holding Snowball and staring at the schoolmistress.

"I think you had better explain fast, Aunt Phoebe," said Miss Prudence.

Mandie and Celia stepped forward.

"Blame it all on us, Miss Prudence," Mandie said. "Aunt Phoebe had nothing to do with it."

"Just what are you talking about, Amanda? Blame what on you? Speak up, young lady."

"Do you remember the noises we told you we heard in the attic? That girl was responsible. We found her last Monday when we came back to school," Mandie explained.

"That's right," Celia said. "When we heard the noises again, we went up to the attic and found this girl pounding on a metal trunk with an old fire poker."

Miss Prudence's mouth dropped open. "You found this girl in my attic?" She gestured toward the silent girl.

"Yes, ma'am, and she had been up there at least since school started," Mandie replied.

"Now, how could she survive up there that long?"

Aunt Phoebe spoke up. "I done been missin' vittles from de kitchen, most ev'ry day, Miz Prudence," she confessed. "But I figures some of yo' schoolgirls was a-doin' it, so I ain't said nothin'."

"You should have reported that to me immediately, Aunt Phoebe."

"Miss Prudence," Celia added, "the girl also kept coming down and taking Mandie's clothes. She was wearing one of Mandie's dresses when we found her."

Miss Prudence drew a sharp breath. "This girl has been stealing clothes, also? We *must* contact the authorities. Find Uncle Cal and ask him to see me immediately, Aunt Phoebe." The schoolmistress turned to leave.

"Wait, Miss Prudence," Mandie said. "You don't understand. There's something wrong with this girl. She can't talk. At least she hasn't said a word since we found her. We can't turn her over to the law."

Miss Prudence whirled in anger. "Oh yes we can, young lady. What else do you think we can do with her?"

Mandie thought quickly. "Send word to my grandmother," she blurted out. "I'm sure she'll take care of the girl until we can find out who she is."

Miss Prudence trembled. She could never let Mrs. Taft come meddling in school affairs again! "Your grandmother has nothing to do with this, Amanda," the schoolmistress said sternly. "This is a matter for the authorities. Aunt Phoebe, I shall be waiting for

Uncle Cal in my office, and you young ladies will both report to me after supper. You realize you have broken rules again."

Miss Prudence closed the door loudly.

"So we're in trouble again," groaned Celia.

Mandie had a sudden idea. "Aunt Phoebe, do you know where Uncle Cal is?" she asked.

"He be down in de flow'r garden wid dat man whut tends to 'em. I guess I'd best be gittin' him."

"Wait, Aunt Phoebe. Would you give me five minutes?" Mandie asked. "I want to find Uncle Cal first, and then you can come look for him."

"Lawsy mercy, Missy, whut you be up to now?"

"Just give me five minutes head start and then you can look for Uncle Cal. All right?"

Mandie didn't wait for an answer. She ran every step of the way down the long slope to the flower garden at the bottom of the hill. She arrived out of breath and tried to explain to Uncle Cal what was going on.

Uncle Cal looked worried. "Dat Miz Prudence, she say fo' me to come see huh?"

"Yes, Uncle Cal. Only I have another idea," Mandie said, beginning to breathe more easily. "Would you please rush over to my grandmother's first? Tell her about our finding the girl in the attic and everything. And ask her to come, just making a call," Mandie directed. "If she acts like she knows about the situation, Miss Prudence will suspect you told her. I don't know what Grandmother can do, but I'm sure she'll do something."

Uncle Cal went along with Mandie's plan. When he told Mrs. Taft the whole story, she immediately ordered her buggy brought to the front door. After arranging for someone to give Uncle Cal a ride back to the school, she climbed into the buggy and headed out. Driving herself, she took the long way around, stopping by the newspaper office. There, she talked to the publisher, Mr. Weston, and his photographer, Mr. Hanback. When they heard the story, they hurried to the livery stables to get their horses.

Next, Mrs. Taft dropped by her pastor's house and persuaded him to meet her at the school. Then when she told the story to the mayor, Mr. Hodges, he promised to arrive soon after she did.

Mandie's grandmother smiled to herself as she urged her horse on. She hadn't had this much fun in years. In a short time, Miss Prudence would have more than she could handle.

Arriving in front of the school, Mrs. Taft tied the reins to the hitching post and hurried inside. She found Miss Prudence in her office, waiting for Uncle Cal.

Miss Prudence looked up in surprise. "Good afternoon, Mrs. Taft," she said. "Do come in."

"Thank you," Mrs. Taft replied. She sat down. "Today is Friday and I thought I'd arrive early and see if Amanda and Celia could come home with me now for the weekend, instead of waiting for Sunday dinner."

"Why, yes, I suppose they could," the schoolmistress managed. She was sure Mrs. Taft had come to start trouble. "I don't believe they have any classes this afternoon. However, Amanda is rehearsing for the play."

Mrs. Taft stood. "She can make up for that later," she said. "Do you have any idea where the girls are?"

"Oh." Miss Prudence hesitated. "I'll send for them."

Suddenly Uncle Cal appeared in the doorway. "Missy Manda and Missy Celia be out at my house with Phoebe," he announced. "Dey say you wants to see me, Miz Prudence."

"So the girls are at your house, Uncle Cal," Mrs. Taft said. "I will go and get them." She started out to the hallway.

Miss Prudence hurried after her. "I'll send for them, Mrs. Taft. Please sit down and rest."

"Thank you, Miss Prudence, but I'd like to visit with Aunt Phoebe for a moment anyway," she replied. She continued down the hall and through the doorway into the kitchen.

Miss Prudence thrust an envelope into Uncle Cal's hand. "Take this note to Sheriff Jones," she ordered. "Quickly, Uncle Cal!"

Uncle Cal smiled to himself and obeyed, while Miss Prudence scurried after Mandie's grandmother.

When Mandie and Celia saw Mrs. Taft, they burst into laughter. "Oh, Grandmother!" Mandie cried. "I just knew you'd come."

"So you two finally found the noise," Mrs. Taft said. She looked at the youngster in the rocker.

The girl stopped rocking and stared at her.

"I've got help coming," Mandie's grandmother assured them.

Aunt Phoebe threw up her hands. "Lawsy mercy, Miz Taft, I guess we all be in trouble," she said.

"Don't you worry, Aunt Phoebe. Just leave everything to me," Mrs. Taft replied.

Suddenly there was a knock at the door and Miss Prudence hurried into the room. "Amanda, your grandmother has come to take you and Celia home with her for the weekend," Miss Prudence announced. "You may get your belongings together—whatever you need for the weekend."

Mrs. Taft faced the schoolmistress. "Mandie and Celia tell me they found this poor girl in your attic. Did you not know she was there?"

"Of course not, Mrs. Taft. I had no idea."

"Who is she? What are you going to do about her?" Mrs. Taft asked.

"Evidently she can't talk. They say she hasn't spoken a word since they found her," said Miss Prudence defensively. "I don't know who she is. I'm going to turn her over to the authorities."

"To the authorities? Do you know what they will do with her? They'll throw her in one of those dirty old cells until they can find out who she is. Surely you don't wish that on this poor child," Mrs. Taft argued.

"That is precisely what I plan to do," Miss Prudence replied. "I have already sent for the sheriff."

There was another knock at the door. Aunt Phoebe opened it to find the newspaper publisher, his photographer, and the mayor standing there.

Miss Prudence drew in a sharp breath as she recognized the three men. "Good afternoon, Mr. Weston, Mr. Hanback, Mr. Hodges," she greeted them. "Shall we go to my office?"

The three men pushed their way into the room so they could see the girl.

"No, thank you, Miss Heathwood," said Mayor Hodges. "We didn't come to see you. We came to see this girl who was found in your attic. And we want to talk to the young ladies who found her," the mayor explained.

Before Miss Prudence could ask how they knew about it, Reverend Tallant came through the open door.

"Good afternoon, ma'am," the minister greeted her. "I've come to see the little girl who was found in your attic."

Miss Prudence caught her breath sharply.

The four men crowded around the girl who had not moved since Mrs. Taft entered the room. Snowball still snuggled in the girl's arms.

Mandie, Celia and Aunt Phoebe stood to one side while Mrs. Taft spoke to the preacher. "How are you, Reverend Tallant? They say the girl hasn't spoken a word since they found her. Maybe you could get her to talk."

He nodded, pulled up a footstool, and sat down in front of the girl. "We're your friends, young lady," he said gently. "How about telling us your name. Can you do that for us?"

Everyone watched in silence. The girl moved her eyes but did not open her mouth.

Just then Sheriff Jones strode into the small living room and walked straight to Miss Prudence, his hat in his hand. "Afternoon, ma'am. Now, where's this girl you want us to take in?" he asked.

Miss Prudence froze as she felt everyone's eyes on her.

The sheriff pulled a note from his pocket. "Your man came by and gave me this note to come over here right away to take in a strange girl," he explained. "Where's the girl, ma'am?"

Reverend Tallant rose to face Miss Prudence. "You sent for the sheriff to come and lock up this little innocent girl?"

Mayor Hodges frowned. "Do you intend to throw this little girl in jail?" he asked.

"What for?" asked Mr. Weston, the publisher.

Miss Prudence took a deep breath. "It's all a mistake," she managed.

Mr. Weston wasn't satisfied. "These two young ladies *did* find this poor girl hiding in your attic, didn't they?" he probed.

When Miss Prudence didn't answer, Mr. Weston turned to Mandie and Celia.

"Yes, sir," they said in unison.

"Tell us all about it," Mr. Weston urged.

"Well, it was like this." Mandie related the whole story, including the two girls' ten-day suspension.

Miss Prudence ended Mandie's story. "And since you young ladies have again broken my rules, the consequences will be much greater this time."

At that moment Uncle Cal pushed his way through the crowd. "Stan' back, please," he announced. "De doctuh man be heah to see de girl."

Everyone moved back as Dr. Woodard and Joe nudged through.

Mandie ran to the doctor. "Oh, Dr. Woodard, I knew you'd come. Please do something. This girl is sick, and we don't think she can talk," Mandie said.

"I know. Uncle Cal told me about it when we caught up with him down the road. I've been away and just got your note yesterday," the doctor explained. "I had to come to Asheville today anyway, so Joe came with me." The doctor glanced at the girl in the rocking chair and then around the room. "Uncle Cal, do you have a bedroom where I can examine the girl?"

Uncle Cal nodded. Mandie tried to get the girl to go into the bedroom, but she refused to budge from the rocker. The doctor ordered everyone to leave except Aunt Phoebe.

Outside, the photographer set up his equipment by the front door to take pictures for the newspaper. Miss Prudence stood apart from the others who were standing around in small groups, talking.

A few minutes later, Miss Hope joined the crowd outside without her sister noticing.

Joe caught Mandie's hand and pulled her over to one side of the yard. "I'm glad you finally found out what was causing that noise. Who would have thought it was anything like this?" he said.

"I told you, Joe, something just urged me to find out what the noise was, and I'm sure glad I did. The poor girl is not well," Mandie told him. "I hope your father can help her."

Miss Hope came up quietly behind them. "So do we, Amanda," she said gently.

Mandie and Joe whirled around and stared.

"This has all been such a shock to my sister, I don't think she knows how to react."

"I never thought about that," Mandie replied. "I guess this could be bad publicity for the school."

"And I'm sure we are both embarrassed that this poor child was shut away in our attic without our knowledge, but I think my sister feels a greater responsibility." Miss Hope looked at Mandie with pleading eyes. "Oh, Amanda, if you had only come to us when you first suspected something."

"I tried to tell Miss Prudence," Mandie insisted, "but she wouldn't believe me."

"Maybe I could have helped," Miss Hope offered.

Joe squeezed Mandie's hand in support.

Mandie looked down at the ground. "I'm sorry, Miss Hope. I didn't mean to cause trouble. I just had this feeling that I should find out what was making those noises. And something good *did* come from it."

"I know your intentions were good, Amanda, and we are all thankful that the little girl is going to get some help." Miss Hope slipped her arm around Mandie's shoulders. "But you made some poor choices in how to solve the mystery. An adult could have been a great help. What if, instead of finding a frightened little girl, you had found an escaped prisoner hiding in that attic?"

Mandie shivered at the thought. "I see what you mean," Mandie said. "I guess maybe rules are there to protect us."

Miss Hope smiled.

Just then Dr. Woodard came out of the cottage. Several people started to question him, but he held up his hand. "I can't tell you much, except that the girl is badly undernourished," he reported. "She can hear, but I don't know about her speech. With proper diet and medical attention, it is possible that she could start talking."

A murmur went through the crowd.

Miss Prudence stepped forward. "But, doctor, the girl can't stay here," she objected. "If you don't want the sheriff to lock her up, someone will have to take her."

Everyone suddenly became silent.

Dr. Woodard walked over to the schoolmistress and raised his voice so that everyone could hear. "Why can't she stay here?" he asked. "Aunt Phoebe told me she would be glad to help the girl. We'll try to find out who she is, but we certainly can't put her in jail in her condition."

Mr. Weston cleared his throat loudly. "My newspaper is going to run a big story on this. We hope someone will read it and identify the girl," he said. "Would you like me to print a statement that you refused to keep the girl on your premises, even though your cook volunteered to care for her in her own house?"

Miss Prudence's lips quivered. "No, Mr. Weston. What I meant was that the girl couldn't stay here in the school with my students," she argued.

Suddenly Miss Hope appeared beside the newspaper publisher. "We *are* concerned about the girl, Mr. Weston," she said calmly. "Aunt Phoebe may certainly care for the child. That would be wonderful. We are quite pleased that she is willing."

"Yessum," Uncle Cal spoke up. "We takes care o' de girl 'til somebody find huh people," he said.

Miss Prudence heaved a sigh of relief and everyone seemed satisfied.

With that settled, Mrs. Taft called to the girls nearby. "Amanda, Celia, bring whatever you need for the weekend out to the buggy. Please hurry. Joe and his father are coming with us."

Mandie turned to Miss Prudence. "Are we still in trouble?" she asked.

The schoolmistress took a deep breath. "It was fortunate that the two of you were able to rescue the girl from the attic," she began. "However, since you have broken school rules, you must pay the penalty. Perhaps we'll take you out of the play as your punishment. Then you and Celia will take the responsibility of helping Aunt Phoebe with the girl."

Mandie swallowed hard. "Yes, ma'am," she replied. She hated losing out on the play, but she would enjoy spending time with the girl.

When the Sunday newspaper came out, it displayed bold headlines: "Unknown Girl Found in School Attic." The front page article related the two girls' part in the discovery and asked that anyone having information about the girl notify the newspaper office.

The following Friday, a poorly-dressed man and woman stopped by the newspaper office.

"We seen your story in the paper about the girl found in the attic," the man said. "We think maybe she's ours. You see, we've got a daughter that ain't all there. We've had to keep her shut up all her life. Somehow, she got out about a month ago, and we ain't seen her since."

Mr. Weston asked them a lot of questions and finally took the couple out to the school. Miss Prudence sent Mandie and Celia to Aunt Phoebe's cottage with them.

When the girl saw the people, she went wild with fright. There was no doubt about it. She knew them, but she was so terrified, she jumped out of the rocking chair, ran into the bedroom, and shut the door. In her haste, she dropped Snowball, and the cat hissed and slapped the man's leg with his outstretched claws. The man tried to kick him, but Mandie snatched Snowball up in her arms.

Mr. Weston frowned at the couple. "Evidently that girl knows y'all but she's afraid of you," he said. "What have you done to her?"

"We ain't done nothin', mister. She's our youngest. The rest of 'em done married and left home. But Hilda there, she ain't jest right, so, like I said, we keep her locked up so she don't run away."

"You mean locked up in a room by herself?" Mr. Weston asked.

"Yep. That's the only way we could keep her at home," the man said with a shrug.

Finally the wife spoke. "We couldn't let our neighbors know what a disgrace the Lord sent down on us. We ain't never lived a bad life, and we don't understand why God give us such a child."

"What's your name, feller?" Mr. Weston asked. "Where are you from?"

"Luke Edney, my wife, Mary. We live on a farm over near Hendersonville," he said.

"Well, your daughter is under a doctor's care right now," Mr. Weston informed them. "I don't think you can take Hilda home with you today. We'll have to see what can be done for her," he said.

A few days later, the whole town of Asheville, and the surrounding countryside, turned out for a parade to escort Hilda to the hospital.

Mr. and Mrs. Edney had been persuaded to commit Hilda to a private sanitarium. There she would receive medical attention, paid for by donations.

Uncle Ned came for the festivities, too, and as soon as Mandie could get a chance to talk to him alone, she confided in him. "I'm still concerned about April," she said. "I'm really glad I never accused her of taking my things, but I have been mean to her," Mandie confessed. "When she comes back to school, I'll ask her to forgive me." She sighed.

"Papoose need ask big people help more," Uncle Ned reprimanded.

"That's what Miss Hope told me," Mandie said. "I guess I did make some bad choices," she admitted, "and I've asked the Lord to forgive me. From now on I intend to stay within the rules and ask for help if there's a problem."

She looked thoughtful for a moment then said, "I might not get to be in the play, but I'm glad Hilda is getting medical help. Maybe someday she'll be normal. I'll pray for her every day, Uncle Ned," Mandie promised.

"Yes, Papoose," the old Indian said with a smile. "We both pray. Big God good."

Mandie smiled. "He sure is, Uncle Ned," she replied. "He sure is."

Then Mandie went to find her friend Celia. Grinning mischievously she said, "Don't you think it's about time we investigate that trunk up in the attic?—After we get permission, of course," she added.

Alarm spread over Celia's face. But then she sighed, "Oh, Mandie, how can I say no?"

MANDIE

AND THE
TRUNK'S SECRET

For My Son
Donn William Leppard
That rootin', tootin' cowpoke boy,
Now grown so big, handsome, and tall;
Life's most wonderful pride and joy,
And God's most precious gift of all.

CONTENTS

CHAPTER ONE

CLEANING UP THE ATTIC

Mandie squirmed in her chair in front of the headmistress's desk. She and Celia, her friend, had been called to the office—again.

Miss Prudence Heathwood, the tall, elderly headmistress, and her sister, Miss Hope, ran The Misses Heathwood's School for Girls, a boarding school where Mandie and Celia were students.

Miss Prudence looked sternly at the two girls. "You, Amanda, will not be allowed to participate in the school play," she said. "And, in view of your complete disregard for the school rules, I believe it is necessary for you both to be further disciplined."

The girls looked at each other, not knowing what to expect.

Miss Hope Heathwood, a little younger than her sister, sat to one side, watching the proceedings but saying nothing.

Miss Prudence cleared her throat and continued. "If you two had not insisted on running around after curfew looking for noises in the attic, none of this would be necessary," she reminded them. "This discipline is not only for your good, but also for the good of every other young lady in school here. We must have compliance with our rules. Is that understood?"

"Yes, ma'am," Mandie replied, flipping her long, blonde hair behind her. Then cautiously, she added, "But if we hadn't investigated the noises, we wouldn't have found that poor retarded girl, Hilda, in the attic."

"That is beside the point," the schoolmistress said firmly. "You must learn to do things within the rules." Miss Prudence sat straight in her chair behind the desk, occasionally glancing at her sister. "How that runaway managed to hide in our attic so long, only the Lord knows," she said.

"At least now she's getting some medical help at the sanitarium," Mandie said as respectfully as she could.

"That's enough," Miss Prudence snapped. "I have heard enough of your excuses. I am hereby ordering the two of you to begin the task of cleaning up the attic. I have asked Uncle Cal to assist you, but you are to sacrifice your morning free periods each day until the job is completed. You two will work while the other girls are enjoying their leisure. Is that understood?"

"Yes, ma'am," the girls said together.

"Very well then," Miss Prudence replied. Rising, she motioned to her sister, Miss Hope. "I'm putting you two completely under the supervision of Miss Hope. You will answer to her at all times on all questions. And let me tell you one thing. You two had better remember that. There is to be no more disobedience in this school or your parents will have to find you another school to attend." She turned to Miss Hope. "They're all yours, Sister. See that they live up to the rules," she said, hurrying out of the office.

Miss Hope pushed a stray lock of faded auburn hair into place and sat down behind the desk. "Now, young ladies, I'm sure we won't have any problems," she told them. "If we all live according to the Good Book, everything will be fine."

"I'm going to try real hard, Miss Hope," Mandie promised.

"Me, too," Celia added.

"I do hope you both remember your promises," Miss Hope said. "Now, about this chore of cleaning up the attic." She paused to clear her throat.

"Miss Hope, please tell us about all that stuff in the attic," Mandie begged. "There's so much furniture up there, and boxes, and trunks, and all kinds of things. How do you clean up an attic?"

Miss Hope laughed. "Now that's a good question," she said. "I suppose Uncle Cal can clean up with a broom and mop, and you girls can sort everything out. Maybe put everything of one kind together. You know, if there are clothes in several drawers or boxes, put them all in one spot. Arrange all the books in one place, and so on."

"Then we have permission to open anything up there?" Mandie asked.

"Why, yes. You may open anything in the attic," Miss Hope said.

Mandie's blue eyes grew wide, and the two girls looked at each other.

"Where did so much stuff come from?" Celia asked.

"It's mostly things the former owner left here when my sister and I bought this place. We've been here about forty-five years, but I don't think we've put much in the attic," the schoolmistress told them.

"Forty-five years?" Mandie gasped.

"Yes, about that long. The house was probably twenty years old when we bought it. The lady who owned it was a widow. Her daughter got married and left her alone. She didn't want to live here in this big place by herself, so she sold it to us and went to live with some relatives," Miss Hope explained. "We bought some of her furniture because she couldn't take it all with her. She told us to throw out anything we found in the attic, but we've never really cleaned it out. Most of that stuff up there is not ours."

"Didn't she ever come back for any of it?" Mandie asked.

"No, I don't think we ever saw her again. In fact, she must be dead by now. She was up in years then," the schoolmistress replied.

Mandie wiggled impatiently in her chair and smiled at Celia.

Celia glanced from her friend to Miss Hope. Apparently Miss Hope was not in any hurry to get the cleaning done.

"Well, when do we begin?" Mandie asked.

"You sound as though you're in a hurry," the schoolmistress said.

"We might as well get it over with," Mandie said, "so we can have our free periods for other things."

"I admire your enthusiasm, Amanda," said Miss Hope.

Mandie smiled. " 'Nothing like paying a debt and getting rid of it,' my father always said. And we do owe the school this work because we broke the rules."

"I'm glad you think that way, Amanda," Miss Hope said. "Some girls who have to be penalized for their wrongdoings seem to think we owe them something. I can see your father was a good man."

"My father was a wonderful man, I miss him so much." Mandie replied with a catch in her voice. "And he died so young . . ." Mandie bit her lip. Then turning to her friend, she added, "And so did Celia's. I suppose that's why we're such good friends. We understand each other."

"Right, Mandie," Celia's green eyes glinted with a touch of sadness.

Miss Hope fumbled with pencils on the desk, looked down at her hands, and then looked squarely at Mandie. "Do you know your father's people very well, Mandie?" she asked.

"Oh, yes, Miss Hope." Mandie brightened. "I have so many wonderful Cherokee relatives. My grandmother was full-blooded Cherokee, you know, but my father never told me for some reason. I didn't know about it until my father died. Then Uncle Ned, his old Indian friend, came and explained everything to me. He told me about my father's brother John, too. I had never even heard of him. But dear old Uncle Ned helped me get to Uncle John's house in Franklin."

"What about your stepmother?" Miss Hope asked.

"Well, you see, I thought my stepmother was my real mother until I went to Uncle John's house. Uncle John found my real mother for me and then the two of them got married," Mandie explained.

Miss Hope leaned forward. "I didn't know all that, Amanda," she said. "I knew your mother, you know, when she went to school here."

"My mother went to school here, too," Celia said, pushing back her thick auburn curls. "Our mothers were friends. Mandie's grandmother told us about it when we went to visit her."

"Yes, I remember your mother very well, Celia," Miss Hope said. "Tell me, dear, how is your mother? Is she adjusting to the loss of your father?"

"I'm not sure, Miss Hope," Celia replied, twisting her fingers in her lap. "You know I haven't been back home to visit since I came here, and Mother doesn't write very often."

"I'll send her a note, Celia, and inquire about her health," the schoolmistress promised.

"Thank you, Miss Hope. I was worried about leaving her at home alone, but she insisted that I come on to school the day after my father's funeral," Celia said, her voice quivering.

"I know, Celia," Miss Hope said, sympathetically, as she rose from her chair. She flipped open the watch she wore on a chain around her neck, then added, "Now, young ladies, as soon as I can find Uncle Cal and set up this cleaning schedule, I'll let you know. But I believe right now it's about time for you to go to the dining room for your noon meal."

The girls stood up.

"Thank you, Miss Hope. I promise to do my best," Mandie told her.

"And I do, too," Celia added.

"That is all I can ask. Now run along," Miss Hope told them.

No talking was ever allowed during mealtime, so as soon as Miss Prudence dismissed everyone, the two girls ran all the way up the stairs to their room on the third floor of the boarding school.

Puffing for breath, they burst into their room and collapsed on the bed, laughing.

"Now we have permission to unlock that trunk we found Hilda beating on," Celia said.

"Right. Miss Hope said it was all right for us to open anything in the attic," Mandie said. "I sure am anxious to see what's inside that trunk."

"Me, too," her friend answered.

Mandie sat up quickly, pushing back her thick blonde hair, which she now wore loose. "But not anxious enough to break any more rules," she said.

"I'm not either," Celia echoed.

"I'll tell you what," Mandie suggested. "If you catch me breaking any more rules, or about to break any, will you remind me of what happened to us the last time we did such a thing? I don't want to get suspended from school again."

"I will if you'll listen to me, Mandie," her friend agreed, "and if you'll do the same for me."

"It's a promise," Mandie said. "I guess we'd better get going. It's time for our class. I hope we can start cleaning up the attic before too long."

"And I hope whatever's in that trunk is worth losing all our free periods for," Celia told her as they descended the stairs for their history lesson.

"Even if it isn't, I guess we deserve the punishment," Mandie said.

"But I have a feeling there's something exciting hidden in that trunk," Celia said.

CHAPTER TWO

THE LOCKED TRUNK

The ten o'clock curfew bell had already rung. All the lights were out. Mandie and Celia, still dressed, sat on the window seat in the darkness of their room.

Mandie stared out the window. "It's about time for Uncle Ned to come," she told her friend. "I'd better go down to the yard."

"Mandie, why didn't you just tell Miss Hope about Uncle Ned's visits so you wouldn't have to sneak out to see him after everyone is in bed?" Celia asked.

Mandie quickly turned. "Oh, no, Celia!" she said emphatically. "I don't think Miss Hope and Miss Prudence like Indians."

"I suppose a lot of white people are like that," Celia agreed. "But I don't see why."

"Well, I don't either, but I'm not taking any chances. Uncle Ned is my father's friend. He promised to watch over me after my father went to heaven. I don't want anything to stop me from seeing him. And rather than take a chance on telling anyone, I'd rather meet him this way," Mandie explained without taking a breath.

"I understand, Mandie, but please be careful. I don't want you to get into any trouble," Celia said. "Give Uncle Ned my love."

"I will, Celia. Don't forget to stay by the window where I can see you from the yard. And close that window in a big hurry if you hear anyone coming," Mandie reminded her.

Celia promised she would, and Mandie slipped out into the hallway and down the servants' stairs to the kitchen. Sliding the bolt on the back door, she stepped outside, then ran around to the side of the house where she could see Celia watching from their bedroom window.

Mandie stood in the light of the full moon, watching the shadows of the huge magnolia trees for her old friend. He was usually on time.

Suddenly, she heard a low bird whistle, and she whirled to see Uncle Ned coming toward her.

Mandie ran to meet him. "Uncle Ned!" she exclaimed, grabbing the old Indian's wrinkled hand.

Uncle Ned stooped to hug her tight. "Papoose, sit," he said.

Moving to a bench in the shadows below the opened window, they both sat down.

"I have some exciting news, Uncle Ned," Mandie began. "Remember that girl, Hilda, that Celia and I found hiding in the attic? Remember how we told you that she was beating on an old trunk with a poker trying to open it?"

"Yes, Papoose," the old man answered. "Put sick Papoose in hospital."

"That's right, Uncle Ned," Mandie said. "Well, as our punishment for wandering around after ten o'clock at night, Miss Prudence has ordered Celia and me to clean the attic during our free periods."

The old Indian looked closely at her. "Papoose not open trunk and get in more trouble?" he asked.

"We have Miss Hope's permission to open anything in the attic. We have to sort everything and make it all neat and clean. So Celia and I are going to open that trunk and see what's in it," she told him.

"What Papoose do with what Papoose find in trunk?" he asked.

"That depends on what it is," Mandie replied. "It might be something interesting. Then again, it might just be some old clothes. Only I don't know why anyone would lock old clothes up in a trunk."

"Papoose must be good," the old man warned her. "If find important thing, must tell Miss Head Lady."

"Not Miss Prudence, Head Lady, as you call her. Miss Hope has been put in charge of Celia and me. We have to answer to her," she said.

"Then Papoose must tell Miss Head Lady Number Two," he said. "Papoose must not make more trouble. Jim Shaw not like. I promise Jim Shaw I watch over Papoose while he go to happy hunting ground."

Mandie sobered quickly. "I know, Uncle Ned." She put her arm through his and squeezed it. "I know my father would expect me to live right. I want to be a good person like my father was. I promise to behave," Mandie said, smiling at the old Indian. "Besides, I love you, too, Uncle Ned."

"Papoose dear to heart," the old man assured her.

Mandie sat up straight. "Uncle Ned, did you bring any messages from my friends back home?"

The old Indian smiled broadly. "I bring message from doctor son, Joe," he said. "He come to Asheville with Dr. Woodard soon."

"Oh, that's a *good* message," Mandie said excitedly. "Are Joe and his father going to stay at my grandmother's house?"

"He say he bring white cat see Papoose," the old Indian told her.

"Snowball? Then he must be going to stay with Grandmother because that's where Snowball is," Mandie replied. "Remember Mother couldn't find him when she brought him on the train to see me? Then after Mother left, there was Snowball, sitting on Grandmother's doorstep."

Uncle Ned laughed.

"And remember how he got into my baggage when I came back to school from Grandmother's? Celia and I found him under the bed in my room," she said, laughing. "He's a smart cat!"

"White cat have own mind," Uncle Ned agreed.

"Any other messages?" Mandie asked.

"Cherokees at Bird-town and Deep Creek send love, too. They say Papoose hurry back home."

"Tell them all I love them, too, Uncle Ned," Mandie said with a smile. "As soon as I can get a holiday from school I'll be back to see them. I miss everybody so much."

"John Shaw and Papoose's mother want Papoose stay in big house in Franklin," he said.

"Oh, I will, most of the time, but I want to really get to know my other relatives. I'm proud to have Cherokee kinpeople. I'm so glad God made me that way," Mandie said.

"Cherokee proud of Papoose. God know how to make us all just right, Papoose," he replied.

"I know, Uncle Ned."

The old man rose from the bench. Mandie, holding his hand, stood by his side.

"Must go now. Papoose go back. I watch," he told her. "I come see Papoose next moon change."

He bent to hug her, and Mandie kissed his withered old cheek.

"Don't forget, Uncle Ned. I'll be waiting for you," she said. "And please tell everyone I send them my love."

"I tell, Papoose. Now hurry," Uncle Ned said.

Mandie, glancing up at Celia standing by the window above, ran across the grass to the back door. Turning to wave good-bye to the old Indian, she slipped inside the house, shot the bolt across the kitchen door, and made her way back up to her room.

Celia met her at their door.

When Mandie had closed the door softly behind her, she blurted out the good news. "Celia," she said excitedly. "Joe is coming to see me!"

"Oh, I'm so happy for you," Celia replied. "When?"

"I don't know exactly," Mandie said, "but Uncle Ned said 'soon.' "

"Did you tell Uncle Ned that we had to clean up the attic, and about that trunk?"

"Yes, and I promised him we wouldn't get into any more trouble," Mandie said.

The two girls slipped out of their dresses and picked up their nightgowns lying across the foot of the bed.

"Let's not forget to keep that promise, Mandie," Celia said, pulling her nightgown over her head.

"Celia, please keep reminding me of that. I really do want to behave. I want to be the kind of girl my father would be proud of," Mandie said, as she sat down on the side of the bed.

"I know what you mean, Mandie. That goes for me, too," Celia told her. "We'll just have to keep checking on each other."

"Agreed," Mandie said. "Maybe Miss Hope will let us know soon when we're supposed to start on the attic."

A few days later Miss Hope called the girls to her office where Uncle Cal, the school's old Negro servant, was waiting.

"This won't take a minute," the schoolmistress told them. "I've talked to Uncle Cal here and explained what's to be done. You two can begin on the attic during your free period tomorrow morning. Uncle Cal will sweep and mop the place this afternoon, so it won't be so dirty to work in. Then he will unlock everything—all the wardrobes, chests, and so on."

The two girls exchanged glances.

"I want y'all to sort everything and create some order up there," Miss Hope continued. "I'm putting y'all entirely on your own and trust you to do the job right."

"Yes, Miss Hope," Mandie said.

"Yes, ma'am," Celia agreed.

"Then Uncle Cal will meet y'all up there in the morning. Now, get on with your classes," she said, waving them out the door.

"See you in the morning at ten, Uncle Cal," Mandie said.

The old Negro grinned. "I'll be there, Missy," he replied.

The next morning at the appointed time, Uncle Cal and his wife, Aunt Phoebe, were waiting for the girls.

"Cal, he say fo' me to help Missies, so heah I be," the old servant woman told them.

"Oh, thank you for coming, Aunt Phoebe, but Celia and I have to do the work," Mandie told her. "I'm glad you came though. I haven't had much chance to see you since Miss Prudence made the rule that we have to get permission to go to your cottage."

"I knows, Missy," Aunt Phoebe said, patting the girl's blonde head. "But I still watches out fo' Missy when she go out in de dahk to see Mistuh Injun Man."

"You do?" Mandie said in surprise. She gave the old woman a hug. "Thanks for watching out for me, Aunt Phoebe."

Uncle Cal jingled something in his pocket. "I'se got de keys," he said, pulling them out and dangling them in front of the girls.

"Uncle Cal, how do you happen to have the keys to everything up here when Miss Hope said all this was mostly stuff the lady left here when she moved?" Mandie said.

"Missy, keys go wid furnichuh. No sense in lady movin' out, leavin' furnichuh and takin' de keys wid huh," he explained.

"You're right. The keys wouldn't be any good without the furniture," Mandie said.

"Lemme see now," Uncle Cal said, trying first one key and then another in the locks of the various pieces of furniture. With some success, he was unlocking wardrobes and chests. Aunt Phoebe walked along behind him, examining the contents of each.

Mandie drew Uncle Cal's attention to the locked trunk on the other side of the attic. "Do you have a key to this trunk, Uncle Cal? This is the trunk that girl, Hilda, was trying to open," Mandie told him.

"I'll sho' see," Uncle Cal replied, making his way over to the big old trunk.

Mandie and Celia watched anxiously as Uncle Cal tried key after key in the lock.

"Missy, don't be no key to fit dat trunk," he told them.

Mandie and Celia both sighed.

"Are you sure?" Mandie asked. "Maybe you missed one. Why don't we go around and leave the key in each lock that it fits and when we run out of keys or locks, we can see what's left," she suggested.

So this they did. But as they finished, there was no leftover key. Every key had been used.

"Were those all the keys Miss Hope had?" Mandie asked.

"Dese all she have in de cab'net. I watches huh git 'em out," the old man assured her.

Aunt Phoebe spoke up. "Dat all de keys, Missy," she said. "Miss Hope done had me goin' all ovuh de house lookin' fo' keys and dey ain't no mo' to be found."

"Do y'all know where this trunk came from?" Mandie asked the old servants.

They both shook their heads.

"Dat trunk done be heah long as I 'membuh," Uncle Cal said.

"I don't nevuh come to de attic," Aunt Phoebe told them, "so I ain't got no idee wheah it come from."

"Maybe the key will turn up somewhere," Mandie said.

Uncle Cal bent to hit the lock with his hand several times, but the lock didn't budge.

"Dat's a good lock. Won't bounce open like some I'se seen," he said.

Mandie's face clouded with disappointment.

"Missy, we'se got all dese othuh things we'se got to straighten out anyhow," Aunt Phoebe said, surveying the room. "That be 'nuff work."

"I know, Aunt Phoebe. Come on, Celia," Mandie said. "You start at that side over there, and I'll start over here in this corner. Let's look through everything real fast and get an idea of what all is here. Then we can decide how to sort things out."

Opening doors and drawers became a time-consuming but interesting chore. The girls held up fancy dresses of bygone days, trying to imagine how they would look in such finery. They modeled ancient hats in front of a mirror on an old vanity. They rummaged through drawers full of quaint trinkets and fancy hair combs. Examining an old wooden box damaged by rats, they found several leather-bound first editions of books long out of print. One drawer of an old chest was crammed full of old yellowed nighties, and a small trunk in the corner contained dozens of pairs of funny-looking ladies' shoes. Everything seemed to be old and worthless.

Suddenly the bell in the back yard rang loudly, bringing the girls back from the old world around them.

"Oh, that's the end of free period!" Celia exclaimed.

"And look how dirty I am," Mandie cried. "Come on, we'll have to hurry." She dropped an old dress she was holding and started for the door. "Good-bye, Uncle Cal and Aunt Phoebe. See y'all later to finish."

"Jes' you be careful flyin' down dem steep steps like dat," Aunt Phoebe called after them.

When the girls reached the bathroom on their floor, they hurriedly washed and then ran to their room to change clothes.

"You might know, that particular key has to be missing," Mandie sighed as she chose a clean dress from the chifferobe.

"Just our luck. All this dirty work and we can't even get that old trunk open," Celia moaned.

Mandie pulled her dress over her head. "We've got to figure out some way to find that key," she said. "I don't want to do all that dirty work for nothing."

Celia finished buttoning her dress, and the girls grabbed their books from the table to run downstairs.

"Don't give up," Mandie told her friend as they reached the classroom just in time. "Where there's a will there's a way. Somehow we'll find out what's in that trunk."

CHAPTER THREE

WHAT'S IN THE TRUNK?

Miss Hope was watching for Mandie and Celia that evening as the girls gathered around the dining room door for supper. "Amanda, Celia," she said, motioning them aside. "Uncle Cal gave me a good report on your work this morning." She smiled.

"Thank you, Miss Hope," Mandie said.

"But we aren't finished," Celia told her.

"I know. It will undoubtedly take more work to complete the task, but that wasn't why I stopped you. Amanda, your grandmother sent a note over here this afternoon. She was asking permission for your friend, Joe Woodard, and your cat, Snowball—of all things—to visit you." Miss Hope laughed.

"Oh, when, Miss Hope?" Mandie said excitedly.

"Joe will be here at ten o'clock tomorrow morning. He and his father are staying with your grandmother during his school's harvest break," the schoolmistress said. "Now I know that's your free period when you two are supposed to be cleaning the attic, but Miss Prudence forgot about that when she granted permission. So I'll excuse you this one time. The work can be continued the day after tomorrow."

"Oh, thank you, thank you, Miss Hope," Mandie replied.

Miss Hope looked into the dining room. "Get in there quickly now. Miss Prudence is coming in the other door," she said.

As the girls hurried into the dining room, Mandie grasped Celia's hand. "Where there's a will there's a way," she said softly.

"You mean Joe?" Celia asked in a whisper. "To open that trunk?"

"Right." Mandie grinned.

Since no conversation was allowed at the table, the girls had to wait until the meal was over to discuss their plans for the next day. And then they talked well into the night.

Mandie and Celia awoke early the next morning and eagerly dressed for the day. They were impatient throughout breakfast and morning classes. When the bell rang at ten o'clock for free period, Mandie and Celia were the first ones out of the classroom.

"The porch," Mandie called to her friend as she hurried down the hallway.

Celia followed close behind as Mandie pushed open the front screen door. Joe was waiting on the porch swing with Snowball curled up asleep on his knee.

Joe was Mandie's friend from back home in Swain County. A tall, thin, gangly lad with unruly brown hair, quick brown eyes, and a determined chin, Joe towered over tiny Mandie. He was very protective of her, but he also liked to tease her a little.

Mandie ran forward and picked up her kitten, cuddling him to her neck. Snowball woke and began licking his mistress's neck with his little pink tongue. Then perching on her shoulder, he began to purr softly.

"Snowball, I'm so glad to see you," Mandie whispered. "Thanks for bringing Snowball, Joe."

"That's some greeting for a friend you haven't seen for so long," Joe teased, as he stood up.

"You know I'm always glad to see you, Joe," Mandie told him, reaching to take his hand.

"I know, but I always like for you to tell me so," Joe said, squeezing her hand.

Celia watched Mandie and Joe with amusement. "Would y'all like for me to go somewhere and come back later?" she asked.

"Of course not, Celia," Mandie said quickly.

"It's nice to see you again, Celia," Joe said.

Just then Snowball jumped down and landed on the swing. Mandie reached for him.

"Mandie, please don't let him get away," Joe warned. "I'd hate to have to track him down."

Mandie captured the kitten and held him tightly.

"Me, too," Celia added. "Remember when he got loose in this house and we found him with the girl in the attic?"

"Speaking of attics, Joe—" Mandie guided the conversation. "Come on. We want to show you that old trunk in the attic." She turned to enter the house.

"The one Hilda was trying to open?" he asked, following the girls into the hallway inside.

"That's the one," Mandie replied.

The three quietly made their way up to the attic. Mandie, taking the lead, pushed open the door and stood back for Joe and Celia to go inside.

"Wow!" Joe exclaimed, looking around. "Some attic! There's enough furniture up here to furnish ten houses!"

"Not quite," Mandie replied. "There's the trunk over there."

She pointed to the one thing in the attic that remained locked. Celia led the way through the jumbled mess of everything they had opened and started to sort the day before. Mandie stood by the trunk with her arms crossed and a disgusted look on her face.

"You see, it's locked and we can't find a key to fit it," Mandie said, banging the lock with her fist.

"You can't find a key anywhere?" Joe asked.

"No," Celia replied. "Uncle Cal had the keys to everything else, but not to this trunk."

"How are you going to find out what's in it?" Joe asked. Then a grin spread across his face. "I suppose that's what you're planning now," he said. "Always poking and investigating and getting into trouble, both of you."

"I'll have you to know, we have permission to open anything in the attic," Mandie said smugly. "You see, Miss Prudence gave us the job of cleaning this place up—with a little help from Uncle Cal. Now if you could just figure out some way to get this thing open, then we could see what's inside it."

"So that's why you really brought me up here. Well, I'm not a magician. If you don't have a key, there's no way I know to get it open," Joe told her.

"You could break the lock," Celia suggested.

"Break the lock? And get *myself* in trouble?" Joe asked.

"Look! There are Uncle Cal's tools," Mandie said. She bent behind the trunk to pick up a screwdriver and a hammer. "Couldn't you use these to pry it open?"

"Mandie, you're asking for trouble," Joe warned.

"Miss Hope said we could open anything in the attic. If you're careful and don't damage the trunk, I think it would be all right to force open the lock," Mandie argued. She turned to Celia. "Don't you think it would be all right for us to use these to open it?"

Celia hesitated for a moment and then replied, "I suppose it would be all right. Like Mandie said, Joe, Miss Hope told us we could open anything in the attic."

"Well, then give me those tools," Joe finally agreed. "I'm not even sure these will work. That lock looks all rusted."

"Joe, please hurry," Mandie urged. "We have less than two hours before we have to go to the dining room."

"And my father is coming to get me at twelve o'clock," the boy replied, bending over the trunk with the hammer and screwdriver. The girls hovered near with Snowball perched on Mandie's shoulder. Joe carefully stuck the tip of the screwdriver under the edge of the metal around the keyhole and softly tapped the screwdriver with the hammer. Nothing happened. The strong metal wouldn't yield.

With a sigh, Joe stood up and looked at the trunk and then at the girls.

"Hit it hard," Celia told him.

"What if that metal breaks all up when I hit it real hard? The trunk would be ruined and we'd be in trouble," he reasoned.

"I think it's just stuck with rust," Mandie said. "If we just had something to lubricate it with . . ."

"Just where would you get anything like that?" Joe asked.

"The oil in our lamp!" Mandie said. "Celia, will you go down to our room and get it?"

Celia hurried out of the attic and quickly returned, holding the oil lamp that usually sat on the table by their bed.

"Here. Let's take the shade off and unscrew this metal thing holding the wick," Mandie told her, taking the lamp apart and giving the pieces to Celia. Then she held up the base with the kerosene in it.

Celia frowned. "Don't use it all up, Mandie, or we won't have any light tonight," Celia warned her.

"If we just pour a little of this on the lock, maybe it will limber up," Mandie said, bending to drip a few drops of the oil on the lock.

At that moment Snowball chose to jump down from Mandie's shoulder. As he did, he hit the lamp base Mandie was holding, and the oil splattered all over the top of the trunk.

Celia snatched a handful of cleaning rags lying nearby and threw one to Joe.

"Quick! Let's clean it off!" she cried, wiping furiously at the oil on the trunk.

Joe helped, but muttered to himself all the while.

"Look!" Mandie exclaimed. "The oil is cleaning the trunk. See how nice it looks where you've rubbed the oil off." Suddenly, bending closer, she gasped. "Why there's a big letter *H* on the lid. Look!"

The three heads bent together to look.

"*H*. That could stand for Hope," Celia suggested.

"Do you suppose this trunk belongs to Miss Hope?" Mandie asked. "But she said the things up here mostly belonged to the lady who lived here before."

"*H* could also stand for Heathwood—or for anything," Joe said. "There's no telling what's in this trunk, Mandie, or who it belonged to."

"Miss Hope said we could open anything," Celia reminded them. "If there was something she didn't want us to open, she would have said so."

"Right," Mandie agreed. "Try it again, Joe."

"If you say so," Joe muttered, his thin face giving them an exasperated look.

The girls watched anxiously as Joe picked up the tools and began tapping the screwdriver harder to force the lock. Snowball roamed through the attic.

"Uncle Cal hit it real hard when he tried to knock it open, like this," Mandie said, hitting the lock with her hand.

"That won't work," Joe said.

"Maybe this will," Mandie suggested. She climbed upon the top of the trunk and stood there. "You stick the screwdriver under the lock and hit it with the hammer. At the same time I'll jump up and stomp down hard on the lid."

"Mandie, please be careful," the boy told her, bending to do as she said. "Here we go—one, two, three, jump!"

The first time they were not together for their assault on the trunk.

Snowball quickly moved away from the noise and stood watching. The second time Joe and Mandie succeeded. The old lock flipped loose from the bottom plate in the trunk lid, and the three of them cheered and laughed.

"It worked!" Mandie cried, jumping down from the trunk. "Help me get the lid up. Those hooks there are holding it."

Celia and Joe released the hooks, and Mandie pushed the heavy lid up. Snowball immediately jumped up on the edge of the opened trunk. As he looked inside he hissed and hunched his back.

The three young people gasped in horror as they stared into the opened trunk.

Celia jumped back.

"What is it?" she cried.

"They're animals or something—all furry!" Mandie cringed.

Joe bent down for a closer look. "If they're animals, they're all dead," he said. Reaching for an old poker which stood against the wall, he poked the contents of the trunk.

"Joe, what are you doing?" Celia cried.

Joe reached into the trunk and began pulling out long pieces of fur. Swinging them in the air, he laughed. "Look! Just old furs!" he declared.

The two girls drew closer to inspect what he had in his hands. Snowball ducked out of the way of the swinging furs and huddled against Mandie's ankles.

"You're right!" Mandie laughed. "They're someone's old furs. And here are some fur hats."

When she pulled the hats out of the trunk, something caught her eye. "There's something metal down under here," she said, digging beneath the furs.

Celia and Joe helped empty the trunk, throwing the furs and hats onto the floor. Finally Joe pulled out an old metal candy box and handed it to Mandie.

"All tied up with pink ribbons!" Mandie exclaimed. She pulled the faded ribbons from around the box labeled *Baker's Chocolates*, and lifted the lid, revealing stacks of old letters.

"Oh, look!" Mandie said, sitting down on the floor to empty the contents of the box. Joe and Celia sat down beside her while Snowball nosed through the pile of papers.

"Let's see whose letters these are," Mandie said.

Celia shuffled the envelopes. "There's no name on any that I can see," she replied. "They're all addressed to 'My One and Only Love.' That's all that's on the envelopes."

"Well, let's look inside," Mandie urged.

Each of the young people opened one of the envelopes. The letter paper had turned to a brownish hue and the handwriting was barely readable.

Joe looked up from the letter he held in his hand. "This one is addressed to 'My One and Only Love,' and it's signed 'Your Truelove,' " he said. "How mushy!"

"So is this one!" Mandie told him.

"And this one, too," Celia added.

"Maybe if we read them we could tell who they belong to," said Mandie.

Joe objected. "Mandie, these are someone's personal property," he said. "You wouldn't want someone reading your private letters, would you?"

"Oh, Joe, these are so old that whoever wrote them is ancient by now," Mandie argued. "They may not even be alive. I don't see any year on any of them, just the month and the day, but the paper is so old it's crumbling around the edges." Mandie returned to reading the letter in her hand.

"Miss Hope said we could open anything in the attic," Celia reminded him again. "Besides, if we fold these up and put them back in the box, who will ever know we read them? We just won't talk about it to anyone."

Mandie looked up. "Listen to this," she said, beginning to read. " 'I waited in vain until midnight last night in the cabin in the woods where we always meet, my love. My poor heart cried for you so loudly, I shouldn't be surprised if your dear heart heard its cry. I know you cannot always manage to keep our tryst—' "

"Mandie!" Joe interrupted. "What do you want to read all that sickening rigamarole for?"

"If these two people met in a cabin in the woods, it must have been a forbidden love affair," Mandie reasoned. "I wonder where the cabin in the woods is."

Celia gasped. "This one says 'the place where the diamonds are hidden must be changed.' "

"Diamonds!" Joe repeated. "Let me see what you're reading."

Celia handed him the letter, indicating the paragraph. Joe quickly scanned the page.

"Well, if there are diamonds hidden somewhere, I say let's find them!" Joe exclaimed.

Mandie sighed with relief. They had won Joe over. She moved closer to look at the letter he was holding.

"But there isn't any kind of a clue about where to look," Mandie said.

"We haven't read all of them yet," Celia reminded her. "Maybe we can find something in another letter." She reached for another envelope and slipped out the folded sheets of paper.

"We'd better hurry," Mandie warned. "I'm sure the bell's going to ring soon."

The three hastily read the letters, stuffing each one back into its envelope when they were finished. Snowball played nearby with the ribbon from the box.

"This one mentions a 'dangerous enemy,' " Mandie said. "This is some mystery."

Joe looked up from the letter in his hand. "Whoever this person was writing to must have been adopted," he said. "This one says, 'I am sure your real mother and father would have approved of our courtship. Your adopted parents treat you as though you were twelve years old instead of seventeen,' " he read. "Well, now we know that the person who received these letters was seventeen years old and had two sets of parents."

"Here's more in this letter," Celia said. "This says, 'I pray to God every day that we will be allowed to marry. We must have faith, my love, and trust in Him to lead us and guide us in the right pathway.' " Celia put down the letter. "Oh, how sad! Two people in love who are not allowed to marry."

"Here's that 'dangerous enemy' again," said Mandie. "It says, 'We must be ever watchful for my dangerous enemy. He could cause us great heartache if he learned of our secret meetings, my love. He is so desperately in love with you, and he knows that you scorn his attention. I am afraid to imagine what he might do if he found out about us, especially since he knows your parents favor him to be your husband.' " Mandie's eyes widened. "Listen. It gets even better."

Dramatically, she read on. " 'It fills my heart with great satisfaction to know that his lips have never touched yours, his hands have never held yours. My heart is humble, my love, to know that you prefer my lowly existence over his wealth and power. My heart is forever yours. For the rest of this world and on into the next, I am forever Your Truelove.' " Mandie sighed. "Oh, if I only knew who wrote these letters! This is all so mysterious. No names are mentioned anywhere."

Just then, the bell in the backyard clanged. The two girls jumped up and quickly began to stuff the letters back into the envelopes, returning them to the box.

"But we didn't get to read all of them," Joe protested, helping the girls with the letters.

"I know," Mandie said with disappointment. "But Miss Hope said you'd be in town while your school is out. Can you come back tomorrow?" she asked. "It would have to be during our afternoon free period because we have to work in the attic in the morning."

"Could you and Celia come to your Grandmother's tonight for supper?" Joe asked.

"And bring the letters with us?" Celia suggested.

"Sure," Mandie agreed. "Just tell Grandmother we'd like to come. She'll have to send a note to Miss Hope."

"Just don't forget the letters," Joe said picking up Snowball, as they prepared to leave the attic.

Mandie hugged the candy box to herself. "We'll take these down to our room right now," she said, quickly leading the way down the stairs. At the landing to the third floor Mandie and Celia said good-bye to Joe and Snowball, then ran into their room to hide the candy box in Mandie's traveling bag.

"I won't be able to concentrate on a thing today until I get a chance to read the rest of those letters," Mandie told Celia as they hurried on down to the dining room for the noon meal.

"Me either," Celia agreed. "This might turn out to be exciting."

"And if that dangerous enemy is still around, it could be dangerous," Mandie reminded her with a laugh.

"But no one knows we've found the letters," Celia said. No one knew then, but someone would find out later.

CHAPTER FOUR

SECRET PLANS

As they sat around her grandmother's supper table that night, Mandie was glad for a chance to talk to Joe's father. "How is Hilda, Dr. Woodard? Have you seen her since you came to Asheville?"

"Why, yes, Amanda. As a matter of fact, I have," the doctor replied. "She's healthier and more alert now, but she still won't talk to anyone. We aren't even sure if she *can* talk. But she seems as happy as a dead pig in the sunshine."

Joe looked at his father with pride. "My father knows the doctors at the sanitarium," he said, "and he really keeps track of how Hilda is doing."

"I'm glad you were able to find some help for her. Thank you for all you've done, Doctor Woodard," Mandie said. "I think about Hilda once in a while, and I wonder if she would know Celia and me if she saw us."

"There's only one way to answer that, Amanda. We'll just have to take you girls to visit her." He glanced across the table at Mrs. Taft. "If it's all right with your grandmother," he said.

Celia looked worried. "What about Miss Hope? Do you think she'll allow us to go?"

Mrs. Taft smiled. "I'll send her word that you two girls will be accompanying Dr. Woodard to visit Hilda as soon as he lets me know when," she said.

"Thank you, Grandmother," Mandie said.

"That would be wonderful, Mrs. Taft. Thank you," Celia echoed.

Mandie changed the subject. "How is the work going on the hospital for the Cherokees, Dr. Woodard?" she asked.

Celia looked puzzled. "What hospital?"

Dr. Woodard laughed. "Why, Celia, I'm surprised Amanda hasn't told you about that." He laughed again. "Your friend is quite a heroine among the Cherokees. She and her friends found a great deal of gold which belonged to the Indians, and they let *her* decide what to do with it."

"Oh, I remember now," Celia replied, "but go on. I like to hear about all Mandie's adventures."

Joe took the plate of chocolate cake the maid offered him and continued the story. "There's not much more to tell. Mandie decided the Cherokees needed a hospital, and it's being built right now!" he explained.

"I think that's wonderful!" Celia looked at her friend with admiration.

Mandie blushed slightly, trying to ignore the praise. "Then the building is going all right?" she asked Dr. Woodard.

"No hitches at all," Dr. Woodard assured her. "Everything is right on schedule. Maybe some day soon you can come and see for yourself what it looks like."

"Could I, Grandmother?" Mandie asked excitedly.

"You know that is up to your mother, Amanda," Mrs. Taft replied. "I'm sorry, dear, but I can't let you go without her permission."

"Why don't you write and ask your mother about it?" Dr. Woodard suggested. "Then we could make arrangements for me to come and get you."

"I will, Dr. Woodard. I think maybe mother will let me go," Mandie replied.

When they had all finished their cake, Mrs. Taft called the maid to clear the table. "You young people may go on into the sitting room while Dr. Woodard and I stay here for our coffee," she said.

"Just remember you must be back to school before the ten o'clock bell rings tonight," she reminded the girls.

Mandie, Celia, and Joe hurried out of the dining room and down the hallway to the sitting room where Snowball waited for them.

"Did you bring the letters?" Joe asked.

"Oh, yes," Mandie replied, finding her school bag in a corner by Celia's. "The candy box is under my books. Here."

She handed the *Baker's Chocolates* box to Joe, and they all sat on the carpet to read the "epistles of love," as Celia had begun to call them. Each of them took a letter and began to read silently. Snowball curled up on Mandie's lap and began to purr.

"I keep finding that 'dangerous enemy' in the letters I read," remarked Mandie, returning a letter to its envelope.

"Here it is again about the diamonds." Celia began to read aloud. " 'The diamonds are not safe. I believe someone saw me last night when I checked to see that they were still there. We're going to have to find another hiding place for them, my love.' " Celia looked up. "I wish whoever wrote these letters had been a little clearer about these diamonds."

"So do I," Joe agreed. "I have an idea this dangerous enemy must have been the one who saw him check on the diamonds. He was probably spying on them all the time."

"I think so, too," Mandie agreed, trying to keep Snowball from pawing the letter she was unfolding. "Snowball, behave yourself or I'll make you get down," she scolded.

"Do you really think that someone was spying on them?" Celia asked.

"If we can get finished reading all of these letters, maybe we'll find out," Joe said. "They seem to be in order by the month. If we read in that sequence I think we'll understand more."

"We'd better hurry," Celia said.

"Yes, we agreed that we wouldn't tell anyone about this, so that means that if my grandmother and Joe's father come in here, we'll have to hide these letters," Mandie warned.

Joe opened another envelope. "This is only one page," he said. "It just says, 'Please make every effort possible to meet me tonight at the cabin in the woods, my love. My eyes haven't feasted on you for three days now. I can't eat or sleep until I see for myself that you are all right. I will be waiting, and I pray that God will show you a way to meet me.' " Joe gave a low whistle. "That's some flowery language," he said.

Mandie looked up suddenly. "Something just dawned on me," she said. "There's no mention in any of these letters so far that the person who received them ever answered back."

"Come to think of it, you're right," Joe replied. "There isn't anything about receiving an answer." He thought for a moment. "But maybe this person had no way of sending him an answer. Maybe she couldn't write to him without running the risk of her parents finding out."

"Then how did she manage to receive these letters without their knowledge?" Celia asked.

"I'm wondering why the girl's parents didn't want her to see this man," Mandie said. "What reason could they have had? What could have been wrong with him?"

"He was poor, Mandie, remember?" Joe reminded her. "There was a letter that mentioned his lowly existence and the other man's power and wealth."

"Why should that make a difference?" Mandie asked, stroking her kitten.

"Oh, Mandie, I keep forgetting you were brought up in a log cabin way back there in Swain County, and you never mingled with the big world," Joe said. "Now please don't take that the wrong way. That's what I admire about you—"

Mandie jumped up, knocking Snowball to the floor. "Joe Woodard, I'll have you to know that you were also brought up back there in Swain County. And just tell me what's wrong with that?" Her blue eyes flashed in anger. "I think these city people are all a great put-on with their silly social graces. They're not honest with themselves or with the world. They're always pretending. At least I was always taught to speak the truth, whether it hurts or not."

Joe caught Mandie's hand in his as she waved it through the air. "Now hold on a minute, Mandie," he begged her. "I just said that's what I admire about you—your honesty and outspokenness. People always know where they stand with you. But you must remember, these city people, as you call them, have always had some strange ideas about marrying their daughters off. Society people have always hunted for a rich man to be their son-in-law—someone they thought would be able financially to take care of their precious daughter." Joe waved one of the letters in front of her. "Evidently this man was not rich or in high society. Therefore, the girl's parents thought he was not good enough for their daughter, no matter how much the two loved each other. Money came first, and if they were fortunate, the money had love attached to it. Don't you understand?"

Mandie plopped back down on the floor and picked up Snowball. "I know what you mean. I just don't see how people can live like that. I don't think God meant it to be that way."

Joe scooted closer to her and again took her small hand in his. "Mandie, I told you a long time ago that I wanted to marry you when we grow up—long before either of us knew that you would inherit your Uncle John's wealth someday," he reminded her. "Everyone knew your uncle was already the richest man this side of Richmond, but when he married your mother with all her money, that probably made them the wealthiest couple in the whole southeast. But we didn't even know about any money when your father died and left you with that terrible stepmother." He patted her hand. "I told you then I would take care of you, and I still plan to if you haven't changed your mind," he promised.

Celia sat quietly, pretending to read more of the letters while Mandie and Joe talked things out.

"Oh, phooey on all that money, anyway. I don't want any of it," Mandie insisted. "I just want my father's farm back from that woman he married, and when he died you promised me you would get it back for me."

"And I intend to keep my promise, Mandie," Joe told her. "It may take a few years, but I promise you I will get your father's property back for you."

Finally Celia shook her head. "Hey, come on. Draw the curtain. We'd better hurry and get these read."

Mandie and Joe smiled at each other and then laughed, returning to their task of reading the faded letters.

"Money again," Mandie fussed as she read on. "I wish I could have talked to this girl's parents to make them understand that love is much, much more important than all the money in the world."

The three young people finished reading the rest of the letters and sat back to discuss them.

"We have to make some plans to solve this mystery—that's for sure," Mandie told the others. "We'll probably be finished with the attic tomorrow, and then we'll have our free period free again." She thought for a moment. "I think we should begin by asking Miss Hope a few questions," she said.

"Like what?" Joe asked.

Mandie stared into space. "Like whether she was adopted or—"

"You don't think Miss Hope was the one who received these letters, do you?" Celia interrupted.

"You never can tell. You have to eliminate a lot of possibilities in order to find the right answer," Mandie replied. "Even though she's old now, Miss Hope is still pretty. Some man could have been hopelessly in love with her."

"What are you going to ask her?" Joe probed. "Are you going to tell her you've been reading some love letters that may have belonged to her?"

"Of course not," Mandie replied. "We won't let anyone know we found these letters. But we could find out if she was adopted. And we could also ask her about the woman who owned this house before. Maybe the letters were written to her."

"Sure, Mandie, I can just see a married woman with a daughter keeping her old love letters in the attic," Joe teased.

"Joe, you have no imagination at all," Mandie said. "Just remember they were locked up in a trunk with no key to be found. But on the other hand . . ." She paused to think. ". . . if the letters belong to Miss Hope, the trunk would have been moved here from her parents' home, wherever that was."

"In that case we'll never find the cabin in the woods the man wrote about," Joe reminded her. "It would have been near some other house."

"I think we ought to search near here for the cabin," Celia told them. "There are woods beyond the flower gardens, and we've never been down there. We don't know for sure it *wasn't* near the school."

"You're right," Joe agreed. "If we can find the cabin we'll know the girl lived in this house."

"Well, not exactly," Mandie said. "We might just find any old cabin in those woods. We won't know for sure that it was the one where they met."

"But like you said, we have to eliminate some possibilities to solve anything," Joe reminded her.

"All right. Celia and I will question Miss Hope," Mandie resolved. "Joe, can you come back to our school tomorrow afternoon? We have a free period from three-thirty until suppertime."

"Sure," Joe replied, his eyes twinkling. "I'd sure like to know more about those diamonds."

"When are we going to visit Hilda?" Celia asked.

"Let's do that Saturday," Mandie suggested. "We'll have more free time then anyway. Is that all right?"

Joe nodded.

"It's fine with me," Celia said. "Mandie, don't forget to ask your grandmother to send Miss Hope a note. You know how strict they are about visitors, and we don't want to break any more rules, remember?"

"I'll ask Grandmother to tell Miss Hope that Joe will be coming to visit us in the afternoon," Mandie promised. "She knows Joe and Dr. Woodard, so I don't think she'll mind." Mandie squeezed Joe's hand. "We'll have plenty of time to explore the woods."

"We sure don't want to get into any more trouble," Celia repeated.

As the three young people made their plans, they had no idea what kind of trouble lay ahead.

CHAPTER FIVE

SEARCH IN THE WOODS

By the time their free period was over next morning, Mandie and Celia had the attic in neat order with the help of Uncle Cal and Aunt Phoebe. The four of them stood back to admire their work.

Mandie glanced around at the old furniture lined up along the wall. Worn trunks and discolored boxes were neatly spaced nearby. "I think we did a pretty good job," she said.

"Me, too," Celia agreed.

"Dis place ain't nevuh been dis clean," Uncle Cal remarked.

Aunt Phoebe gave both girls a squeeze. "Both my lil' Missies make good housekeepuhs someday," she said.

"That wasn't such a big job," Celia said.

"No, but that's because we had Uncle Cal and Aunt Pheobe to help us," Mandie replied. "Without them we would have been working here for days. Well, I guess we'd better get cleaned up before the bell rings to go to the dining room. Thanks for your help, Aunt Phoebe and Uncle Cal," she said, giving them both a hug.

"Lawsy mercy, Missy, dat's whut de good Lawd put us all heah fo', to help one 'nuthuh," Aunt Phoebe said. "Now you gits goin' 'fo' you bees late."

"You Missies don't wanta git in no mo' trouble," Uncle Cal warned. "Miz Hope mought not 'llow de doctuh's son come visit."

As they started down the steps, Mandie turned to the old Negro. "You're going after Joe at three-thirty, aren't you, Uncle Cal?"

"Yessum, Missy. I'se gwine to brang him heah. Miz Hope done tol' me to go," the old man confirmed. "But, Missy, please be careful and don' make no mo' trouble."

"I'm trying real hard, Uncle Cal," Mandie told him. "Uncle Cal, and Aunt Phoebe, have y'all been working here ever since Miss Prudence and Miss Hope opened this school? Did you know the lady who owned this house before they did?"

Aunt Phoebe shook her head, and Uncle Cal replied, "No, Missy. Phoebe and me had jes' got hitched 'bout de time dis school opened up. We lived on a farm. Jes' come heah 'bout twenty yeahs ago. But my—"

The bell in the backyard interrupted their conversation, and the girls turned to run down the stairs.

"See you later," Mandie called back to them.

"Thanks," Celia said, quickly following her friend.

Stopping by the bathroom, the girls hastily cleaned up, then ran to their room to take off their aprons and smooth their hair before hurrying down to the dining room.

"I guess that means we won't get any clues from Aunt Phoebe and Uncle Cal," Mandie told Celia as they walked briskly down the hallway. "They wouldn't know anything about our mystery if they didn't live here back then."

The day seemed to drag as the girls waited impatiently for three-thirty. When Joe arrived, they would explore the woods. The girls' minds were not on their lessons.

April Snow, the tall, dark-haired troublemaker at the girls' school, bent across the aisle and whispered to Mandie. "What kind of trouble are y'all thinking up this time?" she asked.

Mandie felt the blood rush to her face and tried to ignore the girl. April was always trying to start something. Mandie did her best to control her temper.

Even though the girl had called Mandie a half-breed savage one day, creating a stir that resulted in both of them being suspended from school, Mandie had tried to forgive and forget. But somehow she just couldn't be friends with April. And April took every opportunity to make verbal jabs at her.

Mandie fidgeted nervously, silently asking God to help her remain calm. She drew in a deep breath and blew it out.

Miss Cameron paused in her recitation about the battle of Cowpens in the Revolutionary War and looked at Mandie with concern. "Amanda, are you all right?" she asked.

"Yes, ma'am, Miss Cameron. I'm fine," Mandie replied quickly. Sitting up straight in her chair, she tried to focus her attention on the lesson.

"Now, young ladies, as I was saying." Miss Cameron continued with the events that led to the victory at Cowpens.

When at last three-thirty came, Mandie and Celia raced upstairs to leave their books, then hurried back downstairs.

"Well, here I am," Joe said as he met them at the front door. "I didn't bring Snowball."

"That's good. He might get lost. We're all ready to go," Mandie replied. "Let's go outside."

The three young people walked out into the yard beneath the giant magnolia trees.

Joe eyed the girls suspiciously. "Are ya'll sure you want to go down there into the woods with those fine dresses on?" he asked.

"Fine? These are just our everyday school dresses," Mandie told him.

"I remember when that would have been finer than your Sunday-go-to-meeting clothes back in Swain County," he said with a laugh. "Well then, what are we waiting for?" As he turned to hurry down the hillside, the girls followed close behind but paused when they reached the edge of the thick woods.

"Looks like an awful lot of underbrush," Joe commented.

"Just a minute," Mandie said. Running toward a huge tree nearby, she brought out a hoe and axe from behind it. "Here! Celia and I borrowed these from the tool shed. We figured we might have to chop a path to get through," she said. "Joe, you take the axe and Celia and I will use the hoe."

Joe threw the axe across his thin shoulder and led the way into the trees. Mandie followed, using the hoe handle like a walking stick, and Celia brought up the rear. Briars caught in their clothes, tree limbs swept their heads, and unseen rocks in the undergrowth bruised the girls' feet through the thin soles of their dress shoes, but they didn't complain.

Joe stopped for a moment after traipsing through the dense forest for what seemed like hours. "Suppose we get lost?" he asked.

"Impossible," Mandie told him. "Remember, I'm part Cherokee. I've watched my Cherokee kinpeople mark a trail."

"Is that why you've been breaking twigs on bushes all along the way?" Celia asked.

"That's the way you do it," Mandie explained.

"All right, my papoose. Please mark a good trail so we can find the way back," Joe teased her.

"Will do, my brave. You keep a lookout for panthers," Mandie replied, going along with his joking.

The farther they went into the woods, the darker it became. None of them had a watch, so they didn't know what time it was.

But finally Joe stopped again. "I think we'd better go back," he said. "It seems to be getting late."

Mandie sighed. "I wish we could have found something," she said.

"Couldn't we come back later?" Celia asked.

"Later?" Mandie frowned. "You mean after dark?"

"Isn't it the night for Uncle Ned to come visit you? The moon changes tonight," Celia observed.

"He's supposed to come tonight, but he doesn't come until after ten o'clock. That will be entirely too late," Mandie told her. "On the other hand, how about tomorrow? I could ask Uncle Ned to come back tomorrow afternoon and go with us. He would know how to get around in a place like this better than we do."

"That's a good idea," Joe agreed.

"I'll ask him when he comes tonight," Mandie promised.

The three found their way back through the woods and left the tools at the hiding place. As they hurried up the hillside, they saw Uncle Cal waiting with the rig to take Joe back to Mandie's grandmother's house.

"Hurry, Missies. 'Bout late fo' suppuh," the old black man warned as they came up the driveway. "Come on, doctuh's son. Let's go."

The girls ran for the front door.

"See you tomorrow," Joe called to them as he stepped into the rig.

Mandie and Celia hurried down the hallway and joined the line of students as they began filing into the dining room for the first seating of the evening meal. Miss Prudence glanced sharply at them, and the girls suddenly realized that they must look quite disheveled after their trek through the woods. But it was too late to do anything about it.

Mandie patted her hair and whispered to Celia. "We might be in trouble," she said, holding up crossed fingers.

Celia straightened her skirt. "I sure hope not," she replied.

The meal went swiftly, and the girls were dismissed as the second group of students waited outside the doorway. Steering clear of Miss Prudence, Mandie and Celia hurried upstairs.

Standing in front of the long mirror in their room, the two girls could now see why Miss Prudence had given them such a sharp look. Celia had a faint scratch across her cheek. Mandie's chin was smudged. Both girls' hair looked as though it hadn't been combed for weeks.

Shocked at her appearance, Mandie fell across the bed laughing, and Celia joined her.

"How terrible we look and none of the girls at the table seemed to notice," Mandie said between giggles. "Not a single person even smiled at us."

"Miss Prudence noticed," Celia said, sitting up. "I wonder if we'll be called in for it."

Mandie groaned. "I hope not," she said. "But right now I think we'd better get cleaned up a little and make a ladylike appearance on the veranda with the others."

"Right," Celia agreed.

Suddenly Mandie whirled around. "Celia, I forgot," she said. "We haven't told Miss Hope that we're finished with the attic."

"That's right," Celia replied.

"Let's find her tonight and tell her, so she won't expect us up there tomorrow," Mandie suggested. "She ought to be finished with her supper by the time we get ourselves presentable."

Not satisfied with their dirty, rumpled clothes, the girls changed dresses and carefully combed their hair. By the time they left their room, the only remaining trace of their trip into the woods was the scratch on Celia's cheek, which she tried to cover with bath powder.

Downstairs they found Miss Hope just as she was going into her office.

Mandie stopped her at the door. "Miss Hope, we're all done in the attic," she said. "Everything is clean and orderly."

"That's nice," Miss Hope replied. "Come on into my office a minute. I'd like to talk to you girls."

Mandie's heart beat wildly; they were in trouble again! Celia turned to look at Mandie as they followed Miss Hope into her office.

Miss Hope sat down behind her desk, her face giving no indication of her mood. "Sit down. This will only take but a minute," she said.

The girls sat gingerly on the edges of their chairs, waiting for their scolding.

"Amanda, I know Dr. Woodard's son plans to call on you every afternoon this week," Miss Hope began, "but I thought you girls might like to go to the farm with me tomorrow afternoon. As you probably know, the school owns its own farm, which is just a few miles from here. We usually take all the girls from the school out there two or three times during the semester for candy pullings and hayrides, and there's a nice lake which freezes over for ice skating in the winter," Miss Hope told them. "I have to go out there tomorrow to check over the books. Since you girls have done such a good job of mending your ways, I thought it would be a little treat for you to go along."

"Tomorrow afternoon?" Mandie asked slowly. They had planned another search for the cabin the next afternoon.

"Yes, I have to go tomorrow," the schoolmistress explained. "Miss Prudence and I can't both leave the school at the same time, and I don't like going alone, so I thought I'd ask you two."

Celia looked at Mandie, then at Miss Hope. "I would love to go with you, Miss Hope," she said. "Mandie can stay here and visit with Joe. She doesn't get to see him very often."

"Neither one of you has to go," Miss Hope told them. "I can ask one of the other girls."

"I'd like to see the farm," Celia said. "Really and truly. I know you have horses out there, and I've missed mine at home so much since I've been here."

Mandie leaned forward. "I would like to go, too, Miss Hope, but since Joe is only going to be in town during his school break, could I please wait and go next time?" she asked.

"Of course, Amanda," Miss Hope replied. "Now, Celia, meet me here at two o'clock tomorrow afternoon. I'll have you excused from your classes then. And please wear something rough if you plan to explore the farm."

"Thank you, Miss Hope," Celia promised. "I'll be here at two o'clock."

The girls left the office and went out onto the veranda.

Celia explained to her friend. "Miss Hope has been so nice to us, Mandie, I just couldn't let her down," she said. "I knew you didn't want to go. But now you, and Joe, and Uncle Ned can look for the cabin, and I'll go to the farm."

"Thanks so much, Celia," Mandie replied. "Miss Hope didn't say when you'd return, but I imagine you'll be back in time for supper. I'll tell you if we found anything then." Mandie blew out her breath. "Thank goodness that was all she wanted with us," she said.

That night, when Uncle Ned came, Mandie tried to explain to him about the letters in the trunk. "You see, the letters don't have any names on them, and not even the year. They look so old and crumbly," she said.

"Papoose, letters belong to someone. Papoose not get into business of other people. Other people be hurt if know Papoose find letters and read," the old Indian cautioned her.

"We're not going to let anybody know about them," Mandie said. "We haven't told anyone but you—not even my grandmother or Joe's father. We'd just like to solve the mystery. So will you come back tomorrow afternoon and go with Joe and me into the woods to look for that cabin mentioned in the letters?" she begged. "Please, Uncle Ned."

"I come," the old man said as he stood up. "I promise Jim Shaw I watch over Papoose. So I watch over Papoose in woods tomorrow. I wait by great trees in forest for Papoose and Doctor Son."

"Thank you, Uncle Ned. Thank you." Mandie rose to kiss the old man's withered cheek.

"I go now. Papoose go back to big house," he told her.

Mandie ran across the grass in the moonlight, then turned to wave as she entered the back door of the house. Although she couldn't see him, she knew her Indian friend would wait in the shadows until she was safely inside.

Mandie hurried into the kitchen and pushed the bolt across the back door. Suddenly she heard faint footsteps coming down the servants' stairs. Ducking inside the huge pantry, she pulled the door almost shut and held her breath. Her heart pounded loudly.

She listened in fear as the footsteps continued across the kitchen floor. Then there was the click of the bolt as the door softly opened and closed. Whoever it was had gone outside.

Mandie raced up the stairs in the dark, rushed into her room, and ran to the window to look down into the yard. There was April Snow walking across the lawn, and she sat down on the very bench where Mandie had just been with Uncle Ned.

"That was a close call!" Mandie exclaimed in a whisper.

Celia rushed over to see what Mandie was looking at below. "She didn't see you, did she?" Celia whispered back.

"No, thank goodness," Mandie replied softly, explaining what had happened. "She was about one minute too late."

Since their window was open, both girls spoke quietly, knowing their voices might carry in the stillness of the night.

"I'd like to know what she's doing out there at this time of the night," Mandie whispered.

"She's probably spying on you," Celia said. "Remember that night she locked us out, and Aunt Phoebe had to use her key to let us back in? April knows you go out sometimes late at night, but she hasn't found out why yet."

"I sure hope she never figures it out," Mandie replied.

CHAPTER SIX

CABIN RUINS

The next morning Mandie and Celia encountered Miss Hope in the hallway.

Smiling, the schoolmistress smoothed a stray lock of hair into place. "Celia, we'll have another girl with us this afternoon when we go to the farm," she said. "April Snow has asked permission to go."

Celia and Mandie silently exchanged glances.

"Is something wrong, dears?" the woman asked.

"Oh, no, ma'am. We're fine," Mandie replied. "We were just sort of surprised that April wants to go out into the country."

"Surprised?" Miss Hope asked.

Celia fidgeted with the sash on her dress. "You know, we figured she was strictly a city girl," she said.

"Well, yes, I thought so too. But when she heard me telling Uncle Cal to get the rig ready at two o'clock for Celia and me to go to the farm, she asked to go along," Miss Hope explained. "Excuse me now. I must hurry. I have to teach this next class. I'll see you at two, Celia."

"Yes, ma'am," Celia answered as Miss Hope hurried down the hallway.

"This spells t-r-o-u-b-l-e," Mandie said as they went up the stairs to their room.

"I think you're right," Celia agreed.

The two girls plopped down across the bed in their room and began to discuss the situation.

"I think we ought to talk to Miss Hope as soon as possible and try to find out whether she or Miss Prudence could have been adopted. They don't look at all alike," Mandie reasoned. "Miss Prudence is so tall and dark. And Miss Hope is so short and fair."

"Well, maybe." Celia didn't seem convinced. "They certainly don't look like sisters, but then there are some sisters who don't favor each other at all."

"We also need to ask her the name of the lady they bought this house from," Mandie said. "I was hoping you'd have a chance on the way to the farm, but since April Snow is going, we'll have to wait."

"Maybe we could talk to her after supper tonight," Celia suggested.

"We can try," Mandie said. "I do hope Joe and Uncle Ned and I can find the cabin in the woods today."

At three-thirty that afternoon, Mrs. Taft sent Joe over in her buggy with his promise to be ready and waiting at five o'clock when she sent the buggy back for him.

Celia had left with Miss Hope and April Snow at two o'clock as arranged. Mandie waited for Joe in the alcove near the front door.

As soon as she saw her grandmother's buggy approach, Mandie ran outside. "I'm ready, Joe," she told the boy as he stepped down and handed Mandie her white kitten. "Celia had to go to the school's farm with Miss Hope, but Uncle Ned said he would wait for us at the edge of the trees." She rubbed Snowball's soft fur and put him on her shoulder.

"I'll be ready at five o'clock," Joe called back to Ben, the Negro driver of Mrs. Taft's rig.

Joe scooped up Snowball, caught Mandie's hand, and together they hurried down to the edge of the woods. They stopped there to watch for Uncle Ned. Mandie knew the old Indian would not come out of hiding until he knew they were there and no one else was around. Sure enough, he stepped forward from behind the huge tree where they had hidden the tools.

"We make haste," the old Indian greeted them. "Papoose not be late back to supper."

Mandie ran forward and took his wrinkled, weathered hand. "Did you find the hoe and the axe, Uncle Ned?" she asked.

"I find," Uncle Ned replied.

The three of them walked the short distance to the tree where the tools were hidden. Uncle Ned took the axe and handed the hoe to Joe. Then he silently led the way into the woods.

After they had scrambled through the weeds and underbrush for several mintues, Uncle Ned left the path they had chopped out the day before. He veered to the right into the heart of the forest.

"Cabin not on trail," he told them. "I look while wait. Cabin must be by water. Water this way."

They tromped on.

After a while, they heard the sound of running water in the distance, and the old Indian led them straight to it. The peaceful, rippling brook, surrounded by lush, green foliage, invited them to rest a while, but Uncle Ned pressed on, following the creek bank uphill. The birds singing in the trees fluttered away as the intruders passed by.

Suddenly, there was a crash in the bushes. The three froze as a beautiful doe bounded into view. Then the frightened animal turned and ran back into the underbrush. Snowball saw the doe and tried to get down from Mandie's shoulder.

"Snowball, be still. You're not getting down to chase that poor doe," Mandie scolded as they walked on. "Besides, you'd better pick on something your own size." She held him tightly as he squirmed on her shoulder.

Uncle Ned stopped in front of them and seemed to be listening to something in the woods.

"What is it, Uncle Ned?" Mandie whispered.

"Sound. I hear sound," he muttered, stealthily moving forward.

The two young people quietly followed Uncle Ned to the edge of a wide clearing in the middle of the trees, where the creek wound along to one side. Uncle Ned raised his hand, and the young people stopped behind some trees. They stood and listened. There was a sound of clinking metal nearby. It seemed to come from the far side of the clearing. The old Indian moved around the clearing, staying behind the trees. The young people followed noiselessly.

When they reached the other side of the clearing, they came upon some old timbers lying on the ground. A stone chimney stood tall and lonely just inside the cluster of trees near the creek.

Mandie gasped. "The cabin!" she exclaimed.

A loud scurrying noise startled them for a moment. Then they saw two squirrels fleeing from the fallen timber. Snowball broke loose from Mandie's grasp and jumped down to chase the squirrels.

"Snowball! Come back here!" Mandie demanded.

The kitten stopped at the fallen timber and sniffed around. Mandie dashed forward to grab him. As she picked him up, she noticed a piece of an old chain tangled in the logs. Evidently the squirrels had been shaking it as they nosed into the rubble.

Mandie lifted the end of the chain and rattled it to show Joe and Uncle Ned. "Here's the noise." She laughed.

"Cabin been here," the old Indian stated, stooping to look at its remains.

Mandie grinned at Joe. "I think we've found the cabin in the woods—or what's left of it—don't you?"

"Maybe," Joe said. "It must have been awfully old to be all fallen down and rotted like this."

Uncle Ned straightened up from his inspection of the timbers. He pointed to the ground. "Burn," he said. "Cabin burn."

Mandie and Joe bent to look. Beneath the thick greenery growing around the area, Uncle Ned had discovered old blackened pieces of logs lying there.

"How do you know it burned down, Uncle Ned?" Mandie asked. "Maybe this wood just rotted."

Uncle Ned reached down and crumbled the end of a log in his fingers. "Fire make ashes," he explained. "Like powder. Rot not make ashes."

The two young people bent to closely inspect the substance in Uncle Ned's hand.

"Yes, I can see it looks like powder," Mandie agreed.

"Besides, you can still smell the burn on the wood," Joe said. He picked up a small piece of wood to sniff it.

Mandie scanned the area. "I wonder what the cabin really looked like," she said. "I imagine it was romantic looking, surrounded by blooming flowers and trailing green vines, with the stream floating by, and fish swimming in the water."

Joe and Uncle Ned started examining the ground.

The old Indian scratched in the wet dirt and uncovered a corner of the stone hearth beneath the huge chimney. "Hearth here," Uncle Ned told them, pointing. Standing the axe by the chimney, he straightened up.

"And here are the pillars," Joe said, pulling the weeds away with the hoe. "You can tell how big the house was by these. See how far apart they are spaced? It was a good-sized house," he reasoned, pulling away weeds with the hoe to expose the stone pillars.

Mandie stroked Snowball as she explored the cabin ruins. "Here is where the front door was," Mandie called to them. "See, part of the steps is still here. Let me use the hoe, Joe."

The boy handed her the hoe and she beat down the weeds.

"Here spring house," Uncle Ned said, pointing to a clump of weeds. "Now that we find cabin, what Papoose do?"

"Nothing really, Uncle Ned," Mandie told him. "You see, this cabin was just one of the clues in the letters. Now that we know where it is, I would imagine the girl lived in the house where the school is now."

"But, Mandie, we aren't positive this is the cabin the man talked about in the letters," Joe reminded her. "All we've really found is what's left of some old house."

Mandie tossed her head. "I have a feeling, Joe, that this is the one," she replied. "Anyway, we'll say it is and work on the other clues from there."

The old Indian looked up at the sun through the thick trees. "Papoose go back now or be late," he said.

"I suppose it is about time to get back for supper," Mandie conceded. "Uncle Ned, we appreciate your finding the cabin for us. Thank you so much."

"Yes, thank you," Joe echoed.

"Papoose not do bad things, make trouble," he warned her. "Use head to think before body acts."

Mandie threw down the hoe and took her old friend's hand in her own. "I promise I won't get into any trouble, Uncle Ned," she said. "All we're going to do is ask some questions and try to find out who the girl was who received the letters."

"Uncle Ned is right, Mandie," Joe agreed. "I'm as curious about this as you are, but you've just got to stay out of trouble."

"All right, all right. Let's go," she said, picking up Snowball again. Turning quickly, they followed Uncle Ned as he led the way out of the woods back toward school.

At the bottom of the hill below the schoolhouse, Uncle Ned bid the two good-bye with a promise to return on the next change of the moon.

Mrs. Taft's buggy was waiting for Joe at the front steps.

Mandie gasped. "I hope I'm not late," she said. "Here, Joe, don't forget to take Snowball. See you tomorrow."

Handing him the kitten, she raced up the front steps as Joe got into the buggy to return to Mandie's grandmother's house.

Inside the hallway Mandie didn't see anyone about. Glancing at the big grandfather clock standing at the bottom of the stairs, she saw that she had plenty of time to get ready for supper.

She started up the steps and then stopped. It suddenly dawned on her that they had left the tools at the remains of the cabin. What if someone missed them? They had already had them out since yesterday. She didn't want to get into trouble. *Maybe I should run back real fast and bring them back to the shed,* she thought, convinced she could find the way. Now that she knew where it was, it wouldn't take so long. *Yes, that's what I'd better do,* she decided.

Turning quickly, she ran back out the front door. Joe was already gone. With her heart pounding Mandie raced toward the woods. If she hurried she would be back in time to stay out of trouble.

CHAPTER SEVEN

WHAT HAPPENED TO THE TOOLS?

Mandie ran and ran until she was panting for breath. She brushed tree limbs and bushes out of her way and stumbled over the rough ground. Then a pain in her side slowed her down. Stopping by a huge chestnut tree to catch her breath for a moment, she suddenly thought she heard something in the thick woods. She could hardly hear anything except her own hard breathing, but somehow another sound caught her ear.

Her heart pounded. She stood perfectly still, trying to hold her breath as she listened. There it was again! Someone was tromping through the bushes. The noise grew fainter and then went off into the distance.

Mandie immediately hurried to her left in the direction of the old tumbled-down cabin. If she could only reach the clearing and grab the tools, she would have something to protect herself with, coming back.

She should be getting close. There was the faint sound of the creek. As she came into the clearing, she breathed a sigh of relief and ran to the place where she remembered dropping the hoe.

"Oh, where is it?" she cried to herself, looking all around. "It's got to be here somewhere. Let's see, I was right here by the old steps, and Uncle Ned stood the axe by the chimney. Where is that hoe?"

Although she searched thoroughly for the hoe, it was not to be found. She circled the chimney. The axe had also disappeared. Someone had been there, evidently as soon as they left.

Mandie was really afraid now. Someone had those dangerous tools, and she was alone. The afternoon sunlight was growing dimmer inside the thick forest.

Clasping her hands in front of her, she looked through the tree-tops toward the barely visible sky.

"Dear Lord, what time I am afraid I will put my trust in Thee," she whispered aloud.

There, she thought, *God will see me safely back to the school. I don't have to worry anymore.* Taking a deep breath, she ran back into the trees and headed for the schoolhouse.

Without looking back or slowing down to listen for noises, she ran and ran until she came to the edge of the forest. Stumbling up the hill, she collapsed halfway to the top, out of breath.

She was safe now. The sun was still shining. The schoolhouse was in sight. Staring back at the forest while she regained her breath, she relaxed a little and didn't hear anyone approaching behind her. Suddenly there was a loud yell, and Mandie almost jumped out of her skin. Quickly turning around, she scrambled to her feet. When she saw it was only Celia running down the hill, she fell to the ground in relief.

Celia, a little short of breath from running, just stood there looking at Mandie.

"Oh, thank goodness it's you!" Mandie cried.

"If you don't hurry, you're going to be late for supper," Celia warned. "Come on, let's go!" Pulling Mandie up, she turned to go back up the hill with Mandie following.

At the top, arriving on level ground, Mandie questioned her friend. "Celia, when did you, and Miss Hope, and April get back?"

"A long time ago," Celia replied. "Miss Hope came back early. I looked everywhere around the school, but I couldn't find you, so I decided to walk down the hill, and there you were," she explained. "What happened?"

"I'm pretty sure we've found the cabin, Celia. But after Uncle Ned left and Joe went back to Grandmother's, I suddenly remembered we forgot to bring the tools back," Mandie explained, relating her adventures back through the woods alone.

Celia's eyes grew big as her friend told her about her journey into the woods, the noise she heard, and the disappearance of the tools.

"Mandie, please don't ever go back there again *alone*. Something might happen to you."

"Don't worry, I won't," Mandie promised.

Celia hugged her friend, and the girls hurried back to the house. "I suppose I must look a sight after going through all those bushes," Mandie said, reaching up to smooth her long blonde hair.

Celia stood back and looked at her. "Not really," she said. "You don't look as though you've been roaming through that forest. Just straighten your sleeves a little bit and tie your sash."

Mandie did as her friend suggested. Together they hurried down the hallway and joined the line of students as they were entering the dining room.

Almost bursting to swap details of their afternoon adventures, the girls quickly cleaned their plates and impatiently waited for everyone else to finish. When Miss Prudence stood and tinkled her little silver bell to dismiss the students, Celia and Mandie were the first ones through the door.

Rushing up the stairs, they collapsed across their bed.

"You first, Celia," Mandie said. "Tell me about the farm."

"It's enormous. Miss Hope said it has several thousand acres," Celia reported. "And most of it is used, for either cattle or crops. But there are a few acres of woods. And guess what?" she paused. "Uncle Cal's mother and his brother run the farm."

"They do?" Mandie looked confused. "Uncle Cal's mother must be awfully old."

"She's *real* old." Celia nodded. "They say she's still the boss out there, but her son really runs things. He's not as old as Uncle Cal."

"Did April behave?" Mandie asked.

"I suppose so," Celia replied. "She went off by herself as soon as we got there. Then on the way home she asked Miss Hope if it would be possible to bring some of the horses up to the school so the girls could take riding lessons," she said.

"April doesn't know how to ride? I'd imagined everyone knew how to ride a horse," Mandie mused.

Celia laughed. "I sure do. Horses are our family's business in Richmond, you know."

"Well, I guess some of these city slickers never learned," Mandie said.

Celia sat up on the bed. "Tell me what you and Joe and Uncle Ned did," she begged.

Mandie related all the details of the afternoon to her friend, including the fact that Uncle Ned thought the cabin had burned down.

"So you think that's the cabin in the woods where the sweethearts used to meet?" Celia asked.

"Well, there's not much left of it, so I'm not positive. But I'm pretty sure." Mandie thought for a minute. "I just can't imagine who took the tools or why," she said, sitting up. "Why don't we try to talk to Miss Hope tonight? Her group must be finished with supper by now. Maybe we could ask her some questions."

Celia stood up. "I'm ready if you are," she replied.

The girls found Miss Hope in her office alone.

"May we come in, Miss Hope?" Mandie asked from the open doorway.

"Why, of course, girls. Come on in. Sit down," she invited.

"We just wanted to ask you about something that we're curious about," Mandie began.

"Yes, Amanda, what is it?" Miss Hope asked.

"You told us that you and Miss Prudence bought this house from a widow lady. Do you remember her name?" Mandie asked.

"Why, yes. She was Mrs. Scott," the schoolmistress answered, "I believe her whole name was Mrs. Hortense Howard Scott."

"Is she still living?" Celia asked.

Miss Hope thought for a moment. "I don't remember hearing of her death. In fact, we never saw her again after she left here," she said. "But she must be dead by now. That was forty-five years ago, and she was rather old *then*."

"Do you know if her daughter is still living? You told us she had a daughter who married and left her alone," Mandie said.

"No, I'm sorry. I never met the daughter. In fact, I don't believe we even knew who she married, or where she lived. Mrs. Scott didn't go to live with her. She went to her sister's in Charlotte," the schoolmistress answered. "May I ask what brought on this sudden interest?"

"We were sorting all those things in the attic and we figured most of it must have been Mrs. Scott's. You said she left things here when she moved out," Mandie said.

"Yes, most of it did belong to Mrs. Scott. She told us they were things for which she no longer had any use, and she asked that we dispose of them. But we got busy and never really cleaned out the attic," Miss Hope explained.

"Are you and Miss Prudence the only ones who have actually lived here since you bought the house?" Mandie asked.

"Why, yes, except for the students," she replied.

Mandie cleared her throat nervously. "Miss Hope," she said in a rather shaky voice, "were you adopted?"

Miss Hope gasped in shock. "Adopted?"

"Yes, Ma'am," Celia answered.

"Why on earth would you ask me such a thing?" the schoolmistress asked.

"You and Miss Prudence don't look at all alike," Mandie told her. "We thought you might be adopted, or you and Miss Prudence might have different fathers, or something."

"Amanda, what are you saying?" the lady asked. "Different fathers?"

"I'm sorry, Miss Hope. I didn't mean anything bad." Mandie fumbled for words. "I meant that maybe your mother's husband died, and then she remarried, and you belonged to one husband and Miss Prudence to the other," she said, her face turning red.

"No, no!" Miss Hope replied. Rising quickly, she began tidying her desk. "Now if that's all you girls wanted to talk about, I'm sorry, but I have work to finish here."

The girls stood up.

"I'm sorry, Miss Hope. I know you're always busy," Mandie said.

Miss Hope smiled and said, "Never too busy to talk to you girls, Amanda."

"Thank you, Miss Hope," Mandie replied.

"We appreciate your time, Miss Hope. Good night," Celia added.

The girls returned to their room to rehash the conversation.

Mandie sat on the window seat in their room. "We didn't get much information, did we?" she said.

Celia plopped down beside her. "No, I guess not," she agreed. "Miss Hope did seem flustered when you asked her if she was adopted. What do you think?"

"I'd say she might have been adopted and didn't want us to know it for some reason. She did act a little nervous, and then right away she said she had work to do," Mandie said.

"I suppose if a person is adopted, they don't want to go around talking about it. I know I wouldn't," Celia confessed.

"I suppose," Mandie agreed. "Joe is coming back tomorrow at three-thirty. We'll see what he's got to say about solving this mystery in the letters."

"Where are the letters?" Celia asked suddenly.

"In the second bureau drawer where I put them last night, remember?" Mandie said, going over to pull out the drawer.

"Celia, someone has been in here!" lamented Mandie. "Look at all the mess."

The letters *were* still there, but it was easy to see that someone had been rummaging through them.

Celia came up behind her and bent to get a closer look.

"It looks like someone took them all out of their envelopes," Celia said, picking up a handful of the papers. "See?"

"You're right," Mandie agreed. "Let's put them all back inside."

As the girls began carefully returning the fragile letters to their envelopes, Mandie spoke her thoughts aloud.

"I wonder who did this," she said. "Whoever has been snooping must have gotten into these letters after three-thirty. I opened the drawer to check on them just before I went downstairs to meet Joe this afternoon. They were all right then."

"We may never know who it was," Celia said.

"Well, I know one thing," Mandie said. "We're going to hide them this time."

"But where?" Celia asked.

Mandie thought for a moment. "Let me see," she said. "Hey, I know. We can put them all in an extra pillowcase and attach it to the back of the bureau where no one can see it."

"The back of the bureau? How are we going to do that?" Celia asked.

"I remember seeing some nails in the attic. I think the hammer is still up there, too. Let's go get them," Mandie said. "But first let's put these letters under our mattress till we get back."

The girls carefully hid the letters. Then carrying their oil lamp for light, they hurried upstairs to the attic to get the nails and hammer.

"Here they are," Mandie said, finding a paper bag of nails.

"And here's the hammer," Celia replied, picking it up.

"We only need two or three nails, so that's all I'll take," said Mandie. "We can bring the hammer back later."

Back in their room they retrieved the letters from under the mattress. Finding an extra pillowcase in a drawer, they stuffed the letters inside.

The big oak bureau was heavy, but with quite an effort, they were able to move it far enough away from the wall to tack a nail in the back side. Celia tied a knot in the top of the pillowcase, and they hung it on the nail.

"Whew!" Mandie said as they pushed the heavy bureau back into place. "This day has been full of hard work."

"You are right!" Celia agreed.

"I don't think anyone will find them now," Mandie said, satisfied with their work.

But no one else had to. Someone had already read them.

CHAPTER EIGHT

THE STORM IN THE GRAVEYARD

"Hello, Mandie. You and Celia are to come back with me to your grandmother's for supper tonight," Joe told the girls as he alighted from Mrs. Taft's buggy the next day. He handed Snowball to Mandie. "She sent a note to Miss Hope, and I have to give it to her. I'll be right back," he said, running inside.

Mandie rubbed Snowball's fur. "You have to behave this afternoon, Snowball. No running off. Do you hear?"

Celia stood next to Mandie and petted the little white kitten. "Mandie, I appreciate your grandmother always including me in her invitations," she said. "But maybe sometimes you might want to go to her house alone so you could talk together without me around."

"Oh, hush, Celia. Grandmother and I both want you to visit whenever I do," Mandie assured her. "After all, our mothers were friends here in this school together. Besides, you don't have any relatives near enough to visit."

Celia looked down to hide the tears of gratitude welling up in her pretty green eyes. "Thanks, Mandie," she said.

Mandie knew that Celia's mother hardly ever wrote to her. She was still deeply grieving over her husband's sudden death. And Celia had no brothers or sisters.

Just then, Joe joined them on the porch. "Miss Hope said Uncle Cal will be waiting with the rig to take us to your grandmother's for supper at five o'clock," he informed the girls. "Now what are we doing this afternoon?"

"First we have to tell you what happened yesterday after you left," Mandie answered. "Come on. Let's walk down the hill so no one will hear us."

Laughing, the three raced to the edge of the woods and sat down on the grass. Mandie brought Joe up-to-date on the events of the day before.

"Somebody must have been watching us while we were there at the ruins of that old cabin," Joe said. "Then they took the tools as soon as we left, I suppose."

"That's what we thought, too," Mandie replied. "But I can't imagine who it was or how we could ever find out."

"Someone also opened all the letters while they were in the bureau drawer in our room," Celia added.

"Oh, no!" Joe moaned. "You mean someone read them?"

"Evidently," Mandie said. "They were all out of their envelopes and unfolded when we looked in the drawer after supper last night."

"I'd say someone is definitely trying to find out what we're so interested in," Joe remarked, breaking off blades of grass as he sat there.

"Well, are we going to the cabin?" Celia asked. "Remember, I haven't even seen it yet."

Mandie jumped up and dusted herself off. "Of course, Celia. Let's go," she said.

Agreeing to listen for anyone else who might be in the woods, the three tramped silently through the underbrush straight to the site of the tumbled-down cabin.

As they came out into the clearing, Celia excitedly ran over to the remains of the old cabin.

"Is this it?" she asked, looking around at the fallen timbers and the tall chimney.

"We *think* this is the cabin they talked about in the letters," Mandie said. "Or what is left of it."

"Oh, isn't it sad? This is all that's left of that beautiful love story," Celia said, picking her way though the weeds as she looked about.

Joe laughed. "Don't get so sentimental over it. This might not even be the place in the letters," he reminded her.

"But if we can put other pieces of the puzzle together, I think we can find out for sure," Mandie said.

"Why don't we see what else is around here in these woods?" Joe suggested.

"Let's do!" exclaimed Mandie.

"Yes," Celia agreed.

Joe started walking over to the creek bank. "Let's follow the creek and see where it goes," he said.

The three young people pushed their way through the heavy underbrush, wandering still farther from the schoolhouse. Here and there birds flitted excitedly from branch to branch. Squirrels ran up tree trunks and sat there, peeping from behind limbs to watch the intruders.

Although unnoticed by the three young people, it began to grow darker. The sun disappeared behind the trees. The forest seemed to go on forever. Then way in the distance they spotted a high rock wall.

"Look!" cried Mandie, pointing ahead.

The three stopped and stared at each other. Breaking into a run, they rushed to investigate.

As they got close to the wall, they could see a big iron gate in the center. "It's a cemetery," Mandie whispered, stroking Snowball.

Joe walked toward the gate and pushed it open. "Let's go inside," he said.

The girls followed. Inside, weeds grew thick and wild around tumbled-down tombstones. Huge trees stood like guards watching over the dead, and an old stone building cowered in the corner.

Celia hesitated at the gateway. "We can't walk in there," she protested. "It's too grown up with weeds and things."

"Oh, come on, Celia," Mandie urged. "It's no worse than what we've been through in the woods." She walked on ahead and Celia timidly followed. Joe hurried from one grave to another, trying to read the faded inscriptions on some of the weather-worn stones.

Mandie tried to keep up with him but paused to pull weeds away from some of the stones along the way. "If we got some water and scrubbed these stones, I think we could read some of the names," she suggested.

Joe stopped. "Where would we get water?" he asked.

"The creek, of course. We've been walking by it all the way," Mandie reminded him.

"How are we going to carry it? In your apron?" Joe teased.

The two girls laughed.

"I don't suppose we could find a bucket, or something like that," Mandie said.

"I sure haven't seen one lying around anywhere," Joe replied. "Besides, that would take too long."

Suddenly a heavy wind swooped down through the graveyard, nearly blowing the three young people over. Lightning flashed. Thunder cracked. They grabbed each other in fright. Snowball dug his claws into Mandie's shoulder.

"It's blowing up a storm!" Joe yelled above the roar. "We'd better head for the school!"

The girls nodded and held hands tightly as they turned to leave the cemetery. Just then the clouds opened up and unloaded torrents of rain.

Joe pulled at Mandie's hand. "Over here!" he cried, pulling them in the direction of the stone building in the corner.

Instantly drenched by the rain, the girls hurried behind him until they reached the building. They froze in their tracks. It was a tomb!

Joe tried to get the door open.

Mandie screamed. "N-not in th-there, Joe!" she cried.

"Oh, come on," he insisted, tugging at the door with one hand and pulling at Mandie with the other. The door jerked open, and he pushed the girls inside, out of the rain.

Snowball had been good all afternoon, but now he meowed loudly as he licked his fur, trying to dry himself.

Mandie held her kitten tightly and huddled together with Celia. It was dark inside. Both girls were shivering, and they refused to budge from the step inside the doorway.

Joe walked around inside and came back to report. "Nothing here," he said. "Just some old dead people. They can't hurt us."

"Joe, stop it!" Mandie cried, her voice quivering from fright and cold.

Celia was already shaking in real terror, then suddenly something touched her hair in the darkness. She screamed and ran outside into the rain.

Joe dashed after her. "Stop, Celia! It was just an old grasshopper that got in your hair," he told her, pulling at her hand. "Come back in out of the rain."

"A-a g-g-grass-h-hopper?" she cried, finally standing still while the rain beat down on both of them.

"Yes, you've seen hundreds of grasshoppers I'm sure. Come on. We're getting drenched," he told her.

Reluctantly, Celia let Joe guide her back inside the tomb to join Mandie right inside the doorway.

Mandie grasped Joe's other hand while he still held onto Celia's. "We need to ask for protection!" Mandie yelled above the roar. She turned her face upward.

Joe and Celia understood.

Holding hands together, they recited Mandie's favorite prayer. " 'What time I am afraid I will put my trust in Thee.' "

The three smiled at each other, unable to speak.

Outside, the storm raged on. They could hear lightning striking trees. The wind roared as though it were sweeping the whole cemetery away.

The three young people huddled together, their hearts beating wildly. Snowball clung to Mandie's shoulder, meowing in fright.

Then as suddenly as it had come, the storm moved on. The three young people rushed outside in relief. Sunshine filtered through the thick trees. Snowball still clung desperately as Mandie turned to close the door behind them. Only then did she notice the name inscribed on the door.

"Scott! These people were Scotts!" she cried excitedly.

"Let's get out of here!" yelled Celia, running through the wet grass and weeds toward the gate.

"We'd better hurry," Joe agreed.

All three of them were soaking wet. The girls' long, heavy skirts hindered them as they made their way back through the woods to the school. No one said anything. They were in too big of a hurry and too much out of breath for that. As they came to a clearing on the hillside below the school, they could see the rig tied to the hitching post at the front steps.

"We're late!" Mandie cried.

"And in trouble!" Celia added.

Joe tried to help the girls up the hillside, but he was wet, too, and progress was slow. As they reached the front porch, Miss Hope came outside.

"My goodness! You were caught in the storm!" she exclaimed. "Girls, run upstairs quickly and change into dry clothes. Joe, I'm afraid I don't have a thing for you to wear. I trust you won't catch a cold before you get back to Amanda's grandmother's house to change."

"We'll be right back," Mandie told Joe. She and Celia hurried through the doorway and up the stairs to their room.

Joe sat on the steps and talked to Miss Hope.

"Where were y'all? Couldn't you find shelter anywhere?" Miss Hope asked.

"No, ma'am," Joe said. "You see, we were in the cemetery in the woods, and by the time we managed to get inside the vault there, we were drenched to the skin."

"Cemetery?" Miss Hope asked. "Where is this cemetery? I don't remember ever seeing one around here."

"It's way on the other side of the creek beyond the woods down there," he explained.

"Oh, that's not our land," Miss Hope said. "We only bought the acreage up to the creek when we got the house. I don't really know who owns that land now. I don't think it has ever been used while we've been living here," she told him.

"The vault was the only shelter we could find from the rain," Joe said. Then smiling mischievously, he added, "Of course, the girls didn't want to go inside the vault. They were afraid."

"I don't blame them at all," Miss Hope said.

"It's my fault that we're late, Miss Hope. I suggested exploring the woods," he told her.

"We'll overlook it this time," the schoolmistress said. "The good Lord himself must have helped protect you."

Just then Mandie and Celia appeared on the porch in dry dresses, their damp hair combed back and tied with ribbons. Uncle Cal stood behind them.

"Miss Hope, I'm sorry we were late," Mandie apologized.

"Me, too, Miss Hope," Celia added.

"Don't worry about it this time. I just hope y'all don't get colds from this. Now hurry on. Your grandmother will be worried, Amanda, if you are too late," the schoolmistress said. "Uncle Cal, hurry back."

As soon as they arrived at Mrs. Taft's, Joe quickly changed into dry clothes. Then they all went in to enjoy the supper waiting on the dining table.

During the meal, the young people related their adventures to Mrs. Taft and Dr. Woodard but did not mention the letters they had found in the trunk.

"So you got caught in the rain," Mrs. Taft said. "And then had to stand in a vault to wait it out? My, my! That must have been eerie!"

"It sure wasn't fun!" Mandie declared, helping herself to more roast beef. "Grandmother, did you ever know the Mrs. Scott who owned the big house that is our school now?" she asked.

"That was a long time ago, Amanda," her grandmother reminded her. "We weren't living here then. In fact, we were still in Franklin when your mother went to school there. We didn't move to Asheville until about twelve years ago."

"Did you know them, Dr. Woodard?" Mandie asked.

"Well, no. I can't say I did," the doctor replied. "I do remember hearing the name years ago. It seems like Mr. Scott was a right well-to-do man. He owned a lot of land and mica mines, I believe."

"Mica mines?" questioned Celia.

"You know," Mandie said, "that shiny stuff they dig out of the ground. You can see yourself in it, like a mirror," she explained.

"And it's in layers?" Celia asked.

"That's it," Mandie told her. "Dr. Woodard, you didn't personally know them?" she asked.

"No, but I remember my father mentioning Mr. Scott. You see, my father was a doctor here in Asheville," Dr. Woodard replied. "That was ages ago."

"I didn't know your father was a doctor," Mandie said.

"And the older Dr. Woodard was a friend of your grandfather's, Amanda," Mrs. Taft added.

"I suppose everybody knew everybody back then," Mandie said.

Dr. Woodard eyed her curiously. "Why were you interested in the Scotts?" he asked.

"Miss Hope said they bought the house from a Mrs. Scott, and then the vault we hid in this afternoon had the name Scott on it. I just thought it might be the same family," Mandie explained.

"It probably is if the cemetery is not too far from the school," the doctor said.

As dessert was served, Dr. Woodard changed the subject. "Well, are you young folks coming with me to see Hilda Saturday, or did you have something else planned?"

"Oh, yes, Dr. Woodard, I'd love to go," Mandie replied.

"I would, too," Celia answered.

Mrs. Taft seemed pleased that Mandie and Celia were still interested in the young retarded girl. "I'll send the rig over for you girls Friday afternoon, then. You can spend the weekend here," she said with delight.

The three young people looked at each other silently. Mandie thought about how they wanted to explore other clues in the letters. They wouldn't have a chance to do that while staying at her grandmother's house. But what else could they do? They would have to come and visit as her grandmother asked.

Later, in the sitting room, the three young people discussed the situation while the adults had coffee in the dining room.

"We'll just have to bring the letters with us," Mandie said. "Maybe if we read them all over again, we can find some more clues."

"I'd like to hunt for the diamonds the man mentions in the letters." Joe's eyes twinkled. "Now that we think we've found the cabin in the woods, maybe we could track down those diamonds."

"Good idea!" Celia agreed.

"We'll concentrate on that next," Mandie decided.

Someone else was also concentrating on that.

CHAPTER NINE

TREASURES FROM LONG AGO

Friday afternoon Mandie, Celia, and Joe set off for the tumbled-down cabin in the woods. They had all reread the letters and had decided the best thing to do next was to go over the area inch by inch. If the cabin had burned down, there was the possibility that the contents of the house had been scattered nearby.

"Let's split up," Joe said. "Mandie, you begin in that corner over there by the creek and, Celia, you start at that corner over there. I'll work back and forth between these other two corners."

"Don't forget to watch for any stakes, or unusual rocks," Mandie reminded her friends.

"Or there could be some old paths beneath all these weeds," Celia said.

"I can move the logs for you when you get to them," Joe told the girls.

They worked in silence for a long time without finding anything unusual.

Then suddenly, Celia squealed in excitement as she bent over, examining something at her feet. "Hey! Come here!" she cried. "I've found something!"

Mandie and Joe raced to her side. Celia was trying to open a wooden box that had the lid smashed shut.

"Let me find something to hit that with," Joe said. He looked around and picked up a heavy board. "Get back. Let me take a whack at it."

He beat and banged, turning the box at different angles. Finally the lid flew open, and the young people gathered closer to look inside.

"Looks like some old clothes," Joe said, pulling a long piece of black cloth from the box.

"A scarf," Celia corrected him.

"There's something else," Mandie said. She reached inside and pulled out a shiny object. "It's a picture!" she said, holding up a small oval frame, covered with grime.

Using the end of the black scarf, Mandie vigorously wiped the frame clean enough to reveal the picture of a beautiful girl with dark curls and laughing eyes.

"Look!" Mandie handed the picture to Celia.

Celia took it and sighed. "Oh, how sad!" she said. "This must be the girl who received the letters!"

"Probably, but we don't know for sure," Joe persisted.

Mandie kept rummaging in the box. "Here's a handkerchief," she said, holding up a small, dirty piece of white linen and lace. "I suppose these things were her sweetheart's keepsakes."

"That's all that's in there," Joe said. "I wonder why the box wasn't scorched."

"It might not have been inside the cabin," Mandie suggested. "Anyway, we'd better hurry and finish."

Although they inspected the entire open area around where the cabin once stood, they found nothing else.

"Looks like the only thing to do is dig," Joe commented. He sat down on a fallen log.

"Dig? You mean dig up this whole place? Why that would take forever," Mandie told him.

"That's the only way to find anything else. The cabin has been burned down so long the weeds have probably covered what was left," the boy replied.

"We don't have any tools any more, remember?" Celia reminded her friends. "Whoever took them never did bring them back."

"We can borrow Grandmother's," Mandie said. "And speaking of Grandmother, I imagine it's about time to get back to school. We have to go to her house tonight for the weekend, you know. Celia, will you bring that picture, and the handkerchief, and scarf with you?"

Celia picked up the objects and followed Mandie along the path. Joe brought up the rear.

Ben had Mrs. Taft's rig waiting when they arrived back at the school. Leaving Joe downstairs, the girls ran to their room and grabbed their already-packed bags.

"Let's get the letters," Mandie said. "We can put these things we've found into the pillowcase with the letters and take it all to Grandmother's house. That way we'll know where things are."

"Good idea," Celia said.

The girls pulled the bureau away from the wall enough to reach behind and get the pillowcase containing the letters. Celia dropped the picture, handkerchief, and scarf into the pillowcase with the letters. Then Mandie stuffed the whole thing under her books in the school bag she was taking to her grandmother's house.

"Now we know everything is safe," Mandie said. At the last moment she grabbed a red dress from the chifferobe and tossed the dress into her bag.

"For Hilda," she explained, as Celia looked at her questioningly.

Hurrying back downstairs with their bags, the girls found Miss Hope in her office and told her good-bye. Then they joined Joe in the rig for the ride to Mrs. Taft's house.

On Saturday, Dr. Woodard took the three young people to see the mentally retarded girl they had found hiding in the school's attic.

As they rode down the cobblestone streets on their way to the private sanitarium, Mandie questioned him. "You say Hilda has never said a word to anyone, Dr. Woodard?"

"Not one word," the doctor replied. "We still don't know whether she is even capable of speaking, but otherwise her health has improved considerably."

When they arrived at the sanitarium, Hilda was brought to the parlor to visit with her friends. Mandie and Celia hardly recognized her. She had gained weight and was neatly dressed. Her shiny, long brown hair was tied back with a ribbon.

Hilda stared at Mandie and the others. Then a faint smile brightened her face.

Mandie reached into her bag, pulled out the red dress that she had brought her, and cautiously approached the girl. Hilda stood still. When Mandie held out the dress to her, she smiled broadly and took it. Holding it up against herself, she turned this way and that, admiring the dress.

"Remember us?" Mandie asked her. "I'm Mandie, this is Celia, and that's Joe. And you know Dr. Woodard, I'm sure."

Hilda looked at the dress and then at Mandie. With a sudden rush, she put her arms around Mandie and hugged her tightly.

"Thank you!" Hilda whispered, barely audibly.

Mandie whirled to look at the others.

She spoke! "Thank the Lord! She spoke! She said 'thank you.' She can talk!" Mandie cried excitedly. She turned back to embrace the girl. "Oh, Hilda, you can talk! Praise the Lord!"

Hilda nodded her head as tears ran down her cheeks.

Dr. Woodard walked over to Hilda, took her arm, and guided her to the chair nearby.

"Here, sit down, Hilda," he said gently. "You don't have to cry about it. We're all happy. And when you're happy, you should smile and laugh, not cry."

Hilda wiped her eyes with the back of her hand and smiled.

Mandie leaned down in front of the girl and held her hands. "Hilda, what else can we bring you?" she asked.

Celia and Joe stood beside Mandie.

"Hilda, we'll bring you anything else you'd like," Celia offered.

"Would you like another ribbon for your hair?" Joe asked.

The young people continued to talk to Hilda, but she would not say another word. She just sat there smiling at them and hugging the dress Mandie had given her.

"We don't want to tire her out," Dr. Woodard said. "I think we'd better go now. I'll bring you back next time I come to Asheville."

The young people said good-bye to Hilda but she just sat there smiling. As they drove off in the rig Mandie smiled and looked up into the blue cloudless sky. "Thank you, dear God, thank you. Hilda can speak," she said quietly.

"That is indeed something to thank God for," Dr. Woodard said. "Now that we know she's capable of speaking, we'll try to help her start talking."

Mandie looked up into the doctor's kind face. "I don't know if it was a miracle that she spoke those two words or if she really knows how to talk, but I've been praying for her, Dr. Woodard. I think more prayers can still accomplish a lot more," she said.

"Prayers can work wonders," the doctor replied.

At the supper table that night, Mandie asked her grandmother about borrowing some tools.

"A hoe? A rake and a shovel? What on earth do you and Celia want with such things?" her grandmother asked.

"We'd like to do a little digging," Mandie said with a secretive smile.

"Digging? Well, I suppose you will need tools to do any digging," Mrs. Taft answered. "But, mind you, don't do anything that will cause trouble at school and bring your mother down on our heads. I can handle Miss Prudence, but your mother is a different story."

Mandie laughed. "We won't, Grandmother. We promise."

"When we get finished here, Amanda, go find Ben and tell him I said to put a hoe, a rake and a shovel in the rig when he takes y'all back to school tomorrow," Mrs. Taft told the girl.

"Thank you, Grandmother," Mandie said.

Joe and Celia smiled as they caught Mandie's glance. When they returned to school, they would have the necessary tools to continue their search in the woods for the diamonds.

As they drove up in the rig the next night, Uncle Cal was just coming down the front steps of the schoolhouse.

Mandie jumped down and called to him. "Uncle Cal! Would you please do something for us?"

The old man came over to the rig.

"Why, yes, Missy," he said.

Mandie pointed to the tools on the floorboard of the rig.

"Would you please take these tools over to your house before anyone sees them? We borrowed them from my Grandmother, and we'll be over tomorrow afternoon to get them," Mandie explained.

"Lawsy mercy, Missy. Why y'all bring dese when we got sech things right heah?" he asked, picking up the tools.

"But, Uncle Cal, the school's tools disappeared after we used them," Mandie told him.

"Didn't y'all know dey back in de shed? 'Cause dat where dey be," he said, looking from one to another of the young people.

"No," the three said in unison.

"When did you see them there, Uncle Cal?" Joe asked.

"Why I notices 'em yistiddy, I reckons," the old man said. "After I sees Missy April leave de shed, I goes inside and sees de tools be back." He looked around to see if anyone was watching. "Now lemme go fo' somebody done sees us. I leaves dese unduh de front porch fo' you." He walked away quickly, carrying the tools.

"Well, at least we'll have plenty to dig with." Joe squeezed Mandie's hand. "See you tomorrow afternoon," he said. "Good night." Jumping back into the rig, he rode off with Ben.

Mandie and Celia hurried into the schoolhouse.

"So someone brought the tools back, and April Snow was down at the shed. That really puzzles me," Mandie said as the two girls entered their room.

Celia began unpacking her school bag. "At least we won't get in trouble for losing the school's tools," she said, not realizing how much trouble still lay ahead.

CHAPTER TEN

HIDDEN DIAMONDS

"We'll only need the tools we brought from Grandmother's house," Mandie told Joe and Celia the next afternoon. "There are only three of us, so we can use only three tools at a time."

"You're right," Joe agreed. Stooping to locate the tools under Uncle Cal's front porch, he reached under and pulled them out.

Celia picked up the rake. "May I use this?" she asked. "I rake better than I hoe."

"Sure," Mandie replied. "I'll take the hoe and leave you the shovel, Joe."

"Let's get out of sight with these tools before someone stops us," Joe urged, leading the way down the hillside toward the woods.

Arriving at the clearing where the cabin had stood, the three young people began their search. With great enthusiasm, they hoed, raked and shoveled, but they found nothing more than some old rusty nails.

Disgusted, Joe sat down on the cracked hearth to rest. "That was a lot of work for nothing," Joe said, glancing over the clean ground. Taking off his shoes, he shook out the dirt that had filtered inside.

Celia began swinging her bonnet for a fan. "I don't know when I've worked so hard," she admitted. "I guess I'm not very good with a rake either." She laughed.

Mandie wiped the perspiration from her brow and took off her bonnet. "I can't believe we haven't found anything," she said. "This has to be the place." With a sigh, she plopped herself down next to Joe on the cracked hearth.

Celia joined her. "Where would you hide diamonds if you had some?" she asked her two friends.

Joe thought for a moment. "I'd probably pull up a floor board and put them under there," he answered. "But you see, we've dug all around where the floor of the cabin must have been."

"I'd probably stick them up the chimney," Mandie said.

"The chimney? Wouldn't they ruin from the heat?" Celia asked.

"I don't think so, but I don't really know," Joe replied.

"Then what about the hearth? Under the hearth?" Mandie asked. Suddenly she stood up. "The hearth! We haven't looked under the hearth!" she exclaimed.

Joe frowned at her. "How would you hide something under a hearth?" he asked.

He and Celia stood up to examine what they had been sitting on.

"It *is* cracked," Celia observed.

"Maybe it was cracked on purpose so part of it could be pulled up," Mandie cried. "Let's dig it up."

Picking up her hoe, Mandie started banging at the hearth.

Joe took the hoe from her. "Here. I can do that faster than you can," he said.

Joe dug away at the crack until gradually the stone hearth fell apart. There seemed to be nothing but dirt under it. Then the hoe hit something that made a clinking sound.

"There's something there!" Mandie cried.

"Don't get too close. I might accidentally hit you while I'm swinging this thing," Joe warned the girls.

He quickly dug the dirt out of the spot until something metal showed through. As he pushed the dirt aside, the girls squealed with joy at the sight of a small metal box.

"At last!" Joe exclaimed.

Mandie jumped up and down. "This has got to be the diamonds!" she said excitedly.

"It's got to be!" Celia echoed.

Joe pulled the box out of the dirt and set it on the remaining piece of hearth. He tried to open it, but the lid was wedged tightly shut.

"Get back," he cautioned. "I'm going to beat it open with the hoe."

After a few blows the lid flew open, revealing a candy box similar to the one in which they had found the letters. The girls crowded around as Joe opened the candy box. Inside, on a bed of black velvet, lay a set of wedding rings. sparkling with diamonds in the sunlight.

Joe gasped. "Wedding rings!"

The three plopped down on the ground and laughed till their sides hurt.

"Why, of course!" Mandie said when she could catch her breath. "Why didn't we figure that out? They hid the wedding rings here."

"Wedding rings," Joe murmured. "And here I thought I was hunting for diamonds."

"But these are diamonds," Celia told him, pointing to one of the rings. "Look. There must be a dozen diamonds in that one ring alone."

"Now that we've found them, we know this is the cabin in the woods that the man wrote about in the letters," Mandie said.

"Yes, and now that we've found them, would you please tell me what you're going to do with them?" Joe asked.

"We'll take them back to our room until we can decide what to do next," Mandie replied.

Celia kept staring at the beautiful rings. "We still need to figure out who they belong to," she said.

"I have an idea those rings have been here for many, many years. Those letters must be old as the hills," Joe said.

"How are we going to get them to our room without anyone seeing us?" Celia asked.

Mandie thought for a moment. "When we get to the edge of the woods I'll take my bonnet off and cover the box with it," she suggested.

"You'd better be careful," Joe warned her. "That will look suspicious, carrying your bonnet to hide something."

He started pushing the pieces of the hearth back into place as much as he could and the girls helped.

Then Mandie suggested a plan. "Uncle Cal is going to take you back to Grandmother's, Joe," she said. "So if you and Celia can get the tools back under his house, I'll rush up to our room with the rings," Mandie planned. "Will you tell Uncle Cal to take the tools back to Grandmother's when he takes you?"

"Sure," Joe agreed.

Everything worked out according to plan, and Mandie took the box of rings up to their room. When Celia came upstairs the two girls pulled the bureau out and added the box to the contents of the pillowcase on the back.

Mandie started out the door. "I guess we'd better both run for the bathroom to get cleaned up," she said.

"I know the bell's going to ring any minute for supper," Celia agreed, following her friend down the hallway to the bathroom.

Mandie hastily washed up. "I sure hope we can find out who wrote those letters," she said.

"Me, too," Celia replied, washing her face and hands. "I'd like to know who those diamonds belonged to. It's really sad when you think about finding those old letters and then finding the diamond rings and the handkerchief with the picture. They must have really been in love, and for some reason they never got married."

Mandie dusted off her shoes. "I'm going to have to change if we have time," she said. "My dress is dirty around the hem from digging in the dirt all afternoon."

Celia inspected her own dress. "Maybe we should," she advised. Hurriedly opening the door of the bathroom, they came face to face with April Snow who was sitting on the window seat across the hallway from the door.

Mandie paused a second in surprise and then rushed down the hallway to their room. Celia quickly followed.

"Why was she sitting there of all places," Mandie wondered aloud. Grabbing a clean dress from the chifferobe, she moved out of the way for Celia to get one. They quickly unbuttoned the backs of their dirty dresses and took them off, slipping the clean dresses over their heads.

"I don't know why she was there," Celia answered, fastening her dress, "but I hope she didn't hear what we were saying in the bathroom."

"I'll just bet she was listening at the door, and when she heard us start to leave, she probably rushed over to the window seat," Mandie looked at Celia with concern.

"Well, let her listen. She can't figure out what we were talking about because everything is well hidden now," Celia said.

The bell rang for supper, and the girls looked in the tall floor-length mirror in the corner. They rushed out into the hallway, unaware of the pair of eyes that watched them from behind the window draperies in the hall.

Later, as the girls left the dining room, Uncle Cal met them in the hallway. The girls stopped to talk.

"Hello, Uncle Cal," Mandie said.

Celia smiled broadly. "I keep forgetting to tell you that I met your mother and your brother the other day when I went out to the school's farm," she said.

"You did?" The old Negro laughed. "Phoebe, she got to go out theah tomorrow," he said.

"Your mother seemed awfully old to be working so hard," Celia said.

"Yessum, Missy. She be ol'. She done be workin' fo' Miz Prudence and Miz Hope for nigh onto forty-six years now," he said.

"Forty-six years!" exclaimed Mandie as something nudged her memory. "Uncle Cal, did she work here at the school?"

"Yessum, Missy. She wuz workin' heah befo' Miz Prudence and Miz Hope gets dis house. She work heah till me and Phoebe come. Den she go to de farm," the old man explained.

"She did!" Mandie's eyes grew wide. "And Aunt Phoebe is going to see her tomorrow. May we go, too, Uncle Cal?" Mandie asked excitedly.

Celia, realizing the impact of all this information, joined in. "We sure would like to go," she said.

"Y'all hafta aks Miz Prudence or Miz Hope," Uncle Cal said. "Phoebe, she ain't got to go till late tomorrow. Maybe suppuhtime."

"Please tell Aunt Phoebe that we'll ask for permission to go with her," Mandie instructed.

"I'll sho' do dat, Missy," Uncle Cal said, continuing his way down the hallway.

"What a break!" Mandie whispered to her friend.

"Yes, if we're allowed to go," Celia replied. "Joe is coming back tomorrow afternoon, remember?"

"We'll send him back to Grandmother's if he comes before Aunt Phoebe leaves," Mandie suggested. "Otherwise we'll send word for him not to come. He'll understand."

Mandie and Celia waited until they were sure those at the second sitting were finished with supper, then they went downstairs to look for Miss Hope in her office.

As they came to her opened door, they froze in shock. Miss Hope was sitting at her desk, opening the candy box with the rings in it!

They remained motionless in the dim hallway.

"Celia!" Mandie gasped.

"Miss Hope has the rings!" Celia whispered, huddling close to her friend to avoid being seen.

Miss Hope took the rings out of the box and sat there staring at them. "What in the world?" she said to herself, turning the rings over and over in her hand. She carefully examined the candy box, then looked up and saw Mandie and Celia standing in the hallway.

Quickly dropping the rings back into the box, she closed it as she rose.

"Did you girls want something?" she asked.

Mandie and Celia slowly approached her, trying to pretend they hadn't seen anything.

"Miss Hope, may we have permission to go to the farm with Aunt Phoebe tomorrow?" Mandie asked.

"To the farm? With Aunt Phoebe?" Miss Hope questioned. "Aunt Phoebe isn't leaving until late in the afternoon, and it will probably be dark by the time she gets back. I'm sure she will be gone during suppertime."

"That's all right, Miss Hope," Mandie replied. "We'd just like to go with her. I haven't seen the farm yet, you know."

"I suppose you two could eat supper at the farm with Aunt Phoebe. Neither one of you has classes at that time of day. But what about your friend, Joe? Isn't he coming here tomorrow for your afternoon free period?" Miss Hope asked.

"Oh, that's all right. We'll just tell Joe we're going away for the afternoon and won't be here," Mandie said. "He won't mind."

"You may go if you girls promise to be on your best behavior," Miss Hope instructed. "I know Aunt Phoebe is awfully lenient with you two."

"Thank you, Miss Hope. You can trust us to behave like young ladies should in every way," Mandie promised.

"Yes, Miss Hope, we will," Celia added.

Miss Hope looked at them a little skeptically. "I'll let her know y'all are going with her," she said.

The girls excused themselves and practically ran to their room to check on the letters and other articles in the pillowcase. Everything was as they had left it except for the missing rings.

"We might as well take all this and put it somewhere else. Obviously, someone has found it and taken the rings," Mandie said.

The girls laid everything on their bed and slid the bureau back in place.

"I'm worried about those rings," Mandie continued. "How in the world did Miss Hope get them?"

"I don't know, but I'd say there's no way for us to get them back," Celia said. "Why don't we put the letters and everything else in your trunk or mine and lock it up?"

"Good idea," Mandie agreed.

Each of the girls had a small trunk sitting in the corner of their room.

Mandie took the pillowcase full of clues over to her trunk and put everything inside. Locking it up she pinned the key inside her apron pocket. "That's got to be safe now," she said.

"But someone has probably read the letters already," Celia reminded her.

"And someone found our hiding place. I don't understand how Miss Hope could have the rings, but at least we know where they are. We'll just have to find out how they got there," Mandie concluded.

CHAPTER ELEVEN

AUNT PANSY TELLS IT ALL

The next afternoon, Mandie and Celia were waiting for Joe on the veranda when he arrived in Mrs. Taft's buggy.

"Joe! Tell Ben to wait a minute," Mandie called as Joe alighted from the buggy.

Joe did as she said and then quickly ran up the steps. "What's the matter?" he asked.

"Wait till you hear our news!" Mandie began.

"Sit down a minute," Celia said, motioning toward the porch swing.

Mandie tried to choose her words carefully. "Joe, would you mind going back with Ben? We're going away this afternoon," Mandie said.

Joe looked puzzled. "Where?" he asked.

"We're going to the school farm with Aunt Phoebe in a little while," Mandie explained. "Let me tell you what's going on."

The three sat in the swing while Mandie related the events of the day before. She told him about the rings turning up on Miss Prudence's desk, and the fact that Uncle Cal's mother had worked for the Scotts.

Joe listened intently. "Couldn't I go to the farm with you?" he asked.

"No, I'm sure they wouldn't allow that," Mandie replied. "We told Miss Hope we didn't think you'd mind going back to Grandmother's.

I wish you could go with us, but if you can come back tomorrow afternoon, we'll let you know everything we find out."

Joe pretended to be hurt. "This isn't fair!" he teased. "I'm working on this mystery, too." He laughed and flipped Mandie's long blonde hair.

"I know, Joe. But if we start asking for too many favors, Miss Hope might decide we can't go," Mandie explained.

Just then, Aunt Phoebe came out the door and put her hands on her hips. "Come on, Missies, we'se ready to go," she told the girls.

Mandie and Celia quickly rose and followed her into the house.

"We'll see you tomorrow afternoon, Joe," Mandie called back. "I'm sorry you can't go."

"So am I," Joe said, looking a little dejected as he walked down the steps to join Ben in the buggy again.

The girls followed Aunt Phoebe out the back door where the rig was waiting, and soon they were on their way to the farm.

Aunt Phoebe shook her head. "I don't know why y'all wants to miss dat suppuh at de school to go to de country and eat beans and cornbread," she said as she urged the horse down the country road.

"Beans and cornbread? That's the best food I know of," Mandie said excitedly. "I haven't had that kind of a supper since I lived with my father in Swain County."

Celia frowned. "Is that all we'll have, Aunt Phoebe?" she asked.

"Well, reckon we mought have buttermilk and some sweet cake," the old woman told her.

"That sounds better." Celia smiled.

Mandie's head was full of questions. "What's Uncle Cal's mother's name?" she asked.

"Huh name be Pansy—Aunt Pansy Jones," Phoebe replied.

"Pansy? That's a beautiful name. Is Jones your last name, too?" Mandie asked.

"It sho' be. It be Jones evuh since I got hitched up with Cal," the Negro woman said. "And dat be a long time ago."

They had come to a fence along the road, and the old woman stopped the rig. "Well, heah we be," she said, starting to get down to open the gate.

"Let me, Aunt Phoebe," Mandie cried.

Excitedly, she jumped down and swung the gate open. The rig went through and stopped to wait for her. Carefully closing the gate again, she ran to get back into the rig.

"You sho' know how to do dat, Missy," the old woman said.

"Of course, I do. Remember, I was raised on a farm," replied Mandie.

As Aunt Phoebe drove the rig up a winding dirt road, Mandie looked around at the rows and rows of crops growing in the fields and at the large outbuildings along the way. "This must be a huge farm," she said.

"Sho is," the old woman muttered. She pulled the rig up in front of a stable. "De house be up dat away." She pointed up the hill at a clump of trees.

Stepping down into the yard, Aunt Phoebe started to lead the girls up the hill.

"Is that where Aunt Pansy lives?" Mandie asked.

"Yes, Mandie." Celia answered. "I met her when I was here the other day."

"She lib up deah, an' so do Cal's brothuh, Rufus," Aunt Phoebe said.

A tall, young black boy came out of the stables and took the reins of the horse.

Aunt Phoebe turned around. "You git dem vittles loaded. We be leavin' right aftuh suppuh. You hears me, Jimson?"

"Yessum, Miz Phoebe," the boy said. He turned to stare curiously at the girls as they walked up the hill.

Mandie hurried ahead as she spied the house. "A log cabin!" she cried, running up the hill.

The big old log cabin seemed to sit in the middle of a colorful flower garden edged with green shrubbery and gigantic trees.

A huge old Negro woman stood on the porch watching the three approach.

When Mandie saw her, she ran up the steps. "Aunt Pansy, I'm Mandie—Amanda, they call me at school," she introduced herself, holding out her small hand.

The big woman smiled a toothless smile and put her big arm around Mandie's shoulders.

"I knows who you be. I knows yo' ma," Aunt Pansy told her. Turning to Celia, she added, "I knows this missy's ma, too."

"Hello, Aunt Pansy," Celia greeted her. "I'm glad I got to come back to visit again."

"I sees you didn't bring dat snubby gal wid you dis time," the old woman said.

The girls smiled at each other, knowing Aunt Pansy meant April. "Phoebe, bring dese chillen inside," Aunt Pansy instructed. She turned to open the screen door.

Inside, Mandie looked around the parlor. The room couldn't possibly hold another piece of furniture. The walls were covered with pictures of people. There was a comfortable, homey look about the room.

"Y'all jes' sits down now. I gotta tell Soony we got mo' comp'ny fo' dinnuh," she said, leaving the room.

Aunt Phoebe plopped down in a nearby rocking chair. "We'se gonna hafta be leavin' soon's we eats," she informed the girls.

Mandie and Celia sat down on the edge of a small settee.

"In that case," Mandie told Celia, "we're going to have to talk to Aunt Pansy during supper."

Celia nodded.

Overhearing the remark, Aunt Phoebe said, "Missies, dis ain't no highfalutin' place like yo' school. We talks all we wants whilst we eats."

"And you won't tell Miss Hope we talked during the meal?" Mandie asked.

" 'Cose not," Aunt Phoebe said. "Y'all be in *my* charge right now. I decides what's propuh. And I says ain't nothin' wrong wid talkin' at de table." She looked up as Aunt Pansy came back through the doorway.

"De vittles is ready," Aunt Pansy announced to her visitors. "Let's go eat." She turned to lead the way into the kitchen.

The room was a combination sitting room and kitchen. A huge fireplace stood at one end, while a shiny, black iron cookstove beamed heat from the far side. In the middle stood a long wooden table covered with a red checked tablecloth and set with plain white dishes. A young Negro girl was taking the food from the pans on the stove.

"Dis heah be Soony," Aunt Pansy told Mandie. "She be my granddaughter. Willie, my son whut lives heah and whut's gone to town right now, is her pa," she explained.

The girls smiled at the young girl who stared curiously at them.

"I'm glad to meet you, Soony," Mandie said, walking over to the stove. "Here, let me help you, Soony," she offered, taking the bowl from the girl and bringing it to the table.

The two old Negro women watched in surprise.

"Thank you, but I kin do it all," Soony said, filling another bowl from a pot on the stove.

"I know you can, but I'd like to help." Mandie stood there waiting for the bowl to be filled. "Makes me feel like I'm back home in my father's log cabin. We had a big room that looked a lot like this one. And I used to have to help with cooking the food, washing the dishes, and milking the cows."

Soony's eyes widened in astonishment. "But, Missy, you goes to dat fine ladies' school," she said.

Mandie took the bowl from her and placed it on the table. "But that's all new to me," Mandie explained. "And I don't really like it. I'd much rather be back home on the farm."

"Well, I nevuh!" Aunt Pansy exclaimed.

As Soony and Mandie finished putting the food on the table, Aunt Pansy gave them a big smile. "Now y'all jes' find a place and sit down. Phoebe, you sit right heah next to me so's we can talk a bit," she said.

Mandie and Celia, determined to talk to Aunt Pansy, sat down as near to her as they could get. Soony sat on the other side of the table next to Aunt Phoebe.

Aunt Pansy cleared her throat. "Befo' we says anothuh word, Phoebe, you ask de blessin'," she said.

They all bowed their heads as Aunt Phoebe prayed.

"We all thanks you, deah Lawd, for dis fine food and all de othuh fine things you gives us. Bless us all and make us mo' bettuh people. Fo' dat we thanks you, deah Lawd. Amen."

"Amen," Aunt Pansy echoed in a loud voice. She reached for the bowl of green beans near her. "Jes' reach and make yo' selfs to home, Missies. We'se all jes' plain people. We jes' takes what we wants."

Mandie picked up the bowl of corn on the cob near her plate, and took out an ear, passing the bowl on to Celia.

The girls piled their plates high with corn, fried chicken, mashed potatoes, green beans, cabbage, cornbread, biscuits, and butter churned right there on the farm. There was a pitcher of cold tea nearby and a huge jug of fresh milk from their cows.

"Aunt Phoebe, you fooled us," Mandie teased. "You said we wouldn't get anything to eat but beans and cornbread, and look at all this food!"

"Now I can't be knowin' whut Soony's goin' to feed us," Aunt Phoebe said. "But I knows fo' sho' theah goin' to be beans and cornbread. Always is."

Everyone laughed.

"Yessum," said Aunt Pansy. "I always has to have mah beans and cornbread. Soony cooked all dis fo' us, an' all de hired hands dey come an' eat latuh, too."

"Aunt Pansy—" Mandie dared to change the subject. "Uncle Cal said you used to work for Mrs. Scott who owned the house before Miss Prudence and Miss Hope made it into a school," she ventured.

"Well, Missy, I sho' did. Aftuh Cal marries Phoebe and Willie done got hitched with Ella, I gives dem de farm and I moves in wid dat Miz Scott. Dat one nice lady, she wuz," Aunt Pansy said.

"And you stayed with her until she sold the house, didn't you?" Mandie asked.

"Den I stays on to work fo' Miz Prudence and Miz Hope. An' when Cal and Phoebe sells Willie their part of de farm, dey comes to work at de school, and I comes to work fo' de school's farm. Den when Ella dies—dat be Willie's wife—Willie sell his farm, and he come work heah and bring Soony fo' me to raise," the old lady explained.

"Did you know Mrs. Scott's daughter?" Celia asked.

"Which one? She have two daughtuhs," Aunt Pansy said. "Fust one, Missy Helen, she don't belong to de Scotts. Dey 'dopted huh 'cause dey don't be gittin' any chillun. And den, soon as dey gits huh, along come dey own daughtuh, whut dey calls Missy 'Mealya. Sho' is good dey had one theirselfs 'cause dat terrible thing whut happened to Missy Helen."

Mandie and Celia almost dropped their silverware, then leaned forward anxiously.

"What terrible thing, Aunt Pansy?" Mandie asked quickly.

"Lawsy mercy, Missy," the old woman began. "Missy Helen she be promised to dat Mistuh Taylor whut own de nex' farm. Back in dem days de white folks match up dey gals wid some man whut got money. But Missy Helen she don't cater to dat Mistuh Taylor, and she gits huh a sweetheart whut she say she really luv." Aunt Pansy took a bite of fried chicken and continued. "But dis sweetheart he be young and got no money. So Miz Scott and Mistuh Scott dey forbids huh 'sociatin' wid dis man. Well, if you tells Missy Helen she cain't do sumpin' she gonna do it or else."

Mandie and Celia smiled at each other.

"Then what happened?" Mandie asked, breathlessly.

The old woman wiped her mouth on her apron and continued.

"Lawsy mercy, Missy, dat girl jes' got wiped right outa dis world, fast," the old woman said, her voice breaking with emotion.

"She died?" Mandie asked.

"You bettuh believe she die. Wudn't nothin' left of the po' thing but some ashes," the old woman said, wiping a tear from her eye. "Huh tells me all huh troubles. She meets dis othuh man in a servant's cabin down in de trees 'way from de house 'most ev'y night aftuh ev'ybody go to bed. Den one night de whole cabin burn up. Dey found whut wuz lef' of huh inside. No sign of huh sweetheart."

Celia gasped. "Oh, how horrible!"

"That's so sad, Aunt Pansy," Mandie said. "Did anybody know what caused the fire?"

"No, nevuh did. But right afta dis happened dis Mistuh Taylor sell his farm and move 'way off out wes'. Ain't noboby evuh seed him since," the old woman replied.

"Did they think he might have done it?" Mandie asked.

"Dey wuz 'spicious of him 'cause I tells dem afta it happened what Missy Helen say. She say dat Mistuh Taylor done foun' out she wuz meetin' dis sweetheart, and she say he warned huh to stop it 'cause she be promised ta him. But Missy Helen jes' laugh and keep right on seein' dis sweetheart. Po' girl! She was beautiful, all dat dahk curly hair," the big woman told them.

Mandie's heart beat faster, remembering the girl with dark curly hair whose picture they had found at the cabin site. "Did anyone ever find out who her sweetheart was?" Mandie asked anxiously.

The old woman looked around the table and grunted a time or two. Then looking directly at Mandie, she replied, "Dat still a secret. Ain't nobody but me evuh knowed who he be."

"How did you find out who he was?" Celia asked.

"I seed him one night waitin' at de cabin when I goes by from visitin' ovuh at a friend's house 'cross de creek," Aunt Pansy said.

"Y'all bettuh eat up, Missies," Aunt Phoebe warned the girls. "We'se got to go 'fo' long."

"Aunt Pansy, please tell us who it was," Mandie begged. "We won't tell anybody."

"Now y'all look heah," Aunt Pansy scolded. "Whut fo' you wants to know all dis? Ain't none of it none of yo' bidniss, Missy. It all happen long 'fo' y'all evuh was heerd tell of."

"We have a special reason for wanting to know," Mandie begged. "Please!"

"I ain't nevuh tol' nobody," the old woman said.

Mandie's blue eyes sparkled. "We'll tell you our secret if you'll tell us yours," she offered. "We know about something that I'll bet you knew, too."

"Now whut y'all done be messin' in?" the old woman asked. "I ain't tellin' you 'nuthuh word."

Soony leaned forward. "Come on, Gramma. Ain't fair to stop in de midst of yo' story like dat. We wants to know it all."

Aunt Phoebe tapped her foot impatiently. "So do I. Start sumpin', gotta finish," she said.

The big old woman muttered to herself and continued eating her fried chicken.

"Aunt Pansy, what would you say if we told you we found the love letters that man wrote to Helen?" Mandie asked.

Aunt Pansy dropped her chicken on her plate and looked at her sharply. "Whut love lettuhs dat be?" she asked.

"The love letters from Helen's sweetheart. We found them and read them all, but there's no name on any of them," Mandie replied. "We also found what's left of the cabin."

"Lawsy mercy! De past done come alive agin!" the old woman exclaimed. "Well, if dey ain't no name on dem lettuhs, den you don't know dey be from Missy Helen's sweetheart. Wheah you find dese lettuhs?"

"In a trunk in the attic. It was locked and we beat the lock open," Mandie answered.

"So dat's whut be in dat trunk," Aunt Phoebe murmured to herself.

Aunt Pansy turned to Phoebe. "Kin I trust dese heah girls?" she asked.

"Sho' kin. Dey awful good at keepin' secrets," Phoebe replied. "I didn't know 'bout dem lettuhs."

The old woman cleared her throat, wiped her fingers on her apron, and looked from Mandie to Celia. "Dis sweetheart, he be named Heathwood—"

"Heathwood?" Mandie exclaimed. "That's Miss Hope's and Miss Prudence's name."

"I knows. He be deah daddy," Aunt Pansy explained. "Y'see, all dis happened long time ago—long, long time ago, 'fo' Mistuh Heathwood evuh marry deah ma. He wuz young, an' worked on a farm down de road. Afta dis happen he pack up and move intuh town. He go to work fo' de railroad, make big money. Den he marry Miz Hope's ma."

"Is he still living?" Mandie asked.

"No, chile. He die right aftuh Miz Hope be bawn," she said.

Aunt Phoebe stood up. "Now we knows de story, we gotta be goin'. It done be dahk outside," she said.

"I puts my trust in y'all not to 'peat anythin' I tol' you," Aunt Pansy told them as everyone else got up from the table.

"Is it all right if we tell Joe? He's my friend from back home in Swain County. He's visiting in Asheville, so he's been helping us solve the mystery," Mandie said.

"Well, I reckons he be all right," Aunt Pansy consented.

"We won't tell anybody else unless it's absolutely, positively necessary, Aunt Pansy," Mandie promised.

"Yes, it might be absolutely, positively necessary," Celia added.

"Well, I don't see wheah no hahm could be, so I reckons I won't hold y'all to no promise not to tell anybody. Jes' y'all be's careful how y'all tells whut I knows. Don't add no extry embrawdery to it," the old woman told the girls. " 'Cause whut I done bin sayin' be's de honest truth."

"Then we can tell anyone we want to?" Mandie asked.

"I s'pose so, but you be's sure you tells it like I tells it," Aunt Pansy warned her.

They promised and said good-bye to the old woman.

On their way back to school, Mandie and Celia discussed this new information. Aunt Phoebe joined in occasionally when she wasn't urging the horse on.

As they rounded a bend in the dirt road the horse suddenly stumbled and came to a standstill, whinnying loudly.

"Whut in de world done happen now?" Aunt Phoebe said, drawing a sharp breath. "Giddyup, hoss."

But the horse just stood there snorting. When Aunt Phoebe got down to urge him forward, she noticed he was stomping his left front foot. Catching hold of it in the dim moonlight, she felt the hoof and found he had thrown a shoe. No amount of urging could make the horse move.

"He done throwed a shoe, Missies. Guess we gonna hafta leave him heah and walk home. I knows a short cut," she said. "Cal kin come back an' git him."

The girls followed her as she stepped off the road onto a faint path.

Celia gasped. "We're going through the woods!" she said, stopping in her tracks.

"I knows de way. It be fastuh dis way," said the old woman, leading the way.

Mandie took Celia's hand and followed Aunt Phoebe into the woods. The moonlight shone dimly through the trees. They walked on in silence for a while. Then suddenly a big wall loomed up in front of them.

Celia stopped again. "That's the cemetery wall!" she said, shivering.

"We not be goin' in de graveyard, jes' by it," Aunt Phoebe said, trudging on.

Mandie tugged at Celia's hand, forcing her to come along. As they came abreast of the tall wall, the sound of voices reached them.

Aunt Phoebe stopped. A shiver went up Mandie's spine, and she felt the hair rise on her head.

Celia squeezed Mandie's hand till it hurt. "Wh-h-hat's th-that?" she cried.

"Ain't nothin'," Aunt Phoebe answered. "Come on."

They each took a step forward. The voices sounded clearer then, evidently coming from behind the graveyard wall.

"I'll take this 'un and you take that 'un," a male voice said.

"That's a fat 'un. This 'un's a pore 'un," said another male voice.

At last Aunt Phoebe looked frightened and she started to run. "Lawsy mercy," she cried, "de Lawd and de Debil's dividin' up de daid!"

The girls broke into a run after her, and the three didn't stop until they came out of the woods at the bottom of the hill below the school. Mandie's side hurt, and she gasped for air. Celia was out of breath, too, and still shivering.

Aunt Phoebe wiped her face with her apron. Her chest heaved up and down from the hard running. "Nevuh . . . in my bawn days . . . has I heerd sech goin's on . . . in a graveyard," she said between breaths. "De end of time . . . must be heah."

Mandie's blue eyes grew wide. "Well, let's get up to the school before it happens, then," she cried.

"Best y'all tell Miz Hope whut happened. I aks Cal to go aftuh de hoss," Aunt Phoebe called to them as she hurried off.

When the girls got back to school, Miss Hope was waiting for them in the alcove.

"Oh, Miss Hope, Miss Hope! God and the Devil are dividing up the dead down in the graveyard!" Celia exclaimed, white as a sheet.

"What!"

"That's what Aunt Phoebe said," Mandie told her, explaining what had happened.

Miss Hope laughed. "That sounds just like Aunt Phoebe. I'm sure there's some good explanation. I don't think God and the Devil would be doing such a thing. I'll get Uncle Cal to check on it. I promise to tell you what he finds out. Now you girls get upstairs. It's almost ten o'clock."

The girls hurried up to their room. As they dressed for bed, they finished putting together all the pieces of their mystery puzzle.

"Well, now we know who the writer of those letters was," said Mandie.

"And what are we going to do?" Celia asked, still shaky.

"We'll have to talk to Joe tomorrow and see what he thinks," Mandie decided.

"*If* the end of the world doesn't come before then," Celia reminded her.

CHAPTER TWELVE

MANDIE'S REGRETS

The next morning Miss Hope waited for Mandie and Celia as they came downstairs for breakfast.

"Amanda, Celia, I just wanted to put your minds at ease this morning," the schoolmistress told them in the hallway. "When Uncle Cal went back after the horse and rig last night, he found two boys inside the cemetery dividing up chickens they had stolen. So you see, the end of time hasn't come yet."

"Thank you for letting us know, Miss Hope," Mandie said. "I'm so glad Uncle Cal found them. I hope they're punished for stealing those chickens."

"They probably will be. He knew who they were," Miss Hope replied. "Uncle Cal says the cemetery is overgrown with weeds and brush. I know it's not on our property, but I've sent word to ask the boys from Mr. Chadwick's School to clean it up."

Celia brightened at the mention of Mr. Chadwick's School. "Will Robert Rogers and Thomas Patton be in the group doing the work?" she asked.

Miss Hope looked amused. "That can be arranged, I think. In fact, we'll ask the boys to dinner—just the ones who help with the work."

The girls thanked Miss Hope and hurried on into the dining room.

The hours dragged that day. The girls could hardly wait for Joe to come. At three-thirty, as Joe alighted from Mrs. Taft's buggy, the two girls ran down the steps, grabbed his arms, and hurried him down the hill where they could talk. Sitting on the grass within sight of the school, the three young people spoke excitedly.

"We've found out everything!" Mandie exclaimed.

"Everything?" Joe questioned.

"Absolutely everything!" Celia said, waving her arms.

"Aunt Pansy—that's Uncle Cal's mother—knew everything," Mandie explained.

Together Mandie and Celia repeated Aunt Pansy's story, taking turns telling each detail. Joe sat there taking in every word.

"What a story!" Joe said when they had finished. "But there's just one thing I don't understand. Yesterday you told me about seeing Miss Hope with the rings. I wonder how she got them."

"So do we," Mandie admitted. "Now what should we do?"

"I don't know, but I have to go home tomorrow," Joe said. "It's up to you and Celia now."

"Oh, I wish you could stay here in Asheville for as long as I'm here at this school," Mandie moaned.

"You know that's impossible, Mandie. I have to go home because school will be starting back," he said.

"I sure wish we had a school break to harvest the crops like the country schools do," Celia said.

Joe laughed. "I can see you harvesting crops," he said.

"You aren't gathering in the crops, yourself," Mandie teased.

"That's because we have people living on our farm just to do that. You know that," Joe said. "Anyway, let me know what you do about this whole situation. Write me a note."

"I will," Mandie promised. "I suppose the best thing to do is to just give the letters to Miss Hope. They really belong to her and Miss Prudence, anyway, since their father wrote them."

"You could burn them," Joe suggested.

"No, that would be destroying someone else's property," Mandie reasoned.

"Well, I'd say either give the letters to her or destroy them," Joe advised. "Someone might find them and take them. Remember, someone already discovered those letters in your bureau drawer."

"I think we'll give them to Miss Hope," Mandie decided.

After supper that night, the girls went to Miss Hope's office with the letters.

"We have something that belongs to you," Mandie told the schoolmistress as she and Celia stood before her desk.

"Something that belongs to me?" Miss Hope asked.

Mandie reached forward and put the candy box containing the letters on Miss Hope's desk. Miss Hope looked at the girls and then at the box.

At that moment Miss Prudence walked into the office. "And what have we here?" Miss Prudence asked her sister.

Miss Prudence reached forward and opened the lid, disclosing the letters.

"I don't know, Sister," Miss Hope replied, taking an envelope from the box and opening it.

Miss Prudence also picked up a letter, unfolded it, and began reading silently. The two ladies read in unbelief and then looked up at the girls standing before the desk.

"What is this?" Miss Prudence demanded. "Where did you get these?"

"Who wrote these letters?" Miss Hope asked.

"Y'all's father wrote them," Mandie explained.

Miss Hope gasped. "Our father?"

"We found the letters in the attic," Celia added.

Miss Prudence arrogantly shoved the box of letters toward Miss Hope. "Don't include me. He was no father of mine," she snapped.

"My father was not your father?" Miss Hope asked, not understanding.

"You never did know that we had different fathers, did you? My father died when I was a baby and Mother married your father later. Then he gave me his name," Miss Prudence explained.

Miss Hope was overcome. Tears streamed down her face.

Mandie tried to help the situation by explaining. "You see, Miss Hope, your father wrote these letters to Mrs. Scott's daughter, Helen, before he ever knew or married your mother."

Celia cleared her throat. "Since you already have the rings he bought for her, we thought you'd like to have the letters, too," she added.

"Those rings!" Miss Hope exclaimed, bursting into sobs.

Miss Prudence came around the desk and pointed to the door. "Get out of here!" she demanded.

Mandie and Celia, frightened by the outcome, quickly stepped out into the hallway, and Miss Prudence slammed the door behind them.

The two girls turned around quickly, only to find April Snow standing in the hallway.

"So you two are in trouble again, eh?" April laughed.

"Keep out of our business, April!" Mandie said angrily.

"In case you're wondering, I'm the one who put the rings on Miss Hope's desk. They just looked too tempting when I found them in your room, especially after I read those old letters and figured out what y'all were up to," April told them.

"You stole those rings out of our room?" Mandie gasped.

"I didn't steal them. They didn't belong to you," April reasoned. "I had no idea who the owner was, but I knew they weren't yours. I saw you find them out there in the woods at that old cabin. So I took them from your room and put them on Miss Hope's desk."

"Oh, you troublemaker!" Celia snarled.

"Just ignore her, Celia." Mandie tried to calm her friend. "She's just trying to get us to start something. Come on. Let's go to our room."

The two girls hurried up the stairway.

"You've already started something," April called after them.

In their room, the two girls sat on the window seat.

"Celia, we've hurt Miss Hope badly," Mandie said with a shaky voice. "Of all people, I didn't want to hurt Miss Hope."

"But, Mandie, we didn't know all that would happen," Celia said, trying to comfort her. "If Miss Prudence hadn't come in right then, it might not have been so bad. I think Miss Prudence is really angry with us."

"I know, I know," Mandie said, trying to keep from crying.

"Mandie, it's almost time for the ten o'clock bell. Isn't Uncle Ned coming tonight?" Celia asked.

Mandie straightened up, wiping tears from her eyes.

"That's right," she said. "He *is* coming to see me tonight. I'll tell him what happened. Maybe he can help us straighten everything out."

Later that night, Mandie met the old Indian in the yard. As she told him the whole story, her tears dampened the shoulder of his deerskin jacket.

Uncle Ned listened until she was finished, then smoothed back her long blonde hair, and turned her around to face him. "Papoose, let this be lesson," he said, staring deeply into her eyes. "No make trouble with other people's business. You hurt your friend's heart. Miss Head Lady Number Two your true friend, and you hurt her, Papoose. Must ask forgiveness from Miss Head Lady Number Two. Letters private business of Miss Head Lady Number Two. She not know about father's sweet friend. Remember, I tell you, Papoose—must be careful. Not hurt people."

Mandie looked up into his weather-lined face and with a quivering voice, she said, "I know, Uncle Ned. I'm sorry. I'm so sorry."

"Papoose must think with head first. Then do things," he told her. "Always best not to get in other people's business. Would have been best to leave letters in trunk."

"What should I do, Uncle Ned?" Mandie asked.

"Must ask forgiveness from Miss Head Lady Number Two," the old man said. "Papoose also ask Big God to forgive for hurt to Miss Head Lady Number Two."

Mandie gripped the old man's hand in hers, and turned her face toward the dark sky.

"I'm sorry, dear God," Mandie said, softly. "Please forgive me. Please make me a better person. Lead me down a better path than I've been going lately. Please heal Miss Hope's heart. I'm sorry."

Uncle Ned echoed Mandie's prayer. "Papoose learn lesson, Big God. Not hurt people now. You help, I know, Big God," he concluded.

As they sat there on the bench, Mandie kissed the old man's rough cheek. "I feel better now, Uncle Ned. Tomorrow I'll go straight to Miss Hope and ask her forgiveness," she promised.

"Papoose not forget," the old man said firmly. "I go now. Papoose be good?"

"I promise, Uncle Ned," Mandie replied.

The next afternoon during their free period Mandie and Celia went to Miss Hope's office. Feeling guilty, and afraid of the consequences of their actions, the two girls stood at the doorway until the schoolmistress looked up and saw them. She smiled and waved them inside.

"Sit down, girls," Miss Hope told them. "Mr. Chadwick's boys worked in the graveyard yesterday, and they will finish cleaning it up this afternoon. So we will be expecting them to have supper with us tomorrow night."

"Oh, thank you, Miss Hope, but we came to see you to ask your forgiveness for what we did," Mandie began. "I'm so sorry for my thoughtlessness—more sorry than I can express."

"I'm very sorry too, Miss Hope," Celia confessed. "Please forgive us."

Miss Hope hesitated only a moment. "Of course you're forgiven, girls" she replied. She looked down at the desk. "I understand. You two are not old enough, I suppose, to realize the shock of everything that happened. And I did give y'all permission to open anything in the attic."

"But, Miss Hope, we're old enough to know better than to go messing in other people's business. We didn't mean to hurt anyone—especially you," Mandie said.

"I know. Maybe it's just as well that everything came out into the open." Miss Hope sighed. "I suppose the biggest shock to me was finding out that my sister is only a half sister to me. But then I should have been told that years and years ago. It wasn't your fault that I didn't know."

"We are sorry, Miss Hope," Celia told her.

"My sister, Miss Prudence, told me the whole story. She knew about everything. I burned all those letters last night and I'm going to sell the rings to the jeweler downtown. It's all over, so let's just forget about it and not mention it anymore," the schoolmistress told them. "Now, about tomorrow night." She changed the subject abruptly. "I've seen to it that Robert and Thomas will be among the group that comes over for supper tomorrow. You girls will want to look your best," she said with a twinkle in her eye.

"We're so grateful to you, Miss Hope, for everything," Mandie said. Standing up, she walked around the desk and gave the surprised schoolmistress a hug. "We love you," she said. Turning quickly, she left the room, and Celia followed. As the two girls approached the stairway Mandie quickly wiped her eyes and smiled at her friend.

"She's a wonderful lady," Mandie declared.

"She certainly is," Celia agreed. "Now we ought to go upstairs and decide what to wear to supper tomorrow night."

"Right," Mandie nodded, "but first I have to write Joe a letter to let him know what happened. I hope he's not too angry with us."

"I'm sure he'll understand," Celia told her.

The next night, Mandie wore her pale blue voile dress with rows and rows of frills around the full skirt. She left her long blonde hair swinging freely around her shoulders. Around her neck hung the tiny gold locket containing pictures of her mother and father.

Celia's dress was lemon-colored, edged with lace and black velvet ribbon. She tied her auburn curls with a matching black ribbon.

When Mr. Chadwick's boys arrived in the parlor, Robert and Thomas eagerly sought the girls out.

"It's been a long time," Thomas said, coming to stand before Mandie.

"Please sit down," Mandie invited.

"It's been too long," Robert told Celia as he and Thomas joined the two girls on the settee.

"I'm glad to see you, Robert." Celia blushed.

"It was awfully nice of you boys to clean up that old cemetery. I'm sure all those dead people would thank you if they could, but we want to especially thank you," Mandie said.

The girls related the events of their stormy afternoon in the cemetery and their recent experience with Aunt Phoebe.

"So you see, we're very thankful for your work," Mandie concluded.

"I'm glad, Mandie," Tommy replied. "Because now that we have done you a favor, you must do us a favor."

As if on cue, Robert invited Celia to go for a stroll in the yard, giving Mandie and Tommy a chance to talk alone. "My parents have asked me to invite you and your parents for a visit to our home," Tommy began. "We'll be having some holidays before long, and my parents would like to know if y'all can come to Charleston then."

"Oh, Tommy, thank you," Mandie replied. "I'll write to my mother right away and let you know what she says. I'm so anxious to see the ocean."

"I'd like to show you the whole city of Charleston, too," Tommy said. "There isn't another place like it in the world."

"I can't wait to see it all," Mandie assured him. "I'll write to my mother tonight."

Later that night, as the ten o'clock bell rang for lights out, Mandie was just finishing the letter to her mother as she promised.

Mandie told her mother all about the letters she and Celia had found in the trunk, the rings, the tumbled-down cabin, and what they had done about it. She explained that she and Celia had learned their lesson and were doing their best to stay out of trouble.

Then she told her mother about Tommy and his parents' invitation to visit them in Charleston. She begged her mother to accept the invitation, reminding her that her daughter had never seen the ocean.

Would her mother agree to this trip which Mandie wanted so much? Would she think Mandie deserved this after the trouble she had stirred up?

Mandie prayed about it that night and asked God to let her go if He saw fit. That was all she could do. She went to sleep that night dreaming of the ocean.